continued . . .

"Walker pulls it off brilliantly . . . [She] certainly has a future in paranormal and/or romantic suspense." —*The Romance Reader*

"Great romantic suspense that grips the audience."
—*Midwest Book Review*

CHAINS

"This book is a double page-turner. The story is thrilling, and the sex just makes it better—two great reasons not to put it down until the end!" —*RT Book Reviews*

"Breathtakingly wonderful . . . Smoothly erotic . . . Utterly amazing . . . Will definitely keep your pulse racing!"
—*Errant Dreams Reviews*

"Exciting erotic romantic suspense." —*Midwest Book Review*

FRAGILE

"[A] flawlessly sexy suspense novel . . . Exhilarating."
—*RT Book Reviews*

"An excellently crafted mystery and romance!"
—*Errant Dreams Reviews*

"Suspense, romance, and an ending that I can't say anything about—because that would be a spoiler . . . I recommend reading this one." —*The Best Reviews*

"Intense, sexy . . . Ms. Walker has created another unforgettable . . . fast-paced, edgy tale." —*Fallen Angel Reviews*

HUNTER'S FALL

"Shiloh's books are sinfully good, wickedly sexy, and wildly imaginative!" —Larissa Ione, *New York Times* bestselling author

HUNTER'S NEED

"A perfect ten! . . . [A] riveting tale that I couldn't put down and wanted to read again as soon as I finished."

—*Romance Reviews Today*

HUNTER'S SALVATION

"One of the best tales in a series that always achieves high marks . . . An excellent thriller." —*Midwest Book Review*

HUNTERS: HEART AND SOUL

"Some of the best erotic romantic fantasies on the market. Walker's world is vibrantly alive with this pair." —*The Best Reviews*

HUNTING THE HUNTER

"Action, sex, savvy writing, and characters with larger-than-life personalities that you will not soon forget are where Ms. Walker's talents lie, and she delivered all that and more."

—*A Romance Review*

"An exhilarating romantic fantasy filled with suspense and . . . star-crossed love . . . Action-packed." —*Midwest Book Review*

"Fast-paced and very readable . . . Titillating."

—*The Romance Reader*

"Action-packed, with intriguing characters and a very erotic punch, *Hunting the Hunter* had me from page one. Thoroughly enjoyable, with a great hero and a story line you can sink your teeth into, this book is a winner." —*Fresh Fiction*

"Another promising voice is joining the paranormal genre by bringing her own take on the ever-evolving vampire myth. Walker has set up the bones of an interesting world and populated it with some intriguing characters." —*RT Book Reviews*

Titles by Shiloh Walker

HUNTING THE HUNTER
HUNTERS: HEART AND SOUL
HUNTER'S SALVATION
HUNTER'S NEED
HUNTER'S FALL
HUNTER'S RISE

THROUGH THE VEIL
VEIL OF SHADOWS

THE MISSING
THE DEPARTED
THE REUNITED
THE PROTECTED

FRAGILE
BROKEN
WRECKED

Anthologies
HOT SPELL
(with Emma Holly, Lora Leigh, and Meljean Brook)
PRIVATE PLACES
(with Robin Schone, Claudia Dain, and Allyson James)
HOT IN HANDCUFFS
(with Shayla Black and Sylvia Day)

THE
PROTECTED

SHILOH WALKER

BERKLEY SENSATION, NEW YORK

THE BERKLEY PUBLISHING GROUP
Published by the Penguin Group
Penguin Group (USA)
375 Hudson Street, New York, New York 10014, USA

USA | Canada | UK | Ireland | Australia | New Zealand | India | South Africa | China

Penguin Books Ltd., Registered Offices: 80 Strand, London WC2R 0RL, England
For more information about the Penguin Group, visit penguin.com.

This book is an original publication of The Berkley Publishing Group.

Library of Congress Cataloging-in-Publication Data

Walker, Shiloh.
The protected / Shiloh Walker.
pages cm—(Berkley Sensation trade paperback edition.)
ISBN 978-0-425-26443-0 (pbk.)
1. Psychic ability—Fiction.   2. Protection—Fiction.   I. Title.
PS3623.A35958P76 2013
813'.6—dc23   2013020745

PUBLISHING HISTORY
Berkley Sensation trade paperback edition / September 2013

PRINTED IN THE UNITED STATES OF AMERICA

10 9 8 7 6 5 4 3 2 1

Cover art by Tony Mauro.
Cover design by Rita Frangie.

Always to my family . . . my husband, J, and my kids.
I love you so much.

A special thank-you to azteclacy and Ann Aguirre, who helped
so much with the Spanish in this book. And to Ilona Andrews
for an hour-long chat . . . thanks for listening to me gripe, thanks
for the advice about this series . . . thanks for being a friend.

A special shout out to Julaine for naming Tucker's kitty . . .
hopefully, we'll get to read more about Tucker and his
cat in a later book. Julaine was kind enough to bid on the
chance to name a character's pet in Brenda Novak's Annual
Online Auction for Diabetes Research, benefiting juvenile
diabetes.

Thanks to my readers, always. You're wonderful and
I love you. Also, thanks to my editor and my agent. In my
head, I always think that, but for some reason, I never
actually put the words out there the way I should . . .
thanks so much for what you do for me.

ONE

"You want me *where*?"

Vaughnne MacMeans stared at the man in front of her and decided she really wished she'd taken more time off.

Granted, she'd already taken three months of personal time. Then two weeks' medical leave after the case to end all cases went to hell in Orlando, Florida. Maybe she should have made it three weeks. Her head was still so *not* in a good place after that last job.

She could handle another week off, she thought. Another week. Two weeks. Three weeks. Three months. Three years.

Because Taylor Jones just *had* to be shitting her.

"Orlando," he said again.

"No." She crossed her arms over her chest and glared at him. She didn't ever want to see that miserable, forsaken, hellhole of a city again. Just thinking about it was enough to give her nightmares. Thinking about what had happened in that dark, squalid miserable building . . . shit, sometimes she woke still feeling the despair of the women around. She wasn't even empathic and it had gotten to her.

Of course, a person didn't have to be empathic to feel *those* vibes. That much misery was enough to screw with the head of any psychic, even if it was just to leave that cloying, dark layer of despair. She'd been caught in the middle of it, and even though they'd shut that operation down, it wasn't enough.

They'd shut down *one* slave ring. Just one.

Who knows how many more were out there?

"Jones, I don't know if I can handle going back into that kind of work again," she said reluctantly. "Not after—"

"It's not connected to that. It's not about Daylin, at all."

Pain gripped her heart at the sound of that name. The wounds were still fresh and the pain was just as hot, just as vivid as it had been months ago. Was it ever going to fade?

Shooting him a narrow look, she took a deep breath and shifted her attention to the wall behind him. "I don't want to go back there, Taylor," she said, fighting to keep her voice level. It hurt to even *think* about it. To think about that place, to think about those women. Most of all, it hurt to think about her sister. The girl she'd failed . . .

"As I said, it's not about the last case."

She shoved away from her desk and started to pace. An echo of a headache danced in the back of her mind, letting her know that it might not have been a bad idea to take a little more time to recover. Psychics were prone to odd, undetectable injuries sometimes, and she'd wrenched the hell out of something, although it wasn't anything a doctor could diagnose.

Overuse of their abilities could definitely do damage, and these headaches were murder.

Still, she had bills to pay and an empty refrigerator, and sitting at home had been driving her insane.

SAC—Special Agent in Charge—Taylor Jones leaned back in

his seat and pinned her with a direct stare. If one was to try and find paper documentation of their unit, they'd be hard-pressed to do it. A lot of the agents knew vaguely of Jones and his odd team and there were rumors, but if one tried to look up the FBI team of psychics, they weren't going to have a lot of luck. Technically, they didn't really exist.

Vaughnne still wasn't sure just how Jones managed it, but he did.

Just then, he was watching her, his blue eyes cool and unreadable, his face expressionless. That blank look didn't mean anything. He could be madder than hell, he could be amused. Hell, he could have a scorching case of herpes and she wouldn't be able to tell from looking at his face—she'd seen him facing down drug runners, child rapists, and psychopaths with a taste for human flesh with that exact same expression.

Inscrutable bastard.

"It's got nothing to do with that last case," he said again. "It's in Orlando, yes, but it's an easy job, mostly monitoring. It's practically nothing more than babysitting. You can handle a babysitting job, Agent MacMeans."

Sure she could. The problem was it was in *Orlando*.

Clenching her jaw, she stared at him. Babysitting. She wanted to tell him to shove it up his ass.

"Just *who* am I supposed to monitor?" she asked.

"A kid, for the most part. There's an adult male who lives there. My intel is that the kid has a gift, although I'm not sure what. I need them watched, because there are people after them."

Vaughnne ran her tongue across her teeth. "Your intel." That was vague as hell. "And just who are these two? Good guys? Bad guys?"

"Well, as I said, one of them is a child. We don't generally term *children* as the *bad guy*. Beyond that?" He smiled. "I'll give you the info you need once you're in place."

"I still haven't agreed to go," she pointed out.

"Is there a reason why you *can't?*" he asked, watching her the way he might study a suspect before he went in to tear them apart in an interrogation.

Shit.

She was screwed.

She could either take the damn assignment. Or resign. He hadn't said that, and she knew he wouldn't force that on her, but she also knew she couldn't avoid one particular area of the country, either. They were spread too thin as it was, and she wasn't much for playing the chicken shit.

Either she could work and do her job, or she could quit and let him make room on the team for somebody who *could* do the job. He danced on a razor's edge to keep their unit going, anyway.

But she'd worked too damn hard to get where she was just to walk away.

And she wasn't a quitter. Besides, it wasn't like her particular skill set was in high demand out there, and she rather liked being able to *use* them to do something worthwhile. Somehow she doubted any local law enforcement agency was likely to welcome a telepath into their midst. *Sure. Welcome aboard, and instead of using the police radio, just screech out into our minds like a psycho banshee, MacMeans. Look forward to working with you!*

Since she needed to work to live, she had to suck it up, put on her big-girl panties and deal with this. Moving back to her desk, she sat down and crossed her legs. Absently, she started to swing her foot, one heeled shoe hanging off her toes. She was tempted to take it off and pummel Jones across the side of the head with it.

Orlando . . . so many nightmares. So many bad dreams. And the bitter knowledge that she hadn't been able to save the one person who'd always mattered to her.

"You know avoiding it won't make it any easier."

Jerking her attention back to Jones, she stared at him. "This isn't supposed to be easy," she said quietly. "But what in the hell would you know about it?"

For a second, though, as she stared at him, she thought she saw something in the cool depths of his eyes.

Then he looked down and it was gone.

"Just tell me about the job, Jones. I need more than just '*a kid*' and '*an adult male.*'"

* * *

Gus Hernandez pulled the battered, beat-up truck into the driveway of the little house he was renting. It was falling apart, and instead of paying five hundred a month as the landlady had originally requested, he paid three hundred . . . and did repairs. He was good with his hands and always had been. What he didn't know how to do, he was able to learn, and he'd fixed the place up quite a bit over the past few months.

So far, he'd managed to tear up the rotting boards of the porch and replace those. He'd repainted three of the rooms. He still needed to fix the deck in back, and it was an ongoing struggle to keep the yard free of weeds. If he had the money, he'd reseed it, but he didn't. Most of the work he did was using either scrap he found cheap at his other jobs or clearance stuff at the local hardware or home improvement stores.

He still needed to get more work done around the little place, although what he wanted to do was go inside the dark, quiet house and just sit. For a few minutes, with a cold beer and do . . . *nothing*. He didn't want to think, he didn't want to talk. He wanted to do *nothing*. It was a luxury he hadn't been able to indulge in for a good, long while, though, and tonight would be no different.

Although it was a bright, sunny day, he felt like he had a cloud hanging over him.

Always.

Pulling the truck into park, he stared at the old place, studied it, made sure everything looked the way it had this morning when he'd left. He hadn't had a single phone call. Not one. So that was good.

It had taken more charm than he generally cared to exert these days, but he'd managed to convince the lady living across the street to give him a call if she saw anything, and that woman? Old Mrs. Werner was *nosy*. If anybody had been snooping around, more than likely she'd notice something.

It didn't let him breathe any easier, though.

He didn't think he'd ever breathe easy again.

Please . . . you must do this for me . . .

Blocking the echo of a woman's voice out of his head, he pushed the door open. Before he climbed out, though, he reached below the seat and took out the one thing he never went anywhere without.

The butt of the Sig Sauer P250 fit solidly in his hand. He checked it out of habit and then looked over in the passenger seat. A solemn pair of eyes looked back at him. "Come on."

The boy sighed and slid out of the car. "Do we have to do this every day?"

He'd asked the same question yesterday. He'd asked it the day before. He'd keep asking it, Gus knew. It would only get worse, because the boy wasn't exactly a child anymore, and that rebelliousness that always crept out during those years between child and adult was getting ever closer.

Still, there were things in life that didn't care that Alex wanted some freedom. Things that didn't care that the boy just wanted to live a normal life.

Gus's job was to make sure the boy *lived*. Period. Staring into a pair of eyes eerily like his own, he said quietly, "Alex."

That was all he said. Alex's lids drooped and his skinny shoulders slumped, but he climbed out of the truck, plodding around to stand next to Gus and stare up at the old house.

Alex grumbled under his breath. Gus ignored him as he looked around, eyes never resting in one place. Before he shut the door, he grabbed a bag from the back and slung it over his left shoulder and then pulled out his denim jacket, draped it over his arm and hand to hide the Sig Sauer.

"Are you listening to me?"

"Nope."

"There's *nobody* here," Alex said, his voice sullen, bordering on rude. He mumbled something else and Gus stopped, looked back at him. The anger in the boy was getting worse, flaring closer to the surface today than it ever had.

"We've talked about this, Alex," he said quietly. "You want to be angry with me, you got a right. But remember what we talked about."

Gus didn't blame him. The kid had every right to be pissed. Gus wasn't a twelve-year-old kid who'd had his entire life uprooted and *he* was pissed.

"This is so fucking stupid," Alex snapped.

Stopping in his tracks, Gus turned around and stared at Alex. "Watch your mouth," he said. "Your mother raised you better than that."

Alex sneered. "Yeah, she raised me better but she's dead—"

The boy's voice cracked. And as the anger faded away into agony, Gus reached out, hooked his hand over Alex's neck. "Yeah. She's dead. But she wanted you safe. And you'll be safe, Alex. Now come on . . ."

You must promise me . . .

A hard, shuddering breath escaped Alex, but then he pulled away, looking at Gus with glittering eyes. The tears he wouldn't shed still shone in his eyes until he blinked them away. "I told you, there's nobody here."

"Yeah. I heard you. We're checking anyway."

* * *

TWENTY minutes later, while Alex oversaw their dinner of macaroni and hot dogs, Gus stood at the sink, trying unsuccessfully to scrub the engine grease from his hands. He'd worked eight hours at the construction site, then picked up a hundred bucks helping one of the guys from the site do some work on his car. He was filthy, he was tired, and he was hot. He wanted to plunge his head under the cool stream of water coming from the faucet, but he just kept scrubbing at the grease on his hands.

The phone rang just when he'd decided to give up. Hurriedly rinsing his hands, he grabbed it and spied Elsie Werner's number. The sweet, incorrigibly nosy lady from across the street. "Hello, Elsie . . . need me to come clean out the pipes again?"

"Well, now that you mention it, the one in the bathroom is running rather slow," she said.

Gus would swear she clogged them up just so he would come over and she could ogle his ass. He'd had plenty of women ogling his ass in his lifetime. It wasn't a new experience and he'd used it to his advantage more than once. But to his knowledge, most of them weren't old enough to be his great-grandmother.

Still, the lady was kind. She'd made more than a few meals for him and Alex once she figured out neither of them could do anything more complicated than pizza, burgers and fries, macaroni and cheese, or hot dogs. If she had her way, she would have taught them both to cook.

But Gus was intent on keeping his distance. Very intent. Letting a sweet old lady teach him or the kid how to cook wasn't the way to keep a cool distance. It wouldn't help either him or the kid, and in the long run, it could harm her. He had enough blood on his hands.

"I'll come by later tonight," he said. "Although I don't know if I can fix it tonight. I may need to go to the store for the drain cleaner."

"Well, that can wait. I wasn't calling about that, Gus. We have a new neighbor moving in . . . did you see?"

The skin on the back of his neck prickled.

Lifting his head, he looked to the front of the house. "A neighbor, huh?"

"Yes. A pretty girl. The moving van pulled up not long after you arrived. I was thinking about inviting her for dinner . . . maybe you and the boy can join us?"

He relaxed only a tiny bit. They were less likely to send a woman after him. But still, he had to see her. Would have to let Alex see her—*shit*. And it had to be done tonight.

"I don't think dinner will work, Elsie," he said. "I'm pretty worn out at the end of the day and I'm lousy company. But I'll be sure to introduce myself when I see her."

"Well . . . now is a good time." He could almost hear the smile in her voice. "She's out front unloading boxes, Gus. Alone. I'd go help her, but . . ."

The wheedle in her voice was anything but subtle. Gus hung up the phone and looked over at Alex.

If anybody would recognize trouble, it would be the boy. There wouldn't be immediate danger, either. Nobody would want to risk the kid being hurt. They'd try to take Alex alive and Alex would know from a mile away if there was any sort of threat. A fact that, sadly, Gus knew from experience.

He hated it, but he already knew the best course of action. They had problems looking for them, and if they'd found them, it was best to know now, so they could leave.

Alex looked up at him, his eyes solemn.

"It's okay," the boy said softly.

"We need to make sure."

The boy's hand shook as he stirred the mac and cheese. But then he nodded.

TWO

IT should be a damn crime to look that good.

Vaughnne almost swallowed her tongue when she caught her first good look at her target. Well, one of them.

Wow.

Her libido, dormant for the past couple of years, suddenly rumbled to life, and as she stared at the man coming across the street, she couldn't help but think . . . *Come to mama, pretty boy . . . pretty, pretty, pretty boy . . .*

According to the information Jones had given her, he was going by the name *Gus Hernandez*.

It wasn't his real name, though. She'd just about bet on that—Gus Hernandez wasn't too common, but there was *Augusto* and *Gustavo* . . . pair those names with *Hernandez* and you might as well be looking for *John Smith*.

Whoever he was, though . . . he was a fine, fine piece of work.

Leaning back on the porch, she braced her hands on the concrete behind her and pretended to be absorbed in the study of her flip-flops. One thing about this job . . . she could work in flip-flops and shorts. Much better than the skirts and heels, or slacks and heels, she generally wore when she was in D.C. Not that she spent a lot of time in the office, but she wasn't exactly running at full speed just yet and she knew it.

Office work would be her mainstay for the next few weeks if she wasn't doing the babysitting job. Until she could focus her gift for longer than five minutes without a splitting headache, she was useless in the field.

This, though, this was doable. She didn't need to actively use her telepathy to use her instincts and that was a lot easier on the gray matter. And even though she hated Orlando, the uniform here was a lot better.

So she'd just enjoy the uniform, and enjoy the view . . . and pretend she was somewhere else.

The view was fine. Damn fine. Excellent shoulders. Long, loose-hipped gait. Behind her shades, she studied him, black hair tucked under a battered hat, a pair of cheap sunglasses that shielded his gaze from her. He wore a threadbare T-shirt and jeans so worn, they were practically white at the seams. Damn, he wore those jeans well, too.

Because the view was making her throat go dry, she reached for the bottle of Mike's Hard Lemonade at her side and took a long drag off it as she shifted her attention to the other things. Like the backpack he was still carrying. Like the boy.

Her other target.

Two males and both of them were too damned pretty. Family, they had to be, although Jones's information on them was sketchy.

The boy is gifted. I think the man is protecting him. They are in trouble. Keep an eye on them.

Yeah, not a lot to go on.

The boy was already every bit as pretty as the guy walking next to him, although he couldn't be more than twelve or thirteen. He'd break hearts when he was grown, she suspected. His name was Alex, and he had the angriest, saddest eyes she'd seen on a kid in a long, long while. They were a pale, misty sort of gray—set against his dusky skin, those eyes packed even more of a punch.

Yeah. He was going to break hearts, she thought. And she had a feeling he'd be breaking hers before this job was out. Babysit. What in the hell was going on here?

That gaze of his was a punch right to her heart. One that might shatter it, because while she couldn't read emotions worth shit, she knew what fear looked like. The boy was ripe with it. He had so much fear inside, it hurt to look at him. So much cynicism, she figured she probably would have looked idealistic.

And even without lowering her shields, she felt the wide-open power of his mind.

Damn.

That kid was practically a lighthouse on the shore in the middle of a raging storm.

All it would take was the wrong person looking for him . . .

Gifted. *Gifted, my ass*, she thought sourly. A gift like that would be more like a curse for a good, long while. He didn't need a *babysitter*. What he needed was a bodyguard and a teacher. She might be able to handle the bodyguard job as long as there was nothing major going on, but she wasn't equipped to teach a kid like that.

Mr. Gus Hernandez pushed his battered cap back and gave her a sleepy smile. "Hi there," he said.

Okay. If the boy's eyes ripped at her, the man's eyes were going to put her on her knees, but for all the wrong reasons. Wow. If she'd thought the kid's eyes packed a punch . . . again, *wow.*

This guy's gaze was enough to put her out for the count. The color of the mists that hovered over the river in the morning, that was what his eyes made her think of, a surreal shade of gray and so unbelievably beautiful, shockingly pale against the warmth of his olive-colored skin. But it wasn't just the unnatural beauty of those eyes . . . the kid had that.

The man, though, he had a look in his eyes that made her throat go dry.

Sleepy and sexy, like he'd just tumbled out of bed but he'd be more than happy to tumble right back in. Since he was looking at her, the idea was probably to think that he was going to tumble into bed with her, but she knew better.

That look was practiced. Way too practiced and she knew it. Still, it was a good look, and she might as well enjoy it. His smile, too. She was a little disturbed to realize that smile of his was making her feel all warm and tingly down in parts that were *not* supposed to be an issue, considering she was on a job.

He knew what effect he had, too. She could tell. It wasn't arrogance or anything, but he knew. Hmmm. A player? *That* was a harder puzzle, but she'd figured it out.

He was playing at something, but what was it? That was the question, indeed.

Taking another sip from her bottle, she tipped it at him. "Hey, back."

The boy shot her a look from under his lashes and lowered his head. As he shoved his hands into his pockets, she felt it. A ripple of his gift, rolling across her.

She didn't react.

He was young, and unless he'd encountered a lot of psychics, it was unlikely he'd recognize one if she wasn't using her ability. Which she didn't plan to do. Keeping her own thoughts tucked back behind a blank shield, she projected an air of boredom, exhaustion, and because he probably was used to it, she thought a few rather female thoughts about the overall hotness of the long, sexy piece of work standing across from her.

The kid blushed and darted a look at the long, sexy piece of work before he mumbled, ". . . help you move stuff."

Vaughnne reached up and rubbed her ear. "I'm sorry?"

"I think my kid is saying we wanted to see if you needed help."

Those tingling parts started tingling again and she leaned forward, arms crossed over her chest, at the smile he shot her way. Then he glanced over at the boy. "Right, Alex?"

The kid lifted his head, and for a long, long moment, all he did was stare at her.

Seconds ticked away, and Vaughnne would have sworn she heard her heart beating, could have sworn she felt *their* hearts beating as the boy took her measure. And somehow, she suspected if that kid didn't like what he saw, there were going to be problems.

She was prepared for that.

Very prepared, although not quite in the way anybody would think.

But finally, the boy gave her a nervous smile and ducked his head again, and that odd, tight tension faded away. "Yeah. You . . ." He licked his lips and looked over at the man who claimed to be his father before darting her a look. "You got lots of stuff and no help. We don't mind."

Don't mind, huh?

Yeah. She was sure they didn't. They didn't mind so much, and if that kid had so much as whispered one bad word about her, she had a feeling she would have had to unload on the two of them just to keep the sexy piece of work from doing . . . whatever he had planned.

Uncurling from the bench, she let her bottle swing from her left hand as she sauntered off. "Sure. I wouldn't mind a hand, I reckon." She laid it on thick with the drawl and kept her smile wide and friendly. "My name's Vaughnne."

They'd decided it would be best to keep things close to the truth with this one, and as the boy flicked her another glance, she felt that odd ripple again. Yeah. Good call. He smiled again and then glanced over at the man with him. "Alex," the boy said.

It was weird, the vibe between them, but she'd already figured it out. The kid's gift . . . the gift inside him, it was so strong, he almost glowed with it. Considering there was some sort of danger chasing them, it seemed the man had made the hard, but wise choice to use the kid's instincts.

And there was something after them. Only reason why that kid would be so afraid, she figured. Not an easy choice to make. But death, danger . . . plenty of other things were far less pleasant and a lot less easy.

"Nice to meet you, Alex," she said, still keeping her thoughts tucked behind that surface shield of nice and normal. He held out his hand, and once more, that power . . . as their skin touched, she shielded down as tight as she could.

His hand fell away and he looked over at the man, another smile.

Signals. She didn't know what they were communicating with those signals, but they were doing it.

"Gus." The man nodded and gave her another one of those lazy smiles as he adjusted his cap. "So, how much more have you got to move in, Vaughnne?"

She heaved out a sigh. "Too damn much."

* * *

HE'D known beautiful women.

He'd known women so beautiful, they made the eye all but hurt to look at them.

The woman standing in front of him wasn't one of them.

But there was . . . something about her, and Gus realized he couldn't look away from her.

A fine sheen of perspiration gleamed along the warm brown

of her skin, and unlike a lot of the women he'd known, it didn't seem to faze her. Her nose was sprinkled with a few freckles, shades darker than that warm brown, and her eyes, liquid gold, held his with a frank, unblinking stare as she nodded toward the moving van.

"Vaughnne," he murmured absently, turning the name over as he studied her.

Alex had read her. They had a system; it worked. He hated it, hated having to rely on the kid like that, but Gus wasn't going to risk the boy's safety when he had a tool that was just undeniable, either.

Alex didn't offer his name to anybody that set his internal warning off, and he'd not only offered her his name, he'd let her touch him. Alex let very few people touch him.

So she had to be safe enough. Maybe that was why he felt his heartbeat kick up a few notches. It had been . . .

Please. You must do this for me.

As the voice roused from the depths of his memory, he shoved everything else to the back of his mind. It didn't matter if *she* was safe. Alex wasn't.

A slim black brow arched and she cocked her head. A bright red bandanna was wrapped around her head, and underneath, thick, crazy black curls fell in long spirals almost halfway down her back. "If we're going to do this, Gus," she said lazily, lifting a bottle to her lips, "let's do it. I dunno about you, but I'm worn out."

She took a drink from the bottle, and he had the damnedest desire to pull the bottle away, and take a drink . . . from her. It was a disgusting thing she was drinking, but he suspected he wouldn't mind a bit, tasting it on her lips, tasting her. Before the temptation settled too deep in his mind, he turned around and studied the various boxes littering the little front yard. "If you want, you can tell Alex where you want the boxes. You and I can work on the bigger stuff."

He glanced back at her just in time to see her finishing off the lemonade, and he watched as a bead of sweat rolled down the soft brown of her neck. Desire, vicious and painful, twisted inside him. He needed to get laid.

Vaughnne lowered the bottle and then tossed it into a little bin off to the side of the yard. It was a good twenty feet away and it landed squarely inside. "Nice shot."

She smiled blandly. "Thanks. Come on," she said as she turned around. She paused halfway up the walk to bend over and hoist up a box. The faded denim shorts she wore stretched tight over her butt and Gus had to drag his eyes away. "I'll show you all around. The boxes are all marked, so it won't be hard to figure out what goes where."

Gus dragged a hand down his face and then shifted the pack he carried so he had one strap over each shoulder. The logical thing to do was put it down, he knew. But he'd do that, maybe, after he'd gotten the lay of the land.

After he'd adjusted his shirt, making sure the weapon at his back was covered, he grabbed a couple of the boxes that were stacked haphazardly on top of one another. Alex glanced at him and he saw, again, there was none of that blind fear, none of the nerves. Everything was cool.

He should be able to relax now, right?

Technically, they could even leave because, no matter what he'd said, he hadn't come over to help her move her stuff in. They could leave and he didn't care if it made him look like an ass. He'd come to make sure she was safe. But leaving was the very last thing he wanted to do.

* * *

THEY muscled the bed frame into place, and Vaughnne all but groaned as the headache throbbing behind her eyes grew to nauseating proportions. She'd meant to take her time, get half the stuff done today and then work on the rest of it tomorrow, but when the gift horse—or gift stud—had arrived, what was she going to do, say *no*?

Especially as it would have been interesting trying to figure out how to move it all in on her own.

She would have figured something out, maybe calmly worked out a meeting and offered to pay them some money if they helped her unload. Either that, or just found somebody else living nearby. Something would have turned up.

Now she felt like her head was going to explode.

"You know how to put this together?"

The warm, dark velvet of his voice rolled over her skin, and she lifted her lashes to stare at him as she sagged back against the wall. He was enough to make her mouth go dry, especially with the way his shirt had gone a little damp with sweat now, making it cling to muscles that were way too defined for just the typical average Joe.

He'd dropped the backpack earlier, tucking it behind the front door, and although he was casual about it, she'd noticed that there hadn't been a single time when they'd walked through the room and he hadn't checked on that bag.

"Well?"

She blinked and then glanced over at the bed frame. Yeah. He'd asked her a question, hadn't he? Sighing, she studied it for a minute and then glanced over at the mattress propped against the opposite wall.

If she had her way, she'd just knock it down, crawl onto the bed, curl into a ball, and pass out. But that wasn't an option.

"Staring at it isn't going to do the job." He gestured at it. "You know how to put it together?"

There was something about the way he talked, she decided. Something *besides* the fact that his voice was sexy as hell. Low and smooth as silk, rich as melted chocolate and just as sinful.

Down, girl, she told herself absently as she pushed her sore body away from the wall and studied the bed frame. Yeah, yeah, staring at it wasn't going to help, but she was hoping she'd *remember* how it had been put together.

It had been bought at a thrift store and it was pretty. Vaughnne had a weakness for pretty things and she had no problem admitting it. But the pale green patina of the metal looked like a mind-bending puzzle just then. Propping her hands on her hips, she tried to remember the way everything had gone together and then she just sighed. "I have absolutely no fu . . ." Then she clamped her mouth shut and shot a look toward the hall. The kid. She wasn't used to being around kids. "Ah . . . sorry. I have absolutely no idea."

Gus nodded. "I'll go home and grab my tools. But that's about all we can do."

She should tell him it wasn't necessary. She knew that. But he'd offered. She needed to do what was necessary to get them to like her, trust her . . . and if he decided to offer a hand here and there? Why not accept it?

Wiping her forearm over her brow, she gave him a smile. Even though the headache pounding inside her head was about ready to kill her, she didn't let it show. "I appreciate it. Hey, I don't know if y'all ate anything, but I am starving so I'm going to order a pizza."

"We had dinner, thanks."

She arched a brow. "You sure? I've never seen a teenaged boy say no to pizza."

* * *

"ANOTHER box of books?" Alex lugged it over and dumped it on the floor next to the bookshelves she'd picked up. The bookshelves had also come from a thrift store. But the books were hers. Since she didn't know just how long she'd have to be *baby-sitting*, Vaughnne planned to keep herself entertained.

And she'd only brought four boxes.

Grinning at him, she sauntered over and peered inside the box. "Yeah. And that's the last of them, too."

He wrinkled his nose and said, "Is it a bunch more of those stupid girly books?"

"I'll have you know those girly books are awesome," she said loftily. "You'd be amazed at what a guy can learn from reading girly books."

"Girly books?"

That voice. It was too damned appealing. Shooting Gus a look from over her shoulder, she shrugged. "That's what he calls romance."

"Girly books." Gus smirked. "Well, I would likely call them girly books as well. A man won't learn much from them."

"Shows what you know, pal." She sank to the floor and started pulling the books from the box. Once she had some books on the shelves, she'd feel a little more at ease, she thought. Whether she was in Orlando or not. Having something of *hers* around would just make her feel better. "For *one*, a smart guy learns it's not a wise move to go and knock what a lady enjoys reading. If it makes her happy and it's not hurting anything? What's the issue?"

"Books like those are unrealistic," Gus said. He shrugged and reached into his back pocket, pulling out a pristine white hand-kerchief that looked out of place with his battered clothes, the faded jeans.

He had elegant hands, she thought. Very elegant hands.

And she was getting distracted. "Unrealistic," she drawled. Snorting, she pulled her knees to her chest and rested her chin on them. "Riiigggghhhht . . . like *Star Wars* isn't. *Lord of the*

Rings. Lord of the Flies. Bunnicula. Harry Potter and the Sorcerer's Stone."

"None of those books promise that love will conquer over all."

Vaughnne snorted. "Neither does romance make those promises. They are just *books*. Reading them doesn't mean I'm looking for a space pirate to solve all my problems. I can handle my problems just fine on my own."

"Space pirates?" Alex asked, his eyes rounding.

"Yeah . . ." She slid him a sly smile. "And that one got caught by a bounty hunter. Who was a chick."

Gus snorted. Then he shoved off the wall and gestured down the hall. "Milady, your bower awaits. But you'll need to help me get the mattress onto the bed frame."

* * *

HE probably should have tried to do it himself. He could have, but he wanted to make sure the bed was where she wanted it before he bothered. But now, in addition to having images of tasting her mouth, he wanted to see her stretched out on the bed, all that long, wild hair spread out around her as he stripped her clothes away.

He was too intimately acquainted with that body after three hours of helping her drag and move and push furniture, boxes, and every other damn thing she'd had crammed into that truck. Too familiar with those long, lean muscles and the way she moved with more confidence and control than any woman should have a right to.

He had more than a passing acquaintance with females. He'd had lovers whose bodies were honed to an athletic tightness, and others who were so soft and lushly female. Lovers whose bodies had been sculpted by the finest plastic surgeons around, and he appreciated every damned last one.

But Vaughnne . . . his hands itched to strip her naked already and he had no idea just *why*. It had been years since he'd had time to indulge in such a thing, but he hadn't had any trouble ignoring it until today. Until her.

She was a powerhouse of curves and sleek muscles, the kind of muscles that came from a dedication to fitness, yet none of it had affected the sheer female beauty of her. Her hips and ass were still lush and round, her breasts soft and full under the tank top she wore. Every once in a while, her bra strap had peeked out from under the edge of the shirt, simple and black, and it was driving him out of his mind.

"I think this will do."

As she stroked a hand down the mattress, he tracked the motion of her hand for a moment before he schooled his features into blankness and lifted his gaze to study her face. Her features had to be the most unique he'd ever seen. She was pretty, yes. Not beautiful, but pretty.

And unique, with those dark freckles dancing across her nose, a top-heavy mouth, and her smooth, warm brown skin.

"Is the bed where you want it?" he asked. He thought it would do better under the window. Where the morning light would come in and dance across that perfect body of hers.

Vaughnne heaved out a sigh and lifted her arms. She dragged the bandanna off her hair with one hand and used the other to gather her hair into a tail. "At this point, you could have glued the stupid thing to the ceiling and I wouldn't care. I just want it done. I'll take a better look around tomorrow, and if it's not where I want it, I can get it moved on my own."

She fished around in her pocket and pulled out a little black band, snapping it around her hair before shooting a look at her watch. "Now if that damn pizza would get here—"

The doorbell rang.

Alex appeared in the doorway, and although he knew Vaughnne wouldn't see it, the boy's face was taut, tense with nerves.

With that easy smile on her face, Vaughnne said, "It's about damn time. You two sure you don't want some? There are plates and stuff in the kitchen."

As Alex crossed to stand by him, Gus mentally ran through the layout of the house. The kitchen was just up the hall. They could stay out of sight of the front door. Although the backpack was by the front door. Careless . . . he'd gotten careless. A look at Alex's face had him thinking it through again. Alex was nervous . . . nervous, not scared.

This would work. They'd stay out of sight in the kitchen, and if he had to go through bodies to get the bag, then he'd do it. He had the Sig Sauer tucked into place at his back, regardless.

"I don't know . . . you hungry, Alex?"

* * *

VAUGHNNE wondered if that pizza delivery kid would have been so obnoxious if he knew there was a man with a very loaded, very dangerous weapon lurking just about twenty feet away from him.

Granted, she had her own weapons, although she'd wisely left them out of sight, and off her body, as much as she hated it. The man saw too clearly, though, and if he'd seen a weapon on her, he would have been gone.

Hard to guard a body when the body was hauling ass to the state line.

As she sauntered into the kitchen, one large pie in her hands and a box of wings on top, she kept her focus on the kid. Wasn't hard, since Gus wasn't in the kitchen just yet. The first thing he'd done once the front door shut was move out of the kitchen. All lazy, easy moves, from the way he looked, but he'd wasted no time getting the bag he'd tucked behind the front door.

Whatever he carried in that thing, it must be important. As he came back into the kitchen, his gaze sought out Alex. The kid gave him a wan smile and she could all but *feel* a pop in the air as some of the tension drained away.

Pretending not to notice their preoccupation, she dumped the pizza on the table. "I kept it basic," she said, flipping the lid up. "I was kind of figuring you might want something—I hear about how boys your age always have room for food and I figured it was the least I could do to say thanks. I doubted you'd want the garbage truck approach I take to my food."

Alex wrinkled his nose, relaxing a little more as he leaned in and eyed the pizza. "Garbage truck?"

"Yeah." She grinned at him. "I get it loaded with just about everything."

She found the cabinet where she'd already put the plates. One thing about moving in—if you didn't get the basic stuff out, toiletries, dishes, books—books were very basic—then it just made it that much more annoying. She grabbed three of them and passed them out before moving to the fridge. "All I have is sugary stuff," she said, shooting Gus a wry smile. "I've got the appetite of a six-year-old boy. Coke, Big Red, some root beer. I do have milk, but it's chocolate."

"I'll take a Big Red," Alex said.

She glanced at Gus. He shrugged. "That's fine. I'll have water."

"I have beer," she offered. She snagged a Big Red for Alex, another Mike's Hard Lemonade for herself. "And these?"

He snorted and shook his head. "I'll pass."

* * *

SHE shouldn't have had the second lemonade.

Vaughnne could admit that nearly two hours after they left as she emerged from a deep, deep sleep to the sound of her alarm.

She'd set her phone to go off because she wanted to take a

good look around and get a feel for things when she wasn't going to be seen. So that meant . . . at night.

But she was exhausted. If she didn't plan on trying to get some more sleep, she might have gone and chugged a few of the Monsters she had stashed in the fridge, but she was damned well going to get sleep unless all hell broke loose.

She didn't think that was going to happen.

Everything inside her body was just screaming for bed, and if there were problems, adrenaline would be crashing through her and clearing away the clouds. That only made it harder to drag her tired ass out the door once she'd donned a black tank top and some black jogging shorts. She'd thought about going for something a little more concealing, but that kid already had her reevaluating things.

She'd come up with something if they woke up and saw her snooping around. Vaughnne was nothing if not clever and quick on her feet, but if she was dressed up all ninja-like, that was *not* going to set the oh-so-sexy Gus or the oh-so-scared Alex at ease.

Why are you so scared, anyway, kid? she wondered as she started down the street. Right now, the plan was to get the lay of the land. Nothing like a midnight jog for that. Even had an excuse. She couldn't sleep. They didn't have to know she was lying.

It was a quiet neighborhood, she decided. Run-down and tired, but trying to cling to nice, and it looked like everybody here still tried to take care of what they owned.

And . . . each other, she figured out not even eight minutes into her run.

A cop car came around the corner and she grimaced, slowing to a stop, keeping her hands at her sides. She'd put her license in her pocket before she left—not *her* license, but one of the fakes she carried for working so she was in the clear there. Even as the two cops climbed out of the car, she figured it wasn't a total irritation that they'd been called.

She had another piece of the puzzle. The people around here *did* watch things. Would make it harder for her to do what she needed to do. Harder. But not impossible. Also made it safer for the kid. A little, at least.

As the younger cop loitered off to the side, she focused on the older one. A tall guy, his skin nearly as black as the night, smiled at her, a nice, professional smile. "Ma'am."

"Evening." Then she grimaced and looked around. "I guess I should say night."

"Guess so." He smiled a little more naturally. "It's kind of late for a jog. Had a call about a strange woman prowling around."

Damn. Glad I didn't go for the prowling method, Vaughnne thought. Even as she thought, she gave a disgruntled sigh and swiped a hand over the back of her brow. "Do I really look like I'm prowling around, Officer? I'm *running*."

"At one in the morning?" his partner asked.

Younger. Rookie, Vaughnne decided. Still had the shine on him, and the stupid.

"I had a hard time getting to sleep," she said mildly. "I just moved into my new place today and I don't know where a gym or anything is around here. The only thing that helps me sleep when I'm having insomnia is a workout. So I went for a run."

"Where did you move into?"

The response that leaped to mind was, *None of your damned business*. But instead of going with that, she shrugged and waved off to the east. "Westbrook Avenue, a few blocks over."

Somebody who had never had trouble with the law, or didn't work in law enforcement, was just going to answer that sort of question, because they automatically thought *cooperating* made everything better. Sometimes it did. Sometimes it didn't. Right then, it didn't hurt her to cooperate. Vaughnne was an old hand at dealing with law enforcement . . . from both sides. She carried a badge of her own now, but there had been a time when *she* was the one having trouble with the law. Lessons that had served her well more than once.

"Just moved into a new area and you're out running around in the dead of night."

She looked back at the rookie and lifted a brow. "I was told it was a safe area. Was I told wrong?"

"It's a nice enough area," the older cop said, subtly moving so that he stood just a bit between her and his partner. "But you can never be too careful, Ms. . . ."

"Caffee," she said, sighing. "Vaughnne Caffee. Fine. I'll head back home. Unless I'm in trouble for taking a damned run?"

"No." He shook his head and smiled again. "No trouble. You understand, of course, we have to follow up on the calls we get."

"Sure." Without looking at the other one, she turned around and started back down the sidewalk. They watched her for a few minutes.

She took the longer route on the way back to the little house she was calling home. She still needed to get a better look at the setup where Gus and Alex lived. Figure out the best way to keep an eye on things. Although she already had a decent idea how she'd do that. The tricky thing was going to be getting it all set up.

The little house was even smaller than hers. More run-down than most of them, although she could see signs where somebody, probably Gus, was working on things.

Hard to tell in the dark, of course. The windows bothered her. Windows and doors were the most vulnerable areas of a house. Where did the boy sleep? In a room of his own?

There were no lights—

Then one flashed on and she crossed the road. Casual. Jogging across the road, waiting for that prickle feeling between her shoulder blades that would let her know she was being watched.

It never came. But as she unlocked the door and slipped inside, her breathing was coming far too erratic and her heart beat in a harsh, unsteady rhythm against her ribs. Leaning against the door, she edged to the side and peered through the narrow window, watching as a shadow moved through the house across the street.

* * *

IT had been years since he'd slept well.

Too many years.

Usually the dreams that plagued him were full of screams, or broken cries. Desperate whispers and fears and blood and misery.

This time, though . . . well, there had been broken cries. Desperate whispers. And heat. So much of it. He'd been back in that house across the street, but this time, he'd been alone there with Vaughnne, and when she'd gone to tug her bra strap into place, he caught her hand and stopped her.

He could remember how soft her skin had felt in the dream. So very, very soft . . . it would feel like that in real life, he thought. But in the dream . . . yeah. Yeah, she'd been soft. And when he went to strip her shirt away, she'd just stood there, watching him, her eyes intent and quiet, a strange little Mona Lisa smile on that wicked, sexy mouth.

He'd tangled his hands in her hair and feasted on her mouth like it had been decades since he'd touched a woman. It had only been four years, but that was too long.

Before he had managed to get her completely naked and bury his aching dick inside her, the dream had shattered. Gus didn't know what had woken him, but whatever it was, he was awake and he knew better than to lie in bed when his body was suddenly humming with tension.

A quick glance at the clock told him that he'd gotten two hours of sleep.

Not enough.

But it didn't matter. He listened to the silence of the old house as he rolled silently out of the bed, his hand gripping the butt of his weapon. Back to the wall, he checked the hallway out of habit. His instincts said the house was empty, save for him and the boy. He didn't trust them. Creeping down the hallway, he checked inside and saw that Alex was sleeping on his belly, face buried in a pillow.

Alex . . . Alex was asleep. *That* he would trust. Sighing, he sagged against the wall behind him and scrubbed a hand down his face while the adrenaline drained out of him.

Alex wouldn't be asleep if there was any sort of threat within a hundred feet of the house. He was like a living, breathing danger meter.

"Gus?"

In the dim light, he could see Alex lift his head. Forcing himself to smile, he said, "Go to sleep, kid. It's okay."

Knowing the boy would sleep better if there were lights on while he was moving through the house, Gus flicked on the hallway light as he prowled around. He needed a drink, so before he did anything, he bypassed the kitchen and pulled down the bottle he kept stashed over the refrigerator. Tequila, cheap shit, but the only thing he could afford, straight, the burn of it heating his throat and then his belly as he moved through the house, checking it over once more.

Alex slept in the narrow little room he'd claimed for his own. It wasn't intended for a bedroom, but neither of them worried about that. The cot in there wasn't exactly what Gus wanted for him, but what Alex needed the most was to feel safe and he'd sleep better someplace closest to Gus, someplace where nobody could come in through the windows.

If they came in through the windows where Gus slept, they would have an unpleasant surprise, he thought. So very unpleasant.

Pausing by the open entryway, he watched as Alex rolled onto his side, hugging a pillow against him. *You're safe, Alex*, Gus thought. And for as long as he breathed, Gus would do every damn thing he could to *keep* the boy safe.

Every damn thing. He'd make any sacrifice. Give up anything and everything. It didn't matter what rivers he had to cross, what mountains he had to climb, what dragons he had to slay. The boy had lost enough. Gus's job was to keep him from losing anything else.

Knowing the boy wouldn't stay asleep if he remained there brooding, Gus took his tequila and slid outside to sit on the front porch.

Across the street, Vaughnne's house was dark.

She'd be asleep, he thought. She'd been so tired with dark circles under her eyes and exhaustion in every line of her body when they left.

Stop thinking about her. He had no room in his life for that. Not for anything.

The only thing he had room for was the boy.

Alex was his focus, and that was the way it had to be.

THREE

THE cookies smelled too damned good.

Vaughnne helped herself to two of them as they cooled, and she knew if she didn't get them out of there, she would eat more of them. Which meant she'd have to tack another mile onto her run when she hit the pavement later that day.

But with the scent of chocolate, both white and dark, filling the air, and her belly still demanding another cookie, she almost gave in.

If Gus didn't leave the old lady's house next door soon, she *would* give in.

It was turning into a bitch, keeping an eye on him. She'd set up exterior cameras over the past few nights, planted around his property, but not on it. He was too . . . cautious. Yeah, that was it. Jones still wasn't having any luck turning up information on either of them, and that in itself was a puzzle, but the guy was so cautious. So watchful. He held himself in a way that normal people didn't. Like he was ready to fight, ready to run, ready to react to any damn thing.

If she planted cameras on his property, she knew he'd find them in a heartbeat.

Still, around the perimeter, a few here and there, and they weren't exactly watching *him*. They were watching for anybody that might be trying to *get* to him. A nice 360 view of the place. Ideally, she'd wanted one inside the house, but she was reconsidering that plan every time she saw him.

Tipping him off that somebody was watching him just wasn't going to go over well.

Sighing, she checked the window again. The truck was still in front of the house, and nope, he still hadn't left the house next door.

She'd been biding her time, watching the house at night and getting by on catnaps during the day because she couldn't rest as heavily at night as she'd like to. She was on edge, sleeping with one eye open, and this was so *not* the ideal way to get all the way back up to full speed.

Babysitting, my ass, she thought, grabbing a cookie and nipping another bite. She'd like to take the entire plate and dump them over Taylor Jones's head.

The cookies were her way in.

But if Gus didn't get home soon . . .

Her phone rang.

It was an unknown number and that wasn't a surprise. Picking it up, she continued to stare outside, keeping her body positioned so nobody could see her. "Hello?"

"Mac."

Jones didn't introduce himself, but he didn't need to.

"Figures." She took another bite of cookie, but the explosion of chocolate on her tongue didn't help.

"How are things going?"

"Quiet as the proverbial grave," she admitted. "Nothing happens. At all. They get up. They leave. I watch them while he works . . . he keeps the kid with him and nothing happens there. They come back. I haven't seen hide nor hair of anybody. Have you learned anything new about them?"

"Some. Get me some better visuals on the man and I can do more. I have my suspicions, but I need clearer images to confirm. He moves like a man who knows how to avoid being caught on camera, and for the facial recognition software to work, we actually need to see his *face*."

"So . . ." She drew the word out. "You have nothing really to tell me."

"I have some things I *could* tell you; I'm just electing not to until I confirm the information. Just be careful."

"Wonderful. Be careful. Information noted." She grunted, shifting to stare down the street, watching for them. Any minute now and they'd be at the house. She thought. She hoped. "Just what had you sending me down here anyway?"

"I listened to somebody I trust," Jones said simply. "I trust my sources, Mac. In our line of work, we have to."

"And what did your source say?" She rubbed the back of her neck, irritated. He usually wasn't so closemouthed about these things. None of them liked operating in the dark, he knew that.

A moment of silence passed, and then Jones sighed. "There was very little my source *could* say. Just that the boy was going to have trouble . . . and we didn't want anything bad happening to him. I think there are things I'm not being told, but I've learned to trust this person."

"So we're taking a lot of things on blind faith here." She rubbed her temple, going back to watching the house while her gut twisted round and round.

"Do *you* think my source was wrong?" he asked. "If you

think we're off base and there's nothing wrong, fine. I'll call you back."

"Shit, I hate you sometimes," she said. "No, your source isn't off base. The kid has a gift that's waiting to explode, and they both have trouble written all over them."

"What else can you tell me?"

She made a face. "That's *my* line. You're supposed to be the one with the info here, boss, but you won't tell me shit. The guy . . ." She paused, blew out a breath. "The guy isn't your average Joe, if you get what I'm saying. Military, cop. Something. He watches things. Sees things. He's got moves on him, if you know what I mean."

Jones was silent.

She twirled a lock of hair around her finger. "And the kid . . . shit, Jones. Did you know what you were sending me into?"

"I told you the boy was gifted."

She snorted. "Gifted doesn't touch it. He makes my teeth hurt, he's so strong. If anybody with the wrong sort of mind grabbed him, Jones?" Shaking her head, she sighed. "And he's got no idea how strong he is, how much he's casting it out there, either. It's like nobody ever worked with him to tone it down."

"Not everybody has somebody around to teach them," Jones said softly. "You didn't."

"Yeah, but I learned fast how to shut things down." It was that or just suffer more for it. "What about the guy? The kid calls him his dad, but he's not."

"How can you tell?"

"I just can." Some of the others in the unit could read that sort of thing. Read the mind and read the lies. Read the emotions and *feel* the lie. Vaughnne couldn't. She had to rely on the more mundane abilities, and she'd brushed them up as much as could be expected. When people lied, there were just tiny little cues.

Vaughnne had learned to look for them.

The boy, as skilled as he was at it, all but *screamed* "liar" to her. He'd probably convince just about everybody else, including teachers, neighbors, and friends. Probably even a lot of law enforcement, if they had a reason to talk to him. It wasn't even that stupid shit that people *thought* you might see when talking to a liar. He had no problem meeting her gaze, and there wasn't any of the constant fidgeting some people thought you'd see when talking to somebody who was hiding the truth. And he *was* a fidgeter. She'd seen that much when they were moving. He had a problem being still, which was normal for a kid. But when she asked him anything remotely personal, he went oddly still.

And he *lied* . . . like a dog. With easy, polite smiles and practiced, natural responses, he lied. And he did it all while looking her right in the eye.

Gus was harder, though. If she didn't know better, she'd almost believe everything he told her. That bothered her, because she didn't like it when she couldn't see through somebody's story. And it was just a story.

They weren't a dad and a son just trying to make it on their own after the mom decided she'd rather go out and party than help raise a kid.

Not an unusual story. She'd heard it before, had seen it, but that wasn't the case here.

"I think you're probably right, by the way," Jones said, interrupting her mental train of thought and successfully derailing it. "About the man. I believe he does have a background we'd find interesting . . . and that's after we get through the false layers that I'm just now uncovering. I can't confirm until I get better images of him, but I don't think I'm wrong. Also, I'm just about certain he's not the dad."

Spying a familiar form striding down the sidewalk next door, Vaughnne edged back from the window. "I'm surprised you don't have everything from their social security numbers to their shoe sizes already."

"I was hoping you'd fill me in on the shoe sizes. Because that's so important to the case," Jones replied, his voice neutral.

So very neutral, it took her a second to realize what had just happened. "Oh, shit, Jones. I don't believe it, but I think you might have just made a joke."

"I don't joke. They removed my sense of humor when I took the job." She heard him pause, speak to somebody, and then he was back on the phone. "I have to go. I'll stay in touch, Mac."

The line went dead and she went in, cleared it from her list of recent calls before sliding the phone back into her pocket. Standing in the middle of the living room, she continued to stare out the window. She'd bought a wispy set of curtains for a reason. If the blinds weren't drawn, she could see through them just fine, and since the lights were off, unless somebody was looking right at her, they wouldn't be able to see her easily. Considering the white-hot brightness of the sun, it would be pretty damn hard to make her out, standing in her darkened living room.

Gus and the kid were standing in front of the house. To anybody else, it might look like they were talking. Gus had the backpack slung over his left shoulder, a jacket draped over his right hand. Weapon hand, she thought. Something skittered along her senses and she knew, as sure as she was standing there, they were not talking.

Alex stood there, while Gus looked down at him. And the boy looked up at the house. Just watching, kind of like she was watching him.

Then, the next thing he did had her rubbing her temple as the headache flared.

Psychic energy flared, crackled. And it wasn't until the mad energy faded that the tension she sensed in both man and boy eased. Once it passed, the two of them headed into the house.

"What kind of trouble are you two in?" she muttered.

Then she glanced over at the plate of cookies she'd put together. She needed to reach out to them, try to get some sort of relationship with the kid going, but everything in her screamed *caution, caution, caution*—

It was just a plate of cookies.

They could take the cookies or not, invite her inside or not.

It might take more than one or two visits to get in the door, and she was more than aware of that fact. She knew she'd have to take her time getting closer to the boy and *that* was the easier part of the job.

The scary part . . .

Her heart jumped into her throat as she thought about the other thing she needed to do. She slid a hand into her pocket, touched the microscopic little camera, and sighed. She really did need to get eyes on the inside and *not* just because it would be nice to be able to do more than catnap at night. Her instincts were good, damn good, and they'd kept her alive, sane, and healthy for a long, long time—part of the reason she made a good *babysitter*, she figured, but part of a *babysitting* job . . . or bodyguard job? Knowing where in the hell the body was. Watching the damn body. Hard to do if she was catching up on sleep. No matter how badly she needed it.

The lack of solid sleep wasn't going to help her get back to fighting form any quicker, that was certain.

She went to pick up the cookies and then she stopped. Although Vaughnne absolutely wanted to kick herself in the ass, she headed to the bathroom. She wasn't vain. Back when she would have been learning all that shit about hair and makeup, she'd been struggling just to scrape by after her parents had kicked her out on her ass.

Once she'd managed to haul herself out of the hole where she'd found herself, she'd then been busy busting her ass to get up to speed, because she'd figured out just what she *wanted* to do. What she *needed* to do. It had been right about the time she read about a psychic in the newspaper.

Taige Branch. Taige Morgan now. But Vaughnne had figured out then and there, she wasn't alone. So she'd hitchhiked and walked and made her way down to Alabama, determined to talk to the woman who had been helping others out. She hadn't ever gotten to talk to Taige that day, but she had talked to somebody else.

Taylor Jones, who had been playing guard dog at the hospital where Taige was hospitalized. Apparently that happened a lot with her. Taylor had taken one look at her and told her she wasn't ready.

He was right. She hadn't been. Getting her GED, college, all of that shit had eaten up more of her time. But for the past six years, she'd been a part of his unit. She finally had a place where she belonged, and she'd worked damn hard to get here. Not much time to worry about some of the vanities that came with being a girl, not much time to worry about hair, makeup, any of that shit.

But she knew when a guy was interested and she'd seen the look in Gus's eyes more than once the other day. Flipping the light, she stared at her reflection for a long moment. A black woman with a hell of a lot of hair, a hell of a lot of attitude, and grim eyes stared back at her.

"You are *not* going to be charming anybody's pants off with that look on your face, honey." Blowing out a breath, she skimmed a hand back over her hair, but there wasn't a whole hell of a lot to do with it. She planned on washing it that night, but unless she wanted to delay everything else she had to do until she had it washed and taken care of, then she'd just have to leave her hair as it was for now.

Maybe she should have gotten it plaited or something before she came down here, but it was too late to worry about it right now.

Resting her hands on the cool porcelain of the sink, she tried to see herself the way he might. Pretty enough, but nothing to write home about. The freckles were something she'd hated for her entire life, odd, dark little dots that danced across her nose and cheeks. She didn't mind her mouth, though. Or her eyes.

She had a unique face, if nothing else, which wasn't always good considering the life she lived. Sometimes she needed to blend, and Vaughnne's looks didn't lead to *blending*. Neither did her attitude. When she bothered with makeup, she played up the mouth and the eyes, but she didn't think it was a good idea to go for the makeup just then. Anything that might make *their* instincts sound an alarm was going to cause problems.

Okay, so no makeup and she wasn't about to go put on any *come-hither* clothes.

The red tank top and denim shorts were just going to have to work.

One thing she could do . . . wipe away the attitude. Get rid of the frustration and make sure everything was all locked down nice and tight behind her shields. Working around other psychics with stronger abilities had taught her everything she ever needed to know about hiding her thoughts, controlling them. Generally, psychics would only skim surface thoughts, and if they wanted more, they had to establish a deeper connection. She kept everything she didn't want known hidden under strong, solid shields. The kid didn't have the finesse needed to power through those shields without her realizing it, and if he started trying to pull that trick, it would be time to start doing some fast talking and even faster phone calling.

So . . . tone down the attitude. Smooth away some of the rough edges she hadn't bothered to cover, since she was in here by her lonesome. Closing her eyes, she gave herself a minute to do that, and when she looked in the mirror, she saw herself again. But the woman looking back was just a little less . . . rough. A little less ready to go for the throat, she guessed.

Blowing out a breath, she went through a few of the mental exercises she needed to calm her thoughts and relax.

Finally, though, she felt a little less jagged, a little less ragged. And about as ready to face Gus as she was going to be. Gus. And Alex. Really, Alex should be the one to worry her. But who was she spazzing about? The hot guy.

Hell. She needed to have her head examined. Or maybe she just needed to get laid. Or have an orgasm. Something. Sighing, she hunted down the plate of cookies and headed outside.

Thinking about *Gus* and *orgasm* was not good. It undid the past thirty minutes of *mental relaxation*.

He was bad—very, very bad, she decided. Very bad for the female parts of her, very bad for her peace of mind, and if she couldn't keep her mind on the job, he was going to be very bad for her life in general.

* * *

VAUGHNNE was bad for his peace of mind, but Gus had successfully convinced himself that all he needed to do was stay the hell away from her. If he did that, everything would go back to the way it had been.

"It's her," Alex said, an odd tone in his voice. He was at the table working on the day's assignment and he spoke seconds before the knock came. Gus reached for the towel to wipe his hands off as they listened to the next knock, twenty seconds later.

"I know," Gus said. He wasn't psychic, but this was just his luck. He'd decided he needed to stay away from her, so naturally, life had thrown her back in his path.

Alex continued to sit at the table. "Are you going to answer it?"

He really shouldn't.

But the truck was in the drive, and if he didn't, he figured it would only make her more curious. It was a perfectly logical, perfectly plausible explanation.

And it had nothing to do with the simple fact that he wanted to see her again.

"I'll be there in a minute," he called out as he slid Alex a look.

Alex stood up and went into the room off the back of the house. They'd rehearsed it all a hundred times. Probably more. And even though they both knew who was at the door, it didn't matter. Alex did his part. Gus did his, reaching for the Sig Sauer on the kitchen counter and tucking it into place at the small of his back.

"Do you need that?" Alex asked softly, even as he tucked himself against the wall and got ready. Always ready. The backpack was hanging on the back of a chair, and Gus could grab it in a moment. In two minutes, they could be out of this house. Out of the house, and running. Again.

Fury tore into Gus with hot, greedy claws, so abrupt and so all-consuming. It all but leveled him and caught him completely off guard. He'd thought, after all this time, he had dealt with this. Nobody understood the reasons behind this as well as he did. Why *get* angry over something he couldn't control?

But the anger was there, bubbling, burning inside him.

He shoved it down, buried it deep as he looked at Alex. He'd never fully deal with it, perhaps.

This was no life for that boy. None at all. He knew it and he hated it. They lived every day by a set schedule. Up at dawn where they went through a routine, what to do if somebody tried to break in, what to do if somebody *did* break in and managed to get ahold of Gus, where Alex was supposed to go, what he was supposed to do. Gus went to work at his shitty job where the kid sat in the car and did his schoolwork because he couldn't go to school. They lied through their teeth that Gus was homeschooling him because they didn't need the mess it would bring down on them if somebody suspected the boy wasn't getting an education, although that was actually the *least* of Alex's concerns.

If they managed to find him—*Stop it*. He couldn't do this now.

The resigned look on Alex's face was another blow. It didn't cut at him the way the fear did, but it was a blow nonetheless. Like Alex had already accepted this was his life. This was all his life was, would ever be.

Gus didn't *want* that for him.

He wanted to promise Alex that things would get better, that he'd have . . . something. A life, somehow. But he didn't do that. Instead of offering promises he couldn't keep, he stood there and stared back at the boy until Alex looked away. Casually, he adjusted his shirt, made sure it covered the gun. "You know it's necessary."

"But—"

He cut the boy off, speaking softly, in a low voice, and watched as Alex tucked his chin against his chest.

"Yes, sir."

And as Gus turned away and started down the hall, he heard her voice again.

You must do this for me.

Yeah. He knew that. He knew what he had to do. He just wondered if he and the boy would get through it without the boy hating him.

* * *

"HAVE you found them?"

Esteban eyed the boss from under his lashes for a moment before he lowered his gaze back to the floor.

The boss did have a name, but he didn't dare speak it. He didn't even want to be here. The last man assigned to this job had failed. And he hadn't been seen since.

He didn't want to end up the same way.

But he knew it was likely. He had another idea, but whether or not the boss would go for it . . . Swallowing the spit that pooled in his mouth, he managed to keep his voice level as he responded, "No, sir. We haven't found him. Not the boy or the man."

"Why not?"

He had no answer.

After a few seconds, the boss said, "It's been years. You realize this, don't you? *Years*. And a *pendejo* whose claim to fame in life is looking pretty and fucking females has managed to keep that child away from us. It's pathetic. You were supposed to be reliable. To have resources. And what have you done but fail?"

"I have a new plan lined up," he said, swallowing the nasty, metallic taste of fear that rose up his throat. He resisted, just barely, the urge to swipe his hands down the sides of his trousers, but that would wrinkle them and the boss wasn't overly impressed by a man in a wrinkled suit.

The boss wasn't impressed by much, to be honest. He never should have taken this job. If he failed this time, his best bet was to get as far away as possible. At least he'd lined up an escape route.

Skepticism dashed through the boss's eyes, carefully concealed, there and then gone.

But he knew what he'd seen in the other man's eyes. Doubt. Anger. He made a study of recognizing such things. It kept him alive, made him money. Sometimes, one was equally as important as the other.

"Oh?" The boss leaned back and crossed his hands over a belly that had just now started to go soft even though he was almost sixty. "What is this plan?"

Floundering, he wracked his brain for a decent lie. "I am still working to get it together. Once I have more concrete data to present you with, I'd be happy to go into detail with you, sir." He didn't plan on giving him any *detail*, if he could avoid it. Because if this didn't work out, he needed to disappear. No point in making it any easier for the man to find him, right?

The boss continued to watch him, his eyes flat, black . . . soulless. "I would suggest, my boy, that you get that information together. Quickly."

He bowed his head and turned to the door. He had to get back to the search. And he planned on leaving quickly. He was running out of time, he knew. But this new development . . .

Yes. It was the best break he'd had in the past seven months, ever since he'd started hunting for the missing child. As long as it was legit, he might stand a chance.

And he thought it was.

He had a knack for discerning codes, and this website was nothing *but* code. The subtext and innuendos that people used to get across hidden meanings. It was little wonder they didn't want people stumbling across the site, little wonder they used code and subtext.

Psychics.

These people were for real. They were legit, not just a bunch of lunatics or New Agers who *thought* they were psychic. He knew it in his gut. Now he just had to get one of them out in the open. And if that didn't work, he'd just keep going until he succeeded.

The boss called out his name just as he reached the door.

Pausing, he stood there. Waiting.

The next words sent a shiver across his spine. "I hope you realize . . . my patience isn't endless. You are quite running out of time. Very much so."

* * *

As the door shut, Reyes turned and stared out the window.

Four years.

It had been four years.

He hadn't lost hope, though.

Losing hope too easily led to lost focus, and when one lost focus, it was too easy to stray from the path. He would find the boy.

Find the boy, and kill the man who had taken him away.

It was as simple as that.

But he was losing faith in the man he'd hired. Supposedly this one could find the unfindable, do the undoable, finish the unfinishable. That was what all his previous clients had said. His job record was impressive, to say the least.

A record was shit without results, though.

And they had no results. Nothing.

It infuriated him.

It took an effort to keep that fury under control, but he finally managed, and when he reached for the phone, his hand was steady.

Perhaps he wouldn't pull his current man off the job until he saw the results from his latest endeavor, but it was time to start exploring other options, he decided.

But before he could dial the number, there was a knock at his door and a low, throaty voice called out his name.

"Come in," he called out. He could make the call while she was in here, he supposed. It wouldn't hurt.

The blonde came inside, a smile on her mouth, her lips slicked with red, her curves barely covered by a scrap of a bikini the same shade as her eyes. She came around the desk and leaned against it, reached out to trail a finger down his arm. "You've been working all day," she murmured.

Inexplicably, he found himself unable to look away from her mouth. His limbs felt heavy and his blood pumped hotter, slower. Yes . . . he had been working all day, hadn't he?

* * *

VAUGHNNE sighed and glanced out over the yard. She'd knocked almost two minutes ago. If she hadn't heard Gus's voice, she would have worried a little. But she heard movement inside, and none of those movements were the sorts that set her instincts on edge, either.

As the footsteps drew nearer to the door, she ignored the butterflies jumping in her belly and braced herself. She hadn't brought her weapon. She still didn't trust how things would go if Gus saw it, but she suspected things would go . . . *badly*. And he'd peg it from a mile away, the same way she'd known he was carrying.

When he opened the door, she was doubly glad she hadn't brought her Glock. The look on his face wasn't quite the one she'd been hoping for, although it didn't really surprise her.

Each step was going to be a struggle, there was no denying that.

His eyes, that sultry gray, rested on her face, and although that inviting, sexy warmth was there, she sensed a distance. *I'm sorry, but you're not welcome here.* That was the message he was sending out, loud and clear. It was like his eyes said, *I'll take you to bed in a second . . . but . . .* and the *but* spoke louder than everything else.

Well. It was a good thing Vaughnne had always ignored those messages she didn't want to acknowledge.

"Hey." Smiling at him, she pulled the foil back off the plate of cookies and held it up. "I wanted to say thanks for the help. I made you and Alex some cookies."

He glanced down and something flickered in his eyes. It might have been surprise. Might have been caution. She didn't know. But he wasn't going to take the cookies, not just like that. Tugging the foil off, she took one at random and nipped a bite off. "Come on, you have to take them," she said, rolling her eyes. "I already ate three or four of them, and if you don't take them for you and your boy, *I'll* eat them and then I'll have to run double what I usually run. Then I'll be cranky and it will be all your fault."

"My fault."

She licked a crumb off her lips and nodded. "Yes. I made you cookies and you won't eat them . . . I can't let them go to waste, right? But if I eat them, I have to work them off. And running seven or eight miles instead of three or four will make me a bitch . . ." She grimaced and peered around him. "Sorry. Um. It won't make me very nice. See how this is your fault if you don't take them?"

She took another bite from the cookie and then held it up to him. "Try a bite," she offered. "I make damn good cookies, if I do say so myself."

He caught her wrist in one hand and plucked the cookie out, eyeing it narrowly before taking a quick bite. "You could have finished it," he pointed out.

His eyes dropped to the plate. Then something shifted in his gaze. And he reached out. She didn't look down. She'd been tested enough in her life to know when it was happening again. "Here, since you enjoy them so much that you ate three or four . . ."

She wondered if he had some inkling in his head to make her taste-test every one before he let the kid have a damn cookie. And abruptly, her heart hurt. It just *hurt*, standing there staring at him as he pushed a cookie at her and watched her with that sleepy, sexy look in his eyes and his hand now hanging loose at his side.

And maybe she didn't have any ability to read minds, but Vaughnne knew one thing damn well. If she balked about taking that cookie, they would have a problem.

Not only did he not *trust* people, he expected every damn soul around him to try and hurt him.

Why?

She polished off the cookie in two bites, and even though it was like sawdust on her tongue, she leaned forward and studied the plate, poking through them until she found one of the white chocolate macadamia cookies. "I've got to be balanced," she said. "You made me eat a chocolate chip, now I have to have the white chocolate."

She nibbled on it as she eyed him. "You going to share any of those with Alex, or am I going to stand here and be a glutton and eat all the cookies?"

She felt a ripple roll across her skin just then, but it wasn't from Gus. He didn't have a lick of talent in him, unless it was the way he could look at her and make her *want*.

A minute later, he glanced back behind him. "There he is. He probably smelled the chocolate."

"Chocolate." Alex wedged himself in the door, and for a second, the look on his face was that of just any ordinary kid. "Where is there . . ."

Then the words trailed off as he saw the plate. "Cookies." He swallowed and then looked up at Gus. "She made cookies."

"She did." He nodded to Vaughnne. "You should thank her."

Vaughnne was already a little tired of this, and if she didn't already have an inkling about the kind of life these two had been living, she could probably find herself rather pissed off with Gus. But as the kid hurriedly stuck out his hand, she went to shake his, letting some of her puzzled smile show on her face.

Then she stopped and frowned, swiping her hand down the side of her shorts. "I've got cookie crumbs on me," she mumbled. After she'd dusted them off, she shook the kid's hand and felt his mental fingers rooting through her mind yet again. He wasn't as neat that time, and pain ripped through her mind.

She barely managed to keep a grimace from showing as he broke the connection with absolutely no finesse and no care. The pain increased, and she could feel it rippling through her, growing, and growing . . .

Dayyum, he was strong.

Distantly, she made a mental note. This kid needed training and he needed it fast.

Even though she'd been braced for him to do something, his blunt probe through her mind left her off balance. She felt like he'd jammed his hands inside her skull, scraped them through her gray matter like it was muck, and then just shoved her to the side. Stumbling, she tried to catch her balance on the doorjamb.

A hand caught her arm.

Gus—

Trying to breathe through the pain, trying to keep her own mental shields in place, she sucked in a desperate breath before she swung her head around to look at him.

"Are you okay?" he asked, his voice low and tense.

"Headache," she said absently, forcing herself to smile. She needed to leave. Get back to the house and sit down. Maybe lie down. Right inside the door would be fine. Shit. The pounding in her head increased, and she thought she just might puke.

But he was eyeing her oddly, and her instincts were screaming. *Cover*, she reminded herself. *Don't break your cover.* "Probably from all the sugar I've been sucking in today."

Then, because she figured they *both* needed to be aware of the kid's lack of finesse, she reached up and pressed the heel of her hand to her head. It wasn't like she was acting, either. It felt like a freight train was trying to rip through her skull, and the nausea churned through her harder and harder with every passing second. She was going to hurl cookies in a second if she wasn't careful. "Damn, it hit me hard, like somebody just punched me."

Alex's hand froze over the plate.

Any guilt she might have felt died as the pain just continued to grow.

"Maybe you should sit down," Gus said quietly. "Are you well enough to go home?"

"Sure." She smiled at them both and pushed the cookies into

Alex's hands. The pounding in her head was getting worse, though, and she felt something wet on her face.

"What . . ." She went to wipe at her nose.

But before she could, she swayed. The world went dark.

*　*　*

GUS swore as he caught her.

He'd seen the trickle of blood, but it went from a trickle to a flood in a matter of seconds.

Under his breath, a litany of curses ripped out of him as he caught her against him.

From the corner of his eye, he saw Alex, his mouth stuffed full of cookie and his gaze big and round. "Don't eat them, damn it. What if that's what made her sick?"

Alex looked miserable.

But he shook his head and swallowed. As he followed Gus into the house, he clutched the plate against him. "It was me."

"What?" Then he shook his head. "No. Not now. Get me a towel." He laid Vaughnne's still form on the couch and tried not to think about what a very nice form it was . . . lean muscle, lush curves. He could spend hours learning all the secrets of her body and never get tired, he suspected. But even if he could *let* himself take that pleasure, now wasn't the time.

That smooth brown skin had gone ashen on him, and as he shifted to kneel closer to her head, he saw that the bleeding was getting worse.

"Alex, hurry up!"

"Here . . ." The boy's voice was soft and sad as he pushed a towel into Gus's hand, but Gus didn't linger to look at the kid.

Not then. Anger pulsed inside him and he needed to get a grip on it before he spoke. He'd thought they had this under control. But . . . *No. No buts. We just start again. And if it happens* again, *we start over* . . . again. He focused on that as he pressed the towel to Vaughnne's face, pinching her nose lightly just below where the bony area ended to help stem the bleeding.

More than two minutes in silence. He'd give it five before he pulled the towel away, but each second was an eternity and she was so still—

There was no warning.

One second she was lying there, motionless.

Then next, he had a fist flying toward him and his arms full of a woman he very much wanted to hold. He took the punch. It was off center and barely clipped his jaw, but if Alex was responsible, he figured she was more than owed that one hit.

She all but tumbled on top of him, still off balance, and the lush body was a temptation he could barely resist.

But Alex was only a few feet away.

And he had no time in his life for luxuries like this.

"What the hell . . ."

She blinked down at him and then pushed away, moving all too easily considering she'd been flat on her back just seconds ago. That had him concerned. But even as he started to puzzle through that, she stumbled, swaying above him. Rising to his feet, he caught her arms and stared down at her. The bleeding had stopped. That was good.

Her eyes were still cloudy.

That wasn't good.

"What the hell . . ." she muttered again, shaking her head like she was trying to clear it. She pressed the heel of her hand against her temple like that might help lessen the pain he knew she was feeling—and he knew she was hurting. Knew it from experience.

Nothing would help except time. He'd *thought* they had this under control.

He couldn't think about that, though. He'd think about it later. Once he had her out of here and away from Alex.

Focusing on her face, he said quietly, "You passed out." *That is all. Nothing else to it.*

She'd believe it. They all did.

Her gaze rested on his face for a second, and then she looked down, studying the towel in his hand.

He just barely managed to resist clenching his hand in a fist. "Your nose started to bleed," he said, lifting it up. "There's a bathroom down the hall if you'd like to wash up."

She lifted a hand and touched her nose, grimacing a little before looking back at him. With a sigh, she nodded, and as he turned around, he glanced at Alex.

The boy was staring at his shoes.

Wonderful. Like that didn't look guilty as hell.

FOUR

SOMETHING told her this wasn't his first time at this particular rodeo.

As he managed to wedge them both into the tiny bathroom, she kept her face blank and tried to act a little dismayed. It wasn't hard. She was panicked, trying not to panic more. As they'd come down the hall, she'd pressed a hand to her chest, felt the slight bump of the micro cameras she'd decided to tuck inside her bra instead of her pocket. Thank God.

Thank *God* he hadn't found those. If he had . . .

Yeah. It wasn't hard to fake dismay, wasn't hard to act a little off balance. She *was* dismayed. She *was* off balance.

Just not for the reasons he thought, and she had to totally downplay that.

The boy had literally knocked her off her feet.

She'd been helpless at the hands of a man who was capable of God only knew what.

And damn it, her nose was still trickling blood. All from Alex's careless assault on her mind.

Did she know *anybody* with that kind of raw power?

Vaughnne honestly didn't know. She knew plenty of powerful psychics, yeah. But they were all older than Alex, all of them trained. And none of them were going to *accidentally* knock somebody out like that.

The kid was dangerous. And he was running around without any kind of real supervision, nobody to make sure he was learning how to control it and nobody capable of reeling him in if he did lose it.

Talk about an absolute *mess*.

She had been bad enough with her banshee-like voice when she lost it back before she had gotten herself under control, but she'd never had the ability to cause physical harm. Mental harm, yeah. She'd done her share of that. But this boy had caused physical damage. And he was all of what . . . thirteen?

"Here we go," Gus said, turning away from the minuscule closet and facing her.

The bathroom wasn't much bigger than a postage stamp, it seemed. There was room for the toilet, the sink, and the tub. That was about it. With the two of them in there, it was something of a tight fit.

"Ah . . ." She glanced at the rag and then eased closer, but that had her brushing up against him. She held out her hand, but he acted like he didn't notice. She didn't see how *that* was possible as he turned on the water, reaching past her to do so. It brought him even closer, and she could feel the wicked heat of his body and she just wanted to lean against him, wrap her body around his, and rub herself all over him.

The image was almost enough to make her whimper with want.

"How is the headache now?" he asked.

That voice of his—black velvet in the dead of night. Seductive and sinful. Something else that could make her whimper with want. She could just get lost in it.

Instead, she gave him a wry grimace and turned away from him to study her rather macabre reflection. He'd managed to get most of the blood off her face, but it was drying on her neck and her shirt was trashed. "The headache is getting better, but I look like a vampire's chew toy," she said sourly. She held her hand out over her shoulder. "Can I have the rag?"

He pushed it into her hand, but instead of moving out of the way, he lingered there as she leaned in and started to wash the blood away. She had to rinse the rag out twice to get her neck clean. She went over her face again. Finally, though, she'd cleared it all away, and before she turned to face him, she rinsed it out one more time. "I can take it home and wash it if you want."

"No. Not a problem."

From the corner of her eye, she saw his hand move and she tensed.

Slowly, she lifted her head, watching as he stroked a finger across her temple. "How do you feel now?"

The ache still lingered. The dizziness was gone, but she had a feeling she'd be dealing with the aftereffects of this for a while. "Like somebody kicked me in the head," she said bluntly. "I might want to ease up on the sugar intake if that's what caused it. I know teenage boys have a different metabolism, but maybe I should dump the cookies instead of letting Alex have them."

"No. You're probably right . . . just the sugar. Maybe the heat, if you're not used to it." He feathered his thumb over her brow. "If you take a nap, rest for a little while, you'll probably feel better in a couple of hours."

He sounded rather certain, she thought. Shaking her head, she casually eased away. His touch had hot little sparks jumping inside her. Not good. "I dunno, Gus."

"I'm sure it's fine." He seemed undeterred by the way she'd casually shifted her body, his fingers trailing down her cheek to cup her chin, angling her head back until he could peer into her eyes.

A light, easy touch—just the press of his fingers under her chin. Barely any contact at all, and yet she felt it ricocheting through her. Her heart slammed hard against her chest, and if it wasn't for years and years of practice in controlling everything from her physical responses to her emotions, Vaughnne knew she would have been breathing harder just from that light touch as well. She could feel the physical responses that weren't quite as obvious. Her nipples tightened and ached—thank the maker of lined bras. It was the only thing keeping him from seeing *that* reaction, and she suspected he would have noticed.

All because he stroked his thumb across her brow, touched her chin.

All because he'd *looked* at her . . .

What in the hell would she do if he kissed her?

Better off not to know, she warned herself.

Better off.

"Are you still dizzy?"

Dizzy . . . She hadn't mentioned that. She knew she hadn't. Giving him a wide-eyed look, she asked, "Was I dizzy?" Then she laughed a little. "I guess I was, seeing as how I did a face plant, huh? Nah. I feel okay, other than my head."

Wiggling out from between him and the sink, she made for the hallway. So much for trying to figure out a way to plant one of the units in the house.

It was a damn good thing he hadn't decided to search her while she was out. She was going to have to think about alternative methods, maybe, of keeping a close set of eyes on them.

But thinking would have to come at a time when it wasn't sheer torture just to move. She hadn't been honest. She was still dizzy and her head was killing her. Alex's mental probe had come smack up against her shields, and although she didn't think he'd realized what he'd hit, just that impact had been enough to send her reeling.

Rest. Reevaluate. But get the hell out of there first.

The room spun around on her, and despite her determination, a groan managed to slip out of her. Slamming a hand against the wall, she closed her eyes and sucked in a breath.

The kid . . . what the hell . . .

She blew out all the air in her lungs and then took another breath, slower. Feeling a pair of eyes on her, she looked up and saw Alex standing at the end of the hall, a nervous, anxious look on his face.

And he still held that stupid plate of cookies, too.

He looked half-sick with guilt, and the cookie he'd been eating was clutched in one fist, but judging by the look on his face, he'd forgotten about it. Sighing, she closed her eyes and took another breath as he started to say something.

She even saw the words forming in his eyes.

But before he could say it, Gus cut him off. "Alex, why don't you grab her a Coke from the fridge? Maybe it would help if she had a drink."

Sorry. The kid wanted to say he was sorry, but Gus wouldn't let him. She realized the problem there . . . Gus *couldn't* let him, because neither of them realized she knew what had happened.

What an utter *mess.*

Babysitting.

My ass.

She managed not to snarl as Gus closed his hand around her arm once more, but it was a close thing.

And once she got out of there, she was going to have a word with Mr. Taylor Jones. A very painful word.

* * *

"You have to be more careful," Gus said once Vaughnne was tucked safely back inside her house.

"I'm sorry." Alex stood there, his head hanging so low, his chin touching his chest. "I just . . ." He sniffled and then looked up, a defiant look in his eyes. "I just wanted a cookie. Why did I have to do that just to get a damned cookie?"

"Watch your mouth, Alex," Gus warned. "And you know why. So because you're angry about the situation, you took it out on her. Was that fair? Was that kind? You saw what happened, didn't you?"

"Her head felt funny!" Alex snapped. He turned away and jammed his hands into his pockets. "It's not as easy to get inside her head. It's almost like looking in yours and I had to push harder."

Staring at the boy's slumped shoulders, Gus rubbed his neck and tried to figure out what to say, what to do.

He understood, basically, what Alex was saying. Some minds were just more open, easier to read. The more closed the mind, the harder it was for Alex to look inside, but if he really wanted in, Alex would get in. So far, it didn't seem like anybody had been able to keep the boy out. But Alex usually didn't cause pain when he looked, and over the past two years or so, his control had gotten better. For the most part, nobody seemed to even notice anything was going on. Before they'd started working on it, Alex had pushed too hard and people had . . . sensed something. Or just sensed that something wasn't quite right, Gus supposed. He didn't know how to describe it because he was always aware of it when Alex was probing his mind and he knew the look the boy had on his face when he was looking into somebody else's.

But as the boy's control had improved, Gus had stopped seeing those signs of strain, those signs of pain. It happened less and less often, and for more than a year, those occurrences were the anomaly, not the norm.

Until today.

Not only had he caused Vaughnne pain, but he'd sent that woman crashing to the floor. All because she'd brought them a plate of cookies.

Leaning against the wall near the door, Gus stared outside, watching her house, still painfully aware of how she'd felt when he'd picked her up. Solid. Warm. And real. It was a miserable thing, he mused. She'd been unconscious, dealing with a nosebleed, and instead of being wracked with guilt over that, he was too busy remembering how good she'd felt in his arms.

So focused on that, he hadn't taken the chance he probably should have taken. He could have searched her, looked for an ID, some sign of who she was. Although he'd already run a background check on her, using the piss-poor excuse of a laptop he had. According to the information he'd gathered, she was who she said she was . . . had lived in Atlanta, moved after she'd lost the lease on her house. Did data entry for a living and the company she worked for had been around for a long, long time.

He knew there were ways around that sort of thing, but nothing about her set off his danger alert, and more, Alex wasn't scared around her. That was the most important thing.

Still, he should have done . . . something. Instead, he'd thought about how soft she felt. How warm. How much he missed feeling a woman in his arms.

Too long, he brooded. It had been too long since he'd had a woman under him. And something told him it had been even longer since he'd been with one like Vaughnne. Maybe even never. She'd never let him run the show and she'd meet him hunger for hunger . . . he closed his eyes as that hunger tore into him.

If he didn't get this under control soon, they'd have to leave.

He couldn't let anything distract him. Not even something as simple as sex.

Feeling a familiar brush on the edge of his thoughts, he turned his head and stared down Alex. "You know better," he said quietly. "You use it only when you have to, and there's no reason to use it on me."

Gus had no abilities, something he was ridiculously grateful for.

But he'd also learned that one didn't necessarily need psychic skill to know when it was being used. Not once you'd felt it a time or two. Or two hundred, in his case. Since they had no way of teaching Alex, years ago, Gus had made the decision to let Alex practice on him.

But it came with rules.

This was outside the rules.

Alex still had his hands shoved deep in his pockets and he looked miserable. Angry. Scared. "Are you mad at me?"

"I have no reason to be angry," Gus said, shrugging. "You didn't just knock me out on my butt, Alex."

"I tried to tell her I was sorry."

Closing his eyes, Gus shook his head. "You can't. She doesn't know what happened . . . we can't *let* her know."

Alex glared at him for a long, tense moment.

Gus held his stare and waited. Finally, the boy turned his back and stormed out of the living room, and disappeared down the hall. It wasn't a long walk. The narrow little room he'd claimed as his own was all of four feet down the hall. It seemed like the entire house shook as he slammed the door shut. Closing his eyes, Gus rested his head against the wall.

When is this going to end? It wasn't the first time he'd wondered it. It wouldn't be the last.

He knew there wasn't going to be an easy answer.

At this point, he wasn't even expecting an answer, period.

The boy had to be protected, and he suspected *protection* was going to be a problem for them even once Alex was no longer just a boy.

Please . . . you must do this for me . . .

Those words haunted him even now. He'd given his word, and he'd stand by it. With no regrets.

But how much longer . . .

It ends when the threat is gone.

The knowledge didn't improve his frame of mind. Not at all.

* * *

REYES lowered the phone.

He wasn't overly pleased with the fact that the man he had on this job had decided he'd do better if he was working it some-where . . . else.

It made it harder to watch him. Harder. But not impossible.

He'd made a few phone calls about a replacement, but so far, nobody seemed quite right.

One thing that *was* intriguing . . . the information his man had given him. That other avenue he'd mentioned. Reyes had been prepared to dismiss it as a hoax, except he didn't think it was. That was promising. So very promising.

"I want to go swimming."

The woman at his side stroked a hand down his thigh, and despite his decision to focus and make some headway on this problem, he found himself thinking about that idea himself. Her lovely body, cutting through the water. He could join her. Send his men away from the pool. Not too far, of course. Just far enough away to leave them in privacy.

But he really did need to move forward—

A slim hand slid up and cupped his balls. "Come on," she

murmured. Leaning in, she pressed her lips to his cheek. "I'll be bad for you again."

He leaned back, thoughts of work not just forgotten, but *gone*. Like they'd never existed. "Will you, my dear?"

"Hmmm . . ."

* * *

BENT over the computer, Esteban watched as his carefully worded message went live. He'd just gotten off the phone with the boss, and he knew he didn't have too much time left. He'd heard the impatience in the man's voice. He was down to weeks now. Maybe even days. Something had to happen, and soon.

This was his best chance . . . a harebrained scheme. His best chance at survival. Maybe he should just end it now.

Once more, he read through the message, his heart slamming hard against his ribs. He'd spent hours on those words. Hours. And he'd thought it through for an entire day before he even sat down to put pen to paper, tucked inside a hotel in the miserable hell that was known as Miami. *Away* from the boss. Where he might be able to lose himself if he had to.

He'd torn up more than a dozen drafts of the message, carefully burning each shred down to ash. Nothing to trace back to him, nothing to lead the boss *to* him. Or anybody else, for that matter.

But now . . . now it was done. He had all the right words and there they were, out there in cyberspace, waiting for an answer.

He didn't know how *long* he'd have to wait, but something would come of this. It would have to. Because, really, there was no other option.

Leaning back from the desk, he rubbed his hands over his face and stared up at the darkened ceiling as he thought it all through.

No other option. Save for one.

He could run.

It was the last option. The last resort. The thing he'd do only if no other avenue opened up before him, and he'd almost rather put a bullet in his own mouth before he ran. If he ran and he was caught, he knew he'd be better off dead anyway.

But it had always been a faint, almost microscopic possibility.

He knew this, so he'd planned for that eventuality. But he was saving it until there were no other choices.

Right now, this was still a choice.

He just had to wait.

I am trying to locate an item . . .

*   *   *

The message made the skin on the back of her neck crawl.

Nalini Cole had been watching this website for a long, long time, but why the hell had this happened *now*? This couldn't have come at a worse time. She was in the middle of a job that she had to see through.

And this? It just couldn't wait. She had a number of cockroaches she wanted to smash, and a whole bunch of them were involved in a nasty little nest that had connections to this website. They weren't number one on her list, but they were pretty damn close. She'd been watching, waiting for her chance.

One of the problems, though, stayed in the shadows, using the website only in the most circumspect manner, and it made it hard to move in on them. Too many of them had powerful gifts that made it easy for them to pick up on the tactics she'd normally use.

Still, the opportunity would present itself. So she watched. And waited. And worked on finding the number one cockroach on her list.

Still . . .

Locate an item . . . Those words left a bad taste in her mouth and a twist in her gut. Absently, she reached into her pocket and touched the necklace she'd tucked away. She didn't like to wear it, but she couldn't let it out of her sight, either.

When she touched it, she heard a boy crying. Sobbing.

It threw her back into a spiral of memories that threatened to drown her. Choke her. She couldn't go there, not now. She was dancing on a razor's edge with her current job anyway and now with this mess . . . no. She needed her head in the least screwed-up state possible, not the worst.

Squeezing her eyes closed, she whispered, "Just remember . . . you survived." She'd said it a thousand times. She'd say it a thousand more.

Gathering her dreads into a tail, she secured them at the nape of her neck and then focused back on the message. *Locate an item.*

There really was no question about what she was going to do, she realized. There hadn't been from the moment she'd read those words.

Once upon a time, a man had referred to *her* as an item.

The item in question was last seen in Florida.

"Florida." Just thinking about that place made her gut hurt. "Damned, forsaken hellhole of a state."

She'd left there not too long ago, and if she had her way, she wouldn't go back.

But this couldn't be ignored . . . and she was already hip deep in a mess of her own.

Oddly enough, the answer to that particular dilemma was one that made her smile. She pulled her phone from her pocket and dialed a number.

Something told her he wasn't going to be happy to hear from her.

But that was fine.

She'd been looking for a reason to contact this particular man ever since she'd first laid eyes on him.

* * *

THE gray cat sat in the window, watching him with a calm gaze.

There was something almost regal about the animal, Tucker decided.

As he pulled a can from the cabinet, he read off the label. "Chicken and beef?"

The cat slitted her eyes and just stared at Tucker. Sighing, he tossed the can back into the cabinet. "Sooner or later, you need to suck it up and eat the damned chicken and beef, cat."

She meowed. It sounded a lot like, *I don't think so.*

His phone rang. One glance told him everything he needed to know. He didn't recognize the number, so he ignored it. If his housekeeper had been there, he might have told her to answer the phone and tell the caller to fuck off—Lucia wouldn't use exactly those words, but she'd make sure the message was heard. Loud and clear. Sadly, though, Lucia wasn't around.

Ignoring the phone was the best option. "Okay." Studying the rest of the cans, he pulled down two more. "Ocean fish?"

Now Her Majesty flicked an ear.

"Salmon."

The cat lay down. *Yes, you peasant. You may feed me now.*

"You're a pain in the ass." Tucker stared at Heywood. "One would think you'd be a little more appreciative of the home and all."

As he was in the middle of opening the can, his phone chimed. Tension skittered down his spine, and in response, lights flickered in his house. He clenched his jaw and powered it all down. Shit like that wasn't acceptable. Not in any way, shape, or form. As he knelt down to put the plate on the floor, Heywood jumped down and rubbed her head against Tucker's gloved hand. The gloves, lined with a thin, inner layer of rubber, protected the cat.

It was probably overkill, and he knew it, but he didn't care. He'd long since learned how to control himself, but he didn't like to take chances.

Sighing, he stroked a hand down the cat's back before rising.

The phone chimed again.

There was a picture on the display.

A woman.

He knew her.

Just the sight of her was like a visceral, one-two punch.

Long, dense hair, the palest blond he'd ever seen, fell more than halfway down her back. It was done in a series of narrow dreadlocks, and until he'd seen Nalini, he had never paid much attention to that style, but it was so damn sexy. Ever since he'd met her, he'd spent way too many nights thinking about how much he'd love to twist that hair around his hands and feast on her mouth. Then feast all the way on down until he reached the heart of her . . . spread those thighs and . . .

His cock jerked in response as that image whipped through his mind and he felt the answering tension spark through him, a devastating need that spoke of storms and power and heat.

Problems lay down that road, he knew. Hard to get too involved in kissing anybody when his very touch could prove fatal.

One slipup, one loss of control . . . yeah. His encounters of the physical kind were few and far between, and usually with somebody he found only minimally attractive. It was a release valve for him, nothing more.

Snagging the phone, he pulled up the messages and spent a long, long moment staring at her picture. Just staring. He gave himself that before he started thinking things through.

Things like . . . *how in the hell did she get my number?*

As he was puzzling that thought through, he shifted his gaze to the message that had come with the picture.

If you'd like to know how I got your number, you'll have to answer the phone when I call. If you like, I can send you another picture. I'm thinking about sending one of me naked. Are you interested?

Tucker swore.

FIVE

"**H**E'S dangerous."

The second the words left her, Vaughnne felt a little guilty; the boy didn't intentionally want to harm anybody, she knew. But she needed more information and she didn't believe this shit that she'd been given everything she needed to know.

"He's just a kid," Taylor said.

"Just a kid." She sighed and stared out the window, pondering the empty driveway. The one thing she *had* taken a chance on . . . she'd put a tracker on the truck and a mini-transmitter. She'd know when they were heading home, as long as her little toys weren't discovered. She needed to get a better set of eyes and ears inside that house.

This was one of the few times she could possibly manage to get it done, too. The lovely, wonderful, slightly dodgy Mrs. Werner had another plumbing problem, and Gus had agreed to go pick up the supplies to take care of it for her.

After he'd left, Mrs. Werner had confided to Vaughnne that

she actually had a nephew who was a master plumber and could take care of things in a jiffy for her . . . but she'd rather look at Gus than her nephew any old time. Plus, she thought that nice-looking young man could use the extra money.

Vaughnne suspected it was likely equal parts. The lady was lovely, but she spent an inordinate amount of time ogling every halfway attractive male she could. Gus was more than halfway attractive. Vaughnne actually hoped she had that interest in men when she was Mrs. Werner's age.

Checking Gus's location again, she told herself she needed to get this done if she was going to do it. Should she warn Taylor to come looking for her body if she didn't check in soon? Gus was ten minutes from here, getting closer to the hardware store.

"Just a kid." Then she reached up and massaged her aching temple. Did she lay it out? Or did she bide her time? She didn't think Jones would do anything that would threaten a kid. She really didn't. But . . . "Yeah. It's not the kid I'm worried about," she lied. She did it with ease and she did it without batting a lash or feeling any bit of guilt. "It's the dude with him. The guy walks around carrying a Sig Sauer that would put a pretty damn big hole in me. He acts like I'm trying to poison them if I make *cookies*, Jones. *Cookies*. Trust me, the kid isn't the problem. The guy is."

"So . . . like we've already discussed, use caution."

She glared at the phone and thought about using it to beat the bastard bloody next time she was in D.C. "Use caution," she drawled. "That sounds like an excellent plan. I'll get right on it, Jones."

"You do that." There was a pause and she heard a shout, followed by a flurry of voices, the rush of excitement. Jones spoke again and some of that excitement actually came through in his voice. He might have even smiled a little. "I have to go. Something is about to come apart at the seams."

She wanted to say *good luck*, but he was already off the phone.

Sighing, she hooked up her headphones, checking the tracker once more before shutting the app down. Anybody who looked at the phone wouldn't know what it was, and it wouldn't open without her password. She'd do a run around the block . . . and detour around the back of Gus's house. If he was still far enough away, she'd see about getting the shit planted.

* * *

SHE wasn't even running long enough to work up a sweat. She hit the back street behind Gus's place, checked his location. At the hardware store. Perfect. She should have plenty of time to get this done.

What took a damn long time was getting inside the house, setting up the devices, and then letting herself back out.

On her way out, she was just about ready to set the damn lock, too. On her way out.

And she glanced down, saw the tape over the door. Just the smallest piece.

Damn it, Gus. Sourly, she crouched down and peeled it off, rolling it up to tuck inside her waistband before she spent another five precious minutes scrounging for where he'd tucked the rest of it.

She pressed the tape back into place and then looked around, checking the windows. That was when she saw them, all those little traps. Nothing overt, just something to let the owner of the house know if somebody had been in and out. She spotted strips of tape on the windows, along the fridge. One windowsill held three coins, and she had no doubt they'd been very precisely arranged. Grimacing, she started to look closer and saw other traps. There were three staples placed in what looked like a haphazard manner on the floor in front of one kitchen window. Near the boy's room, a few bits of paper. She hadn't gone near his room. She couldn't have disturbed that.

"Gus, you're a distrustful bastard," she muttered. Simple, basic, nothing high-tech. If they were trying to avoid calling attention to themselves, high-tech was not the way to go. It got noticed. Made people ask questions. Cost money, too, and if you plunked down a lot of money, people remembered that. Used plastic? Left a trail.

Storming back into the kitchen, she went to the back door and glared at it for a minute before she peeled the tape away. Then, narrowing her eyes, she shut the door, still on the inside, watching.

It stuck in place. Not tight and snug, but close enough. She tugged the piece of tape off, wadded it up, and fetched another. She smoothed the new piece down, over and over, and then eased the door open, eyeing the piece of tape. Hoping.

She wouldn't know if it closed or not because she had no way of seeing inside the damn house.

Well, she *hadn't*.

She did now. It was possible she'd be able to see the tape from her setup back at her place.

She'd check.

But until she got there . . .

It was a few more breath-stealing, soul-eating minutes before she made it to the alley running between the two houses. Once she was there, she settled back into a jog. The minute she reached the street, she put everything she had into it and ran hell-bent for leather, determined to get home.

* * *

"No."

Nalini stared at the screen. She was almost obsessively refreshing her screen. No takers. Yet. Some bites, yes, but nothing solid. *Just stay that way*, she thought.

She had a real live psychic in Orlando she wanted on that job. Assuming she could get him to do it. If he took it, she could get him to grab the kid and get him someplace safe. She even had a good idea of where *safe* was.

She just had to convince him.

"Come on, Tucker," she said, smiling a little as she leaned forward and scrolled down the page to check out some of the other posts on the forum. Sooner or later, she thought. Sooner or later, those thugs were going to come out to play. "What have you got to lose? You already live there."

He grunted in response. A few seconds ticked by. "What's this about?"

He would ask that question.

She stroked a finger down her brow. "I'm trying to figure that out, but when I look at this post, I hear screams. My gut goes tight. Somebody hurts if this happens, Tucker. You know enough about hurting, I imagine."

"I don't know what your poison is, blondie, but stay out of my head."

She chuckled. "My poison?"

"Yeah. Whatever voodoo you do . . . keep your powers out of my head, keep your paws to yourself, whatever you want to call it. I don't want you screwing around in my head," he said sourly.

"Tucker, sugar . . . if I decide to screw around with you, it's going to involve you, me, and a bed. That's all. Well, if you're into kink, we can maybe play around with that, but trust me, if and when I decide to screw around with you, it's going to involve actual physical contact . . . it's more fun that way." There was no *if*, though. At least not on her part.

Silence stretched out. Hot, heavy, and tense.

Then, finally, in a voice thick with regret, he said, "Now, darlin', that sounds absolutely perfect, but it's not about to happen.

Me and bare skin aren't a good combination. But it's a nice thought, nonetheless."

You and bare skin, huh . . . she thought about the way he'd looked the few times she'd met him. Black gloves on his hands. Wicked sexy tattoos twining up his arms. That fiery red hair and his face set in unyielding lines. She thought about seeing him naked and stretched out on her bed, and the image was so clear, so vivid, she realized with startling clarity that it *would* happen.

She wasn't sure just *how* that was going to come to pass, but it was going to happen.

"You sound awful certain of this."

"Because I have to be." His voice flat, the kind of voice that said, *We're done discussing this.*

She'd let it go. For now. But the other thing—

"Just what is it I need to find in Orlando?" he asked, catching her off guard.

* * *

An item.

Tucker stared at the website, running his tongue over his teeth and scratching Heywood's head. The feline purred and butted her head harder against Tucker's hand, but Tucker didn't pick her up. "Yeah, yeah, you purr away."

Item. The wording on it was enough to make his skin crawl. Something he'd figured out over the past few years . . . many psychics had only one gift, but some did have one stronger gift, and a second weaker one.

Just about all of them, though, had a hyperaware set of instincts, and right then, his were on red alert.

There was something seriously wrong with that message.

An *item.*

Finally, he dialed Nalini's number back. She answered so fast, he suspected she'd been waiting for his call. "Two questions . . . is this tied into what we were doing with Dru and Crawford? Because if it is, she could still be in trouble."

"No." Nalini paused for a moment and then added, "At least, I don't think it's tied in. I've been watching these people a very long time and I don't believe there's a connection at all. If there is, it's peripheral."

He grunted and read the message again. "Okay. And what's this 'item'?"

"Well . . ." She laughed a little. "If you promise not to get frustrated, I'll be honest with you. I'm not entirely certain, but I think it might be a child."

* * *

ROCKING back on the hind legs of her chair, Vaughnne stared at the back door.

She'd magnified the screen and gone as close on it as she could.

And the tape was clearly visible.

It was only barely clinging to the doorjamb. It *was* touching, but it wasn't a smooth fit at all.

If she'd had any time, she would have tried to figure out a better plan, but she'd checked the tracker app and Gus had been on his way back. This was the best she could do. The trained FBI agent. Outwitted by a piece of scotch tape.

When the truck appeared in the driveway, she almost groaned. She covered eyes. "Let this work."

From where she'd positioned herself, she could see the truck. And she watched as Gus went through his normal routine. Backpack, check, jacket, check. Gun, check. Kid, check.

Study the yard under the pretense of stretching that long lean body . . . check.

Her belly did a mad little flutter and she tried to ignore it. A bag from a local hardware store came out after all that was said and done, and Alex leaned backed against the truck, nose all but buried in a book.

As Gus reached up to shove his ball cap back, she slid her gaze to the boy. He had his head bent and was caught up in the book he was reading. Even after Gus said his name—at least that's what Vaughnne assumed he was doing, the boy just continued to focus on the book.

For a minute, Gus just stood there, staring at the kid's bent head, and something about his posture, the way his shoulders went tense, the way he tipped his head back . . . all of it, every last movement he made, and every one he didn't make, made her realize something.

The man was tired.

She didn't know what was going on, didn't know what he was running from. But whatever it was, it had him so worn out, and so tired.

Then, even as her heart ached a little for him, he shook his head, like he was just shaking it off. Then he said something. Judging by the way Alex reacted, the boy heard him and lifted his head, his mouth moving as he responded. Something angry and defiant danced across his features, but Vaughnne had no idea what was being said. She could have adjusted the volume and found out, but she wasn't doing this to invade their privacy. She just wanted to make sure they stayed safe.

Gus reached up and hooked a hand over the boy's neck, hauled him close. The boy went and they stood there like that a moment, the kid's face pressed against Gus's chest while the man looked around, as though he was seeing monsters in every corner, behind every tree.

Then, finally, they broke apart and headed across the street to Mrs. Werner's.

* * *

THEY'D finished the damn plumbing thing over at the old lady's house. Alex sometimes got tired of going over there, but anything was better than being stuck in this little house with just him and Gus. Even if the old lady did sit there and think about how much she wished she were thirty years younger. Sometimes, he had to hide his face because of her thoughts, too. She wasn't quiet with them at *all*, and those were the sort of thoughts that were hard to block out. Like ignoring the music from a radio blasting at full volume in the middle of the night.

Still, she was nice to both of them, and when Gus was done, she always made them dinner, and then she'd pay Gus. Gus didn't like to take the money, but he did it anyway, because the more money they had for when they had to run again, the better.

Everything was for when they had to run again and Alex hated it.

Just like he hated what he had to do when they went home. Each and every time.

While Gus checked every stupid thing in the main part of the house, it was Alex's job to check the windows and doors, make sure nobody had come in while they weren't there. Alex did it because while Gus could handle anybody that was actually *in* the house, Alex would be able to sense if anybody *had* been in.

It had happened before, back when they were in Oklahoma. Alex didn't like to think of that day. The man who had broken in hadn't been trying to hurt them—he'd been looking for cash and drugs, but he'd hit the wrong house.

No, Alex didn't like to think about that. Instead, he focused on what he had to do here. Check the stupid windows, make sure nothing felt off. That wasn't hard.

Everything felt fine. Tape there. Tape here. Tape everywhere. Coins where they needed to be.

His heart jumped into his chest, though, as he found the tape in the kitchen. That piece by the door. It wasn't sealed . . . well. It was. But it wasn't pressed down tight the way it usually was.

Swallowing, he glanced around.

Everything *looked* fine. He dropped the mental wall he kept around his mind and looked . . . *harder*. It wasn't easy to explain the difference, but he *felt* the difference. His heart was racing by the time he finished, but everything felt fine.

It was all *fine*, damn it. He didn't want to run again, didn't want to leave again. He was so tired of having to run . . .

Hands sweating, he reached out and smoothed his finger down the strip of tape, flattening it into place as he heard the solid, sturdy sound of Gus's boots.

"Everything clear in here?" he asked from the doorway.

Alex turned around and stared at him. "Why wouldn't it be?"

And his stomach twisted inside, guilt rising and making him feel more than a little sick. But nobody had been in there. If they had, he'd know, right? He'd feel it. He was so tired of running. He probably hadn't smoothed the tape down when he put it on last night right before bed. That was all.

No big deal.

Feeling Gus's eyes on him, he looked up.

The man was watching him solemnly, quietly.

And the guilt just got worse.

A big hand came out and hooked him over the back of the neck, tugged him close. As Gus wrapped an arm around his shoulders, Alex sniffled and blinked back the tears that suddenly decided to choke him. "I know this is not easy," Gus said quietly. "I know this is not what your mother had planned for you. It is not the life I would have wanted for you, either. It's *not* the life I want for you. But you're alive . . . and you're safe."

Alex pulled away and stormed over to the fridge. "I've heard this before. It's not what we planned. But it's a life. Right?" He pulled out the pitcher of water and poured himself a glass. "Yeah. It's a life. A shitty one."

"Watch how you speak," Gus warned him.

Jerking his chin up, Alex said, "Or what? You going to spank me?"

Gus stroked his chin, studying him. "I think you can go to your room now. You want to act like a petulant child, then do it elsewhere."

* * *

As Alex disappeared down the hall, Gus dumped the bag on the table and dropped down into the chair. With a sigh, he covered his face with his hands.

There were days when he swore that this was some hell that had been dropped on him because of the life he'd led. The lives he'd taken, the lies he'd told. He hadn't intended to go down that road, but it had just . . . fit. And some roads, once you started that walk, you couldn't turn back.

Too bad Gus hadn't realized it until it was too late. By the time he had, his hands were bloody, his soul was gone, and the life he'd thought would be his was just . . . a dream. So he distanced himself from his family. The world saw a scheming, womanizing bastard who'd had a few runs of good luck and he'd used it all to his advantage. His pretty face got him in doors and he played with the rich and famous, made connections—and while they weren't looking, he slid a stiletto into the heart of a man who'd been planning to kill *el presidente*.

A few years later, he'd been some rich woman's man-whore—that was the story she told everybody, including her husband. When she whispered to him one night about a ménage à trois at a pretty, private little villa, he agreed. And then he arrived thirty minutes sooner than planned, slit her throat, broke the husband's neck, and set the stage to make it look like a robbery. He wasn't even questioned and they were mourned by many at their funeral. He often wondered how the world would react if they knew the husband and wife had been in control of a child slavery ring, selling runaways or indigent children they found on the streets of Mexico into the sex trade.

Deeper and deeper into that life he fell.

And now, he was out of it and all he could do was hope he was fast enough, strong enough to keep Alex alive if trouble found them.

Because it would.

Whether it was karma or just shitty luck, he didn't know, but they wouldn't be able to run forever.

Sometimes he wondered if this was God's way of punishing him. He'd taken lives . . . but if this was a punishment, then he would have been the one who had died that night.

Not Consuelo. She'd been the one who had made that ultimate sacrifice, and here he was, trying to make sure he honored her wishes.

Please . . . you must promise . . .

"I'm trying, love." He tried every single day, and every single day, he was so very certain he was screwing this up. Keeping one step ahead of people who had endless resources, the money to buy and sell more than a few small countries, people who would just as soon kill you as argue with you.

And the boy was angry.

So very angry.

Sighing, he stood up and tugged off his cap, leaving it on a peg near the door before he retreated into his bedroom. He'd give Alex a while to calm down, then they could tackle his schoolwork. They'd eaten over at Mrs. Werner's after he'd repaired the fill valve on her toilet, while she ogled his ass . . . again.

Inside his room, he stripped out of his dirty, sweaty clothes and pulled on a pair of worn cotton pants before dropping to the floor. Sit-ups. Push-ups. He had a few weights that he kept with him and he did the most thorough workout he could with them. He moved on to conditioning, although he was limited in how much he could train there. Without a partner, again he was limited.

He was working on teaching Alex. Alex was still a child, though, and his sessions with the boy were all about training Alex to defend himself more than anything else.

More than an hour passed before he was done and he was dripping with sweat, tired and sore.

And still frustrated. Still angry.

Judging by the silence of the house, Alex was still unhappy with him as well.

He moved out into the hall, passed by the boy's narrow, small room, and saw the kid lying on his cot, staring up at the ceiling with no expression on his face.

Gus turned away.

There was nothing, he knew, that could be said or done.

Nothing.

* * *

"WELL . . . THE cameras work." Vaughnne stared at Gus's naked, muscled back.

His very *nice* naked, muscled back.

As the bathroom door shut behind him, she groaned and leaned back in her seat, covering her face with her hands.

The cameras worked. The audio feed worked.

The motion sensors she'd placed at the doors and windows worked. The cameras were tucked snug inside the smoke alarms, and she'd been watching him through the tiny little slats and feeling like a pervert.

She'd also had a front row seat to what the boy had done.

He'd seen the tape. Her mistake. That fatal little flaw.

Her heart had dropped like a stone when he moved over to it, but then she'd realized what he was doing.

Fixing it.

And then he lied.

When Gus asked him if everything was okay, he'd turned around, looked the man in the eye, and *lied*.

She didn't know what was up with that. Part of her wanted to continue with her own little lies, insisting to herself that she *didn't care*. But she couldn't. She needed to know everything about these two males and she needed to know it *now*. And it was already for reasons that went beyond the job. It had been from the very beginning. For Alex, it was because she understood that fear in his eyes. With Gus . . . hell. She couldn't even explain that mess, although it might have something to do with the way her heart skipped up a few beats when he looked at her and it might have something to do with the way he watched over that kid.

It got to her. She couldn't deny that. Her father had tossed her out like she was nothing more than trash. But this guy . . . there was no denying that he would tear down mountains to protect that kid. It got her, right square in the heart.

Maybe that's all it was. Admiration for him. A little bit of lust.

"Yeah, right," she muttered.

Swearing, she skimmed her hands back over her hair and tried to focus her brain on the job. The *job*. These two males were the *job*. That was what they were and what they *had* to be. She couldn't do her job if she kept letting other things get in the way.

"Just the job." She shoved back from the computer and rose to pace.

She'd done the main thing she needed to do—she had eyes

inside the house now, and so far, they hadn't been discovered. The first few minutes, she knew, were critical. That was when somebody was going to sense something was off. That was when their instincts would scream the loudest, if it was going to happen, and at this point, nothing *had* happened.

Between the eyes she had inside the house and the motion detectors she'd set up on the perimeter, hopefully she'd done enough to catch anybody before they could move in on the two.

There were times when she wished she had something other than a psychic's banshee wail. Being able to talk to anybody she needed to talk to was nice enough, she guessed, although she couldn't *hear* anything unless the person was also a telepath. This was flying blind, though. She had no ability to sense anything more than what her instincts were able to tell her, and while those instincts were pretty damn sharp, she hated relying on just those and her wits.

Something caught her eye and she glanced down at her monitor. "Damn."

The word gusted out of her in a rush as she stopped to stare. It was Gus.

He'd come out of the bathroom, a towel slung around his hips and water rolling down his chest in tiny little drops. One bead rolled down the midline of his torso, arrowing down over the flat plane of his belly before it caught up on the towel. Her heart slammed once, hard, against her ribs, and she licked her lips. She was pretty damn certain she'd never been so thirsty in her life.

He glanced down the hall before heading toward his room, and she groaned as she found herself treated to another view of that fine, muscled back. And his ass. Nice, nice ass.

She needed to quit ogling. She needed to—

She wheezed out a breath as he dropped the towel just inside the door and grabbed a pair of faded jeans off the foot of the bed.

"Oh, hell, he's going commando." She passed a hand in front of her eyes and tried not to drool.

She dropped her hand, fast, though, leaning forward and staring at him before he dragged those jeans up over his hips, hiding that perfect butt from her view. And it really was a perfect butt. Hard and muscled, it made her just want to bite him.

"You need to get laid. Or buy a vibrator. Something."

SIX

Psychic skill, in Bruce Watkins's opinion, really wasn't as uncommon as people thought. Not everybody was going to be able to read minds, that was certain, and he knew the average Joe wasn't going to be able to float candlesticks across the room, either.

But if more people listened to their instincts, if more people paid attention to what that still, quiet voice in the back of their head tried to tell them . . . well, people would be amazed at what they could accomplish.

Refined instincts and psychic skill weren't the *same*, by any means. Psychic ability was the next step up. But there were some people out there who *thought* they just had really good intuition, and what they had was a rudimentary psychic skill they just never bothered to improve upon.

He wasn't a particularly strong psychic, but he knew how to listen to those instincts, and he'd worked to improve his skills.

He made his living listening to those instincts, selling his skills in an odd sort of manner.

It wasn't always easy to come by work, but when he did, he tended to hit a windfall.

His skill wasn't anything special. He could feel the abilities of others. Basically they just exerted a pull on him—their rampant energy tugged at him and drew him in.

That was why the ad on the site that operated on the dark web was so appealing to him. He read between the lines pretty damn well, although the initial posting hadn't given him much to go on. But then somebody had asked for more information just a few hours ago.

The response:

This item is something that should appeal to certain people here. It's very valuable to me.

There was a wealth of unspoken information in those cryptic words.

The question was . . . just how much money were they offering?

So that was the question he had to ask. If he liked the answer, he'd offer his very valuable services.

If not?

Too bad. Their package could swelter and rot in Orlando for all he cared.

He typed out a reply, keeping it every bit as vague and obscure as the initial message was, asking for more information, hinting as his experience, his special skills.

The final few words danced around the issue of money, and he hated to be so crass, but it was an issue that had to be addressed.

* * *

LOCATING *such an item can come with expenses.*

He smirked as he read the final few words and then he rose,

pacing around the office as he pondered his own response. It had been three days since he'd put the ad out there on the web, and this was the first time anybody had shown any *real* response.

There had been more than a few fishing expeditions, which he had expected, and somebody had asked for more information. But nobody had shown promise. A couple of quacks had suggested they meet so they could show how they could use his aura to help locate his missing *item*. Others had told him they could use divination.

All nonsense and he knew it. He'd been prepared for some nonsense, though, so that was fine.

Three days.

It had taken three days to get a serious inquiry.

Nervous tension ripped through him, but he finally got it under control and started to figure out just the right way to answer.

* * *

AN *item*.

"You're sure they are talking about a person?" Tucker asked as he climbed into the car. He had the phone on speaker, which was annoying as hell, but it was easier to talk to Nalini that way than to try and juggle the phone and drive. Plus, his first stop was going to be Starbucks. He needed coffee like he needed to breathe.

It had been raining all damned day and that was a good thing. Rain altered the current in the air, which made him steadier, and he needed to be just then.

Talking to Nalini, even if it was just on the phone, left him *damned* off balance. He'd been so unsteady last night, he'd ended up jacking off in the shower. Normally, that wasn't a problem. Thanks to his issues with touching people, he had a good relationship with his hands, sad to say. But this time, he had actually let himself think about having somebody *else* involved.

Nalini.

That hadn't been wise. It was like everything inside him had exploded, including the raw, chaotic energy that he absorbed and it had surged out of control. *That* led to him frying the electrical shit in the house and tripping the circuit breaker.

So rain was good.

He didn't have to deal with the wild electricity rippling through the air, and he didn't have to worry about toning things down.

"If he'd lost his address book or his car keys, I doubt I'd be this worked up over things, Tucker. I was drawn to this for a reason and I don't get pulled in on *things*. It's people . . . always people," Nalini murmured, her voice distracted. "There hasn't been an answer to the reply yet."

"If they are seriously looking for somebody to grab, they'll probably be extra cautious, especially after the shit that went down here recently." Tucker jammed the key into the ignition and turned it. It didn't start. Sighing, he glared at the engine. The damn car was old.

Tucker loved his car. Flat-out loved her. It was the first thing that had ever been his, and he planned to keep her going as long as he could, but she was contrary at the best of times.

Today wasn't the ideal time.

Closing his eyes, he let himself check things out and then he tried again, using his own energy to trigger the dead battery.

"Are you okay?"

He grunted as the engine rolled over. "Yeah. Dead battery. It's good now." If only the rest of the car's problems were that easy to fix.

Nalini was quiet a moment and then said, "Well, if you've dealt with the car problems, can we discuss how we're going to locate this item?"

He shot the phone a dark look. "*We*, sugar? I hate to tell you this, Nalini, but *we* aren't doing anything. I'm looking for this item. You're wherever you are, doing whatever you are doing, and jumping when those FBI boys tell you to jump. I'm only doing this because I hate to think about somebody being hurt in my neck of the woods."

"Your neck of the woods . . . where are you from, Tucker?"

He clenched his jaw. "Originally? Georgia. And what does that matter?"

"Oh, nothing. That drawl of yours just gets to me. Right down in my lady bits."

He dragged a hand down his face and shoved the car into reverse. "Your lady bits. Nalini . . . do you want me to do this job or not?"

She chuckled. "Of course I do. I just want you getting used to the fact that, at some point, I plan on testing that theory of yours on you and bare skin. I bet you can handle it better than you think."

He handled bare skin contact just fine as long as no stress was involved. But looking at her did something bad to the way his brain functioned—something he'd figured out already—and he suspected he'd go on overload if he spent too much time touching her. One slipup and she'd pay the price. He already knew for a fact what happened when he lost control. That wasn't happening. Not with her.

"How about we focus on the job?" he suggested softly as he whipped the car around.

"You are just no fun, Tucker. How can you be so cool and controlled when I'm sitting here squirming and thinking about you and me and bare skin?"

He disconnected the call. She'd call back in a second; he knew it. So he took the brief moment to drag a hand over his face and force his recalcitrant body under control. The leather of his glove slid over his face, smooth and worn from years of use. He'd had the gloves specially designed. He pulled them on first thing in the morning, and pulled them off right before he went to bed. He stripped them off for certain things, of course, but for the most part, those gloves were as much a part of him as breathing.

They protected everybody in the world from the wild charge that lived inside him. It seemed his body was one big, giant conductor of electricity half the time, although it wasn't that simple. He pulled the energy from somewhere, he knew, and he could channel it out when he was focused. When he wasn't focused, when he was pissed, he also affected the ebb and flow of electricity around him.

Once, he'd unintentionally stopped a person's heart because of it.

Bare skin on bare skin. Terror pulsing out of him.

Yeah. Control was pretty vital to him.

And Nalini managed to shatter it.

When the phone rang a few seconds later, he was as much in control as he could expect to be. After a ring or two, he answered with a curt, "Yeah?"

"Wow. I must really be getting under your skin. Okay, we'll focus on the job," Nalini said, her voice heavy with amusement.

The woman was bizarre. Most women get hung up on and they are irritated. He does it to *her*? She laughs.

"Why don't you just give me a better idea of what I'm looking for and then we can be done with the chatter?" Tucker said.

"I already explained I'm not sure what you're looking for," she said, her voice low and soft. There was a long pause and he thought he heard a rapid series of taps. Like somebody firing away on a keyboard. "I . . . I just think there's a kid involved. I'm almost positive the *item* is a child. I hear one . . . in my head, if you get my drift. He's screaming. I think it's him. And I think they are looking for him because he's . . . well . . . unique."

"Drop the codespeak, Nalini." He slowed at a stop sign and then turned left, taking the highway that would lead him into Orlando. He didn't live in town. That just wasn't smart for a guy like him. But his place was only a few miles out and already traffic was closing up around him. "You mean psychic."

"Yeah. Yeah, I mean psychic."

"Why?"

"Because that's what this site is for. It's where people go to find others, it's where they go to connect . . . and I think others go to recruit. It's bad news, though, because sometimes people disappear."

"Disappear." He stared at the license plate of the car in front of him and tried to blank his mind. Wild, chaotic energy crackled inside him and he had no place to put it, no place to direct it. All he could do was focus and ride it out until it eased off. "And you think a kid's the next mark?"

"Yes . . . but this is different. Usually, they recruit here. This isn't recruiting. It's . . . hunting," she said, her voice grim.

Hunting—

Just thinking about that had his hands tightening on the steering wheel and he wanted to hit something. Pound it bloody and then do it all over again.

Seconds ticked away, and then softly, Nalini asked, "Are you okay?"

"I'm just fine, darlin'." Everything built to a screaming roar in his brain and he shunted it off, splicing that part of himself off until it was like two people rode inside his mind. Tucker who was in control, pressing on the gas as the cars around him started to move. Tucker who was ready to fry the next thing he touched. He could control it. He'd spent the past twenty years of his life learning how to do just that, and control it was exactly what he'd do.

"How certain are you that your boss isn't behind any of those disappearances?" he asked dispassionately. He knew more than a few federal types who'd tried to make people like him disappear. One had tried to make *him* disappear. Permanently. Not long after—

The car shuddered around him and he cut that line of thought off. Couldn't go there. Not right now.

"I couldn't be more positive if I had to. Jones and his unit are clean. I know you don't have any reason to trust me, but they aren't dirty. They aren't behind any of this."

Nalini continued to talk, her voice soft and low, and even though he barely heard her words, he let himself focus on the low, soothing sound of her voice until some of that rage banked, until the energy surging inside him ebbed down.

"So. You got any idea how to help me out here?"

Tucker spotted a familiar sign up ahead and hit his turn signal. "Yeah. If the kid I'm looking for is psychic, I just go trolling. The human mind is an electrical construct, basically. And the mind of a psychic feels different. I'll just keep circling and hoping I'll find something."

"That . . . could take a long time."

He grunted. "Yeah. But there's already been something around here moving. I've been ignoring it. Guess it's time to check it out." He got in line at the drive-thru. "Is that all?"

"Yes. Thank you."

He didn't say anything as he went to disconnect.

"Hey, wait . . . you can *really* sense things just by the way our minds feel?"

"Yeah." He rubbed his brow.

"And you can sense the minds of all the people around you, too. All the time?"

"If I let myself." He'd already lowered his shields a little and he knew, within a fifty-foot range, there were one hundred and fifty-two people. One of them had a pacemaker. He felt that as well.

"Doesn't that drive you crazy?"

He pulled forward in the line. Softly, he said, "Yes."

SEVEN

VAUGHNNE didn't run because she liked it.

She didn't hate it, but she sure as hell didn't love it, and in her expert, professional opinion, all of those who talked about a runner's high were just deluding themselves. The only time she got *high* off exerting herself was after a bout of particularly good sex.

Which she hadn't had in so long, she could *be* delusional.

No, she ran because she knew it was necessary.

Keeping her body in top physical form was just part of the job.

It was the same reason she lifted weights and the same reason she trained in a variety of fighting styles, ranging in everything from standard tae kwon do to kickboxing to muay thai. Even though she'd spent so much time on the streets, she couldn't rely on street fighting to get her everywhere, and she didn't. There was always room for improvement, so improvement was what she pushed for.

After the shit way she'd felt ever since the last job in Orlando, she'd been knocked down to where she could barely manage three miles on average, and the first few times she'd run, she'd been hard-pressed to make two.

She was back up to five now, and today, she planned on going for six. It was annoying as hell, having to do it in this neighborhood. Pounding it out on the busted-up pavement wasn't much better than running on a treadmill in the gym. She preferred the park back home, but she wasn't leaving this area unless she had to, and she definitely wasn't leaving it to run.

Right now, it was just after six; Gus and Alex weren't home. According to the tracker, they were at the grocery store, just a mile away, and although she didn't feel right not being there, hiding just out of sight, she hadn't followed them that day.

She couldn't explain why, but she'd felt the need to stay here. Instinct, she knew. Still, her gut was a wild, tangled mess, and she wished there was a way she could have planted a tracker on the damn kid.

She felt almost glued to this place, though. Thanks to the wonders of technology, she had the video feed coming to her live on her iPhone and she kept checking it every few minutes as she ran. At their house, everything was calm, everything was quiet.

For now. But it wouldn't last.

Something was going to go down. The knot in her belly, the tension crawling through her. All of it added up to something, but the question was what. Yet again, she found herself checking the video feed . . . nothing.

Nothing unusual had activated the alarm sensors that fed into the program she'd set up, either.

It wasn't perfect, but it was good enough.

She was less than half a mile away at the most and could be over there in no time.

Stop it, she told herself. She was working herself up—

The camera feed caught the image of a car. It cut between the cameras she'd set up at her place and the house directly across from hers, rolling down the street slowly. Slowly, but not *too* slow.

Everything about it set her hair on end.

The camera feed on her phone wasn't good enough for her to be able to make out anything about the driver, but everything inside her was already screaming. Long and loud.

It wasn't screaming *danger, danger, danger.*

But the *warning* alert was bad enough.

Wheeling around in her steps, she laid on the speed and hauled ass back.

Son of a bitch.

She'd expected things to make a shift soon. Just not *this* soon.

The question was . . . *is this for the better* . . . or the worse.

* * *

TUCKER eyed the house.

Somebody who lived in that house was a problem. Whoever it was, they weren't home now and all Tucker could pick up was a weird little buzz, kind of like an echo.

One hell of a strong echo.

If it was this strong and the person wasn't even here, then how strong was he?

A kid. Assuming Nalini was right, and it was a kid involved. She seemed to think so, though, and he wasn't inclined to dispute her gut feelings. People like them, they lived and died by those feelings.

Sighing, he cut around the corner and headed north, trying to decide what to do. He'd told Nalini he'd take a look around, see if he could find this *item*. He'd be willing to bet this kid was the *item*—and if so, that kid was a walking, talking hazard. If anybody in the entire town could possibly be drawing the absolute *wrong* kind of interest, it was the person living in that house.

Absolutely no idea how to control what he had in his head,

very little control period, and more power inside him than Tucker had ever sensed in his damn life.

Swearing, he arrowed the car over to the curb, and under the pretense of making a call, he pulled out his phone and punched in the phone number for his house. He didn't have an answering machine and Lucia was there only a few days a week, so all it was going to do was ring. And ring. It would buy him a few minutes so he could think. That was all he needed to do. Take a minute and think.

Sighing, he held the phone to his ear and stared straight ahead, focusing on the vibrant energy still riding in the air as he tried to think up a plan.

He would have been better off checking behind him. Then he might have seen her coming.

As it was, he didn't see her until she already had her gun pulled.

"Well, well, well . . ."

* * *

VAUGHNNE didn't know whether to cuss or heave out a sigh of relief.

The tattoos spiraling up his arms weren't what had clued her into whom she was dealing with.

It was the fiery red hair spilling down into his eyes and down over his collar. Tucker couldn't have tried any less hard to attract attention, she figured. Muscle car. Brilliant red hair . . . not carroty red, but that deep, rich fiery red that a bunch of women would probably sell their soul for, and tattoos that twisted and twined around a rather nice pair of arms. She had to admit that. He had a great set of arms.

Even as she saw them tensing, his hands tightening on the steering wheel. She pressed the gun a little harder against the area behind his ear and moved in, using her body to hide it as best as she could. He'd parked in a damned conspicuous area, so this was going to be hard.

But she wasn't about to let Tucker, whoever in the hell he was, disappear without finding out why he was here. Because she knew better than to believe this was a coincidence. "You don't want to go grabbing for my gun, sugar," she said, smiling at him. "And don't go trying any of that electrical shit I know you can do. Remember what I can do . . . I'll shriek inside your skull until you're ready to gouge out your own brainstem just to shut me up."

He angled his head around just enough to look at her.

Brave guy. He apparently didn't seem to think she was going to pull the trigger.

She probably wouldn't, but still.

"I won't go pulling any of my shit if you don't make me," he said levelly. "How about you lower the gun and we can talk . . . Vaughnne, right?"

"We can maybe talk. But we aren't doing it here." Arching a brow, she held out a hand. "Gimme your keys and your phone. I'm getting in and then you can have them back."

"I can hot-wire the damn car quicker than you can get around to the other side."

"Probably." She smiled a little. "But you're here for a reason . . . I bet it's got something to do with why *I* am here."

His brown eyes bored into hers, a scowl darkening his face. Finally, he jerked his head in a nod and tugged out the keys. "I'm doing it to make you feel better, darlin'. You know it's a waste of time."

"I'm all about feeling better . . ." She smiled at him. "Darlin'."

He tossed her the keys. She barely had time to pocket them before the phone came flying at her. It was an iPhone, and she went into its settings, putting it in airplane mode and shutting down any of the apps that might use the GPS. It wasn't a surefire thing, but it was all she had without destroying the phone. She didn't think she had to take that step with him. She'd hold it in reserve, though. As she turned the phone off and slid it into her pocket, she headed around to the other side of the car, fully aware of the weight of his gaze, boring into her.

Broody bastard.

She wondered if Jones had tried to recruit him yet. He'd fit in *really* well.

Sliding into the passenger seat, she kept her gun in her lap, a firm grip on it, but aimed it away. "See? It's aimed elsewhere. Better?"

Tugging out the keys, she tossed them at him and nodded behind them. "I'm living across from the house you were probably checking out. Let's see if you know where it is. Go park in the alley behind my place."

"See, that's the problem with you federal types. Got to be all subterfuge, all the time. You can't just give me the damn address," he muttered, checking the road before he pulled out.

She shrugged. "Well, I *could*. I just want to see if my hunch is right."

He slanted a narrow look at her. "The kid I'm looking for has a brain that glows like neon. He doesn't know how to shut down. Anybody who knows how to look for people like us can see it."

Damn. She didn't let her reaction show, but her heart sank as she caught a glimpse of the look in his eyes. "So why are you looking for him?"

"I had a . . . request," he said, turning into the alley just behind her street. She wasn't surprised when he pulled into the narrow little space behind her house. "So did I pass the test?"

She just grunted as she climbed out. "Come on. Let's get inside." She used the cover of the car to hide it as she tucked her gun back out of sight and started toward the house.

He waited until the door was shut before he came for her.

She barely managed to duck out of the way, and the only reason she managed it at all was a weird tension in the air. It was like the air went all tight and crazy right before a bad thunderstorm. He was fast. He was quiet. And she thanked God and Taylor Jones for all that brutal, awful training he'd thrown her way before he'd agreed to let her in the unit.

It was the only damn thing that kept her out of Tucker's reach as she spun and drew her weapon—why in the hell had she put it up, anyway? "Do we really have to do this?"

"Put that down before I decide to get pissed off," he suggested.

"And what are you going to do if you get pissed off?" She curled her lip at him. "Call down the lightning on me or something?"

Something flashed through his eyes. "You think it's a joke."

"No. I got a good idea of what you can do and it's pretty damned amazing. I'm impressed. But I'm not looking at a killer. You're not going to hurt me, so shove the empty threats up your very nice ass, Tucker."

Lights flickered. "I don't have to kill you to get you the hell out of my way. Give me my phone. Get out of my way and let me do my job. Do that and we can call a truce before anything gets out of hand." A strange smile curved his face and damned if it was a little bit unsettling. "Before *you* get hurt."

"You can have your phone . . . after we talk and I'm certain you're not a threat to the kid I'm supposed to be protecting." Jerking her head to the table, she said, "Why don't we sit? Talk . . . and you can have your phone back. Heaven forbid you miss an important call or something."

The lights flickered . . . and went off.

She clenched her jaw and braced herself for an attack.

But it didn't come from him *directly*.

Darkness swarmed in on her mind. And she knew her mind

well enough to know *one* thing . . . it wasn't natural. It was like
something was pressing in, pressing down—

She sucked in a breath and felt her muscles weaken, felt her
weapon hand lower.

Instinctively, she sensed him moving and she threw herself
backward.

Knowing she only had a few seconds, she did the one thing
she knew would work.

She screamed. But she didn't scream with her mouth.

She screamed right inside his head, with all the force of her
ability.

* * *

It was a vicious, brutal shock to his system—it was like somebody had taken the power of a sonic boom and combined it with
the loudest wail of a siren, and found a way to make the noise
loud enough to cause physical harm. Except it wasn't happening
audibly. It was all inside his skull and he couldn't block it out.

Shuddering under the shock of it, Tucker sucked in a breath as
his control faltered. He had to either break his connection or risk
hurting her. It was a hard-ass thing, interfering with all those
little electrical connections that happened inside the human
brain. Too much and he'd kill her. Too little, and it wouldn't be
enough.

As the screaming in his brain continued, he groaned and hit
the heel of his hand against his temple, spinning away as he severed the link.

And still the screaming continued.

"*Enough*," he snarled.

Seconds ticked by before it slowly faded away.

Silence, sweet, *sweet* silence fell between them and he shuddered as the raw power inside leaped and burned, clawing to
get out.

Anger triggered it all, and having a gun leveled at him, having anybody threaten him . . . well. It pissed him off. He'd had it happen too many times, and most of the time, it had been because certain people from his past had been trying to drag him back to places he'd never go.

"You might be able to shut my brain down, but if you do, I'll damn well make sure you suffer every second," Vaughnne said from behind him, her voice harsh. "Are you and I going to sit and talk, or do we try to kill each other?"

"If I'd wanted to shut your brain down, I could have done that on the street," he snapped. Without looking at her, he stormed over to the small dining room table and flung himself into one of the chairs. "But I'm not here to chat and I'm not here to make friends with the FBI. I'm here because I've got a job to do and that kid across the street is a hazard."

Vaughnne kept her distance from him. It had just occurred to her that her table was one of those vintage sorts of dinette sets . . . shiny top, chrome plating. It looked like something you'd find in a fifties diner. Too much metal, especially considering she didn't know just what this guy could do with electricity. Electricity and metal were a *bad* mix.

Instead of sitting down, she tucked her gun back into place and adjusted the holster. The damn thing was rubbing her skin raw, but there were only so many places she could carry a weapon when she was out jogging unless she *wanted* somebody to know she was armed.

She studied him through her lashes. "You think I don't see how much of a hazard that kid is?"

"Then why aren't you doing something?"

"I am." She angled her chin up. "I'm babysitting. That's my job for now. That's all."

"That's not—"

The shrill ring of her phone cut him off and she grabbed it, swearing. That ring tone would go off for only one reason. She took off running down the hall even as she checked the display.

Somebody had activated the motion sensor she'd set up in Gus . . . *stop. You're here for the kid. Think about the kid.*

"Time's up," she said quietly as she moved to crouch in front of her laptop, staring at the monitors.

"You bugged his house?"

She shot Tucker a dark look. "Unless I'm expected to never *sleep*? Yeah. I bugged his house."

They watched for a moment as two men prowled through the back, lingering the longest outside the window to Gus's bedroom.

"They're looking for the kid." Something sick spread through her.

"That's why I'm here," Tucker snapped.

"You knew they were coming?" She continued to watch them, eyeing the time. Keeping an eye on the monitor, she checked the location of the GPS tracker she'd planted on Gus's truck. Crap. Leaving the store. A few minutes away at best.

"Yes."

Tucker's low, intense voice shattered her concentration and she glanced up at him, puzzled for a split second before she remembered. "You knew somebody would be here today."

"Not today." He shrugged and moved to the window, staring across the street. "One of them is psychic. I feel it. Not strong. But it's enough. Used it to locate the kid."

"They didn't locate the kid. They located his house."

Tucker shot her a dark look. "Same thing. They pull back, they wait until the kid shows up, and then they move in. That boy has no clue how to protect himself, does he?"

She rubbed her temple, thinking of how her head had felt, like somebody had reached inside and just helped themselves to her brain matter and sanity. "He might have a better handle on it than we think, but it would be purely instinctive."

"If you're supposed to be babysitting, why are you *here*?" he asked. "Isn't part of bodyguard detail just that . . . *guarding the body*?"

"I'm listening to my instincts," she said, curling her lip at him. "My gut said stay here today. If I'd followed, I wouldn't have been here to see this happening."

Ignoring the guilt tugging at her, she stared at the camera for another moment, debating.

Did she go over there?

If she did, her cover was blown.

Shit, it was about to get blown anyway. She shot another look at the phone and then started to swear viciously as she saw how very close that little dot was getting to the house. That dot—Gus's truck was on the move.

"Can you sense the kid, Tucker?" she asked quietly.

He turned his head, stared at her.

After a long moment, he nodded.

She shoved upright and headed into her room. In under a minute, she emerged, wearing jeans and strapping her weapon into place where it belonged. "I need your help," she said as she pulled her boots on. "The kid and his guardian are on their way here . . . *now*. And if I'm going to get them out of this place and on the road safely, I don't have time for chatting up our boys over there, playing B and E."

A muscle ticked in his jaw, and she pushed past him to grab her bag and shove the laptop and cords inside, pausing only long enough to check once more to make sure she had her Bureau ID, her wallet, and her keys. The other things she needed the most were tucked inside the cleverly disguised piece of shit car in her driveway. It looked like a piece of shit, but it would move and it would move fast.

She climbed inside, checking the location of Gus's truck once more.

Couple streets away. They had a few minutes at best. She headed outside.

A hand came down on her roof.

She barely managed to resist jumping.

Turning her head, she stared into Tucker's glittering eyes. "I can hold them up. But don't be surprised if I show up to keep you company, darlin'. I said I'd take care of the kid. Didn't say shit about putting him in the hands of the FBI."

It was good enough.

It was going to have to be.

Gus's truck had just turned down the street.

EIGHT

THE absolute last thing he needed after the day he'd had was to see some big bastard bent over Vaughnne as she sat in her car. Alex had been sick all damn day and he had gotten worse as the day progressed. He'd hoped it would improve once he got him home, but halfway there, he'd remembered they were out of Tylenol, so he'd had to backtrack and go get the medicine.

Gus knew how to handle a sick boy. He'd been taking care of Alex for years now and had nursed him through strep throat and the flu several times. But this seemed worse. He was so hot and he had that look—that *sick* look. It gave Gus a terrible feeling, but he couldn't let himself panic.

This was one of his fears, that the boy would take ill and he'd need medical care and they'd have to expose themselves at the hospital.

Shit.

Gus didn't fear much. He had no room for it in his life. But for Alex, he felt fear, and it was crowding through him now, churning in his gut. He slowed at the stop sign and glanced over at the boy for a minute and then looked back up, eyeing the big bastard hovering over Vaughnne.

Idly, he thought about ripping the man's balls off. Strangling him with them, for daring to even be near her.

The man was big. Red hair, a deep, dark red, the kind of color that would be remembered. And as he straightened and smacked a fist on the roof, Gus caught the sight of black ink twining around his arms.

The man's eyes cut his way.

Alex groaned.

"*Tío* . . . I'm going to be sick . . ."

"It's Gus, Alex, remember." He reached over and touched the boy's brow, and the fever-hot feel of it had him biting back another curse. The Tylenol wasn't helping. "We're almost home, okay?"

No time to worry about the man over there at Vaughnne's.

Man. With Vaughnne.

No time to worry about how much that infuriated him. Or *why* . . .

His truck sputtered just a block down from his house, and this time, he wasn't able to keep the stream of curses inside as the car came to a stop right in the dead middle of the road.

"*¿Qué carajo clase de mierda jodida es ésta?*" He glared at the engine, as though it might answer him back.

* * *

"FIGURED it would be better if you had him a little stuck," Tucker said as Vaughnne stared at the unmoving truck. "Away from the house and all."

"This isn't going to help his frame of mind any," she said sourly as she threw the car into drive. "Deal with the others. Hold them. As long as you can."

He canted his head to the side. "Well, that might be problematic. If I'm here, I can hold them forever and that won't happen. I'll give you a head start, though."

As she gunned the engine, Tucker eased back into the shadows. For a big, red-haired bastard, he actually did a better job at avoiding notice than she would have expected.

She slammed on the brakes just as Gus had managed to shove up the hood of his truck, glaring at it like that would magically fix it.

She pulled out her ID and slammed it down next to him. "Now if I had to pick a movie to go with this moment, I'd go with *The Terminator*," she said as his gaze flicked to the ID and then up to her face. She saw him bracing, preparing to move. "The line would be . . . *Come with me if you want to live.*"

He backed away and she saw the gun in his hands. Double-handed grip, braced and ready, like he could stand there forever. So fast. He was so damn fast. Yet again, she had to wonder, just who in the *hell* was he . . . and what in the *hell* had he done before he gave up that life to go on the run with that kid? A kid he'd die to protect. Always so ready to fight, she thought. To defend.

"I don't care who you are," he said quietly. "Get away. Give me your keys, or I'm going to shoot."

"You can shoot me." She held his gaze. "But it won't stop the ones who are chasing you. You know that. And if you shoot me, instead of just running from *them*, you're running from the FBI, too."

"Unless I kill you, they won't be too worried about me," he said, shrugging. "I don't need to kill you, just slow you down."

She smiled at him. "Gus, unless you *kill* me, you won't stop me. I'll track you down again."

Somebody shouted, and she slid a look past him, watched as

the two men who'd broken into his house came boiling out on the porch. Gus swung around, shifting his attention between her and the house, his grip on that weapon all too competent, all too ready.

"They broke into your house ten minutes ago. I don't think they are here to talk about baseball or discuss Alex's home-schooling life."

Tension slammed into the air as one of the men lifted a gun. It all but sucked the life out of her, although it didn't look like it hit Gus very hard. His lashes flickered but that was it.

The men went down, though.

Hard. Wow. Tucker really packed a punch.

As soon as they did, Gus shifted the gun back to her. Oh, lovely. She just loved being the center of attention. He thought *she* had done that?

"What in the fuck did you do to them?" he demanded.

Yep. That was exactly what he thought.

She lifted her hands. "I'm just here to make sure your kid stays okay," she said quietly. "And I'm going to do whatever it takes to make sure that happens."

Okay, so a little lie thrown in there . . . she accepted it and let it settle into place. Wasn't her favorite thing to do, but if it helped get the job done, then she'd do it. And it wouldn't hurt her cause for him to think she was capable of *that*, she figured.

He plowed his left fist down against his truck, still holding the weapon with his right. It was a Sig Sauer P250 and it remained pointed at her, steady and level. She had no doubt he could put a hole through her. Maybe he'd regret it, maybe he wouldn't. But he could still do it and that wouldn't help any of them.

"Get out of my way, Vaughnne," he growled.

"I can't," she said quietly.

"I'll shoot," he warned.

Time to get him to focus on the one thing she knew he cared

about. Glancing toward the car, she said softly, "And if you do, you condemn that boy to running even more."

"He's going to be doing that anyway," Gus whispered.

"Is that what you *want*?"

His lashes flickered over his eyes. "No."

"Then get in the car."

Off in the distance, sirens wailed and she gestured to the car. "The cops are coming . . . you can't get away from them without endangering him now. I can get you away. Trust me, Gus. I'm not going to let anybody hurt him. I promise you that."

* * *

Please . . . you must promise . . .

Trust was painful, he realized. For so many years, he'd trusted no one. Trusted nothing but his instincts. The problem was that *now* those instincts screamed that he trust something else. Someone else. Staring into Vaughnne's whiskey gold eyes, with the ghostly voice of a dead woman dancing through his mind, he made a decision.

"If you fuck me over, I'll hunt you down. I'll hurt you. I'll make you pay so badly, you'll wish you'd never been born."

"Understood."

Without wasting another second, he moved around and jerked open the passenger-side door. There were only three things he needed. His weapon, the bag he never went without, and Alex. Slinging the bag over his shoulder, he kept the weapon ready and then headed around the truck and jerked open the door. Alex moaned as he lifted him out. "*Tío—*"

"Shhhh," Gus murmured. "It's time to move on, Alex. We have to go now."

"I'm going to be sick," Alex whispered, his eyes glazed, like he didn't even hear what Gus had said.

The kid's weight pulled at him. They'd found a few months of peace and quiet here, something that almost resembled *safety*. In those months, Alex had shot up several inches and gained some weight.

Shifting the boy in his arms, he turned to face Vaughnne, not bothering to shut the door to the truck or grab anything else. There were things back at the house that might have been useful—more money, their clothes, weapons. But he had everything that was vital with him. Alex, and the bag.

He was always ready for this—ready to run at a moment's notice. Vaughnne had the back door open and was eyeing Alex narrowly. "He's sick," he said sourly.

She just nodded.

In just seconds, they were heading down the street. A nice, sedate speed and he was burning inside with the need to tear out of there. *They found him. They found him . . . I failed.* "Can't you go any faster?"

"Sure. The best way to avoid the notice of the police," she said drolly.

"You're the FBI." Warning flickered inside him.

She sighed and tossed her ID into his lap. "Yes, I am. But unless I want to get into a jurisdictional pissing contest, it's better to *avoid* them noticing us. I don't exactly know *what* you're running from, so I figure it's best to play this nice and quiet like."

Picking up her ID, he rubbed his thumb over it, studying it for signs that it was a fake. He knew what to look for. But then again, he'd carried one of these himself, and had convinced more than one or two agents that *he* was a federal agent. They'd believed him, too. If he could get fake credentials that looked real, others could as well.

"*Tío . . .*"

He closed his eyes, both at the pitiful sound of Alex's voice, and at the connection he'd tried to hide for the past few years. "Close your eyes, Alex," he said, his voice gentle. "Try to rest."

"I'm going to be sick," he said again, and this time, the conviction in his voice was even stronger.

A collapsible blue bag was shoved into Gus's hands, and he shot Vaughnne a look. She shrugged. "I believe in being prepared."

He turned around in the seat and pushed the bag into Alex's hands just as the boy lost control.

As the sour stench of vomit filled the air, Gus hooked a hand over the boy's neck and rubbed. "I'm sorry," Alex whispered. "I . . ."

Another spasm ripped through him.

"It's okay, kid," he said. "You're sick. Nothing to be sorry for."

A few seconds passed and then Alex slumped back against the back of the seat. Gus caught the bag and fisted his hand around it to close it. "Any better?"

Alex nodded, his head rolling over as he huddled against the seat cushions.

"There are plastic bags beneath the seat," Vaughnne said softly. "Just tie it up in that. We'll dump it when we stop. You can put the windows down."

A few moments of strained silence passed while he did that, and not only did he discover bags, but he found a small pack of hand wipes and hand sanitizer. "You often expect people to vomit in your car?" he asked tightly.

"It's happened a time or two." Then she shot him a look and shrugged. "Sometimes with me. I used to get carsick a lot when I was younger. It's better now, but for a while, even up until my twenties, I got sick almost every time I climbed into a car."

He narrowed his eyes, not quite believing that, but even as he decided he'd call her on it, her phone rang.

Her nose wrinkled and the look caught him off guard. It was a look of disgust, but it was so damn . . . cute. That was it. It was cute, that look of aggravation on her face.

"Not now," she grumbled. She didn't ignore the call, though.

* * *

"You pick the worst times to call," she said without waiting for Jones to say anything.

"Are there police there looking for the kid?"

"No." Vaughnne checked the mirror, eyeing the kid in the backseat. He was almost asleep, his dusky cheeks flushed with fever, his eyes closed.

"Agent MacMeans, do *not* bullshit me."

She heard a snap of temper cut through his voice and she let herself smile a little. She so rarely had the pleasure of being one of the ones to irritate him. He rarely *got* irritated, so this made it a double pleasure. "I wouldn't do that, boss. The cops aren't here. Now they might be back at the house, but I'm currently headed up International, on my way out of Orlando. And the kid is with me."

Five seconds passed.

"You had to blow your cover."

"Afraid so." She flicked a look at Gus, brutally aware of the fact that he was watching, and listening. Her skin prickled from the intensity of that look, and she prepared herself for whatever may be coming. "Listen, the kid is sick. I get the feeling we shouldn't take him to the doctor . . ."

"No," Gus barked out.

At the same time, Jones said, "I don't know if that's advisable."

Rolling her eyes, she said, "Well, that's sort of what I was just *saying*." She raised her voice and shot a dark look at Gus before focusing her attention back on the road. It was a tricky situation driving, as it was, watching her tail, talking to her boss, dealing with the hotness that was Gus, even if he was glaring at her. Oh, and not wrecking.

"Look, the kid is sick. He just puked in the car and his . . . guardian would appear to be worried, although I don't think he'd worry over a cold. He looks like he's running a fever, although I can't check while I'm driving." She cut into the right lane and turned off International. This road wasn't going to be much better but at least it wasn't one of the busiest in town. Taking five minutes to breathe and get her bearings wouldn't hurt, either. Pulling into the parking lot of a gas station, she put the car into park and swiveled around, eyeballing the kid. "He's also half out of it, if I'm not mistaken. What does it matter if I'm keeping them safe if he ends up dog-sick with pneumonia or something?"

"We're not taking him to the hospital," Gus growled.

She ignored him. The hospital wasn't her destination. Jones would have an alternative, she knew it.

"Jones?"

Five more seconds passed and then he asked, "Where do you plan on going?"

"I plan on getting the hell out of Orlando for starters, and then I need to get somebody to look at the boy. Preferably soon." In the backseat, Alex groaned, a pitiful little sound that twisted her heart. "No. Not *preferably* soon. It has to be soon."

"Just drive. When you get an idea where you're heading, let me know. I'll get a doctor to you."

She hung up and tossed the phone down.

She hadn't even managed to put the car into drive before she saw the gun leveled at her, digging into her rib cage, out of sight of anybody who might just happen by the car, unless they were outright looking. *Please . . . don't let anybody look*, she thought tiredly. That was the last thing she needed.

Turning her head, she met Gus's eyes.

"If you try to take us to the hospital, you'll be needing one yourself," he warned. "Although they won't be able to fix the damage I'll do to you. You'll just end up in the morgue anyway."

"I'm not taking him to a hospital," she said. "My boss will get a doctor to us."

A nerve pulsed and ticked in Gus's cheek. She had the insane urge to reach up and stroke, try to soothe away the tension, the fear she knew was raging inside him. *Tell me why you're so afraid for him,* she thought. *I can help, I swear . . .*

But she knew he wouldn't believe her. She'd just have to show him.

"That doesn't sound like standard FBI procedure."

Lifting a brow at him, she said, "You know a lot about standard FBI procedure? What, you watch a lot of TV or something?" Then she took a chance and looked away from him, putting the car into drive. "It's not standard FBI procedure, but I don't work with a standard unit."

As she pulled out into the flow of traffic, she felt the impact of his stare.

"What in the hell does that mean?"

Sighing, she shot him a look and then focused on the road. What in the hell did she tell him, she wondered. She needed him to trust her. She needed to know what in the hell he was running from and what—or *who*—he was protecting that boy from. But she couldn't *get* his trust without giving a little first.

"I do work for the FBI," she said slowly. "But it's a special task force, and if anybody knew I was telling you this, I could lose my job. I'm telling you because I need you to trust me, at least a little."

She flicked him another look as she wove in and out of traffic, taking the most direct route out of town. *Get out, get away, move fast . . .* it was a scream inside her brain, an instinct to get a hell of a lot of distance between her and that quiet little street where Alex and Gus had managed to live undisturbed for some time.

"I don't trust *anybody*," Gus whispered.

"You're going to have to learn." She wished she could make him understand just how vulnerable that kid was. How exposed.

"You're doing your best to take care of him, Gus, I get that. But that boy is like an exposed nerve bed. He's got no training and too much raw power. Anybody who knows how to look for psychic skill would be able to find him in a heartbeat."

Tense silence stretched out, before a low curse shattered it.

"*Mierda*," Gus snarled, his voice furious and hot.

Vaughnne's grasp of Spanish was pretty limited, but she understood that one. Lifting a brow, she said, "*Shit* doesn't even cover it."

"How did you know?"

"I just told you. He's exposed. He has no idea how to hide himself. Hell, he's like a neon sign in the dark. Anybody who knew how to look could find him," she said. "And if the *wrong* people come looking? He's got problems. Today, the wrong people came looking."

Then, from the corner of her eye, she saw him shake his head. "The boy reads people. He can see danger. He'd know—"

"He never saw me."

Silence, once more, fell between them and she had to fight not to cringe under the weight of that deadly stare. Her instincts were screaming again. *Danger, danger, danger*, a terrible litany that had her wanting to run, and hide. Far and fast. Hide from Gus.

Finally, he broke the silence, his voice almost terribly gentle as he asked, "What does that mean?"

"He never saw me. I'm not a threat to you, but he had no idea that I'm psychic, that I was there to watch him. He has no idea that people out there, like *us*, can sense him. He doesn't know how to hide what he is. He may be a force to be reckoned with, but he didn't realize there was another psychic right in front of him. And Gus? I'm not all that. If I can hide what I am, there are plenty of others who can do the same. Others who can hide what they *are*, what they *think*. He's powerful, but he's just a kid . . . a scared, untrained one."

"And how do I know you do not lie to me?" he demanded, his voice edgy and harsh. The gun was jamming into her ribs now, hard enough that it was going to leave a bruise. "You could be lying now. You say you're—"

The first time I saw you walking up my sidewalk, I thought to myself . . . the view was fine, Vaughnne whispered into his mind. Her gift was telepathy and it worked best in words, but if she had to, she could project images. It took more thought, and it worked best if the emotion was strong.

Fortunately, she had plenty of *strong* emotion when it came to Gus. Lust definitely counted, right?

She projected the image of how it felt, that first look, the sight of him, how it had sent heat and appreciation flooding through her.

Then as she heard his harsh intake of breath, she shifted the focus of her thought. *Then I looked at the boy and I was caught between nerves and pain. He's too young for the burden he's bearing, Gus . . . and you know it. I don't even understand what his burden is, and I know it. I can see it on him.*

She pushed the image that she carried of Alex into Gus's mind. That first image, Alex, all long, skinny limbs and big, scared eyes, and a fear he tried so hard to hide.

"Enough," Gus said, his voice flat. "Enough."

She cut off the flow of her thoughts and focused on the area around them, checking the rearview mirror, the cars. Nobody was following them, but she still had that burning, pressing urge to get the hell away from there. *Now.*

She could breathe easier, though. Gus was no longer trying to drill the nose of that Sig Sauer into her ribs. That helped a little.

* * *

He's too young for the burden he's bearing . . .

Did she think he didn't know that already?

He shoved a hand through his hair, knocking his ball cap off in the process. He hurled it to the floorboard and turned his head, staring outside as the landscape zipped by.

The view is nice . . .

Innocuous words.

But what she'd pushed inside his mind . . .

He did not need that inside him just then. The knowledge that she felt the same heat he'd felt. No. He didn't need that at all, yet at the same time, part of him . . .

Part of him wanted to grab her, haul her into his lap, and just . . . feel. Give in to what he had inside him, what she obviously had inside her. Skim his hands up that long, slender back and tangle them in her hair as he feasted on her mouth.

That greedy, selfish part wanted to strip her naked and ride her until they were too drained to even move. That part of him knew just how long it had been since he'd had a woman, touched a woman, kissed a woman . . . wanted a woman. How long it had been since his life revolved around anything beyond watching over Alex, nights spent pacing the house as he worried. Worried about whether they'd get through another night without having to run. Worried about whether they'd both survive when the time came, would they be caught . . .

That part that wasn't focused on the fear and everything else, *that* part of him wanted to touch her. *That* part of him wanted to glide his hand through her hair and draw her mouth to his, see if she'd taste as wild as he'd imagined. She wouldn't be a sweet and gentle woman in bed, he didn't think. He'd had sweet and gentle lovers. She'd be heat and power and passion, and he'd lose himself inside her.

If he could have given in to it.

But it wouldn't happen.

Alex . . . his focus was, and would always be, Alex.

"How long have you been running?" she asked quietly.

He slanted a look her way and then looked back out the window. "Too long."

Four years. Six months. Twelve days. He flicked a glance at the clock, calculated the time change. *Thirteen hours and nine minutes.*

Since Alex was eight . . . the day the boy's youth and innocence and life were shattered, right in front of him.

The night his mother . . .

He closed his eyes and tried to stem the flow of those memories. *Please . . . you must promise . . .*

He was trying. *Carajo*, he was trying. But he was so useless at this. Caring for somebody, protecting somebody. A direct opposite of the life he'd been living. And what a life that had been. Pointed in a direction and told to fight, he fought. Told to kill?

He did that, too.

Told to fuck this woman and learn more about her drug lord lover? Absolutely. And more than once, the women he'd been with had probably suffered for it once it was all said and done. But he'd kept it up, because that was what he did.

Now he was expected to care for another. Protect another. When life had never been anything but a race, a gamble, a challenge before this.

It was still a gamble, he supposed. One he'd lost. One his sister had lost.

His job now was to make sure his nephew didn't lose as well. "Who is after him?"

Gus closed his eyes.

Vaughnne sighed. "Gus, I can't help unless you talk to me."

"You can't help." He rested his head against the back of the seat. *FBI.* He didn't know how they'd caught the attention of the FBI. He'd been careful. He'd broken laws, he knew, but he'd done his damnedest to fly under their radar, and that was one thing he knew how to do . . . very well.

Nobody had reported the boy as missing, because they couldn't afford the attention.

So it wasn't that.

How, though?

Not that it mattered.

As soon as Alex was well, they would run. They'd disappeared before. Gus was becoming remarkably good at . . . disappearing. Perhaps his nephew could do tricks that would make David Copperfield look like an amateur and maybe he could do things that might turn a person's mind to mush if he wasn't careful, but Gus knew how to disappear and get lost in the world.

They'd done it several times over.

They'd just keep doing it.

And keep doing it . . .

Unconsciously, his hand clenched into a fist.

"You'll never stop running if you don't make a stand," Vaughnne said quietly.

"Do *not* read my mind," he bit off. He swung his head around to glare at her, but she was focused on the road, like nothing mattered except the stretch of pavement. "Ever. Do you understand me?"

"Oh, completely." A smirk twitched her lips and damn if that wasn't appealing, he thought. Appealing as hell. "I couldn't, Gus, even if I tried. I can talk inside your head as much as I want. As *loud* as I want. And I can do it from pretty damn far off, once I have your . . . channel, so to speak. But I couldn't read your mind to save my life. That's not my gift."

"Do not lie to me," he said.

She rolled her eyes. "I'm not."

"Then how do you . . ." He stopped.

Vaughnne shook her head. "I know what somebody looks like when they are running, Gus. And people don't usually *run* like you do just because it's fun. They don't drag around a kid they love just for kicks and giggles. You only live like you've been living because you feel like you have no choice."

"There isn't one."

"Because you haven't looked at all the options," she said, a sad smile curving her lips. "Or maybe the other options hadn't been there until now. But I'm giving you another option now . . . trust me."

"I don't know you." Gus couldn't see Alex, but he didn't need to see the boy to remind himself of the fact that the child had been the driving force in his life for so long now. Everything revolved around him. Everything would continue to revolve around him.

"No." Vaughnne nodded in agreement. "You don't. But you're going to. I'll help you take care of him, Gus."

"I don't need help." He couldn't need it.

"If you've got the kind of trouble coming that I think you've got, you need all the help you can get."

NINE

L YING to the cops came easy to him.

Maybe it was a sign of how screwed up Tucker Collins was, but he could sit there on Vaughnne's porch, sucking on a beer he'd swiped from her fridge, and lie to the cops without blinking an eye.

And that was exactly what he did, all while keeping his hold on the two assholes across the street.

One of them was a pretty damaging hold, too. Tucker wasn't too beat up over it, even when he'd heard somebody shout, "Tell the paramedics to hurry it up—this guy is seizing on me!"

He'd squeezed too hard. He didn't care. The guy had that dark, malevolent feel to him that told Tucker one thing . . . the man had murder on the mind. It was amazing the things a guy like him could pick up just from reading the vibes in the air.

Like now.

The cop standing in front of him knew that Tucker was lying. His name was Officer R. Rand.

R. Rand, Tucker thought. Well, Officer R. Rand had a good poker face and Tucker couldn't read his mind. Thoughts and emotions were closed to him, but he could read the vibrations in the air . . . all of that crackled around the cop, hovered in the air around him, snapping like microcurrents, and those? Tucker read those things like they were the morning news.

And the cop knew Tucker was lying.

Tucker lifted the bottle to his lips and took another sip. Coors. Cheapest shit beer around, if you asked him. He hated it, but it would do in a pinch. Just then, all he wanted to do was look nice and laid-back. Uninvolved. He'd go for harmless if he thought he could pull it off, but that wasn't going to happen.

"You want to tell me again, Mr. . . ."

Tucker smiled. "It's Curtis. Rick Curtis," he said, tossing out the fake name he'd decided to use for this job. He'd already turned over the fake ID and he was well aware he'd have to kiss it good-bye, both the ID and the persona, because the scrutiny he was getting from the cop was just not good. The ID would pass muster, for a while, he knew, but he had a feeling he just might have some problems on his hands. Shit. He hated that. He'd been here for years and he liked it. Liked his house, liked Lucia. Liked the work he did.

It was over now, though.

It wasn't like he'd expected any of this to last forever, right?

Bastards like him were remembered. It wasn't the height, it wasn't even the tattoos. It was the hair. Sometimes he thought about shaving it all off or dying it, but that required upkeep, and since he rarely got involved like this . . . why bother?

Now he was wishing he'd bothered.

"So." Rand smiled. "Mr. Curtis. Can you tell me again what happened?"

"Sure." He slumped deeper in the seat, resting his chin on his chest as he eyed the house across the street. "I was hanging around here waiting for my girlfriend to get back. She was just heading out to pick up some food, maybe a movie, some beer that's actually drinkable." He shrugged and eyed the bottle he held with acute dislike. "Anyway, I heard a noise—people shouting. So I come out, see those guys on the porch, and you all are there."

"Your girlfriend supposedly had the guy across the street hop in the car with her."

Tucker heaved out a sigh. "Yeah? I'm out of town half the time and she's out running around on me." He gave the cop a dark look. "Women suck."

The cop didn't even bat an eyelash. "Nobody around here recalls seeing you before."

"She just moved in." Tucker shrugged. "I'm only here about a week out of the month because of my job. I live in Louisiana, actually . . . as you can see by my license. Work keeps me traveling a lot."

"And what exactly is it that you do?"

"I'm a field service engineer." He watched as the guy's brows arched up into his hairline and he started to ramble on about how he spent nearly seventy percent of his time either taking QA calls or traveling to fix this, and that, which he had to do because the stupid motherfuckers who called the main office couldn't handle the troubleshooting steps that he always outlined to them on the phone.

Halfway through his little rant, Rand's eyes started to glaze over, and once he launched into a detailed breakdown of his last "job," the cop abruptly lifted a hand and nodded.

"Okay, so you're on the road a lot."

Hiding his smile behind his beer, Tucker drawled, "Oh, yeah. A damned shame I worked out a few days to come visit my lady and then I hear she's out running around with some dumb-ass. When I get ahold of that guy . . ."

The cop flicked him a look.

Tucker gave him a shamefaced look. "Shit, I'm sorry. Vaughnne and I . . . well. Never mind. I'll work that out when I see her."

"And that will be . . ."

He frowned and pulled out his phone. He eyed the messages like he was waiting for one to magically appear, and damn it, it would have to be magical, because he didn't think he'd given her his number.

"I don't know. I'm going to have to call her."

"Would you mind giving me her number?"

Tucker straightened up. "Why?"

Gesturing across the street, Rand said, "Well, we do have a bit of a problem across the way. The neighbor's house was broken into. She was last seen with the neighbors, not that long ago, if you'd recall. It seems we should get to the bottom of it." He gave Tucker a friendly smile.

Tucker smiled back as he settled comfortably into the seat. "It seems you should. But, you see . . . Vaughnne didn't really do anything except drive away. I don't really feel comfortable giving you her phone number."

"Maybe you'd feel more comfortable down at the station."

Tucker lifted a brow and dropped the shucks, Southern boy charm. "Maybe you'd better produce a reason for taking me there first." He shrugged and stood up, eyeing the mess going on across the street. The paramedics were there now, working on the men, calling out terms and phrases that Tucker was more familiar with than he cared to be. One of them would be fine, once Tucker dropped his hold.

The other one, though . . . nah. That man's mind was toast.

He kept having seizures and Tucker didn't give a damn. That son of a bitch had gone after a kid.

"Do I need to look for a reason?" Officer Rand glared up at

him, looking unperturbed by the fact that Tucker had a good eight inches on him, and unperturbed by the fact that Tucker was still on the porch while the officer was on the ground.

"If you want me to go to the station, I'd suggest you find one," Tucker said. He hooked his thumbs in his pockets and decided when he ran into Nalini, he just might paddle her ass. And not just because she had such a nice one, either.

If he got hauled in over this, there were going to be problems. A lot of them. There just might be . . .

The sight of the black car pulling up in front of him didn't do a whole hell of a lot to settle his mind. It didn't do his temper much good when the door opened and a rough-looking bastard climbed out.

The guy was even bigger than he was.

Their eyes met over the distance and Tucker tipped back his head and sighed, staring up at the white painted roof over his head. He didn't bother looking away from it even when the newcomer approached Rand, no doubt flashing his shiny little FBI credentials.

"Special Agent Joss Crawford."

As Rand introduced himself, Tucker figured he'd studied the ceiling boards long enough and he lowered his gaze, staring at Joss Crawford from under the veil of his lashes. A little while back, he'd sort of worked with this guy . . . *sort of* . . . without really realizing it. Crawford had been working the FBI side of things, while Tucker did what he did best—work his side of things.

Their sides had collided because one of Tucker's few friends, Dru Chapman, had ended up right in the middle of the mess. Dru and Joss were shacking up now. Tucker thought she should get her head examined, but what did he know?

"I'm afraid I'm going to have to take this man into custody," Joss said, slipping Tucker a narrow look.

Well, now. Tucker might not be able to read minds, but he could read that look easily enough. It clearly read . . . *keep your damned mouth shut.*

Rand rested a hand on his gun. "And just why is that?"

"I'm afraid I can't discuss that, Officer, but it's regarding an ongoing, sensitive federal investigation. This man has information on my case and he's going to have to come with me."

"I am, huh?" Tucker stared Joss down. Yeah, he read the look, all right, but he didn't do the whole *do-what-you're-told* thing well.

Yes, a voice snarled into his mind. *Or would you* rather *go to the police station? Keep your trap shut and you can walk away with me and I'll get you out of this. Otherwise, you're on your own and I don't care if Dru gets upset.*

As that voice, strong and powerful, echoed through his mind, Joss just smiled and said to the cop, "I have the warrant, if you need to see it. Unless he's under arrest here?"

Tucker curled his lip. "They can't arrest me for not ponying up a phone number." He slid Joss a narrow look and thought hard. *Stay out of my head.*

Joss didn't bat a lash. "Let's not make this any harder than it has to be, son."

Son. Tucker snorted. Well, at least he hadn't given up his real name. Sighing, he headed down the steps and fell into place at Joss's side. Once they were halfway down the walk, Joss shot him a dark look. "Behave, dickhead. Where the hell is Vaughnne?"

"Fuck off."

Joss laughed.

"The sentiment is mutual, buddy. Now get in the car. I was in the middle of something when the boss called and I'd like to get back to it."

Once they were in the car, with the windows rolled up, blocking out the sound, Tucker stopped behaving. He gathered up the remnant energy rolling through him as he shot Joss a look. "You don't even want to think about trying to take me to the FBI, Crawford. You hear me?"

"Oh, suck my dick," Crawford said, looking unperturbed.

Tucker snarled and went to claw off one of his gloves. Even as the red of rage rolled through him, a gun jammed into his ribs. "You want to think long and hard about doing anything else. I know what you can do, Collins—in great detail. The only way you can *stop* me is if you *kill* me. I know killers. You're not one. So either we call a truce or you cross a line you don't want to cross. Which is it?"

"You don't get the gun away from me, you're going to find out."

The air in the car all but crawled with tension as Tucker turned his head, stared into Joss's eyes.

A mean grin slanted Joss's mouth. "I think I could almost like you." Then he withdrew the gun.

Tucker slumped low in the seat. "If you try to take me anywhere, I'm going to cause you more grief than you can possibly imagine, Crawford. Keep that in mind."

"I don't plan on doing anything but getting you out of the way so Agent MacMeans can do her job."

"Well, then, that is a problem." Tucker closed his eyes. "You see, I made a promise that I'd make sure the kid she has with her was safe and I can't do that if I'm out of the way."

He cracked one eye open and looked at Crawford. "I don't break promises."

"You might have to break this one," Joss muttered.

As they neared the end of the block, Tucker had just one thought in mind. He wanted him to turn left. That was all he needed. A left turn. And then he'd take it from there.

And sometimes, he actually *got* what he wanted.

Crawford turned left, driving right past the little alley where

Tucker had parked his car. Satisfied, Tucker focused and reached out. The car sputtered to a stop and died.

He was out of the car in a heartbeat, Crawford reaching for him a split second later. He slammed the door and focused again, listening as the locks snicked shut. All the electronics in cars these days . . . it made some things so interesting.

Crawford swore and drove his fist against the window, and Tucker flashed him a grin before spinning on his heel.

The big, mean black muscle car was still waiting behind Vaughnne's house and he climbed inside. He could feel his hold on Crawford's car lessening, bit by bit, but that was okay. Once he was out of sight, the man would have a hard time tracking him down.

He supposed he could have blown the engine, not just killed it.

But in the end, antagonizing the FBI wasn't going to do him any good. All he wanted to do was make good on his promise to Nalini. Then he'd relocate. Get a new phone number. Get lost in the world so that the frustrating little work of sexual art could never find him again and make him wish that for once, just once, he could actually lose himself inside a woman.

* * *

"WHAT's the status?"

"Beats the hell out of me." Joss shot the phone he'd dropped in his cup holder a dirty look and wished like hell he'd actually finished his job here on *time*. He was wrapping up the loose ends from the assignment from hell. And it *had* been the assignment from hell. Somehow, it was one that had Joss both thanking God and cursing fate, all in one breath. He'd met Dru . . . *found* Dru, because of that job.

And he'd almost lost her, almost died because of that job.

Assignment from hell, in a nutshell.

"Crawford . . . I need to know what is going on in Orlando," Jones snapped, his voice about as close to pissed as Joss had ever heard him. "There's a kid's safety at stake, you understand me?"

"Yep." He cut left on the street up from where Vaughnne had been staying and did another drive by but he already knew he wasn't going to find anything. Tucker Collins had kept him locked in his car, like he'd been trapped inside a damned tuna can, for a good three minutes, and by the time Joss had been able to get the car to turn over or the doors to unlock, the man had already vacated the premises.

And his phone hadn't come on for a good *hour* afterward.

He was debating on whether or not to fill the boss in on all of that. They hadn't ever had anybody in the unit that could play with electricity like that. He'd almost bet Jones would get a hard-on at the idea. Figuratively speaking, of course.

But he also knew, even if he hadn't picked it up from Collins's mind, there was no way that guy wanted in the fold.

And thanks to the gift he had riding hard inside him, he had more than a few blips from the other psychic. Up until a few minutes ago, Joss had been convinced he was the freak show of all freak shows. The label he'd been stuck with was *mirroring*. He could pick up the psychic gifts of anybody he'd been imprinted with and the gift would stick until he synched with another psychic and was imprinted with another gift.

It was a weird-ass gift, he knew.

But Tucker made him look almost *normal*.

The man had shut down his car. *Locked* him in his car. And he'd shut down his phone.

He's like a walking electrical rod, basically, Dru had told him. *He can do crazy shit, and I don't know just how much crazy shit he can do, Joss.*

That had been a few months ago, back when he and Dru had been piecing together everything that had happened, both while they were working together, and when they'd been working toward the same end without realizing it. Tucker had been at her back, all along. It was one of the few things that made the nightmare of those months just a little more palatable. As in, he no longer woke up about to choke on his vomit as he thought about the hell that Dru had been living in. She'd had a way out. Tucker had been the way out. One scary-ass way out, but Dru trusted the guy and that meant something.

That meant, basically, that Joss was going to trust him, too. Dru's ability wasn't one that he was going to discount. Not now. Not again.

"Listen, Jones," he said as the silence stretched on. "Vaughnne isn't here. There are cops all over the place and I saw an ambulance. I don't know what the deal is, but unless you *want* them being alerted to the fact that we are nosing around, we might have to stay in the dark for now." He elected, on the side of wisdom, not to bring Tucker into the picture. Sooner or later, he might have to, especially if he got pulled into this job, but he wasn't sure if that was going to happen.

He had his own mess, one that he was specially suited to, and Vaughnne was already handling this one. They were spread pretty thin as it was. If Jones had wanted him on this assignment, he would have been put on it from the get-go.

"You hooked up with Taige Morgan before you headed back to Orlando, Crawford. You can find things out without talking to *anybody* if you try," Jones said.

Joss rolled his eyes and headed back for the street where the cops were camped out. He'd been out of his mind hoping that maybe the boss wouldn't think about that. Definitely out of his mind.

The second ambulance was pulling away. He only knew it was the second, because the first had gone blowing past him on the way in and he was pretty positive there wasn't another emergency going on anywhere in the neighborhood just then.

Reaching for the police scanner, he turned it on.

Yeah, he had a telepathic gift crammed into his mind.

But maybe he could just use good, old-fashioned investigative skills on some of this.

*   *   *

THE little hotel room was one tucked on the bottom floor in the corner of a Red Roof Inn that had seen better years. Better decades. But it was clean and that was all that counted.

After Gus had laid the sick boy on the bed, Vaughnne knelt at his side and touched his forehead, wincing at how hot he felt. He mumbled a little and batted at her hand before curling in around himself and clutching at his belly.

"How long has he been feeling bad?"

Gus was quiet.

Sighing, she tipped her head back and stared at him. "I need to call my boss and give him an update, let him know where we are so he can get somebody here to treat the kid. It would be *helpful* if I could give him some background on the kid's condition."

Long, tense moments passed and then Gus nodded slowly.

He held out a hand, and although she didn't trust him any farther than she could throw him, she placed her hand in his, let him offer her assistance she didn't need to rise to her feet.

He kept hold of her hand as he guided her across the room and toward the one area where they might have a modicum of privacy. Out of habit, she checked the bolt on the door. The latch was secured. The door was locked. Nobody had followed them and Vaughnne wasn't about to let anybody near that kid. If they tried, she'd blow a hole through them or scramble their brains—whichever seemed to work best at the time.

Still . . . she checked.

Seconds later, the bathroom door closed at her back.

And then, *she* seemed to be the one who needed protection.

Gus went from the quiet protector to the warrior who'd leveled a gun at her, fully prepared to kill her. Before she could even catch her breath, he slammed her against the door, his forearm at her throat, pressing hard enough that she couldn't draw her breath to scream.

She could have fought back.

She knew that.

And she knew how.

But as his misty eyes stared into hers, her heart slammed against her chest and she couldn't breathe, could barely even think.

It wasn't *fear* that seemed to crowd out all of her thoughts, though. Fear she could have handled.

This was so, so much worse.

"You need to understand something." He leaned in, pressing his mouth to her ear. "And I want you to listen to me, very, very closely . . . Vaughnne. Is that even your name?"

She was pleased that her voice was almost steady as she said, "Yes. It's my name. I gave you a false last name, but my first name is Vaughnne."

"Hmmm." He nuzzled her neck and little licks of pleasure shot all the way through her. "And FBI . . . are you really FBI?"

"Yes." She closed her eyes as he pushed his thigh between hers. Oh, hell. What the hell was this? "You can call D.C. They can verify."

"They routinely give out names of their agents, Vaughnne?"

He licked her. What . . . the . . . hell? She shuddered as he crowded in closer. His forearm was still wedged against her throat, preventing her from moving, but it was no longer pressing against her so tight that it was a chore just to breathe. Well, it *was*, but that was because of the sheer, burning weight of lust. He traced his tongue down the line of her neck. "You did not answer me."

Accent, she noticed dimly. He had an accent—she hadn't ever

heard it before. And she would have *noticed*, too, which meant the man's skills just went from Category 4 straight to Category 5. At least.

Swallowing, she focused on his question. "Generally, no. But if you call and ask for the man I tell you to ask for, he will verify."

"And isn't that convenient?" He laughed a little, resting his free hand on her hip. His fingers flexed and she felt the imprint everywhere he touched. Every single place, from his thumb, to his little finger, curving over her flesh, kneading back and forth . . . "You give me a false number. A false name. So easy to fool me, you think?"

As his mouth came to cover hers, she averted her head. Finally, her brain was engaging.

Sex as a weapon. Not something she'd ever had directed at her, but whoa. Damn. That's what this was and he was potent as hell. "You can look the damn number up on Google. I'm pretty sure I can't control Google, although if I can get them to give me some major shares in the stock, hey, I'm game to try. You call that number, I'll tell you how to get connected to the man who can vouch for me."

His knee pushed between her thighs, and this time, no matter how hard she tried, she couldn't keep from shuddering. Couldn't keep from whimpering as he drew her in until she was all but riding his thigh. *Oh. Hell.*

"And what will he tell me when he vouches for you? What happens then? Somebody comes in here to take the child from me? I don't think so, Vaughnne."

"Nobody wants to take him away," she snapped. And then she curled her hands into fists to keep from reaching for him as he shifted and settled his hips squarely between her own. She felt him now. *All* of him, the ridge of his cock, hot and thick, and damn it, if he hadn't been aroused, this would have been easier, so much easier.

But sex as a weapon wasn't really useful if the weapon wasn't primed and ready to fire, she supposed.

Summoning up what little strength she had, she closed her eyes. She went through her options and discarded all but a few. As she was busy with that, he shifted the forearm he had wedged across her upper body. Cooler air kissed her flesh and she hissed as she realized he had freed the top button of her shirt.

No. Absolutely no.

As he reached for the second one, she opened her eyes and stared at him.

He stared right back at her.

She didn't have a lot of room to maneuver, she had next to no leverage, and she'd rather not wake up Alex. The kid had already been through hell and was sick on top of everything else in his life.

She didn't really want to hurt Gus. Assuming she *could*. She might want to bloody him in that very second, but he was trying to protect the kid. She thought maybe she could understand that drive. Maybe.

As pissed off as she was, she understood the basic need to protect.

When he leaned in, she slid a hand around the back of his neck, careful to keep her expression blank. As he covered her mouth, she held herself still. And as he went to sweep his tongue across hers, she bit him. At the same time, she tangled a hand in his hair and jerked. He muffled his response, doing exactly what she'd expected—trying to avoid waking Alex, scaring him. He went to grab her and she jammed her fist into his throat. He had to breathe, right?

Even as he was struggling to do that, though, he was already reaching for her. He was too well equipped for this, she thought. She evaded his hand and lashed out with one weapon he *couldn't* prepare for. Blasting her voice into his mind, she watched as he stumbled and slammed a hand against his temple, caught off guard.

She jerked the door open, taking advantage of the few precious seconds she had. The second she was out the door, she cut the scream off, pulling her weapon as she set her stance.

He came for her, pausing only at the sight of her weapon. She held his gaze.

"We're not doing this, Casanova," she said quietly. She licked her lips and hated the fact that she could still taste him. Her entire body throbbed, ached. Burned for him. And if he hadn't been trying to pull . . . whatever he'd been pulling? She might have been just fine with letting him do anything he wanted to with her. Even with a kid sleeping a few feet away. They'd been in a bathroom, right? She knew how to be quiet.

But he *had* been up to something and she wasn't going to be used. Wasn't going to have any man use sex against her. No matter what the goal was.

"Nobody is going to hurt him," she said as he edged out of the bathroom, moving closer and closer.

She backed away. And still he kept coming. Eventually, she ran out of room and he stood there with his chest pressed to the muzzle of her Glock and no emotion on his face.

"Nobody is going to hurt him. Nobody is going to *take* him. I'm here to help keep him *safe*," she said.

"Nobody can keep him safe," Gus said, his voice a monotone. "You don't even know what is after him."

"No," she said, shaking her head. "I don't. Because you haven't told me. But I do know that I work for the FBI, and if anybody stands a chance of protecting that kid, it's the people I work for."

* * *

"THE people you work for." Gus stared at her. Stupid woman. She didn't come off that way, but she had no idea what she was dealing with, when it came to protecting Alex. Up until the past few years, *Gus* hadn't even had a clue. And he'd thought he had. Considering the life he lived, he should have been damned well aware.

Holding her gaze with his, he reached up and went to grab her wrist. She spun away, but he'd already noticed the fact that she was determined to be quiet. Taking care not to bother Alex. Considerate . . . he had to appreciate that. Maybe she was being honest. But she was still naïve. Naïve, foolish . . . and she fit against him better than anything he could ever imagine outside of a wet dream. That strong, limber body had vibrated as he'd leaned into her, all but ready to kill her if it came down to it. But had she stared at him with fear?

No. It had been desire he'd seen in her face. Maybe the fear had been there, but the desire had been stronger.

Damn him straight to hell, but he wanted her. More than he wanted his next breath.

"Crazy woman," he whispered as she shifted to give herself more room to maneuver. He shot a look over her back, saw that Alex had rolled over onto his belly and had his face buried against the mattress. Concern warred inside him. It was a different sort of battle raging within him then. They had to move, had to run, had to hide and remake themselves all over again. But Alex was ill . . .

"You know, I'm getting a little tired of this," Vaughnne said. "Back off. Sit down. Chill out. We can talk."

"Better idea," Gus suggested. "Get out of my way. I take my boy and we leave. You tell your . . . boss . . . that you lost us and everybody is happy."

"And when the people chasing you finally catch you?" She lifted a brow at him. "Don't you get it, you big dumb idiot? Those men waiting outside your house tracked you *down* . . . by tracking *him*. You can't hide him. He's not trained, he's hitting puberty, which means he's going to get *stronger*. He's a hazard to himself and everybody around him until he learns how to control that gift of his."

Something cold lodged in his heart. He wanted to brush it aside. She was wrong. She had to be. "We have done well enough for several years. They were lucky."

"No. They were smart. One of them was psychic, you jack-ass." Her eyes narrowed on his face. "You don't have any idea what to *look* for when it comes to people like us, do you?"

Through his lashes, he studied her. "I don't need to. The boy does." Gus could *feel* it when their kind used their abilities, but no. He didn't recognize them. It wasn't an issue, though. Not with Alex. The boy could see them well enough. He always had before.

"*Again*, he didn't recognize me—if I can hide, what's to stop somebody else from doing the same thing?" she said quietly. She glanced at her gun and then sighed. "I'm putting this away, but if you come at me again, you and me will go another round. But I'll pull the gloves off this time."

There was something so sexy about the way she glared at him that he was tempted to do just that . . . go at her again. But he was already a raging, aching mess of want, and he suspected that if he kept putting his hands on her, his control was going to snap. Masking everything he felt, he brushed by her and moved deeper into the room, pausing to linger by the bed. He reached down to touch Alex's shoulder, intending to wake him up.

"We can't . . ." *stay*. The word was on the tip of his tongue. They couldn't stay.

Somehow, someway, he'd get the boy to a doctor, even if he had to kidnap one, but they couldn't stay—

Except Alex seemed even hotter now.

So hot he nearly burned Gus's hands.

Closing his eyes, he went to his knees by the bed. *Please . . .*

That was the only thought clear in his mind.

Just *. . . please . . .*

A hand touched his shoulder.

Woodenly, he said, "The fever seems to be getting higher. I have no way to check."

"Let me call my boss," Vaughnne said quietly. "You know he's ill. He's half out of his mind with his fever at this point. If you don't get him help now, it could be too late by the time you *do* try."

The absolute last thing he could do was say yes.

The absolute last thing.

But then Alex groaned and rolled over onto his side, shuddering, shaking a little as he doubled over. *"Tío . . ."* he whispered, opening his eyes. But his gaze was glassy, and Gus had the oddest feeling the boy didn't even see him.

"I'm here, *m'hijo*," he murmured, brushing Alex's hair back from his face and fighting back the fear that crowded up his throat at the hot, dry feel of fevered flesh under his hand.

"¿Mamá? ¿Dónde está mi mamá?"

Gus closed his eyes while a howl built inside his throat. His mother. Son of a *bitch*—the boy was asking for a woman who had been dead for years. Stroking a hand across Alex's brow, Gus said softly, "Get some rest, Alex." He didn't know what else to say.

Alex blinked and then shook his head. *"Tío . . ."* When he looked at Gus again, there seemed to be a little more focus in his eyes. "I hurt. My back. My stomach."

"I know . . . I'll get you a doctor, *Ale* . . . I'll get you a doctor." He caught himself just before the name slipped out, but he realized he'd already lapsed, calling the boy an endearment that just wasn't one he should have used. Shoving his cap back, he rubbed his hand over his hair and then resettled it on his head before rising and meeting Vaughnne's eyes. Nodding to the door, he waited until she had followed him, playing out the words he needed to say. Praying. Planning. Hoping.

He hadn't trusted *anybody* in years. Not since Alex's mother had died. He didn't want to change that now, but he had to get the boy help. The fever was bad enough, but if Alex was so sick that he was asking for his mother . . . he couldn't wait any longer.

Hearing the soft fall of Vaughnne's footsteps behind him, he turned and studied her face. Her dark gold eyes met his and he stared at her, hard. He'd never guessed, he realized. Not once had he guessed that the sleek, sexy woman living across the street from him was FBI. He'd thought it was *possible* she might have been there to watch them. And he'd been prepared. Had even mentally gone through the steps he'd take to kill her and dispose of her body, if it came to that. He'd been prepared for the wrong sort of bad guy, he realized.

Not the cops. Not the FBI. He hadn't seen this coming.

"How does the FBI know about us?" he asked quietly.

Vaughnne inclined her head. "Now that's a question you'd have to ask my boss. But I imagine one of the others picked up on something from the kid."

"Others?"

She hooked her thumbs in her pockets and rocked back on her heels. "Oh, come on now, Gus . . . you've done some research on this, I'm sure. Psychic skill isn't like homogenized milk. You've got a whole variety of flavors . . . abilities. Some of us *see* things . . . things from the past, bits and pieces of the future. Some of us can talk into another's mind." A faint grin curled her lips and he didn't have time to brace himself before her voice, low and smooth and potent as whiskey, curled through his mind.

And he realized he'd been wrong . . . yet again. He'd *thought* he'd feel it when a psychic was doing his thing because he always felt it from Alex. But he didn't feel a thing from Vaughnne—he felt nothing, but he heard something . . . her voice, rolling through his mind, as low and sexy as if she'd been whispering naughty little nothings in his ear.

That would be me, by the way, as you probably figured out, she told him. Then she shrugged. "There are others who have the ability to track missing people. We usually call them bloodhounds. Some key into . . . ghosts."

He curled his lip. "Ghosts."

"Yes." She smirked at him. "Don't tell me you believe in psychic skill, but not ghosts."

He shrugged dismissively. Ghosts weren't real. That was all there was to it. If they weren't real, then he didn't have to think about the one ghost who *should* be haunting him, every day, for the rest of his life.

"Well, that's an answer." She shoved her hair back and sighed. "And that's neither here nor there. You've got a sick kid over there. Sick and getting sicker. Are you going to deal with it, or stand there and brood and worry and breathe your paranoia all over us until he needs to be hospitalized just to fix whatever is wrong with him?"

Closing the distance between them, he bent down until he was nose to nose with her. Then, holding her defiant gaze with his, he said quietly, "There is nobody, and I mean this with every bit of strength I have in me, absolutely nobody who means as much to me as that boy. I can, and have, killed for him. I will do it again, without blinking. Am I understood?"

"You're quite understood." Her eyes flashed. If they could have burned, he suspected he would have been singed all over.

But that didn't stop him from reaching up and catching one of her wild, soft curls and twining it around his finger. He half expected her to pull away. She simply stood there, though, as he rubbed his thumb along the thick, silken curl, holding his gaze levelly. "You can call your boss . . . Vaughnne. I want a doctor here. If there isn't one here within the next few hours, I'll take the boy and I'll go find one." If he had to kidnap one, that was just fine with him. "But understand me, nobody will take that boy from me. Not while I breathe."

He let go of her hair, watched as she swallowed. Then, as she went to turn away, he caught the back of her neck and hauled her against him. *Show me that you're afraid, damn it*, he thought, staring down into those wide, dark eyes. Her lashes swept down low, shielding her gaze from his. If she would just be *afraid*, he could maybe throttle this painful need down. He would continue to scare her. He had no issue with using fear on anybody if it kept Alex safe. Alex was *all* that mattered, and in the end, when he had to pay for all the sins he'd committed just to keep that child safe, he would simply offer that up and hope it was enough. He'd been protecting the boy.

But he couldn't do this . . . couldn't want this. Couldn't want her.

The fear he needed to see wasn't there, though.

She lifted her lashes and met his gaze, straight on. "I've already told you, and the promise stands. Nobody is going to hurt him, not if I have anything to say about it. And we don't want him *taken away*. I was sent down here to watch *over* him. Not steal him from you."

"Hmmm." He dipped his head and caught her lower lip between his teeth. The need to do more, to take more . . . take *everything* was so strong he could hardly stand it. If it wasn't for Alex, wasn't for the fact that the boy was ill, he'd be buried inside her already, Gus knew it. He bit her, still staring into her eyes, and he felt the shudder as it wracked her body. Stroking his tongue along the area he'd nipped, he resisted the urge to do more. Instead, he held there, his mouth pressed to hers. "So you say. But fuck me over on this, Vaughnne, and every nightmare you've ever had will look like a sweet memory by the time I am done with you."

TEN

LISTENING to the police scanner, Esteban leaned back and crossed his hands over his belly.

He hadn't expected anything to come of this. Still, he'd flown to Florida and checked into the Peabody, just in case. As an added bonus, he was away from the señor and it gave him some breathing room as he planned what to do next, where to go next.

If the boy and his uncle were there, he had to take care of it personally. But he hadn't expected anything to happen so soon.

It had, and he hadn't been there in time.

Now the boy and his uncle were on the move, and the man he'd hired was in the hospital. So far, the señor hadn't called and he hadn't had to explain anything. That was good. He'd already bumped up the offer on the website, and another had accepted and was on the move.

This could all be fixed.

So simple. After all this time and all it had taken was that website.

It was too bad the initial man he'd hired had been inept. He should have sent more than one. Esteban realized the error of his ways now. The second offer had come from a man who outlined a plan of attack that included working in teams. He had a partner he worked with and they'd both move in on the child and the reward would be split. A much smarter approach. The first one had just hired some muscle and that hadn't been enough.

He was paying for his lack of foresight now. In the hospital. The boy's handiwork? Esteban didn't know and he hadn't been able to get much information out of the hospital. He'd claimed to be Watkins's next of kin, but the nursing staff hadn't given him anything useful.

For a moment, he eyed the phone and then he shifted his attention to the police scanner. The other one was likely still sitting in a jail cell. Had he talked? Not that he could have said much. Watkins wouldn't have told the muscle why he was needed. It was good, over all, that they hadn't told him why his services had been required, and even better that he'd only been paid five hundred up front. Esteban had agreed to that added expense and he was glad it had been a minimal one.

Whoever would have thought that such a pretty little manwhore would turn out to be such a pain in the ass?

That was all he had ever been. He'd done a stint in the military, but it hadn't lasted—they booted him out, after some disciplinary measures. Since then, he'd drifted through life, fucked his way into some money, and put that pretty face to use. He excelled at whoring around, gambling. He could hold his own in a fight, but he had no real use in life as a man. Esteban had done his research over the years. Eliminating this one man should never have been this complicated. Tracking him *down* should never have been this complicated.

But it had been.

And if he didn't find those two soon . . .

The phone rang.

Part of him didn't want to answer. Closing his eyes, he said a quick prayer that his voice wouldn't shake.

Then he answered. His bowels almost turned to water as nothing but dead air greeted him.

Seconds of silence ticked away, and unable to handle it another moment, he said, "I have promising news. I tracked them down to their most recent location. They've been living here for a while, I believe."

"And do you have my son?"

Squeezing his eyes closed, he clenched one hand into a fist. "No, señor. I don't. But we're getting closer and I have found more useful tools to help locate them. Now that I have, it shouldn't be long."

"It had better not be. I've been far more lenient with you than with your predecessor. Do not make me regret that, Esteban."

Esteban swallowed the spit pooling in his mouth. "Of course not. Thank you for your trust. For this opportunity. I will—"

The phone went dead.

* * *

REYES stared outside.

Turquoise waters glistened under the sun. Carefully tended gardens with vivid bursts of flowers stretched out in all directions.

His domain.

His property.

He'd worked hard for this.

He was respected. Feared.

People knew his name and knew to stay out of his way. Some of the most powerful men and women in the world owed him. He had secrets of those powerful people tucked away that could be used to destroy so many lives.

He had more money than he could ever hope to spend in his lifetime.

But the things he wanted the *most* eluded him. He wanted his son back in his home, and he wanted that *pendejo* dead.

Simple. It should really be simple.

There was a knock at the door.

He ignored it, rage still churning inside him.

"Ignacio, may I come in?"

Despite his anger, the woman's low voice pricked at something inside him. She . . . she was like a drug to him. He'd never touched any of the products he sold. They were the fall of too many men, he knew, and he wouldn't be like them. But this woman . . . she was a safe addiction. And only his. Turning, he called out her name and watched as she entered.

Her long hair, pale and thick, fell to her hips. A bikini, lush and red, barely covered her curves, and he brooded as she came to him.

He had money.

He had power.

He had this beautiful woman.

And yet he couldn't get his hands on the child. That child . . . the absolute *pinnacle* of his power. But was he here? Where he belonged? No.

Reaching out, he touched his finger to her lower lip.

She closed her hand around his wrist and smiled at him.

"You're not happy," she said softly. "Is it the same problem bothering you?"

"Yes." He hooked an arm around her waist and pulled her against him. "The man I've hired to solve it isn't working out. I think I need to remove him from the equation and find somebody else."

She pushed her fingers into his hair. "Maybe you can worry

about all of that later . . ." She arched against him and pressed her lips to his jaw. "Worry about me for now."

* * *

IT was a lousy, long-ass forty-five minutes and Vaughnne felt like she was going to come out of her skin.

Her very hot, tight, itchy skin.

She just felt that much worse, every time she looked over at the bed and saw Alex huddling in on himself, clutching at his belly as he slept fitfully. His dusky skin was flushed, and the few times she'd touched him, he'd felt hot enough to burn her hand.

Each time she'd touched him, she'd felt the weight of Gus's gaze slamming into the back of her head, like he was ready to snap her neck if she so much as moved wrong around the boy. She had no doubt he was ready to do just that.

His words echoed through her mind, over and over.

There is nobody, and I mean this with every bit of strength I have in me, absolutely nobody who means as much to me as that boy. I can, and have, killed for him. I will do it again, without blinking. Am I understood?

He'd been trying to scare her, she knew. Yeah, some part of her had been a bit thrown by his intensity, but he obviously had no idea just how far *she* would go to protect somebody she loved. She'd been ready to throw her badge away, her life away. Everything, if it would have saved her sister.

She hadn't been able to save her.

So she'd been ready to do the same thing just to avenge her.

Daylin . . .

Her heart ached as an image of her sister's smiling little face flashed through her mind.

Daylin had been just four the last time Vaughnne had seen her. Four years old. Vaughnne had been fifteen years old the day her father threw her out into the streets, when he realized he hadn't been going crazy, that Vaughnne really was able to whisper into people's minds. He'd thought it was the devil's work. That was what he'd claimed. She knew better now.

Psychic ability tended to stick to families. If one person was psychic, chances were there was somebody else in the same gene pool who had abilities, too. It could range from just being very, very astute with an insight that just seemed way too sharp to be natural, to abilities like Vaughnne's. To freaky-ass shit like Tucker could compel, and everything in between.

She'd gotten her abilities from her father. She realized that now, with the wisdom that came from distance and age. She'd often wondered why he'd hated her so much, and now she knew. It wasn't hate . . . it was fear. Fear of something he hadn't understood, fear of something inside himself that he'd never been able to control.

She had no idea what his ability had been, but she knew she wasn't wrong.

He'd chased her away, while her mother stood there, wringing her hands and crying. They'd just . . . thrown her away, and Vaughnne had never seen her sister again. She never would have known her baby sister was missing if she hadn't been watching things on her own. He hadn't once tried to call her. She'd found out nearly a week later, when she'd been doing one of her infrequent stops by his Facebook page, one he'd never bothered to make private. There had been a plea to help find his baby girl.

And Vaughnne's first look at her sister in more than a year had been on a *missing* poster.

The grief still hit her hard.

"Why the FBI?"

Pulled out of the pit of grief and memory, Vaughnne looked up and found Gus watching her from his position by the window. Abruptly, she realized there was something . . . practiced . . . about the way he stood. Too practiced. Not like he was posing, although she'd seen enough of that, too. No, this was the carriage of a man who knew how to . . . protect. How to fight. How to hunt. Attack.

Fighter. That much, she knew. She'd seen the clues and already pieced them together, but it went deeper than that. There were fighters, like cops. And then there were those who were modern-day berserkers, warriors without any real equal. Navy Seals, Airborne Rangers . . . but she didn't think he was from here. Where had he learned . . . whatever he did, she wondered.

He'd turned all the lights off save for a dim one by the bed, enough so that the boy could see. He stood lost in the shadows, his hands empty . . . empty, and ready.

"Well?"

Swallowing, she looked away from him and shrugged. "Why not?"

He snorted. "I can think of a thousand reasons. Why work for the government? I don't imagine it's for the money, or the glory."

"All about the glory," she said soberly, shooting him a quick glance. "I get up every damn morning and do my workout and my mantra is *for the glory of the FBI.*"

Gus just stared at her.

Obviously, her sense of humor wasn't appealing. Rolling her eyes, she rose from her chair and started to pace. "It just fit. I was a kid in trouble . . . a lot of trouble. The man who heads up my unit has a knack for finding the people who'll fit best into his unit. I'd just come off a stint in juvie and—"

"Juvie?"

She lifted a brow. "Juvenile detention center. I was something of a problem child." That last trip in, she'd stolen some food, and when she'd gotten caught by the store owner, she'd beaten the shit out of him. Not because he'd *caught* her. But when he did catch her, he'd decided he'd take it out of her in a rather inappropriate manner. Of course, nobody had believed her.

The story was a little different when he was arrested for sexual exploitation of a minor two years later, but by then, she was out of the system and busting her ass to get her GED so she could get into college. Still, it had been a pleasure to see that man going to jail.

"Anyway, it was right before I was eighteen and I was reading in the paper about this woman who'd found a kid down south. She was one of the bloodhounds in the unit, although I didn't really know about them. I headed down there—my gut told me that was what I needed to do. I wanted to talk to her. I hadn't realized there were others like me until then and I . . . hell, I don't know. I wanted to talk to her. She was in the hospital—I never did talk to *her*, but her boss? I did talk to him. He told me I wasn't ready. Had to get my GED, had to go to college. Had to get myself together and under control—in other words, I had to stay out of trouble. He helped me get my life together, and he was there walking me through the mess while I did just that." She shrugged self-consciously and looked away. "When I got out of college, I told him I was ready. He didn't have much to say to that, but a few days later, the paperwork showed up at my place."

"Paperwork?"

She lifted a brow. "You don't just walk into the FBI and say, *Hey . . . I want a job*, Gus."

Swiping her palms down her jeans, she moved over by the bed and touched her palm to Alex's brow again. "He's still so damned hot," she muttered.

"We should put him in a cool bath."

Vaughnne shook her head. "Bad idea. I've taken basic first aid courses . . . sometimes it comes in handy. Doctors don't always think that's the wisest thing these days. Sometimes the body reacts by the fever shooting even higher."

Rising, she checked the time. "The doctor will be here soon."

Gus looked like he wanted to argue, but after a moment, he

just went back to staring out the window. "You never really answered. Why the FBI?"

"Because it fit. I've seen too many monsters, too many assholes in my life. I know what it's like to be victimized and I hate it. With the Bureau, I have a chance to use what I can do to help people. I don't have to hide what I am all the time and I can actually use it to make a living." She shrugged and then suppressed a wince as the movement sent pain streaking up her neck to echo through her skull. She was too damn tight, too damn tense. Somehow, she didn't think she'd have time to work in a massage or anything in the next few days, next few weeks, either. "Nothing else is going to come up in my life that lets me use what I can do the way this does."

"And how can you use it?" Gus continued to stare at her. "How does your . . . talking . . . thing make you at all useful?"

"Pair me with a telepath who can receive as well as send and the two of us can go infiltrate damn near anything without having to worry about being spied on or caught because we had to reach out and make contact with the unit. For that matter, I can *always* be in contact with my unit. My range is pretty much limitless." She smirked at him and added, "Just in case you're thinking you can use me for hostage purposes or something. It's a bad idea. I can reach out and touch somebody, so to speak, anytime I want."

One black brow arched fractionally as he studied her face. "Anybody?"

"I have to have had a connection with them. Even if I've just seen them face-to-face one time . . . that's all I need. If I know them personally, the contact is stronger." She didn't mention that distance could be a factor. No point in making her ability look less impressive. Sending a message to Jones in D.C. from here wasn't an issue. She'd be in debilitating pain for a long, long while afterward, but if the need was extreme, she could do it several times over as long as adrenaline kept her going. She'd just pay for it afterward.

"So you have to have seen the person," he said slowly.

"Yes."

His eyes narrowed. "Did you see the men earlier? Those who came to attack us?"

Ahhhh . . . I see. Smiling a little, she inclined her head. "Yes. I did." Then she shrugged and turned away. "But I'd rather not reach out and make that connection blindly, so don't go asking me to play messenger girl."

"Why?"

She shot him a look. "Because they tracked your boy. If I send a message without knowing just how capable they are, it's entirely possible they can track *me*. And my job is to keep him safe. I can't do that if I'm leading his attackers to his door, now can I?"

Any answer he might have made was cut short. She saw him stiffen at the window, watched as he pulled out that deadly Sig Sauer he liked to shove in her ribs every few hours.

"Somebody just pulled into the parking lot," he said quietly.

Vaughnne pulled out her phone.

Gus continued to stand there, watching. "They are just sitting in the car—"

Her phone chimed with an incoming message.

You asked for a house call? -Grady

* * *

"If I *had* to guess, without doing any kind of lab work, I'd say a UTI."

Gus stared at the doctor like he thought she was going to chop off the kid's hands and feet and feed him to alligators. Vaughnne carefully kept her body between them, although Dr. Grady was probably used to working around temperamental, pissed-off people. She didn't even seem perturbed at being called to come to a hotel in the middle of the night.

"A UTI." Gus spat the words out like somebody had shoved his mouth full of horse shit.

Vaughnne glanced over at him. "A urinary infection. Somewhere in the kidneys or bladder."

"I know what it is," Gus said, giving her a withering look. "But how would he get one? He is a healthy boy."

"Anybody can *get* one," Dr. Grady said gently. "He's also a preteen boy. Boys his age are often too busy to slow down and drink as much as they should. That can predispose you to a UTI. Sometimes their body hygiene starts to slip."

Something flashed in Gus's eyes, and as he took a step forward, Vaughnne slammed a hand against his chest. "Throttle back, big guy," she warned. "She's not wrong. I've known more than my share of kids his age. You tell them to get in the bath ten times before they do it and they are out in the blink of an eye. They barely have time to get wet, much less really *bathe*. She's *not* saying you're not taking care of him and she's not calling him a sloppy little heathen, either. So chill out."

Dr. Grady's brows had arched up high over her eyes by the time Vaughnne was done. "Exactly so, Vaughnne. If he's not drinking adequate fluids, if he's not using proper body hygiene . . . that could do it. Is he circumcised?"

Gus's face went tight and harsh flags of color rode on his cheeks. "No, I don't think he is."

"Good grief." Vaughnne rolled her eyes and turned to the doctor. "Gus has only been his guardian for a few years. The parenting gig is a new thing for him. I think some of this is making him uncomfortable." She shrugged as she tossed it out there and gave the doctor a look that hopefully conveyed . . . *guys, what can you do?*

The doctor studied Vaughnne consideringly and then turned away. "If he isn't circumcised, that's more of an issue, then. It's even more important that he's cleaning himself properly. I need a urine specimen." She reached into her bag and pulled out a cup, as well as a little square packet. Holding them out, she looked back at Gus. "We need to wake him and you need to get him to void."

If the kid hadn't been so damn sick, if the entire situation hadn't been almost painfully serious, Vaughnne might have laughed at the look on Gus's face. He stared at the cup like it was about to bite him.

Sighing, Vaughnne said, "If you can't do this, Gus, I'll do it. But I suspect it will be easier if it's his uncle helping him, not some chick he barely knows."

Gus nodded shortly. "Leave us for a bit."

Vaughnne met the doctor's eyes and the doctor inclined her head. "I'll wait on the patio," Vaughnne said.

The doctor could cover the hall. If Gus was going to try to escape, it would most likely be this way . . . closest route to the car.

And if he did go through the hall, the doc could send her a message. Vaughnne wasn't terribly friendly with Grady, but she knew her. Jones had sent one of the doctors from the Bureau. She didn't practice medicine much, but Grady knew her stuff.

And she carried a weapon, so if Gus tried to intimidate her, he'd be in for a surprise.

Of course, if he pulled the methods he liked to use on her . . .

Stop it, she told herself as she slid out onto the patio. She had to stop it and preferably now.

The last thing she needed to be thinking about was Gus using that damn near overpowering sexuality of his. Especially on another woman.

* * *

It took a good twenty minutes to get Alex to wake up enough to get him into the bathroom, and by the time they were done, Gus wasn't sure who was more embarrassed. He'd bet on himself.

If Alex wasn't so miserably sick, the boy probably would have died from mortification.

It was a shame that when Gus looked in the mirror, he saw a man who was red-faced. A simple fact of life and he couldn't handle it without feeling like he needed somebody to walk him through it. *Consuelo, could I mess this up any more?* he wondered as he made sure Alex washed up before they left the bathroom.

They'd have to deal with that embarrassing hygiene thing, too, he realized. Things Consuelo would have handled with grace and calm and ease, and he was all but tongue-tied just trying to figure out how to even approach it.

It took another five minutes to get Alex situated back in the bed. "I'll bring the doctor back in." He brushed Alex's hair back.

Alex's eyes opened wide and panic flared across his face. "Doctor?"

"Yes." Sighing, he cupped the boy's face. "*M'hijo*, you are sick. She thinks it might be an infection in your . . ." He grimaced. "They call it a UTI. It's all the parts that lead up to where you make the urine, then empty it out. She thinks there is an infection and they can get serious. Your mother had them a lot as a child."

It occurred to him, then, perhaps he should have mentioned that to the doctor. Did that run in families? He didn't know. He wasn't used to handling sick children. He hadn't ever been prepared to handle *children* period.

You must do this . . .

The ghost of that voice danced through his mind and he

shoved it out. Bad things to think about when Alex was so ill and likely to be less in control than normal. "You needed a doctor. We have a doctor."

"But what if—"

There was a knock at the door and the boy went white. So pale and white and scared. Gus's heart twisted in his chest and he rested a hand on Alex's shoulder. "It's okay, *m'hijo*. I'll take care of you. You know that."

He rose and headed to the door.

He was two feet away when the patio door opened.

Vaughnne came inside, sleek, dark, and silent, her eyes moving to linger on the boy. Alex stared at her as she came to kneel by the bed. "You can look in my head again," she said quietly. "I won't hide this time."

The look of shock, shame on the child's face was another blow to Gus's heart. He'd put too much pressure on the boy, he knew. But when you were fighting an unwinnable war, fighting to protect a boy, you used whatever weapons you had. Even if the *boy* was the weapon. "I think we didn't have you as ready to face things as we thought, Alex," Gus said quietly. "That is my failing. Not yours. You're still young."

"Let the doctor in, Gus," Vaughnne said softly.

He watched for a moment as she caught Alex's hand. Then he turned away. He needed to get the boy better. Then he could figure out where to go from here.

* * *

"I gave him an injection. It should help him if it's a UTI. It was a broad-spectrum antibiotic, so even if it's not a UTI, it may give some coverage. I'm betting on the UTI, though. I did a finger stick and got enough blood to run a blood count, although I wish I could have talked his guardian into letting me draw enough blood for blood cultures." Grady sighed, a disgruntled look on her face as she met Vaughnne's eyes. They stood out on the patio, and through the window, they watched as Gus sat on the bed with the boy. "I'm leaving you some antibiotics, too. If it's not a UTI, they aren't going to help much. I'll run some tests on the urine . . . I'll have a better idea within a day or so."

Vaughnne nodded.

"You'll leave a number?"

"Jones has it."

"Okay." Grady nodded, a concerned look on her face. "He needs rest. He's pretty sick and everything in me tells me that he should be in a hospital, preferably hooked up to an IV for a day or two. He's getting dehydrated, and if he gets any worse, he'll *have* to go into a hospital, Agent MacMeans." She paused, studying Vaughnne's face. "Am I understood?"

"Yes." Rubbing the back of her neck, Vaughnne looked up at the sky. "If I thought it was safe, I'd try to talk them into going now. But I don't think it is. I can't risk him, I can't risk the casualties that might come up if I took him to an unsecured facility. We'll head north. If he has to go into the hospital for a day or two, I'd rather it be closer to where Jones can provide more protection."

"Taking him to D.C.?"

Vaughnne snorted. "I don't think that will go over well, although that might be where he is safest."

"How much trouble is he in?"

Sliding the doctor a look, she said quietly, "My gut tells me you're better off to forget you ever saw them. They have that much trouble trailing after them."

Grady pursed her lips for a moment. Then she nodded and pushed a small plastic bag into Vaughnne's hands. "I brought the basic meds with me, just in case. An antiemetic in case he starts having issues with nausea, one of the better antibiotics for a UTI. I'm leaving a setup with you to collect another urine specimen in a few days."

"I don't know if we will be anywhere to get it tested."

Grady waved a hand. "I'll take care of that. But if it's a UTI, we need to know it's clearing up. It doesn't do you any good to keep his neck safe if he ends up with a kidney infection that could kill him, now does it?"

Vaughnne closed her eyes. "Shit."

"Yes." The doctor touched her arm. "Head to D.C. Be close to there, if for no other reason than so you can get him medical treatment if he needs it, and if the antibiotics don't kick in, he'll need it. Jones has people who owe him favors. If he had to, Jones could put the boy up in his home and I'll take care of him there. I could use a few days off. But we need to keep him healthy if we want to keep him alive, right?"

* * *

TUCKER'S brain felt too wired.

Trying to lock on the wildfire that was the boy's erratic ability was almost impossible right now.

Crashing in a hotel five hours north of Orlando, he tossed a ball up in the air over and over, letting the repetitiveness of the motion calm the ragged edges of his mind. Or that was the *plan*. And the *plan* was failing.

Swearing, he jacked up into a seated position and grabbed the phone. He jabbed in a number and it wasn't until Lucia's tired voice came on the line that he realized how late it was.

"Shit, Luce. I'm sorry. Ah . . . I just wanted to make sure you remember to feed Heywood."

"Mr. Collins, I'm hardly about to let the cat starve," she said, sniffing a little. "I might let *you* starve, but not the cat."

He laughed a little and then reached up, rubbed the back of his neck. "You've got the alarm and everything set, right?"

"Of course."

She had the alarm set. He'd gotten the notice on his phone.

And if he knew Lucia, which he did, she'd also have her weapon handy. He and Lucia understood each other well. She was one of the few people he allowed around him with a weapon, because he knew she'd kill for him. Just like he'd kill for her. She was one of the few people in this world that he actually trusted. He might even almost love her, if he understood how to love anybody. She was definitely one of the few people he'd call a friend. He didn't like being here and her there, with all of this going on.

"Is everything well, Mr. Collins?" she asked softly.

He closed his eyes. He didn't know if he could answer that without lying, without worrying her. Lucia worried was a bad thing. People had died because Lucia worried. Not often, and he couldn't say the people hadn't deserved to die. He'd been flat on his back, dealing with one of the attempts to . . . return him. It had also been the last attempt. Something about the fact that he'd fried a half dozen of the men who'd been involved and Lucia had gone after the others . . .

There was something to be said about having a former mercenary as your housekeeper, he guessed.

Not to mention the fact that she was a killer cook.

"I'm not sure, Luce," he finally said. "I'm doing a job. Involves a kid."

The silence between them went strained. Seconds ticked by and finally Lucia said softly, "You didn't agree to harm a child, Mr. Collins."

He suspected if he answered in a way that displeased her, she might decide to come hunting *his* ass. Lucia had lived by few rules in her life as a hired killer, but one of them had been hard and fast. No children harmed. Ever. The reason she'd gotten out was because her handler had decided to try and push that line. When she'd refused, he'd sent people after her.

That was when Tucker and Lucia had met up.

She'd been bleeding out in an alley while he'd been working

his own job-collecting information on a drug runner that he'd planned to sell to whoever wanted to pay the most money for it.

He could have walked by. Probably should have.

But when he'd paused by the older woman and looked into those defiant eyes, he'd been sunk.

That had been fifteen years ago. She'd moved out of the life and for a while had acted as a "security" specialist and she and Tucker had often exchanged information, or sold it, depending on the job. But problems from her past life had continued to emerge, and after one of them had landed her in a bloody heap at Tucker's door, she'd confessed to him that she was tired. All she wanted was a quiet, normal life.

She'd never have one, but Tucker could hide like nobody's business when he had to. He didn't mind having somebody around to watch his back, either.

They were a good pair, all in all.

As long as he didn't cross her lines, and she didn't cross his.

Her lines were kids.

He smiled a little. "You know me better than that, Luce."

"Naturally." Her voice had thawed and Tucker slumped back on the bed, staring up at the cracked, water-stained ceiling over his head. The bed was miserably hard but he'd slept on worse. Hell, he'd spent more than a few years *without* a bed. This was almost paradise.

"So what is this situation that may or may not be a problem?"

"People after the kid. I stopped the immediate problem, but . . ."

Again, he lapsed into silence. Lucia picked up the ball. "You don't know if the problem will return."

"Oh, no. I'm positive it will. Right now, I need to find the kid and my brain feels like it's been hot-wired."

"Then perhaps instead of waking me up, you should go find a way to burn the excesses off and clear your mind, focus. So you can do your job."

"If it was that simple, I'd do it," he muttered.

"It's only complicated if you choose to *let* it be complicated, Mr. Collins," she said, her voice unconcerned. "Is there anything you need me to do, or may I go back to sleep?"

He blew out a breath. "I think we need to plan on shutting up things here locally and moving on. You think you can handle it?"

There was a long, tense pause. Then, Lucia said, "Do we have . . . past issues aggravating matters, Mr. Collins?"

"No." Lights flickered. He couldn't think of those *past* issues and stay calm, but the flicker was quick. He only saw red for a second. "But I had to give a fake ID to a cop and you know how that goes. So once this is done, we'll have to move on anyway. You might as well head on out and set things up at the new place."

"I see. Very well, Mr. Collins. I did enjoy Florida, though. Now . . . why don't you see about burning off those excesses?"

The phone went dead.

He scowled and muttered something that likely would have had her punching him if she'd been here.

If Lucia Frazier was twenty years younger, he might risk the fact that touching her was a hazard to both her and him. Assuming he wasn't afraid she'd break him in bed. The woman was scary as hell.

Burn off the excesses.

Shoving to his feet, he grabbed a clean stack of clothes, his gloves. He'd stopped to rest, thinking he might be able to get a better lock on the boy. But that hadn't happened.

Might as well shower and get back on the road. Maybe he'd get lucky and find some relatively therapeutic way of burning off those excesses.

* * *

NALINI had no trouble tracking Tucker Collins down.

But she *did* have trouble getting out of her current mess for two days. The people she'd buried herself with weren't exactly the kind who thought it was okay for her to just . . . waltz out. Even though she'd done just that off and on for several years, hoping to intrigue a madman.

It had worked.

Now she had the madman good and hooked, which was the bad news. He was a possessive, jealous piece of work, that was for certain. Another bit of bad news—she was working the job solo, and if she got jammed up, she was screwed. This wasn't a contract case with the FBI or anything. This baby was all hers. The one bright spot was that she knew a phone call would get her out of said jam. Assuming she had time. But she was good at reading that sort of thing.

Somehow, she thought Jones might be really, really interested in what she'd uncovered over the past few days.

It went pretty damn deep, too, and she'd just scraped the tip of the iceberg.

If she knew anything about Jones and his unit, they'd just love to bust that iceberg apart. Blow it straight to hell.

But her job, first. All of that had to be done because once Jones brought his people in, the man *she* was looking for would either bury himself or Jones's people would bury him.

She wanted to be the one to do that.

"So close," she muttered. Pulling all those little threads, weaving a careful web, drawing closer and closer to the man she'd been hunting for so long.

And now she was at a standstill, because she couldn't concentrate. The boy. Screaming. A dying woman . . . no. Dead now. Nalini had connected with her in the moments of death, and there was no way that woman had survived. She'd been hurting so much, and death had almost been a sweet release. Almost. Nalini would never go gladly into that good night, that was for damn sure. She couldn't do anything to help the woman, but she could focus on the boy. Maybe help him.

That was why she was here. Sighing, she tugged the jeweler's box from her pocket and flipped it open to study the necklace. It had been given to her a few weeks ago. It was a pretty piece of work, she had to admit. Flawless rubies, diamonds, and gold. Nalini knew her stones and this was worth a lot. It should be worn, admired . . . locked away in a safe when somebody wasn't wearing it, not shoved into a pocket.

But she couldn't stand to have it on her skin. When she wore it, the sound of screaming was that much louder. So she kept it in a jeweler's box and the box was tucked inside the inner pocket of her light jacket. Heaven help her if she was mugged . . .

Then she smirked a little, just thinking of it. Not that it was likely. She could make any man who touched her do just about anything she wanted for short periods of time.

When he'd put this necklace on her, she'd almost made him put a bullet through his own brain. It had taken most of the night to bring herself down off that ledge.

Killing him wouldn't be a bad thing.

But she had to do her job first.

And she couldn't do it while she was so worried about what was going on with the boy. So she was here . . . all because she'd touched a necklace.

Her main skill was the ability to influence people through touch, to take their energy and . . . work with it. Jones had called it impressions. She could get inside a person's head, in their soul, and leave an impression. While she was there, she could manipulate a person's energy, their will. Nalini could channel that person's energy, if she put her mind to it, and drive people to do either very *bad* things, or very *good* things. Since she tended to hunt down scum, she was usually driven to make them want to do *bad* things . . . to themselves. When she wanted to, though, she could do useful things. When she pulled back, she could filter away some of the negative shit. She didn't do that much. But then again, when you worked with the scum of the earth, you didn't have much of a chance to want to do nice things.

The impression/emotional manipulation shit was her main ability, but there was another one, a weaker one that sometimes got in the way. That ability was the reason she was here now and it hadn't just *gotten in the way* this time.

It had almost tripped her up in the middle of the job, and if she wasn't careful, it would get her killed.

A woman crying.

A boy screaming.

A man, almost brutally handsome, staring at the woman, and the woman had known her life . . . and death . . . were in his hands.

Then there was just death.

And the knowledge that the boy was still alive.

She'd gotten a glimpse of him, just that one flash.

She'd lied to Tucker. Lies were, sadly, something she dealt in. She told them, sold them, used them. Half the time, she didn't know what was truth and what was reality, in part because she sold people another reality entirely, depending on what she needed to accomplish to get her job done.

To accomplish *her* goal.

Her goal . . . finding one man, one who'd proven to be very, very hard to find. But she had to find him if she ever wanted her life back. It was one of the reasons she wasn't ever going to *officially* work for Taylor Jones. He claimed he could help with all of that, but she wasn't about to let her name into the system, or her prints, or anything else. It was easier to just push some information his way and take the money he'd give her when he was in the mood.

She wasn't going to barter money or info this time. What she wanted was to point Jones and his group toward that kid. In her gut, she knew why the boy was wanted. Why his mother—and the woman had to be his mother—had been murdered. If anybody could care for a damaged kid, it would be Jones. And if the kid had psychic skill, even better that Jones be the one taking care of him. But first they had to find him.

Narrow things down a bit. That's where Tucker came in.

Then she'd just give Jones a nudge and sit back, watch while Jones worked.

He might deny any psychic ability, but she'd never seen *anybody* who could locate their kind the way he could. It was like he had some inborn compass that pointed only to psychics and trouble. She'd once called him Professor X, just to get a rise out of him.

He hadn't been amused.

She'd almost think he didn't have a sense of humor. Except she'd gotten that glimpse into him. He had humor. He had heat. He even had a heart, surprisingly enough. He also had a wife, a fact that Nalini had found a damn shame, right up until she'd laid eyes on one Tucker Collins.

There weren't too many men she'd be willing to drop her guard around. Jones had been one, but he'd never noticed her interest.

Collins, though . . . he was aware of her interest.

And he was interested in return.

She realized they had a complication or two, but that was nothing she couldn't work with. She'd dealt with volatile types before. She was almost certain she could handle him.

Except instead of walking up to the hotel where she knew he'd rented a room, after more than twenty minutes, Nalini was still standing outside, leaning against her car and staring up at the dark night sky.

A slice of light came spilling out of one of the rooms, and she turned her head. He was too far away and it was too dark out for her to see his face as clearly as she'd like.

But she didn't need to see him. Tucker's face was all but imprinted on her memory.

As beautiful as he could possibly be, with those high, arched cheekbones, a jawline that looked like he could take a punch or ten . . . and had, a mouth that would have made her sigh with want if she was disposed to such things. As it was, she just *thought* about sighing over that mouth. Most people would look at him and think that his hair was the most memorable feature. Deep, dark red . . . completely beautiful. It wasn't the hair, though. Nor was it the tattoos that crept up over his arms, winding around them and disappearing under the sleeves of his T-shirt. Dressed, she thought, shoving off the car. Even this late at night. Or early in the morning.

What a pity.

No, it wasn't the hair. Wasn't the tattoos. Wasn't even his size and Tucker Collins was a big guy. She'd never been much into that until she'd laid eyes on him.

The thing that made Tucker stand out were the eyes.

A person looked into those eyes and realized very clearly that this was a man who'd clawed his way through life and was going to keep on doing it. He'd killed. She knew it just by looking at him. Death stained the soul and she knew the soul. He'd killed and he didn't regret it. Nalini was fine with that. She'd killed a few times herself, and she didn't regret those deaths, either.

His eyes told a story. One of a man who'd caused, and solved, a helluva a lot of trouble.

If Nalini was smart, she'd steer very, very clear of him.

With a slow, lazy smile that felt entirely fake, she shoved off the car and headed toward the open door. The wedge of light framed Tucker too damn well. She stopped just a few feet away, close enough that she could feel the soft buzz that was another psychic's energy against her skin. Far enough away that she didn't have to tip her head back to see his face.

She really did like his face.

If it wasn't for a boy who was in trouble. If it wasn't for everything that was so damned complicated . . .

If it wasn't for the screams that echoed in her mind every time she let her thoughts drift for even a minute . . .

"How did you find me?" Tucker bit off even as she let another *if it wasn't* . . . dance through her mind.

Smiling a little, she reached out, thinking only that she was curious to see how he'd feel under her hand. That was all she wanted.

A gloved hand caught her right wrist.

The black leather covered his hands from the wrists down, and being the deviant that she was, she had an image of those leather-covered hands covering *her*. Gliding over her skin, while she straddled him.

"What's with the leather?" she asked, not bothering to disguise the soft rasp in her voice. "You planning on playing cat burglar or something?"

"Bad things happen when I touch people without them," he said. He squeezed her wrist once in warning and then let go. "Bad things can happen when people touch *me*. Just something to keep in mind."

"Just how bad?" She stared into his eyes. "'Cuz I think it might be worth it."

* * *

THE woman was a menace.

He'd been in the shower when he felt somebody approach and he'd lowered his shields just enough to figure out who it was. Everybody had a different feel, and nobody felt like her.

He'd spent the last few minutes in the shower with a raging hard-on and it had yet to subside.

He had more wild energy sparking inside him than he normally had to deal with and there she was *taunting* him. She had a smirk on her beautiful face and the mole by the corner of her mouth was just driving him nuts.

He was tempted. He *thought* he could touch her without hurting her. He doubted he'd ever be able to sleep with her. He'd lose control and that was one thing he couldn't do during sex.

But he could touch her . . . just to see what happened.

Except if he touched her, even once, he suspected he'd need more. And more. And more—which couldn't happen.

Still, she needed to get an idea of what she was doing. It wasn't even fire she was playing with. It was lightning and that was way worse. Holding her gaze, he reached up and tugged off one of his gloves. "Worth it, huh?" Still staring into her eyes, he reached out and caught one of her narrow dreads. Fire licked inside his veins, jolted out of his skin, and he smiled a little as she swayed closer. He flooded the air with electricity. The lights flared. In the room behind him, out in the parking lot. Lights halfway down the strip of rooms went out, and he shoved out as much of the power as he could without it going into her.

Behind him, the light bulbs exploded as he shoved more voltage in them than they could handle. Took a lot to do that, but Tucker manipulated energy as easy as he breathed.

As the room was blanketed in darkness, he cut off the current.

The only sound Nalini made was a harsh intake of breath.

And then he felt her hand on his chest.

"Wow. That's quite a demonstration . . . got any other parlor tricks you can show me?"

He backed away, glaring at her as his eyes adjusted to the absence of light.

She was still smiling, although he thought maybe it was a little more strained this time around. "Parlor tricks?"

"Hmmm. I'd love to see them . . . just not tonight. I need to know where the boy is. He's in a hell of a lot of trouble."

He snorted. "You bet your ass he is. He's got an FBI agent with him. If I was the kid's guardian, I'd get my ass as far away from her as I could."

Nalini tensed. "FBI agent?"

"Yeah." He shoved a hand through his hair and stared at her. "You work with them. Don't you all ever talk?"

ELEVEN

Morning brought better news.

Marginally.

Alex's fever was down.

And when Vaughnne came out of the bathroom, the small hotel room was empty.

That was the *marginal* part of the better news.

Sighing, she gathered up her stuff. Fortunately, she'd been smart enough to pack everything before she disappeared into the bathroom. She was going to have to learn how to go without little things like toilet breaks if he tried this again.

On her way out of the hotel, she paused in the little alcove where the vending machines waited.

Reaching up on top of the ice maker, she pulled off the distributor cap.

She'd asked the doctor to hide it the night before. Good thing she was prepared.

She came out into the parking lot just in time to see Gus slip behind the wheel of a small, pale gold sedan that had seen better days. It wasn't theirs. He caught sight of her and slammed his head back against the seat. She pointed a finger at the tires, gunman style, and cocked her thumb.

He got the point without her saying a word.

He climbed back out, and a second later, a tired, wan-looking Alex did the same. As she crossed the distance between them, she asked, "Did you even bother to take the medicine Dr. Grady left for him?"

"Yes." He inclined his head. "I can make him take a pill as easily as you could. Easier, as he is my child."

"Your nephew, you mean?" She displayed the distributor cap in her palm. "You'll get farther with this."

He went to grab it.

She jerked it out of his reach. "You can have it when I'm behind the steering wheel, and the kid is in the backseat."

"He's my responsibility," Gus said, forcing the words out through clenched teeth.

"I get that. And I'm trying to help you." Shaking her head, she gestured around her and then looked at the boy. "You've got a kid there that's going to just get more out of control. He's going to hurt himself, or somebody—"

"He's not a danger!"

Vaughnne arched her brows. "Tell that to the migraine he sucker-punched me with. Or the nosebleed he walloped me with. And he wasn't even *trying* to hurt me. What happens when he gets frustrated with some kid who picks on him and he really hurts him?"

"He wouldn't," Gus said.

"You don't know that. Not for sure." She saw the doubt in his eyes, hated herself for playing on it. But he had to realize the danger he was messing with. "Or what about when he gets mad at *you* and just loses control? He's a kid, Gus, and you don't know how to train a psychically gifted child. How are you going to keep everybody safe from him if he *is* getting stronger? Keep him away from anybody and everybody for the rest of his life?"

"If that is how to keep him safe, then yes."

"And if there's a better option?"

"There isn't one!" He closed the distance between them and fisted his hand in her shirt, jerking her up onto her toes, hauling her up until they were nose to nose. "Don't you get it, you stupid little fool? There *is* no option. He is hunted by men who would kill anything and anybody just to be able to *use* him."

She curled a hand over his wrist. "Then you find people who know how to fight back. And you have to do it soon . . . he's going to get stronger and he needs to learn control *before* that happens. Before he hurts people who've done nothing wrong. You want him to live with that?"

"He . . ." Gus clenched his jaw and looked away. "Why are you so certain he's going to get stronger?"

"Puberty." Vaughnne shrugged and gave him a wry smile. "It usually manifests then, but for those who already show a gift? It just amps it up and he's hitting puberty, hard, I'd say. He's going to have to start shaving soon, I bet. He's already got that long, skinny look of a kid who can't eat enough to keep up with the growth spurts. If he's not hitting it now, it's going to be soon."

He stared at her, his eyes dark, menacing. "You're certain of this."

"There's no guarantee, but roughly ninety-five percent of those who are already showing the ability before puberty? Yeah. It jumps up. And it gets harder to control then, too. The theory is that the hormonal swings and shifts that come with puberty play into it." She sighed and shook her head. "Trust me, Gus . . . he needs help and he needs it from somebody who has *been* there. He's not the only one of his kind. There are others, and they'd be willing to die to protect a child." She reached up and touched his cheek. "You asked why I did the FBI . . . this is why. Because this way, I can help. I know what it's like to lose somebody. I won't let them take him away from you."

"How can I trust you?" he demanded, his voice raspy and raw. Almost broken. "I don't know you. How can I trust you with that boy? You don't know what he's gone through."

"No. I don't. But I can tell you what I went through—"

Her skin prickled. Everything inside her went cold, then hot. It wasn't anything she attributed to her abilities. This was just instinct. Jones liked to say that psychic skill ranged from everything just above a hyperaware set of instincts to those abilities like his agents possessed.

This? Just instinct. And her instincts were screaming.

Something bad . . .

That thought crawled through her brain as she took a step back. "Get him to the car," she said quietly. "Now."

And she pulled the weapon from the holster at her back.

"What?"

As he spoke, Alex stumbled over to them. Eyes wide and black. Full of terror. "*Tío* . . ."

"Shhh, *m'hijo*," he said, cupping a hand over the back of the boy's neck.

"The car, Gus," Vaughnne said, keeping the gun low, out of view along her thigh unless somebody was looking.

They'd be looking, though—

Absently, she was aware that Gus was hustling the boy to the car. She swore and looked down at the distributor cap she still carried. "Shit," she muttered. "Gus!"

Turning, she hurled it at him. She didn't wait to see if he caught it before she went back to looking around.

The black SUV came pulling around the corner a few blocks down. Even with all the other cars on the road, her gaze was drawn to it and she felt like a moth pinned to a board, trapped, helpless, and certain they were staring right at her.

That was the fear inside her talking.

Her brain kicked in as the SUV moved into the center lane. Turning aside, she started to move like she was heading over to one of the cars, keeping the vehicle in her line of sight even as the ice in her gut spread.

The SUV had already passed her by. *Yeah, that's right. Keep driving—*

They hadn't noticed her. As long as she didn't draw physical attention to herself, she was fine. The main problem was hiding from any of the psychic bloodhounds, and *she* knew how to hide what she was, unlike the boy.

But Alex . . .

Shit.

Tires squealed on the pavement and she moved to the side. Gus stopped and she went to open the door. It was locked. *You son of a bitch,* she thought. *Don't even—*

A second later, it unlocked and she jerked it open. "Drive," she said. "Preferably without squealing the tires again or anything else that will call attention to you. Unless they've got a damn good bloodhound, they aren't going to realize right away that he is in this car. They'll just know he's close. If we get some distance between us and them before they lock on him, we stand a better chance."

"Bloodhound," Gus muttered. "You keep saying that."

"Somebody who can track. People. Psychics. Anything." She shot a look back at the kid. "Anybody they get a lock on, that is. If they had somebody go through your house, then they've got all sorts of shit they can use to track him with, even if he wasn't casting out signals like crazy."

"Would you shut up?" Gus snarled.

She looked back at him, but not before she saw the boy flinch. "What do you want me to do? Pretend he isn't dangerous, the state he is in?"

"So help me God, you'll be silent or—"

She ignored him and looked back at Alex. Focusing on the chaos that was his mind, she spoke directly inside his head. *You're sick, you're scared, and this isn't a good time to do this . . . but if you want to be safe . . . or safer, you need to let me help you learn how to shield better.*

She saw his reaction in the way he flinched, the way his mouth dropped open.

Then, to her utter disgust, he asked, "Shield? What does that mean?"

She dropped her head against the seat.

The boy had absolutely no clue, she realized.

None at all.

* * *

GUS followed the directions Vaughnne gave him for one reason.

He'd just figured out how very little he understood his nephew's ability.

Bloodhound . . . ¿qué carajo? What did that even mean?

Vaughnne had explained in short, terse terms, but just *how* somebody could track . . .

"Shit."

He glanced over at Vaughnne and then up ahead at the cars slowed down around them.

"Get off the highway," she said. "Now."

He shot her a dark look. "Thanks, but I'd already figured that much out."

Unfortunately, several hundred other cars seemed to have the same idea. Moving to the exit ramp wasn't the easiest process in the world and he was about ready to bite something by the time he hit the red light a half mile later. "Where now?" he asked, forcing his voice into a flat, level tone.

"Whichever way seems to have cars moving the easiest," she said. "The biggest thing is to keep moving, and stay moving . . . away from the city."

That was all she said before she looked back at Alex. "You have to try again."

Gus shot her a narrow look and then checked the mirror, cutting over into the left lane in front of an eighteen-wheeler the second the light turned green. He maneuvered through the traffic, keeping an eye out for cops and watching Vaughnne.

Something about her changed when she was doing that . . . talk . . . thing.

He'd done some reading up on psychic abilities and he thought it was called telepathy. And when she was doing it, although her features didn't change, there was just . . . something. A slight shift in her eyes. The way she held herself. He couldn't quite describe it, and if he hadn't spent many, many years doing nothing but studying people . . . studying women, he likely wouldn't have noticed it.

But then again, with Vaughnne, maybe he would have.

She couldn't seem to breathe without him noticing.

Right now, she was using that ability to talk to Alex.

And he didn't like it.

As they came to another stoplight, he made a decision. Pulling into the parking lot of a crowded McDonald's, he nosed the car into a parking spot. He hadn't even gotten the car into park before she was glaring at him. "We need to keep moving," she said.

"Leave him alone."

"Do you *want* those people finding him?"

"We're thirty miles from where we were," he pointed out. They couldn't track somebody from that far. It wasn't like they were sharks in the water. These were just people. The SUV hadn't shown up once, and if they were being followed, he would know. That much, at least, he would know.

"It doesn't matter. We could be on the other side of the *globe*, and if he can't shut it down, I know people who could track him. He needs to shut it down . . . now." She turned her head away from him and focused on Alex, the boy huddling in the backseat. "Again, Alex."

Alex groaned and Gus shifted his attention to the rearview mirror, watching as the boy closed his eyes. "It's hard, Vaughnne." Little lines of pain bracketed out from his eyes, and as Gus stared at him, he clamped his mouth so tightly shut, his lips went bloodless.

"Enough, Vaughnne," Gus said quietly.

She ignored him.

This . . .

He blew out a careful, controlled breath. He hadn't wanted it to come to this, but apparently, they didn't have much choice.

* * *

SHE caught the danger just a second too late.

Just a fraction of a heartbeat sooner and she would have been able to move. But she'd been concentrating on Alex, trying to guide him through the shielding process without being able to see inside his head—she was so woefully inadequate for this—

By the time she saw Gus moving, he had her pinned against the door. And she couldn't even strike out—*fast*, she thought. He was too fast. Her head was spinning with how fast he moved and she jerked up a leg to get between them. And that was another mistake. She felt the sharp sting penetrate her leg, and then the burn as he injected her with something.

"Damn it—"

That was what she tried to say.

Her tongue was too thick.

Help—

Help. She needed help. A face formed in her mind. *Tucker—*

Even as she screamed for him, she was distantly aware of Gus easing her around in the seat. "I'll leave the windows down," he said, leaning in to murmur against her ear. "You'll sleep for thirty minutes, no more. The keys are in your pocket."

The words barely made sense. The darkness came on harder, faster.

"You . . ." She licked her lips. That sense of dread kicked up and ran down her spine. Adrenaline chased back the fog a little. "They'll find the boy," she whispered. "You stupid jackass. You . . . just fucked yourself . . ."

"No. I'll keep him safe. It's my job."

TWELVE

Tᴜᴄᴋᴇʀ damn near fell to his knees out in the parking lot.
The shriek threatened to turn his brain into mush.

High and desperate, lasting forever.

And then . . . just like that . . . it was gone.

A hand gripped his forearm, but he was so shaken, it didn't
dawn on him until nearly thirty seconds later that Nalini was
touching his bare skin.

He was hopped up high on fear, and energy crawled through
him, but she was touching him—

Dazed, he stared at her hand, her skin pale against the tattoos
that twined around his arms. Blood roared in his ears and his
heart pulsed and throbbed in his throat. For a minute, he couldn't
see anything but her hand on him. And then, reality shifted,
twisted. And settled.

"Vaughnne," he whispered.

Nalini's hand tightened. "What?"

Carefully, afraid something sparking inside him would leap out and scorch her, he tugged his arm away and focused on the broken, busted pavement of the parking lot in front of the seedy motel. They'd spent most of the night going over all the information they had, and Tucker had gotten on the phone with Lucia, giving her an abbreviated version, despite Nalini's furious arguments.

Nobody could dig up information the way Lucia could and he needed more info on the website. The website . . . an underground craigslist for psychics.

Now this.

He closed his eyes and thought of that desperate scream. "It was Vaughnne," he said, worry riding him hard. "She just screamed in my head. I think something bad happened."

Nalini went pale. Her skin was smooth and delicate as ivory anyway. Now, it was like she was just a shade away from snow.

She drilled a hand against her temple and swore, spinning away so fast, her dreads whirled up around her. "Shit."

"Yeah. We can cuss about it on the road. We need to go find her."

Nalini just stared off toward the office, her shoulders stiff, her spine a long, rigid line. Long seconds passed before she slowly turned around. "I can't," she said, her voice low. "I have something else I'm caught up in and I can't abandon it for this."

Tucker hadn't heard that right. He knew he hadn't. Closing his eyes, he counted to ten and then looked back at her. Calmly, he said, "I don't think I understood that."

"Yes," she said gently. "You did." She reached into the little purse she'd slung over her shoulder, the strap lying between two small, firm breasts. She tugged out a card and a pen, scribbling something down furiously. "Call this number once you're on the road. It's the SAC for the unit. Jones. You may or may not have met him, but tell him your connection, Tucker. You can trust him. Vaughnne does. I do. He'll get help—"

He stared at the card and then turned away. "I hope to hell

that's not a friend of yours I just heard screaming in my head, Cole."

Part of him just wanted to leave. He could. Technically. *Nothing* bound him to this. He said he'd watch out for the kid but nothing required him to do it. He wasn't getting paid and he didn't have a stake in this.

But he liked Vaughnne.

She had balls.

And . . .

Shit.

She'd reached out and asked . . . no . . . *begged* him for help.

He hadn't had too many people do that.

"Damn it, Tucker!"

He flipped her off without looking over his shoulder. If he looked at her again, something inside him was going to turn to ashes. He'd thought . . . hell. Never mind.

He was behind the wheel of his car before she caught up with him. The look in her eyes might have meant something if he hadn't picked up on the fear he'd heard in Vaughnne's voice. He hadn't realized it would happen like that, that a telepath could put *that* much emotion in her voice. It had been like she'd been right there in the room, screaming, and he'd felt every bit of the terror she'd felt.

His skin heated and he had to shove the rage down inside. He'd let it out once it was safe to do so, but now wasn't the time. Now wasn't at all the time. As he jammed the key in the ignition, Nalini slammed her hands against the window. "Roll it down, you moron," she snarled.

He ignored her and shoved the car into drive.

"Listen, you dickhead. I'm already working a dangerous case. I can't just *drop* everything for this. You don't even know if she's in danger."

"Yeah, I do. I don't think she screamed for help because she wanted to ask me about the weather. If somebody doesn't go after *her*, she might die. The kid you wanted me to watch? She's watching after him. So he could be in danger, too. But hey, that's fine." Tucker shrugged. "I know the FBI has its own sense of priorities."

"I'm not FBI. I'm freelance." She glared at him through the window.

Freelance. He ran his tongue over his teeth and shook his head. "That didn't help the situation any, sweetheart. You don't have a boss jerking your chain back to work? And you'll still walk away?"

Her pulse raced in her neck, and for one brief second, he wished he would have kissed her. Just once. Just so he knew what she tasted like. Shaking his head, he looked away. "Stay away from me from here on out, Cole. You want to play the hero, but when it comes time to getting dirty, you pull back."

He pressed down on the gas, and as the tires squealed, she just stood there.

* * *

THE car Gus had decided to take was one he'd seen an employee climb out of just moments earlier. Hopefully the kid wouldn't come out for a smoke break or anything anytime soon.

Even as he urged Alex into the seat, he found himself looking back at Vaughnne's car, though. Her head slumped against the door, the long tangle of her hair blowing in the breeze.

He'd stolen the fast-acting sedatives some time ago. He hoped they still had the kick in them that he needed. They'd expired six months earlier, but it was all he had and breaking into a medical facility wasn't as easy as one might think. Or maybe it was every bit as hard as one might think, depending on the person.

He needed to replenish his supplies, but that was a problem for another day.

"Why did you do that, *Tí* . . . ah . . . why did you do that?" Alex asked, correcting himself as Gus slid behind the wheel.

"She was hurting you."

"No. It . . ." Alex closed his eyes and curled up in the seat, looking so lost, so young and scared. "It was just hard. It's a weight in my brain. And if I have to do it . . ."

"You don't." Gus set his jaw and focused on hot-wiring the car. That needed to be the focus because they needed to get out of there. Get on the road. Head west, he figured. Northwest, he was thinking. Oregon, if they could make it. Hell, if they *could*, he'd like to get out of the country. Maybe he could get in touch with one of his old contacts. Someone who could help them leave the States. It might take exchanging a favor or two, but if it would get them out of the country and farther away . . .

"What if she's right?"

Gus put the car in reverse and wished the boy would just be silent. Twenty minutes of peace, so he could think. So he could plan. They had next to nothing. His bag of weapons and the stash of cash he'd always kept. It wouldn't last them forever. He had several caches of money and weapons scattered across the country—the nearest was in Macon, Georgia. That was the destination for now, he guessed.

But he needed to think.

To plan.

And he couldn't because every time Alex mentioned Vaughnne, he was hit with guilt for what he'd done. But she'd been pushing the boy, hurting him—

"*Tío*, what if—"

"It's not *Tío*. You have to remember, I'm not your *uncle*, I'm your father, as far as anybody is concerned," he snapped, glaring at his nephew.

Alex immediately dropped his gaze, staring down at his lap.

Gus spied a local highway sign and turned, heading north.

They hadn't been away from the interstate long enough for the traffic to have cleared and he'd rather not sit around in traffic anyway. Silence wrapped around him . . . the silence he'd been wishing for just moments earlier. But this tense, heavy silence was choking him.

"I'm sorry. I shouldn't have snapped." Guilt settled inside him, with sharp, jagged hooks. "But you keep messing up, Alex. You can't do that."

Alex nodded slowly and turned his head, staring out the window.

A few more moments ticked by, but the tension didn't let up. Alex had never been the sort to stay angry with him. They'd spent too many years with just each other, and Gus knew, as unhealthy as it was for the boy, he was all Alex had. It wasn't anybody's sort of ideal, but Alex rarely reacted like a boy his age should. He didn't get angry over silly things; he rarely got angry at all. But as the minutes bled away into almost an hour and Alex still hadn't spoken, Gus wondered just how much longer he could force the boy into this hellish life without it taking a toll.

It already has. The boy lost his mother. He has no home. No friends. Let him be angry, he told himself when he finally took time to stop for lunch. It was just fast food. He was so tired of fast food. He missed real meals. A pile of hot tacos, some fresh salsa. A steak and a potato . . . anything but fast food.

As Alex bit listlessly into a chicken nugget, Gus pulled the amber bottle of pills from his pocket and shook one out. "It's time for the medicine."

Alex took it without comment and washed it down with his soft drink.

"How are you feeling?"

The only response was a shrug.

"Alex, I already apologized," he said, sighing. "How much longer are you going to be angry with me?"

Alex turned his head, staring at him with dark, miserable eyes. "I'm not angry. I'm scared."

Gus felt his heart break. He went to reach out, but Alex shrank away, leaning against the door of the stolen car. Gus had stopped at a busy outlet mall thirty minutes earlier and swapped out the plates. Hopefully, it would buy them more time, but by nightfall, he'd have to steal another car.

Sooner or later . . .

No. We will not be caught, he thought darkly. It wasn't a thought that he could risk thinking about. He knew how to evade such things and he would. He'd never had to do it with a boy in tow, but Alex was smart and he knew how to listen.

Watching as Alex started to tear his food apart and drop it down without eating it, Gus tried to figure out what to say. In the end, he just went with the same lie he'd been telling himself for years. "You don't have to be afraid. I can take care of you. I *will* take care of you. He will never get his hands on you . . . I swear that."

Of all the things he said, the one promise he could be sure of was the very last. Because he'd do anything and everything to make sure the monster who had fathered Alex would never touch him. No matter what it took, no matter what it cost.

"You won't be around forever." Alex stared at him, fear in his eyes. "And I won't be a kid forever. What happens then? When I'm grown up? Do I live my life running?"

It was a question that haunted Gus. It bothered him that the boy had already started to ask it, though. "Let me worry about that, *m'hijo*," he said gruffly, tossing the rest of his uneaten sandwich in the bag and starting the car. "We need to go."

"What if she was right? What if they can find me just because of what . . . what I am?" Alex asked, his voice shaking and nervous, but there was an underlying thread of steel inside it. "I *felt* something. When she was in my head . . . and when I hurt her that day, I felt something in *her* head. Like a wall. It's different from what is in my head. That's what she was showing me. If she was right about the wall, about shielding, then maybe she's right about the rest of it."

Gus didn't want to think about that.

Couldn't.

Because if she *was*, if she hadn't lied, and if there were psychic bloodhounds on their tail . . .

Dread twisted his gut and he did the same thing he'd done with his terrors over the years. He shut them down and blocked them out. He'd get Alex and him through this. That was just all there was to it. There was no other option, really.

* * *

IT could have been ten seconds since Vaughnne had closed her eyes. It could have been ten minutes. She doubted it was ten hours, because it was still early in the day, judging by the angle of the sun in the sky. What small glimpse she had of it when the door was jerked open out from under her and she was grabbed by a big, smelly-ass man who looked like it had been years since he'd seen the inside of a shower.

It might have even been his stink that woke her up.

Adrenaline cleared the rest of the fog from her brain, but it was another few minutes before she could get the rest of her body working.

By *that* time, Vaughnne was the unhappy occupant of the big, black SUV she'd glimpsed earlier. With a gun shoved against the underside of her chin. The man leaning in and glaring at her didn't look happy.

He was about to get even more unhappy, she decided.

Once she knew she could move. And fight.

She'd bloody him.

Then she'd find Gus and bloody *him* for leaving her drugged and helpless.

"Where's the boy?" the man asked, his voice low and soft.

Vaughnne arched her brows. "Boy? What boy?"

A second later, that gun that was digging against her chin came flying through the air and she tasted blood. She swallowed it down, along with any sound she might have made, and focused on breathing. Then she tried to wiggle her toes. Ah . . . perfect. They moved. So did her ankles.

"The boy," he said again. "Where is he?"

"I don't know what you're talking about!" she said.

He went to hit her again and she pretended to flinch, using her hands to protect her face; she could move. Thank God. She could move almost close to normal. Eyeing the man in the driver's seat, she used her arms to protect her head and give her cover as she looked around. They were on the highway. Driving. Driving *fast*.

"Listen, you stupid bitch. I saw you earlier and I know what you are. Don't lie to me because it don't work," he said, grinning at her and revealing a pair of teeth that badly needed brushing. He leaned in close and she decided he could also use some mouthwash. "So don't lie to me again. Where is the kid?"

"Look, I don't know which kid . . . I was hired to grab a couple of them for my boss, okay? He likes them young." She swallowed and darted him another look, wondering if he was buying this. He wasn't all that strong, she suspected. Something about him just felt . . . off. Chaotic, like he was struggling to use his gift even at the level he was using it. So he was probably self-taught and not all that well. Good. That was good. Taking a deep breath, she said, "You have to help me a little. Which kid? I grabbed a bunch of them."

Silence stretched out.

"Your boss. What are you talking about, bitch?"

She licked the blood from her lip and then darted a look up, pretended to be nervous. "Ah . . . yeah. Um. Well, he . . .

you know. He doesn't dig girls. He likes boys. Young ones. So I was—"

A hand gripped her throat. "The one from this morning. I saw you in the parking lot. You would have had a boy with you. I know it."

Did she go with mock innocence here?

If she decided to let loose with the screams considering how fast they were driving, then they were going to be hurt. Maybe she could get them to stop the car . . .

"Listen to me, bitch." He squeezed harder. "If one of the others get to him first, I'm going to rip your throat out and fuck your dead corpse. You hear me?"

Vaughnne lifted her lashes and stared at him. *Others* . . . Letting a tremor of fear enter her voice, she whispered, "I can't tell you. But . . ." Shit. If this didn't work, they were so screwed.

The gun, a big-ass Desert Eagle 357, returned to press into her neck. If he pulled that trigger, it wouldn't matter if they were driving or not. She was dead. But on the flipside, if he pulled that trigger, he wasn't going to get whatever information he wanted, and he had to know that. He didn't care if he killed her, but he wanted that money so he'd wait to kill until he had the information he needed.

She hated dealing with unknowns like this.

"But what, sweetheart?" he asked, cupping her face with his free hand. "Come on. Just tell me where to find the kid and you walk away from this. It's not your mess."

Walk away. Like hell. She gathered up her strength, because regardless, Jones had to get his ass down here and she only had this one shot. She started to jabber out, randomly, anything and everything but the truth—that was the key when stringing somebody along. Keep it as close to believable as possible, but don't throw the truth in there. If he started to hurt her and the truth slipped out at some point, he'd have a hard-ass time telling truth from fiction by the time she was done, especially considering his damned faulty control.

She gathered up her strength, started to focus her mind. When she had to put out a call over a long distance, it wasn't like making a damn phone call. Took a bit more juice and this was going to take everything she had.

But as she started to reach out and touch someone, she felt the air go tight and heavy, wrapping around her. At the same time, the hairs on the back of her neck stood on end.

She recognized that feeling. And just in time, too. She let loose with the scream building inside her—the call she'd intended to send out to Jones—she split her focus, a mindless shriek at the foul-breathed thug even as she called for Jones.

Distantly, she was aware that the thug in front of her had flinched away, swearing as he clapped his ears. He was pale, his eyes rolling back in his head.

Desperately, she fumbled with the Glock at her back. She'd like to use it and put a bullet between the bastard's eyes, but those instincts of hers were screaming—

Hurry, hurry, hurry—

She dropped the weapon on the floor and it hadn't been out of her hand for more than a second before all that crackling energy in the air seemed to . . . contract. All around her. Her ears popped, something cracked, and the stink of scorched air flooded her nose, even as she realized something was burning.

And then somebody screamed.

That was the last thing she knew before the SUV jolted, then swerved off the road. She smashed into the door and everthing went dark.

* * *

TUCKER jerked open the door and stared inside.

Vaughnne's limp body all but fell into his arms and he swore.

Even as he caught her, though, she moaned a little. "Thank God." Okay. Okay. This was good.

She was alive.

He'd hoped for that much, at least. Spying a familiar-looking weapon on the floor, he grabbed it and jammed it in the back of his jeans before he slid his arms under her.

But before he could pick her up, the man across from him spoke.

"Don't . . . she's mine."

Considering the man could barely move, Tucker wasn't overly concerned at the moment. First, get Vaughnne out of there.

Then, he'd deal with this. He carried her a few feet away from the car, painfully aware of the few cars driving by, slowing down. One of them almost looked like she was going to stop. But then, at the last second, she sped on by. *Good thinking, lady.* As he reached the car, he saw that the occupant in the backseat had managed to get himself moving, more or less.

The guy in the front was dead.

Cardiac arrest, probably. Happened sometimes when a serious amount of voltage was directed into the body. Tucker didn't entirely blame himself for the guy's death. After all, nobody had made him kidnap Vaughnne. Tucker was just the tool used to help alleviate that situation; that was his story.

The other guy, well, whether he lived or died, it was his own choice.

And his odds lowered as he lifted his gun. Tucker really hated it when people pointed guns at him. The bastard held it at his side, partially blocking it with his body so those on the highway wouldn't see. Tucker saw it, though, and that was the big problem.

"You should put that down before you get hurt," he said, smiling a little.

"Are you here for the boy, too?" the man asked, his eyes bleary, but focusing more and more with every second.

Alarm flickered in the back of Tucker's head. "No. I'm just here for her," he replied easily. "I got her. I'm good."

"Can't have her. She's our ticket to the kid . . . put her back in the car, shithead. Then walk away."

"Can't do that." He eyed the man as he stepped out of the SUV, swaying a little. Blood spilled down his face from a cut on his forehead, and he slammed a hand against the vehicle to brace himself.

"You *will* do that," the man said. His face folded in what Tucker assumed was supposed to be a menacing snarl, but as he continued to sway there, so close to that big pile of metal . . .

"You know, you've got about five seconds to decide if you want to live or die," Tucker said. "If you want to live, get back in the truck. Otherwise . . ."

He let his words die off.

The guy laughed. "Dumb-ass. *I* am the one with the gun."

"Yeah. But that gun can't do this . . ." He emptied himself of the remnant energy boiling inside him. First on the man, forcing his way into the man's mind and shutting down the electrical impulses, holding that until he saw the man stagger. The arm holding the gun lowered as the strain on his brain weakened him. Once the gun was no longer pointing at Tucker, he said one more time, "Last chance. If you want to live, you're better off in the SUV."

"Stu . . . stupid fuck."

Tucker gave up holding himself in check.

It was almost like an orgasm, just letting go like that.

It would have been a beautiful thing, except he was painfully aware of the stink of burned flesh, painfully aware of the foul miasma as the man's bowels and bladder released as he died, painfully aware of the gun as it hit the ground. Most modern weapons were equipped with safety features to keep them from accidental discharge, but still, Tucker wasn't relying on that as he jerked to the side. Just in case. He didn't trust *safety features*. He didn't trust jack shit. Not even himself, most of the time.

With two dead bodies and no visible sign of what had killed them, he headed back to get Vaughnne. The entire exchange had happened in under two minutes. He knew this area. It would only take county cops five minutes, maximum, to get here. He had to move.

He was taking a chance moving her without knowing if she'd been injured, but he had to do it. They had to get to that kid.

That jackass back there, he hadn't been at all surprised that somebody else might be looking for the kid. Which meant . . . what? He'd been expecting it?

Not good.

THIRTEEN

IT was an innocuous, dark blue sedan following them.

Gus had noticed it nearly thirty minutes earlier, and in those thirty minutes, it hadn't once gotten any closer than it was now. Staying about a good fifty feet back, usually more. Sometimes two or three cars would get between them. Sometimes it would veer over into another lane, keeping that easy, casual distance, but there was no mistaking it . . . the car was following them.

And Alex was scared. It didn't help that his fever had come back, either. Some Tylenol knocked the fever down, but nothing took the fear from his eyes. Sweat that had nothing to do with illness beaded on the boy's forehead, and he sat there with his hands clenched in his lap, his entire body trembling.

Terrified.

"They found us again, *Tío*," Alex said softly.

He didn't respond. Fear spread through him, but giving voice to it wasn't going to help Alex. It curdled in his belly, a twisted knot, but he accepted that fear, swallowing it down and welcoming it. He'd channel it. Make it his own, and use it.

They'd moved back onto the highway halfway through the afternoon and had made good time, leaving Florida behind nearly thirty minutes ago. But now, driving up I-65, speeding through Georgia, he felt like he was bashing his head against a brick wall.

He didn't know where to go.

He'd been so sure if they just hit the road and got some distance between them, they'd be okay. Every other time somebody had tracked them down, all it had taken was a few hours and some distance and they'd lost them. Gus knew how to lose people.

You've never had to run from people who can track a psychic child, though, the dark, ugly voice of self-recrimination whispered from deep inside him.

No. He hadn't had to do that before, had never realized it would be a concern. Even when Vaughnne—

Stop. Looking back wouldn't help now. He hadn't trusted her, and in all honesty, there had been no *reason* to trust her. He didn't know her, had no reason to trust a total stranger. His experience with Alex over the years had served him well enough.

Things had changed and he'd fucked up.

Now he had to fix it. First, he had to get the hell away from the people trailing them.

He couldn't take the boy on a high-speed chase. Not in the car he'd stolen.

And he had to ditch the car soon.

There was no way around that.

But if he stopped . . .

"They are going to hit us soon." Alex's voice was low, thin.

Gus swore.

Gripping the steering wheel, he looked back in the mirror and then at the cars all around them. "How are you feeling, *m'hijo*? How is your stomach? Your back?"

"I feel better with . . . um . . . that." He shrugged, a restless jerky motion, and his cheeks were a dull, ruddy red. "I guess the medicine stuff is helping."

Gus nodded shortly. "Good."

"My head hurts . . . I'm . . ." Alex swallowed and looked away. "I'm trying to do what Vaughnne was showing me. It's giving me a headache, but I don't feel like I did yesterday."

Vaughnne—

Mierda. He'd been trying not to think about her. She'd been right. He'd been wrong. There was no other explanation for how they'd been tracked down.

Psychic bloodhounds.

They'd tracked them down. Somehow. Gus didn't know if it was because of something they'd *done* or what, but somehow they'd tracked them down. Maybe it was really as simple as she'd said and it was something Alex was unintentionally doing.

And it was something that did him no good to worry about now. They were hours away from where he'd left her and no telling where she was now. He had no way of finding her, which was exactly how he had *thought* he'd wanted it.

For now, he had to figure out the best way to take care of Alex.

Get those men off their tail.

"You think you can get in their heads?" Gus asked slowly, hating that he had to ask, but knowing he didn't have much choice.

"You mean—"

"You know what I mean, boy," Gus said quietly, staring straight ahead. "We need to be away from here. We need another car. We need to get you safe. But we have to make sure they can't follow us, can't try and take you from me. We need to make you safe."

Alex swallowed, and the sound was terribly loud in the silence of the car. "If I do it out here, they'll wreck. People will get hurt."

Gus nodded. "Then we leave the highway."

It would be better that way anyway. If they could find a quiet little road, someplace where they thought they might be safer to make a move, it would be easier for Alex to focus on them. Fewer people around to get hurt. Gus was willing to do whatever it took to protect his nephew, but if possible, he didn't want to harm a bunch of innocent people.

He was already too close to becoming the monster he was trying to protect Alex from as it was.

They had to get off the highway, and fast. He checked the upcoming exit, mentally mapping things out. He'd spent long, long nights going over his exit strategies for the time when he and the boy had to leave. He wasn't as familiar with this area as he'd like to be, but he knew the major interstates and the highways as well as he could hope to.

If he took the upcoming exit and headed east for a while, they'd get away from the traffic. There was a smaller county road that went north. There . . . they'd try to make it there.

"Okay, Alex," he said, leaving the fast lane and watching as the car back there casually did the same thing. "This is what we're going to do."

* * *

VAUGHNNE woke up in more pain than anybody should have to feel without pharmaceutical intervention.

And when she opened her eyes a slit, she could see the highway speeding by. *Not* the bright lights of an ER, either. That was what she'd rather see. An emergency room. With a nice doctor . . . preferably a sexy one so she could have something to focus on while she waited for pain medicine, because *damn*, she hurt.

That wasn't happening, though, she didn't think.

She continued to sit there, breathing shallowly while she did a mental check. She had all of her body parts, and even though she *hurt*, she didn't think she was in bad shape, considering she was pretty certain she'd been in an accident. Might have something to do with the fact that, even as scared as she'd been, she'd still been pretty limp and lax from whatever Gus had pumped into her system—

Gus . . . shit. Alex.

Fear flooded her, crowding up the back of her throat in a metallic, nasty rush, and she had to battle it back. Okay. Time to figure out what was going on—

"Calm down, Vaughnne," a tired, *familiar* voice said. "It's just me."

She went to turn her head, and pain streaked through her, just from that. She winced, barely managing to keep the cry behind her teeth as she found herself staring at Tucker's profile. "You." Closing her eyes, she blew out a breath. "You heard me."

"Yeah. Kind of hard not to. You wail like a banshee."

She might have flipped him off if she could have moved without it hurting. Instead, she just sat there, letting her body adjust to being awake. Her body didn't like it. Not at all.

"What happened?"

"I . . ." He paused and tapped a gloved fist against the steering wheel. "I might have forced the car you were in to wreck. Overloaded the system with a discharge."

"A discharge?" She stared at him, trying to figure out what he was saying. The words *sounded* like English, but they weren't, because he just wasn't making sense. Or maybe it was the pain in her head.

"Yeah. It's . . ." He blew out a breath. "I manipulate electricity, basically, and I store it inside me. Science says it isn't possible, but then again, look at what most scientists would say about people like you." He shot her a glance and shrugged.

"You . . . you store electricity." Yep. It was official. He wasn't speaking English. Okay. Whatever. "What are you talking about, discharging the car?"

"Think of a lightning strike. I took what I had in me, sent some of it into the car."

"Then why weren't we electrocuted?" Her brain was too muddled for this.

"The car." He shrugged again. "I wanted to stop the car, and I did, but the car's metal exterior protected the people inside . . . well, except for the guy driving. And the other guy. He got burned. Had his gun. He was touching metal."

She narrowed her eyes down to slits, glaring at him. "*I* had a weapon on me, you ass. I dropped it like five seconds before you did . . . whatever . . ."

He grimaced. "Sorry. I was reacting on instinct, going with the best plan that seemed viable at the time. I knew you were there. And I . . . hell. Every one of us feels different, but those who don't have a problem killing anything or anybody just have a different sort of vibe to their minds. I can't read them—that's not my thing—but you were in the car with a couple of people who would just as soon kill you as look at you. I didn't figure you'd want to be dead so I took the chance."

She closed her eyes. No. Dead wasn't what she wanted. "They had information about the boy. Were tracking him. I needed to know who else was doing it—it would have been good to talk with them and figure out what in the hell was going on."

"I can help you there." He grabbed something from the back-seat and dumped it in her lap. It was an iPad.

She turned it on and stared. "Now what?"

"Go to Safari. It's the only page open. You'll see."

She blew out a breath and opened the browser, trying to think past the pain pounding in her head. Five seconds later, the pain was forgotten as a rush of adrenaline slammed into her.

Item.

Swallowing, she licked her lips.

"Please tell me this item isn't what I'm thinking it is."

"I'd be lying."

She shot him a look, and this time, the jolt of pain that went screaming up her neck barely even slowed her. Absently, she reached up and rubbed her neck, although it didn't do a damn thing to help the stiffness there. "It's damn vague. It could be anything."

"Scroll up to the top . . . read what the site is about. Who it's for," he said quietly. "Then decide if you think it's nothing."

She flicked her finger across the screen and found herself staring at the header. It was just an eye. The words were a jumbled mess. Shaking her head, she said, "I'm not getting it."

"It's a code." His hands tightened on the wheel. "It's called *The Psychic Portal.* An underground site for psychics . . . people like us. And they put up a want ad for the kid, Vaughnne. Anybody with the ability to pick up anything is going to know that isn't an *item* being talked about. And there are no requirements for moral fiber to get in there."

Her lids drooped as fear closed an icy, cold fist around her throat. Scrolling through the page, she started to dig deeper and then her heart jumped up and slammed against her ribs, hard. "This . . . this says they've got almost ten *thousand* members."

"Yeah." Tucker's mouth was a tight, narrow line. "I bet a bunch of them are fakes and wannabes. And a lot of them aren't going to be interested in going after a kid. But think this through to completion . . . you know there are plenty of scum out there who'd kill their own mother for a few hundred dollars. Grabbing some kid they don't know?"

"*Shhhhittttt . . .*" she whispered, breathing the word out as her mind started to process that. "Tucker, we have to find them. Whether Gus likes it or not, we have to find that boy and get him in. It's his only chance."

Tucker's lashes swept down over his eyes, and she recalled just how loudly he made known his dislike of the FBI. Damn it, if he started fighting with her over this—

He flicked her a look and gave a short, single nod. "I don't know if turning him over to the FBI is the best idea, but he needs to be protected. We can agree on that much."

"Good. That's good. Thank God." She shifted on the seat and groaned as her abused body screamed out at her. "I feel like I was run over by a truck."

"You're not far off." He sighed and lifted one hand to his mouth.

She watched, wary as he used his teeth to strip off one of his gloves.

"Let me see your neck," he said.

She just stared at him.

He blew out a breath. "Come on, Vaughnne. This will help."

"Aren't you the one who was telling me all the crazy shit about how you carry electricity inside you? And you want me to let you touch my neck?" He was out of his *mind*.

"Haven't you ever heard of electrical stimulation therapy?" he asked, giving her what was probably supposed to be a charming smile. It failed. By a long shot.

Tucker looked too devilish to ever pass for charming.

Narrowing her eyes, she tucked herself more firmly against the seat.

"Come on." He smiled again. "Chiropractors use it all the time."

"I heard about this one chiro who was doing an adjustment on a woman—he severed her carotid artery. She ended up in the ICU, all because of his *adjustments*," Vaughnne said, smiling at him.

"Well, I'm not going to give you an adjustment. I just want to help with your neck, seeing as how I helped put it in the shape it's in." He sighed and shrugged. "But if you want to sit there and suffer . . ."

He went to pull his hand back.

"You think you can really help?"

"Well. If I didn't, I wouldn't offer," he said.

She muttered under her breath and then eased forward. As his hand came close, she squeezed her eyes closed and prayed. The first brush of his fingers wasn't anything. Then, as she went to glance over at him, she felt something buzz against her skin. Hissing out a breath, her eyes widened.

But before she could say anything, it hit her again, and again.

He pressed against her neck, and the heat of his palm, combined with whatever the hell he was doing, managed to ease that horrid pain. "Oh . . . hell," she mumbled, sagging in relief.

She needed to start to think. And she would soon. Really soon. Once they had an idea where they were going.

It was almost too soon when Tucker pulled his hand away. "I can't do much more," he said softly. "I have to limit how much I touch others, but that should help."

Eyes closed, she sighed in bliss. "That was enough. I almost don't hate you now."

He laughed a little. "Gee, thanks." A few seconds passed, and then he asked, "Why don't you give me an idea just what we need to do here, Miz FBI? You got a plan?"

"Gimme a minute," she groused. "This has been one lousy day for me, okay? Car wreck. Kidnapped. Oh, and hey, I was drugged this morning, too. Not to mention losing the kid I was supposed to be protecting."

"Drugged?"

There was an odd, heavy note of tension in Tucker's voice.

She cracked one eye open to peer over at him. "Yeah. Gus, his . . . ah, the kid's guardian, he drugged me. Gave me some sort of short-acting sedative, if I had to take a guess. Caught me off guard. I woke up when they were shoving me in the car and I probably hit my head or something, because I went out again for a few minutes. I don't know where Gus and the kid disappeared to."

"I can help there." Tucker stared ahead, his face grim. "I'm tracking the kid's . . . brain waves, basically. He's got an electrical signature that's pretty unique. If nothing else, it will make it easy for me to find him. I'm keyed into the electrical shit."

"I can't imagine that. Really." She made herself move her head, checking it one way, then other. Oh, bliss. She could move her head without major pain. The rest of her body was still in major protest, but other than that, there didn't seem to be any problems. Wrenched a few things, probably. No major damage, she didn't think. "How far?"

"It's faint. We're closing in on them, but if I had to guess, I'd say twenty miles or so." His dark brown eyes were flat. "The kid isn't the only one out there, though. I don't think he's been grabbed. I think he's being followed or something, but there is at least one or two others close by. Probably looking to grab the kid."

"So we just get there before that happens."

Tucker muttered under his breath, "Yeah. That's all we gotta do. Easy, right?"

*　*　*

NALINI came upon the accident scene only moments before the cops did. She sighed and climbed out, although it was just going to slow her down.

She had to get out there, because she needed to get her hands on . . . something. Her psychometry wasn't going to kick into place unless she touched something, and she had to know what was going on so she could figure out where to go from here.

Mexico.

That was where she *needed* to go.

Except she was needed here, too. And she couldn't be in two places at once.

Forcing herself to focus, she made her way over to the truck and studied the dead bodies there. The sirens wailed, closer now, and she knew she was missing out on her chance to grab anything from the scene.

Bracing herself, she made her way over to the body and touched the man who lay on the ground.

Images slammed into her.

Tucker.

Vaughnne.

Memories piling into her head, too hard and fast, fractured and burning hot in her brain. That was normal. She shoved them to the back of her mind, where she could pick through them when she had time to breathe . . . and time to not worry about local law enforcement.

What she *needed* was buried deeper and it was fading. The human body wasn't exactly like an inanimate object. Inanimate objects held imprints longer. Human bodies were like the sand on the beach. One good, hard wave was all it took to wipe the slate clean and death was one hell of a wave. But it was there . . . just . . . *there*—

She grabbed it, took it.

Memories of the promise of money. The boy. It all circled back to the boy. She should have headed straight back to Mexico, she realized. None of this would stop until that damn listing went off-line. She severed the connection and sucked in a gasp of blood-drenched air. The night was thick with death and she closed her eyes, tried to process everything she'd just taken in.

It was too much.

This wasn't her strongest ability, and she'd never perfected it as much as she should have. But a few things were clear.

They had been hunting the boy.

That wouldn't stop until somebody made it stop. That was actually one thing she could probably do, all on her own. That one listing wasn't going to rock the boat too much, she didn't think.

The crunch of gravel was as loud as the crack of a weapon fired in the night, and Nalini was glad she'd had all those years of practice, all those years dealing with shock and fear and surprise. All those years had given her another gift, one that had nothing to do with psychic skill. She wiped every emotion *she* felt off her face and then replaced those emotions with the emotions she suspected she *should* feel. Horror, nerves, a bit of anxiety.

Keeping her breathing level, she lifted her gaze and summoned up the saddest expression she could, let tears fill her eyes as she looked up at the sheriff coming her way. "I . . . I think he's dead."

* * *

Not long now, Gus thought, brooding, as he stared into the rearview mirror. They'd just passed a slow-moving old farm truck, loaded down with four people in the cab and four in the truck bed. As it passed around a bend in the road, he glanced over at Alex. The boy was fiddling with his seat belt, tugging at it where it rode over his chest. "Leave the belt alone, Alex," he said quietly. His muscles were tense, and deliberately, he relaxed them. "What do you feel?"

"They'll be doing something soon," Alex said, his voice reed-thin, his skin pale.

Reaching over, he checked the boy's forehead. No fever. He felt clammy, actually, and Gus wasn't sure if that was a good thing or not. "We'll do this and you'll be safe."

Miserable, Alex stared at him. "If Vaughnne's right and they can *feel* me or track me, how can I ever be safe? I don't know how to stop . . . doing whatever I do."

"I'll find a way to keep you safe," Gus said, his voice flat and level. He didn't know how, but he'd do it. Vaughnne's face flashed through his mind. The way her gaze had bored into his.

And how many times had she *told* him that she'd help keep Alex safe?

I'm here to help keep him safe . . .

Carajo. He should have trusted her. It was too late now—

Abruptly, Alex's hand, small but strong, reached over and clamped down on Gus's forearm. His mouth opened, but no sound emerged.

He didn't have to say a word. Lifting his gaze to the rearview mirror, Gus saw that the car behind them was closing the distance and fast.

"Block them out, Alex. Hurt them if you can." He checked the Sig Sauer. It was loaded. Ready. He knew how to kill; had done it more times than he could even count, really. There was blood on his hands, and it didn't even bother him for the most part. He could do it again and it wouldn't haunt him at night. Not any more than anything else, at least.

As the car came bearing down on them, faster and faster, he slammed on the brakes. Tires squealed. "Hold on, *m'hijo*," he ordered. He whipped the car around and found himself staring at a surprised face. The driver slammed on his brakes, watching them.

A moment later, he felt a pressure shoving against his mind— familiar, that, but nothing he hadn't felt from Alex—and he ignored it as he aimed, squeezed . . . the pressure disappeared as the man's head exploded in a mess of blood, bone, and brain matter.

Without waiting another second, he hit the gas and took off barreling down the highway.

He'd made it maybe five hundred yards before the car went airborne.

* * *

"WHAT in the hell . . ."

Vaughnne watched as the car a few hundred yards ahead went flying, up and backward, flipping over the dark blue sedan parked in the middle of the road.

Tucker jerked the steering wheel to the side to avoid having the car plow into theirs, and for the second time that day, she had the pleasure of having her body flung about. This time, the seat belt stopped her, but it wasn't really that much of an improvement. It still *hurt*.

The car flipped upside down, landing in almost the exact spot where Tucker's car had been three seconds earlier.

Neither of them took a second to breathe a sigh of relief, although Vaughnne did say a quick prayer of thanks as she fumbled for her seat belt. She was out of the car, weapon in hand, before Tucker even had his car at a complete stop. Every muscle in her body screamed and she suspected she was going to crash, and hard, sometime soon. For now, adrenaline, determination, and fear were the only things keeping her going.

"Stop," she said, positioning her body as a man climbed out of the passenger side of the dark blue sedan still sitting in the middle of the road. He had blood splatter on his face, she noticed. Blood splatter, and either he didn't notice, or it didn't bother him.

She peered around his body and saw the driver, slumped over the steering wheel, and although she couldn't see him well enough to be certain, she had a bad feeling she knew where the blood had come from.

The man took another step toward her, hands lifted in the classic pose . . . *Hey, I surrender, don't shoot me* . . .

It might have worked, if he hadn't been walking toward her, if he hadn't had blood all over him, if she hadn't recognized his vibe. Psychic as all get-out, and since *something* had sent Gus's car flying through the air, she was going to assume this bastard had something to do with it.

"Hey, I just wanted to help . . . I saw the accident," he said, smiling a little.

"Yeah. Sure." She braced her weapon with both hands and hoped he couldn't see the fact that she was swaying a little. "Stay where you are, man."

Something nudged her. Hard.

She couldn't see it, but she damn sure felt it.

His eyes tightened when she didn't react.

The push came again, harder, and this time, she stumbled a little.

"Sir, you are going to desist," she warned him. "Now."

"I'm just standing right here," he said mildly.

"And I'm Santa Claus," she snapped.

"Ho, ho, ho . . ."

This time, when he pushed, she went down and he lunged.

"Do I get to play, too?"

*   *   *

TUCKER moved between them just as the man would have grabbed Vaughnne. Intercepting them, he smiled a little as the man fell back. Apparently he hadn't realized there was a third party lurking around. Tucker decided he liked that . . . being the third party.

Stripping off one of his gloves, he tucked it in his back pocket. Something shoved at his chest. He didn't know what it was, but he figured it was the guy. Telekinetic, he decided, able to move things with his mind. Tucker wasn't impressed.

Snaking out a hand, he caught the man by his throat, using his still-gloved left hand. "I want to play, too. Let's start with twenty questions. Who is after the kid?"

Something gripped at his hand—it was like he could *feel* something trying to pry his fingers off. "Stop it," he warned.

"Fuck off or I'm gonna fuck you up," the man gasped out.

"Oh, really?" He laid his bare hand on the man's face and did a quick discharge.

A scream split the air, and when Tucker lifted his hand, there was a red imprint of his palm left on the man's face. "Electrical burns . . . such a bitch. You know, I think I'd do the most damage. Want to have a pissing contest or are you going to tell me what I want to know?"

"I don't know who is after him . . . but it's a lot of money." Eyes wide, the man stared up at him. "A shitload of it, and if we don't take him in, somebody else will."

"Oh, it won't be you." Tucker slammed everything he had into the man and watched as the life faded from his eyes.

Nobody who hunted kids deserved to live.

As he rose, he watched Vaughnne steady herself as she got back to her feet. "Please tell me you did not just do what I think you did."

"Hey, his heart gave out. That's all."

"*Damn* it."

"What was I supposed to do? Just let him walk?" Tucker shrugged as he tugged his glove back on. "You think you can arrest him and tell the judge . . . *Hey, Judge . . . he wrecked that car with the power of his mind. Yes, sir. He really and truly did.* And they'll believe you and lock him up until . . . oh, wait, it won't happen."

She glared at him.

He just shrugged and headed over to the car. He was five feet away when the driver door budged. He heard somebody grunting and then there was another smash as whoever it was kicked it again. Determined son of a bitch.

He surveyed the damage to the door and glanced over at Vaughnne. "That door isn't opening without some serious assistance."

She grimaced and went to one knee, peering down.

A gun was shoved in her face.

Tucker swore and went to kick it away, but she lifted a hand to stop him.

Sighing, he turned his back and stared off into the distance.

* * *

THE battered face staring in at him was the very last one he'd expected to see. For a minute, he thought perhaps he hadn't lived through the crash. But then Vaughnne stared at the gun he held for a long, long minute before shifting her dark eyes to his. "You know . . . I don't think I've ever had a man spend as much time threatening me as much as you do without me doing him serious bodily harm. I'm contemplating just how much I'm going to make you suffer for it once this is all said and done, Gus," she said, her voice tired, husky.

He just glared at her. Alex was behind him, his breath coming in harsh, panicky little stops and starts, and the one thing that Gus knew . . . they were trapped. They were completely trapped and he was out of options. The only chance he had was the woman in front of him.

And Vaughnne knew it.

"Don't you think it's about time you start trusting me?"

He gripped the Sig Sauer, staring into her eyes.

You must promise me . . .

That voice danced through his mind, teasing, taunting.

Promises.

Trust.

Behind him, Alex sobbed softly.

His gaze locked on Vaughnne's, he laid the gun down. Her hand caught his, and gently, she squeezed.

Gus closed his eyes.

FOURTEEN

"A simple babysitting job, you said."

She had to give him credit, SAC Taylor Jones had the grace to look the slightest bit shamefaced as he joined her at the door. A doctor had cajoled her into being treated, but not until somebody else had shown up to stand guard over the kid.

Somebody was Taige Morgan. She freelanced for the unit. Taige now spent more of her days playing mama to her own gifted child, but Vaughnne knew she could trust the woman to guard that kid while she was poked and prodded by the doctor.

Taige was currently sitting by the boy's bed, and although the doctors had told him to rest, she was holding his hand and going over some of the basics that Vaughnne had tried to explain to him. Taige would get further. She had a limited telepathic ability, not as strong as Vaughnne's, but her overall psychic skills were a lot stronger. If anybody could get that kid on the right path to shielding, it was Taige. She'd trained herself, and her abilities had come on her young as well.

"He needs to be resting," Vaughnne said tiredly. "Instead, he's being taught shielding."

"He needs to survive," Jones said bluntly. "So he's being given the tools he needs to do it." He looked over at her, and although his eyes were expressionless, she knew he wasn't the cold bastard he seemed to be. It was just better if he came off that way, she guessed. "If he keeps broadcasting the way you seem to think he is, he's a walking target. Best way for him to get any rest is for him to learn how to lock it down. Morgan can do this without scaring him or pushing him too far, and while she's at it, she can build some passive shields around him that will last for a little while, even when she's out of contact."

She nodded and glanced at her watch. Gus was out, getting his turn with the doctor. Now that he'd finally *taken* it. He'd been gone only twenty-eight minutes. If he made it thirty—

A shiver raced down her spine and she angled her head around, looking out the door to see him striding down the corridor toward her. Grim-eyed, stone-faced, and so damned beautiful. She suspected he'd given them hell every second he'd been gone—given them hell, or terrified them. *He* had made her look like a little pussycat when it came to stubbornness.

She shot a glance at his arm as he came through the door, and she studied what she could see under his sleeve. A few stitches were visible.

"Wow. You were generous," she drawled. "You gave them almost a half hour."

Gus flicked her a look. There was a bruise forming along his right cheekbone. It made him look even darker, more dangerous. Deadlier. Sexy as hell.

Shit. Everything the guy did was sexy as hell.

He looked away from her to stare daggers at Taige's skull, although Taige didn't spare him even a glance, focused intently on Alex.

She needed to let the kid get some rest. They were all damn tired.

By the time they'd gotten both Gus and Alex out of the car and the emergency medical personnel had gotten the two to the hospital, it had been nearly six. Then Jones had arrived on the scene, and Vaughnne hadn't been surprised when he'd decided to relocate the two to a different hospital—in Atlanta. A more secure one, a bigger one. More anonymous. By the time they'd been transferred to Atlanta, both Gus and Alex had been assigned new aliases.

How long they'd stick, Vaughnne didn't know. How long Gus would hang around, she didn't know.

But for now, the kid was getting something he desperately needed . . . some teaching. For now, he was safe, and he was getting some much-needed rest, too. Or he would, once he stopped talking to Taige.

Or rather, when Taige decided he'd had enough, Vaughnne amended a few minutes later.

"That's enough for now," Taige said quietly.

"But—"

"No." She shook her head and stood up. "You've had enough for the day and you're already making some progress. Get some rest and I'll do some more tomorrow, but for now, you need some sleep. You're not going to be able to do your best anyway if you're not resting."

"But—"

"Alex." Gus spoke from the shadows of the room, standing in the corner. All he said was his name, his voice soft, almost gentle, but that was all it took.

Alex closed his eyes and turned his head, muttering under his breath.

Taige grinned wryly and flashed Vaughnne a look. "Man, I wish I could command instant obedience like that from my kid," she said. She rose from the chair and came over to stand at the door. "I'll see if I can hunt down a chair and I'll be at the door . . . in case I'm needed."

She didn't say anything else as she passed between them.

But as she passed by Vaughnne, she slid her a narrow look. She hadn't even gone five feet when Vaughnne felt the press against her mind. She let the other woman in.

That kid has more fear in him than I've seen in a long, long while, Taige said, her mental voice as strong and steady as her normal one, and just as clear.

I know. I don't know what they are running from, but I'm going to find out.

There was a pause and then softly, Taige said, *It has something to do with his father. I caught that much. I can try to look deeper tomorrow, but he's got a lot of talent. No skill . . . yet, but a lot of talent, and he's been living on wit and instinct a long time. If I try too hard, he might pick up on it and that's going to make him shut down and it might freak him out. As strong as he is, I'd rather not have him freaked out. It could get ugly.*

Vaughnne kept her face blank, but she was hard-pressed not to snort as she recalled the headache from hell the boy had blessed her with. *Ugly. Yes, it could get really ugly. Do me a favor, if you can, because he won't quit doing it when he feels the need. He somehow uses his ability to read others and he comes down like a sledgehammer. Show him the right way.*

There was a soft sort of sound, almost like a sigh, and from the corner of her eye, Vaughnne saw Taige shake her head. *Reading people. He's too young to have to be using himself as a weapon, Vaughnne. You know that.*

Yeah. She did. *I think it's been the only way they could keep him alive. What were they supposed to do?*

Taige didn't answer, and after a few minutes of silence passed, Vaughnne figured they were done. For now. Focusing on the boy, she studied the slow, steady rise of his chest and realized he'd already gone to sleep. She looked over at Gus and then nodded to the other bed. "You should sleep," she said quietly. "You're both safe here."

His eyes glittered at her in the darkness, and although he had no ability at all, she felt like he could see clear down to her soul, see every last secret. "What were you talking about?"

She stared at him.

Tense, heavy silence stretched out between them, an icy shroud. Finally, she lifted a brow. "Excuse me?"

"With her. You were both talking, I know it."

"Oh? And since when were you any sort of psychic?" she asked lazily, leaning one shoulder against the door.

His eyes narrowed on her face.

Vaughnne sighed. "Don't worry about it, Gus. She's been going over shielding with Alex—was explaining what she worked with him on, how to help him more if I have to." She lied through her teeth and did without blinking.

Gus continued to stare at her, the disbelief on his face clear. "Remember what I told you, Vaughnne."

Next to her, Jones tensed.

She shot him a look and shook her head. "It's okay, Jones. He's just . . . jumpy."

She moved to the hard-ass chair just inside the door and settled down. Every muscle in her body screamed at her as she did it; maybe she should take one of the pain pills the doctors gave her. Once Taige got back. Or half a pill. She thought she could still stay awake on half a pain pill.

"I had them keep the room across the hall open for you," Jones said, dipping down to murmur in her ear. "Go lie down for an hour."

"I'm fine."

"You're not. Consider it an order, Agent."

She turned her head and glared at him. "I said I'm fine."

He slid out of his jacket, revealing the side holster and the weapon he hadn't bothered to remove earlier. As he hung the jacket on the back of the door, he glanced over at her. "If you're so fine, then you can do it just to humor me."

* * *

Gus hated hospitals.

He'd avoided them as much as he could, for as long as he could. Even now, as he stood there in the dark, watching as Alex slept, he was plotting out the escape routes. Just in case.

He'd told Vaughnne he'd trust her, and he was trying to do just that.

But there were too many unknowns here. Far too many.

He hurt.

He had bruised ribs, lacerations on his face and hands; the worst one had fifteen stitches, but that wasn't even the big concern. His left knee was jammed and that was a problem. He needed rest almost more than he needed to breathe, but he couldn't afford to take it. He was going to make do with the anti-inflammatories and ice for his knee. He'd dealt with worse—far worse.

"If you fall down, you're not going to do him any good."

Flicking a look at the blond man by the door, Gus went back to ignoring him. While he hadn't made Vaughnne for a cop, he'd made this one the minute he'd seen him. Well, not a cop. FBI. Federal agent . . . much worse than a cop. A federal agent who had an interest in psychics. That made him a threat in Gus's mind, and he couldn't relax around a threat.

"Do you trust Vaughnne?"

Gus closed his eyes. "I trust nobody."

A soft sigh drifted through the room. "It won't be long before you have to trust somebody, son. Whether it's me or Vaughnne, you need to pick your poison. The boy is in more trouble than you can possibly understand."

A harsh laugh burst from him before he could stop it, echoing through the room. "Oh, I *know* the danger, *son*," he bit off, shoving up from the chair. "It is this danger that has us running all these years. I *know* the danger."

"Do you?"

Turning his back, he stared out the window. The parking lot was quiet, thank God, and he could see the highway—easy access if they had to steal a car. The first thing he'd made note of.

A bright glow lit the room and he turned back around.

The agent, Jones—Vaughnne had called him Jones—sat in his chair, holding out an iPad. "Vaughnne brought this to my attention earlier. I realize you are running from *somebody*, Gus . . . I hope you don't mind me calling you Gus. You haven't given any other name." Jones paused.

Gus just stared at him for a long moment before looking down at the iPad's screen.

Jones shrugged and held the tablet out. "One of my freelancers apparently shared this information with . . . an acquaintance. The information was then given to Vaughnne, who shared it with me. You should read it."

Gus closed the distance and took the tablet, even as a weight settled heavy and cold in his gut. His heart jumped into a fast, hard gallop, and his throat went tight. His palms felt damp as he started to read. Automatically, his brain broke down the code in the heading.

The Psychic Portal—

He set his jaw and fought the urge to hurl the iPad across the room.

"The website's banner is encoded. I'm having somebody on my team break it down—"

Cutting Jones off, Gus shook his head. "It reads *The Psychic Portal*," he said gruffly, glancing up at him.

Jones's brows arched over his eyes. "You can tell that with a glance."

Gus shrugged and continued to read. It was the modern version of *Abandon all hope, ye who enter here* . . . with a quick welcome to those who might actually *fit* in.

"This website . . . it's for . . ."

"Psychics," Jones said, inclining his head. "Assuming it's legit. As I was saying, my team is looking into it. But there's enough—well, troublesome material there to make me think it *is* legit."

Gus continued to skim through it. It wasn't until he reached the bottom of the page that anything really jumped out at him.

And then, it was like the very earth had crumpled under his feet.

Orlando.

The iPad hit the ground with a clatter and blood started to roar in his ears. Run. They had to run—

His brain zeroed down to that goal, and for a few seconds, nothing else existed. Nothing but the plan. Nothing but the goal. Nothing but Alex and making him safe.

Get Alex up.

Get Alex out of here.

Get Alex away.

A voice, annoying like a gnat buzzing in his ear, caught his attention after a few seconds, but he brushed it aside as he grabbed his bag and started for the bed. A car. Plenty of them in the parking lot. Run. *Hurry, hurry, hurry—*

"Gus?"

"Ah, Jones, I wouldn't get too close if I were you . . ."

The voices were a rush in his head and the only thing he could think was . . . *run.* They had to *run.*

Somebody moved in—he saw the man from the corner of his eye.

He swung out. The man was fast, very fast, and evaded. He didn't manage to evade the second move, though, and as Jones crumpled over, gasping for air, Gus brought up his fist, ready to slam it down on the back of the man's vulnerable head.

Before he could, something grabbed his throat. "Come on," a soft voice said. "Don't make me get rough."

He clawed at his neck, but there was nothing there. Just his own skin. Except something was *holding* him—tighter and tighter, too. Eyes wide, he looked around, but Gus didn't . . . there. It was *her*. Taige.

Gray eyes stared into his, and she had a look on her face that was . . . almost sad. "It's okay," she said quietly. "We can help with him, but you have to stop panicking every time somebody tries to help."

He tried to suck in a breath, tried. Failed. Darkness edged in around him and he swung out again, his aim so far off, he didn't even come within a foot of her. The darkness crept in closer . . . closer . . .

And in the back of his mind, a voice murmured . . . *You must promise me . . .*

Just before he slipped under, he heard Vaughnne's voice, *Don't you think it's about time you start trusting me?*

FIFTEEN

"**D**ID you have to choke him?"

Over the bed, Vaughnne glared at Taige.

Taige shrugged easily. "Hey, I was just trying to avoid (a) getting hit, and (b) having him take that kid out of here. You and I both know that's not going to end well if he does that. Besides . . . it got him to rest, right?"

Dropping down on the chair, Vaughnne stared at Gus's battered face. Now he had a ring of bruises around his neck. Lovely. "Yeah, you got him to rest, all right. But how long has he been out?"

"Happened right after you went down." Taige shrugged. "It's been about two hours. And it's *not* because of what I did. His body needs rest and once he went down? Mother Nature took over and forced him to take what he needs. Relax . . . he's fine. I hear his thoughts if I try and they are just . . . well, not fine, but I didn't do him any damage. The guy is almost as scared as the kid is, but he's fine. He's determined. He's a wily bastard, that one.

But he's exhausted." She covered her mouth as she yawned. "So am I."

Vaughnne curled her lip. "Yeah, that trip up from Gulf Shores was just exhausting, wasn't it?"

"Actually, it was the sex last night, but hey." Taige just shrugged and smiled.

Vaughnne cringed. "There's a kid sleeping behind you. Is that necessary?"

With a grin, Taige retreated to her chair just outside the door. "I'm going to crash for a few, since you're up and moving. Don't know how long Jones plans on needing me, but I need a few minutes' downtime."

Sighing, Vaughnne stretched out her legs and focused on the two males in the room. Both of them slept, but neither did so easily. Alex's rest was fitful and he tossed and turned, occasionally muttering in his sleep or crying out. Although Gus was still and silent, even in sleep, he looked ready to battle. His hands were clenched, the muscles in his arms bunched, like he was ready to lunge into action at any moment. Ready to fight. Ready to protect.

Without thinking, she reached up and stroked a hand down his arm, thinking only to soothe him.

And what a mistake that was—

A split second later, her wrist was trapped and she had to bite back a gasp as he twisted it and jerked her forward. Caught off guard *again*, she landed against his chest and glared down at him.

His eyes were foggy but clearing every second as he glared up at her.

Taut silence hung between them.

She licked her lips.

His gaze dropped to her mouth and a hunger like nothing she'd ever felt exploded through her. If it hadn't been for the boy in the bed just a few feet away, Vaughnne suspected she would have stripped off every damn piece of clothing she wore and rubbed herself against him like a cat. She might have begged him, might have pleaded . . . just one night. That was all she wanted.

Well, no. She wanted everything, but one night would suffice.

She sucked in a breath, and just like that, the moment shattered.

He let go and she shoved away from him, pushing her hair back from her face and clambering out of the chair as he sat up, looking around. His gaze lit on the boy in the bed, and she said softly, "He's fine. He's sleeping."

"We need to go." The underlying urgency in his voice cut into her heart and she reached out, despite how stupid that had been a minute ago.

But this time, as her hand caught his arm, all he did was freeze.

"Go where?" she asked quietly. "You know what's after him now, right? I know Jones showed you."

"That's *why* we have to go."

"And how are you going to hide him from all that can come from that? Can you protect him from an army?"

Gus's hand shot out, fisting in the front of her shirt. He tugged her closer and lowered his head, pressing his brow to hers. Hell warred in his eyes as he stared at her. "Can *you*?"

"By myself?" She laid a hand on his cheek. "Hell, no. But I'm not *alone. You* are."

* * *

ALONE . . .

Yes.

That was something that Gus was painfully aware of.

He'd spent so many months alone. So many years.

Most of his life, really. Ever since he'd left the family, staying far away from them once he'd somehow landed in a life that he'd never planned. Never *wanted* for himself, but it had found him anyway. He'd joined the military—there had been no choice. He was on a road to trouble, going nowhere fast, and it was either join the armed forces or find his ass in jail. He'd chosen the military. It might have been better if he'd gone the other way, though, because somehow, he caught the eyes of the man who'd put him on this road.

Almost from the beginning, they'd been watching him and the persona he'd worn—the playboy, the brawler, the man who'd played at modeling, fucking, and fighting. It had been planned almost from the time he'd agreed to *talk* to the men who'd shown up on the base.

Within a few months, he'd known it was probably a bad choice, but there was no turning back then. Not if he wanted to protect his family.

He'd sent back money, had thought it would be enough to take care of them. To make sure his mother and Consuelo were cared for.

This life, it was like he'd been made for it.

Quick to learn, fast on his feet, good with his fists, good at . . . other things.

He'd settled into that life, but it was a dangerous one, and the only way to protect his family was to make like he had none.

Then he'd gotten that simple call.

I need you . . .

Consuelo's voice, a voice he hadn't heard in years. He hadn't even recognized her at first. He hadn't gone home, not when their mother had died, although he would have, if possible. For that, he would have returned home. But he'd been busy recovering from an altercation that had damn near killed him. By the time he'd emerged from surgery, their mother had already been dead, and by the time they had told him about her passing, she had already been buried.

He'd almost walked away from the life then. Almost.

But he'd been told, more than once, *It will follow you. It will take everything and everyone you love. Why risk them?*

Them? There is no them . . . there is just my sister.

Except his sister had been pregnant.

A new life, a new innocent he had to worry about protecting. That had been more than a decade ago. So he'd stayed away . . . again.

But then she'd called him.

How could he stay away when his baby sister had called him? Had needed him?

Please come home, Gustavo. . . I need you. Please. There . . . I can't tell anybody else. Nobody else will protect him.

That was all she had said.

Then she'd hung up and she wouldn't answer his calls, wouldn't answer his e-mails.

Her husband, a bastard if ever there was one, was a man that Gus should have killed the second he had figured out just *who* his sister had married. He was a drug dealer, but there were worse crimes in Gus's mind. Still were. But Gus hadn't thought the bastard was going to go that low.

He had been wrong.

And now, every day, he had to live with that knowledge. Every day, he had to live with what his hesitation had cost him. He hadn't wanted his sister to look at him, or think of him, and wonder.

Now she wouldn't because she was gone.

And her evil, twisted husband lived.

While Gus and Alex fled for their lives.

If it had *just* been Gus involved, he would have gone for the bastard and not blinked twice. It would have been a risk, and the risk was one he would have taken happily. All men died, after all.

He doubted he'd live a long life. But it wasn't a risk he'd take without knowing Alex would be safe.

Alone . . .

Hell, yes. He was alone.

Glaring down at Vaughnne, he opened his mouth to tell her . . . something. Anything. He needed her out of his way. Preferably someplace *far* away from him, because if she was *far* away from him, then he wouldn't be tempted to do just what she seemed to think he *should* do. Trust her.

She reached up and closed her hand around his wrist. "If you don't stop running now . . . you never will," she said quietly. "Surely, somewhere in that beautiful, thick-as-stone head of yours, you have to realize that, right? Either you take a stand or spend the rest of your life running. The rest of *his* life running. And it's likely to be a short one, because those people will *not* quit hunting you. And we can't keep chasing after you to protect that kid when you make it clear you don't want our help."

"Why?"

She blinked, her lashes sweeping down to hide her dark eyes. The scattering of freckles across her cheeks caught his gaze, and before he could stop himself, he lifted a hand, cupped her chin. Stroking one thumb across the silk of her skin, he waited.

"Why what?" she asked, tugging away and backing out of his reach.

"Why do you want to help at *all*?" He shook his head and gestured to Alex. "You don't know us. We're not even here *legally*."

She smirked and rolled her eyes. Then she turned her back and crossed over to the chair opposite the bed. "I'm so shocked by that, I think I just might faint, Gus. I really might." She dropped down in the chair, wincing a little as she stretched out. "I mean, never mind the fact that you've pulled a gun—probably an *illegal* one—on me more than once. Never mind that you've drugged me. Threatened me. But you're here *illegally*. That's just over the line there."

He glared at her and tried to ignore the nasty crawl of shame rising up the back of his throat. How many times had he threatened her? More than once. More than a half dozen, easily. And yet she sat there, watching him with a level, steady gaze, and no anger in her lovely, dark eyes.

"You want to know why?" she asked softly.

"If I didn't, I would not have *asked*," he pointed out.

"Okay." She nodded slowly and then shifted around and reached into her pocket. He watched, more than a little curious, as she opened what looked like a wallet. No purse for Vaughnne, it seemed. She tugged something out, and although he couldn't see it well, it looked to be a picture.

* * *

"WHEN I was fifteen, my father threw me out on the streets and my mom just stood by and watched," Vaughnne said softly, stroking a finger down the ragged edge of the picture. It was one Jones had managed to get for her. She had a bunch of them, thanks to her boss, but this was her favorite. She needed to make some copies of it, but she just hadn't gotten around to it. The picture had been taken at Christmas, right before all the . . . voices . . . had started. It was her with Daylin. Her little sister. The girl she'd tried so hard to save months ago. And when she couldn't save her, she'd settled for avenging her.

Feeling the weight of Gus's gaze, she looked up. "My dad didn't believe in psychic ability, you know." She shrugged and said, "Kind of crazy, because I got it from him. I always felt that . . . buzz around him. Nobody else in the house. And I'd *talk* to him more. Bad call there, because it made him think he was going crazy. Once he figured out it was me, he threw me out. I never saw him again, never saw my mom . . . or my little sister."

She looked back down at Daylin's picture. "I used to check up on my sister, though. She joined Facebook, and although I didn't friend her or anything, I'd . . . well. Watch her. Peek in on my dad's profile even, because he'd post things about her grades and some pictures and stuff. I could see her face every now and then, and it was better than nothing. She didn't lock her profile, either. I hated that, because that's so stupid, so unsafe, but at the same time . . .?" She sighed. "It was the one connection I had with her. I could see what was going on in her life. I used to think about how I'd wait until she was eighteen then I wouldn't have to worry about my dad. I could look her up and see if she wanted to have anything to do with me."

The grief rose up, threatened to slam her to the floor, but she fought it back. Now was so not the time. Sucking in a breath, she waited until the pain ebbed before she went on. "Then, last year . . . she disappeared. My father tells the cops she was kidnapped, but I think she was out flirting with the wrong guy, maybe went to meet him—it fits with some of the stuff I saw on her page when I was digging around. She'd been talking about this one guy. Had plans to meet somebody she'd met on-line . . . so, so stupid. I think she met him and he grabbed her. It wasn't reported for a few days . . ." She rubbed a finger down the edge of the picture again, barely even aware she was doing it. "I didn't know anything about it—was on a case—and then I got home and see he'd logged into her Facebook and put up an alert. That's how I find out my baby sister is missing. An alert on Facebook. He doesn't *call* me, even though I found out he knew damn well how to find me, knew what I did. I'd been hurt once, and Jones . . . well, he called them, thought they might want to know. My dad denied even knowing me. But he knew where to find me. Jones had left the contact info and everything. He didn't even bother trying to get in touch with me. I'm a federal agent and he doesn't bother to reach out to me when my kid sister is taken."

Hearing the soft tread of Gus's footsteps, she looked up just as he knelt down in front of her.

He took the picture from her unresisting hands, and she stared at his face as he studied the image.

"She was seventeen," she said quietly. "Seventeen years old. Smart as a whip. Wanted to be a doctor. And some scumbag son of a bitch kidnapped her. They wanted to sell her."

"Sell . . ."

"Yeah. They talk about slavery like it's a thing of the past, but it's not. A few months ago, we busted open a small ring. It was the monster who organized my sister's grab. But it wasn't in time to save her. They killed her because they couldn't break her. And the only thing *I* could do was help stop the people who hurt her."

Gus looked up at her.

"You want to know why I'm willing to help that kid?" she asked, glancing over at Alex asleep in the bed. He was so still, so quiet. So vulnerable. "It's because for every monster I help take out of this world, it's one sister, one brother, one more set of parents we don't have to worry about going through what I'm dealing with. And trust me . . . *nobody* should have to live with this, Gus. *Nobody.*"

He sighed, and reached over, laid the picture facedown on the table beside the chair. "I don't doubt your determination, Vaughnne. Or your willingness. But you don't even know what we're running from."

"Other than a whole mess of psychics?" she said, taking her picture and tucking it away. "Well, you're out of Mexico, and I can only imagine the fun there. Drugs and slavery are just the top of the barrel, am I right?" Leaning forward, she caught his gaze. "And I'm going to make a few guesses with you . . . either you're military or mercenary. You don't learn to move like you do just from a few years of running. You don't get the drop on an FBI agent just because you've had a couple of bad run-ins with the law. If you weren't able to handle the problem on your own with whatever your background is? Then it's bad, I get that."

Something moved in the back of his eyes, and if she had any sense at all, she should have backed off.

But sense had never been her strong suit.

"It doesn't matter which one it is," she said, shrugging. "You made it clear more than once that you can and will kill to protect him. I should make it clear—I'm willing to do the same."

"You're bound by the laws of your government," he said gently. "By your job."

A faint smile curled her lips. "If people are hunting an innocent boy, I'm doing my job . . . protecting him. And I could do it *better* if you would just tell me who is after him. If we can stop *him*, we can make this a whole lot easier on all of us."

A muscle pulsed in his jaw.

"You already pointed out he now has a whole mess of psychics after him. What makes you think that's going to end anytime soon?"

"Well . . . we're working on that," she said quietly. "All we have to do is deal with that website . . . or at least that listing. It goes away if people realize they won't get paid. At least, he'll be safer from *that* threat. But he isn't safe until we deal with the original threat."

Silence fell, interrupted only by the soft sound of Alex's breathing, and the occasional murmur from out in the hall. Gus stared at her, his gaze watchful and sober. As the seconds ticked by, tension wrapped around them, and when he finally spoke, his words shattered the tension like a hammer against glass. "How can you stop somebody who is feared . . . *worshipped* . . . by millions?"

Vaughnne's heart slammed into her chest. "Millions?"

Gus reached up and caught one of her curls, wrapping it around one finger. In a soft, casual tone, he said, "When my sister was twenty, she met a very rich man. He swept her off her feet. Wined her, dined her. Made her feel like a princess, and within a few months, they were married. She was . . . naïve. She was from a small village and she was one of those people who saw the best in others. Maybe that was why she didn't see the evil in him until it was too late. It wasn't until a few years later that she realized she'd married a man that much of Mexico feared. Those who didn't *fear* him worshipped him. His name was Ignacio Reyes—"

Vaughnne hissed out a breath.

Gus's smile did not reach his eyes. "I take it you've heard of him."

"Ah, yeah. Yeah, I've heard of him." Rich bastard. Drug dealer. Plenty of her counterparts on the more normal side of the FBI had an interest in him. And if he was tied into anything having to do with this kid, Jones was going to take a very avid interest in him. Reyes wouldn't like Jones taking an interest in him.

Come to think of it, she didn't really like the idea of Jones taking an interest in that guy. People who got interested in Reyes disappeared.

But her job didn't change, no matter who the target was.

"That's Alex's father," she said softly.

"Yes. That's his father." Gus continued to stroke her hair, but his hand had moved lower now and the back of his knuckles brushed up against the upper slope of her breast. It could have been an innocent touch. Could have been . . . but it wasn't. Somehow she suspected nothing this man did was innocent. "When Alex was five years old, he guessed the winner of the Kentucky Derby, then the Belmont, the Preakness. A few months later, he guessed the winner of the Indy 500 and then he told his father that there was going to be a bad wildfire and he thought one of his father's men was going to die. It all came to pass. After that, his father started having him sit in on business meetings . . . at first, it seemed Reyes just thought he was a lucky boy and Alex loved the attention. Loved the toys and presents he would get when he made a *good* guess. But then they had a man come to one of their *parties* who had heard about Alex's *luck*." Gus curled his lip. "Alex tells me the man had planned to kidnap him if he guessed right—so he guessed wrong. And the man . . . Alex still has nightmares about the images he saw in the man's head. When Alex told his father the wrong information, on purpose, his father beat him. He couldn't walk for a week."

Vaughnne closed her eyes.

"After that, Alex was unable to see anything for almost six months, and each time he failed, he was beaten . . . again. And when his mother tried to stop it, she was beaten. It all changed when she threatened to kill both herself and the boy. Reyes laughed," Gus said, his voice still so soft and gentle. "He just laughed at her, and backhanded her. I learned of this years after, when I could do nothing to make it better, that she lay there, bleeding, and he pulled out a gun. And that was when Alex had another vision. He told his father that men were going to come, in three days, a raid. Alex gave him names that he couldn't possibly know, told him information that no boy of eight could under-stand. His father stared at him, and that was when he started to realize it was more than just luck. Reyes had always had an inter-est in the . . . unusual, it seems. All this time, his boy had been seeing things. It wasn't just luck, wasn't just perception. He had a walking gold mine . . . and the boy had just saved his ass."

Gus let go of her hair and lowered his hand to curve it over her rib cage. "Three months passed. They'd evaded the raid—moving all of the drugs—and my sister thinks Reyes used the names Alex gave him to kill those who turned on him. He used their son . . . to kill. And she knew he'd do it again. That was when she knew it had to stop. She tried to take Alex and run. He beat her."

"Why didn't she just call you?" Vaughnne demanded.

"That was why she ran," Gus said. "She ran only to the next town. She knew she'd never get far enough away. So she ran to someplace where she could make one phone call that wouldn't be traced."

"She had to know how he'd react." Vaughnne stared at him.

"Of course she knew," Gus said, his voice gentle, but his eyes were pure hell. "Killing her would never be a problem for Reyes. He cared nothing for her. She was a pretty toy for him. But Alex . . . he's everything." He eased in closer, dipped his head, and pressed his lips to her ear. "He cares nothing for how many die. He cares nothing for who he hurts. He will stop at nothing. Half the government *fears* him. The others? They either want to fuck him or befriend him. Very few will stand against him. How do you think your FBI will stop him?"

Then he pressed his lips to her neck. "As much as I'd like to think you can help me protect the boy from his father, it cannot be done. We have to run."

He pulled back, and the second he wasn't pressed to her, she felt cold. It wasn't just from the temperature in the room, though. It went so much deeper than that.

He paused by the bed, staring down at the sleeping boy.

"There's another option," she said, barely aware of what she was going to say.

Gus looked up at her. "As long as Reyes lives, there is no other option for us. We run."

What are you doing? She stared at him, hardly able to believe she was saying this. If she took this step, she might as well be swimming into shark-infested waters while bleeding. It was so damned dangerous, it wasn't even funny. She might not make it out, and if she *did*, she could end up living out the rest of her life in jail.

"There is always another option," she said, forcing the words out through a throat gone tight with nerves.

"I'm done discussing this." He turned away. "We run."

"Which were you, military or mercenary?" she asked. If she was serious about this, she needed to know what she was dealing with—*whom* she was dealing with, although whether or not he'd answer, she didn't know. Still, it mattered. Military, mercenary, each one came with certain benefits, but one would have better contacts than the other.

He glanced back at her, one brow lifted. Then he surprised her with something she'd never expected. An actual answer. He shrugged. "If you really want to know . . . my government trained me to be an assassin. But they'd never recognize me if I was caught or captured. I'd be on my own."

Okay. Not what she'd imagined. But . . . that was even better.

"Being an assassin, you'd think you'd have already figured out that third option. You take Reyes out. Once he's gone, your nephew should be safe."

A soft sigh escaped him and he turned back to face her. "Do you think I haven't thought of that? A hundred times? A thousand? But I haven't the resources to pay somebody to do it—I have to use everything I have to make sure *he* is taken care of. Taking Reyes out is a job that would require a substantial amount of money. I can't call in a favor for this—nobody is going to take that man out over a *favor*, and even if somebody owed me such a debt, I used up any favors I had coming my way just to get out of Mexico. *I* can't do it because I have to stay with Alex and keep him safe. I'm all he has, and if I go after his father alone, it's entirely likely I'll end up dead. Somebody has to care for him."

"I'll go with you."

He gave her a scathing once-over. "An FBI agent isn't precisely the sort of person I'd need at my back."

"Could you do it alone?"

"If I had to, and if I wasn't worried about coming back? *Yes.*" He bit the word off as if it had a bitter, ugly taste. "And if it wasn't for the boy, I'd do it in a heartbeat. But I have to take care of him."

"Let Jones take him."

Gus stilled.

Then he shook his head. "No."

"Hear me out." She held up a hand. "If Jones takes him, he's protected. Better than you can imagine. Take me with you. Maybe I'm just an FBI agent and that's not much in your eyes, but I'm a little more equipped than the typical agent and I've got . . . well, abilities that others wouldn't have. Trust me, I'm useful. One person at your back is better than nobody."

He shook his head.

"Why not? You won't be alone, and you'd have somebody protecting that boy. Reyes wouldn't stand a chance at getting to him once he's under Jones's care."

His eyes narrowed and he took one step toward her. "We're done discussing this, Vaughnne," he said softly.

She folded her arms over her chest, resisting the urge to flinch away from the look that had crossed his face. For a split second, she'd been scared. Absolutely terrified of the man in front of her.

"Nobody, and I mean, *nobody* in the damn country can keep him as safe as Jones can, next to you," she said, closing the distance between them. "He can put the kid up at HQ, surrounded by a shitload of psychics who would feel any threat coming before it even breached the horizon. You want him safe? Surround him with the kind of people who are hunting him—there are psychics who can passively shield him and *keep* anybody from even sensing him. He'd be *safe* there and he could get *trained*. So he's not making himself a walking target. Until you *do* that? Even if you take Reyes out, he's still not safe. Somebody else will figure out what he is and try to grab him, or he'll hurt somebody. He's a danger until he gets that gift under control."

"No," Gus said again, shaking his head.

He turned back to the bed.

And then, Alex startled them both by turning his head and looking up at them.

He'd been awake, Vaughnne realized. The entire time.

Guilt grabbed her by the throat, but as she watched the boy, she realized she hadn't said anything Alex didn't already know.

He was staring at his uncle with dark, unhappy eyes.

"Do it, *Tío*," he said softly as he sat up and faced his uncle.

"We're not discussing this, *m'hijo*," Gus said, his voice flat and cold.

"I'm tired of being afraid." Alex drew his knees to his chest and gazed at Gus, his face miserable.

"Let's go."

Alex hugged his knees to his chest, staring up at his uncle with defiance written all over his face. "I'm tired of running."

Gus went to pull the sheets back.

And Vaughnne felt it coming—it was too late to react, though. Far too late.

Alex had already reached, slamming into Gus with that massive, untrained power of his. Gus made a sharp, startled sound, and before she could reach him, he hit the ground.

SIXTEEN

"You want me to do what?" Jones said again, his voice patient and level.

"Take the kid." Vaughnne eyed Alex and hoped that the boy knew what he was doing, because if he didn't, she just might be dead in a few hours. Gus hadn't been issuing empty threats. She already knew that. "He needs to be someplace safe, he needs to be trained, and he can't get any of that if he's constantly being dragged around the country."

"You want me to take a boy away from his legal guardian," Jones said slowly. "That's kidnapping, Vaughnne. Never mind that it can cost me my job and what it will do to the unit. It can get me arrested. It can land me in jail."

"He's not my legal guardian," Alex said quietly. "I don't think. I think my guardian would be my father."

Jones spun away, scrubbing his hands over his face. "And where is your father?"

Vaughnne lifted a hand, silencing Alex. With a sweet smile,

she met Jones's look directly and answered, "His father is a drug dealer in Mexico. A pretty infamous one. The kid is in danger from him. These are extenuating circumstances if ever they existed. Gus kidnapped him to keep him safe, but the kid's gift is raging out of control and Gus isn't going to let him get trained . . . what do you want him to do? Hurt somebody by accident before we step in and help?"

Jones turned away and stared out the window. He was so quiet, standing there calm as could be like he was riveted by the scenery. Of course, there wasn't much to admire. A busy parking lot. Atlanta traffic. Nothing fun. He stood there, hands in his pockets, shoulders straight, gaze locked on something only he could see.

"Alex, you know for certain your father is involved in the drug trade?"

Alex shot her a glance.

With a tired sigh, Vaughnne met his eyes. "Tell him the truth, Alex. We've already come this far."

"Yes, sir," Alex said, his voice soft but steady.

Jones looked back, eyed Gus's still form. He hadn't stirred once in the past thirty minutes. Alex said he hadn't ever hit anybody as hard as he'd hit his uncle, but he had to go at him hard—
he's harder to read than most.

Some people were just more immune to psychic abilities. Harder to read, harder to touch. Vaughnne had to work harder to whisper into his mind, so it wasn't a surprise that it took more to affect Gus. It was probably that thick-as-stone skull of his.

Alex shot her a look. "He's okay," the boy said, his voice nervous. "I wouldn't have hurt him. Really."

"I know." Vaughnne smiled at him.

Taige had done a mental probe a few minutes ago—the man was out, but fine. Still, Vaughnne didn't like the pale, grayish look to his skin. This whole thing was messed *up.*

"Are you going to help or not?" she asked quietly, looking at her boss.

"Help," Jones muttered, shaking his head. He slid a look her way. "And what are *you* going to do?"

She gave him a look of wide-eyed innocence. "I'm just going to stay here and try to talk some sense into him, of course." Make sure he didn't tear off after his nephew. "Ah . . . although I'm thinking it would be best if you didn't head straight to D.C."

Jones snorted. "Yeah, that's assuming I'm crazy enough to do this." He paused. "I can't believe I'm even considering it."

"You have a better idea on how to keep this kid safe?" She stared at him. "If you do, I'm all ears."

She heard something crack and looked down, saw that Jones had one hand clenched into a fist—a tight one. His knuckles were bloodless. "You already know I don't. I've got a source who is working on the website. She tells me that she's working on disabling the link. Once that's done, he'll be safer, but it's going to take her some time, I'm afraid."

The link—yeah, that little *I'll pay you to kidnap a boy* ad. The website. Good. If they got that down, things were already improved. But not enough.

Nothing would be enough, not until Ignacio Reyes was dead. But she couldn't exactly tell her boss that she was planning on helping an assassin go all assassin on somebody, right?

Shrewd, steel blue eyes narrowed on her face. She kept her expression bland, although she wasn't expecting that to get her very far. Jones might not have shown any of the traits in the psychic testing he'd developed, but the man could read people the way others read a book. Absently, he ran a hand down his tie and then shook his head. "You're not telling me everything."

"I'm telling you what you need to know." She shrugged. "I'm telling you what's the most important information . . . for *you*. And if you're going to do something to protect the boy, the time to do it is *now*. You won't have another chance like this. Gus is down, he's out, and he's going to move slower for a little while."

A heavy, taut silence hung between them, and although she said nothing else, she knew damn well Jones was picking up on all the things she *wasn't* saying. Even some of the shit she'd rather him not be aware of.

But then, slowly, he nodded and looked over at Alex. "Son, you realize what we're talking about, don't you? If I do this, I'm taking you away from somebody who may or may not have a legal right to take care of you . . . but I have none." He slid Vaughnne a dark look. She didn't read minds, but she didn't have to read anything to know what that look meant. *I'm out of my mind to do this.* "Do you believe you're in that much danger that I should do this?"

Alex stared at his knees, his thin shoulders trembling, shaking. "I don't sleep, sir. Not much. I'm always afraid they will come. That they'll someday kill my uncle and there will be nobody to stop them from taking me back."

"Back to where?" Jones asked.

Alex shot him a look and then he shifted his eyes to Vaughnne. *Tell him*, she thought, hoping the boy's gift was as strong as she thought it was. *Tell him what you can . . . make him understand.*

The boy seemed to wilt. His eyes closed and he dropped his face to his up-drawn knees. "Back to my father," Alex said. "He'll make me do it again. Use . . ." He waved a hand in front of his face. "This. He did it before and killed people."

Now he looked up at Taylor and Vaughnne, and it was hell written in his eyes. "Please. I can't go back, but if we keep running, they'll catch us. My uncle is going to die. Others will. If we keep going . . . it just won't stop. And it's getting harder for me to keep it in control on my own. All the noises. Everything in my head." A sigh shuddered out of him and he whispered, "It's just getting worse and I can't do this much longer."

A shiver raced down her spine, but she fought to keep her face blank. Just how much of that was fear, she wondered. How much of it was something more?

My uncle is going to die . . .

"You're afraid your uncle is going to die?" Jones asked quietly.

"No." Tears welled in the kid's eyes, and when they started to roll down his cheeks, it was as though he didn't even notice. "I feel it . . . see it. Something. It's in my head. We're running. They catch us . . . and he's just gone, and then they have me. I can't go back there and do what they want me to do. I can't lose Gus. I—"

"Okay." Jones lifted a hand and turned away. "I understand, Alex. We'll get you away. Until Vaughnne can . . . talk sense into your uncle." The irony in his voice was heavy, and she just stared at him as he watched her for a long moment.

He passed by her as he headed toward the door. "I'm going to get him out of here. Stay with him. I won't be long." He went to head off and then stopped, looked back at her. "Watch the lines you cross, Vaughnne. I understand the desire, but I can't help if you go too far."

Looking out the window, she said, "Not sure what you're talking about, boss. I'm just here to help with the kid."

He wasn't fooled.

But then again, she'd never expected to fool him for very long.

* * *

THE second he opened his eyes, Gus knew there was a problem.

It wasn't just because Vaughnne was sitting on the bed where Alex *should* have been, either.

It wasn't just the look in her eyes, either.

It was the tension in the air.

It was the fact that the door was closed.

And there was also the fact that she had a gun in her lap. He'd been forced to turn over his Sig Sauer when they were checked into the hospital. He could have managed to get it inside, except Vaughnne had been pretty clear that if he didn't turn over the weapon, she'd make things unpleasant. He could have handled that and might have been willing to deal with it, but his concern for Alex—and maybe a flicker of trust in her—had him giving in.

A trust that was obviously misplaced.

Vaughnne wasn't going to have those pesky little problems. She could keep her weapons with her, he supposed, thanks to those FBI credentials, the ID hanging around her neck. She had her hand resting on the butt of the Glock, and he knew without a doubt she'd be very comfortable using that weapon. Some people weren't comfortable with firearms. Others were. She held it like it was an extension of herself.

Her mouth was a firm, flat line, and the warm, smooth brown of her skin looked just a little paler than it should. Her freckles seemed darker in contrast. He wanted to haul her against him, kiss her, strip her naked, and take her. Then he wanted to shake her.

He wasn't going to have a chance to do either because he suspected he was going to wring her damn neck in a moment.

Slowly, he sat up.

She just continued to watch him.

"Please tell me they took Alex for tests," he said quietly.

"I could do that." She shrugged. "I'd be lying."

The muscles in his body immediately tensed, and he made himself relax. "I told you what I was going to do if you fucked me over."

"I haven't," she replied. "I told you I'd help you take care of him, and that's exactly what I did. I got him to the safest place I could possibly think of . . . so you can do the one thing that's going to make sure he *stays* safe."

Rising from the bed, he paced over to her.

She remained where she was, although her hand curved around the weapon's grip. Her pulse slammed away in her throat, and her eyes watched him with a world of caution. "*I* keep him safe," he said softly. "Call your boss and bring him back."

"No."

Shooting out his hands, he grabbed her arms and jerked her upright. Nose to nose, he leaned in, staring into her eyes. The scent of her went straight to his head, straight to his dick. Why had she done this? The last thing he could do now . . . actually, the last thing he should have done *ever* was trust her, want her . . . and yet that was what he wanted to do. But she'd let them take Alex.

"Call him," he said again. "Or you're not going to like what I do when you refuse this time."

She reached up and laid a hand on his throat. "Well, here's the problem. If you *hurt* me, I can tell you this, right now, Jones is never going to turn that kid back over to you. It's just not going to happen." Her thumb stroked over his skin and that light touch seemed to echo through every damn inch of him. "Of course, I realize that isn't necessarily going to stop you. I remember what you said you'd do and I'm prepared—"

"Prepared." He cut her off. Fury and lust tangled inside him and he lowered her back to the floor. Eyeing the door, he crossed over to it and grabbed the chair, wedging it under the handle to keep it shut. It wouldn't last for long, but he wouldn't need long to make his point, he figured. Turning back around, he stared at Vaughnne. "You have about thirty seconds to use that gun or you'll regret it."

A slim black brow arched.

Then, she laid the gun on the table by the bed. "I'm not using it on you. I'm not calling Jones. You do what you think you have to, Gus, but I did what *I* had to. You want Alex safe. You make him safe. Eliminate the threat." Her eyes narrowed and she added softly, "FYI . . . *I* am not the threat, but if you're too stupid—"

The rest of the words were caught against his mouth.

* * *

SHIT.

Vaughnne should have taken those thirty seconds to breathe, she decided, because now it was too late.

His mouth, brutal and hungry, crushed down on hers. She went to shove him away, but he caught her hands and, in a blink, had them pinned at her back. His tongue probed at her lips and the need to open for him almost sent her to her knees. Well, it might have, except his body was pressed to hers. Long, lean, and powerful, and so amazing.

Against her belly, her chest, she felt the hard wall of his chest, the muscled plane of his belly . . . and, oh, hell.

The ridge of his cock pressed against her and any thought of self-preservation went out the window. She opened for him, and as his tongue swept into her mouth, she welcomed it with a greedy moan.

He stilled, for just a second, and then lifted his head, staring at her through slitted eyes. She licked her lips and watched him, breathing raggedly. "If that's supposed to make me run for cover, sugar, they taught you some crazy shit down there in Mexico," she said.

The room spun around them and she sucked in a breath right before he slammed her against the cool, hard wood of the bathroom door. The bruises on her body screamed out at her. The need *inside* her body screamed louder, and she reached up, curled her hands into his shirt. "That's not doing it, either, Gus."

He closed one hand around her throat, pressing his thumb lightly.

It didn't hurt.

But the threat was obvious.

Something dark, dangerous glinted in his eyes. "If I told you that I've killed some of your fellow agents, would you still be laughing at me, Vaughnne? Still be taunting me?"

Some of the heat inside her eased back, but she didn't look away. "I'm pretty sure I'm familiar with what an *assassin* is. You've killed. So have I. I'm still not running."

"And if I tell you that I've fucked a woman and then killed her the next morning . . . what then?" He dipped his head and nuzzled her neck. "I could break you, Vaughnne. So easily. You're strong, and you're fast. But you haven't had to do the things to survive that I have. I could take you now, and then if I don't get what I want out of you, I could break your neck and walk away."

* * *

THE fear he needed to see in her eyes just wasn't there.

Instead, as he issued a threat he really doubted he could follow through on, all Vaughnne did was angle that arrogant chin of hers up. Challenge glinted in her eyes as she smirked up at him. "Yeah? Then do it."

He *could* kill her. At least a few minutes ago he could have. But then she'd put that damned weapon down.

I did what I had to. You want Alex safe. You make him safe. Eliminate the threat. FYI . . . I am not the threat . . .

Eliminate the threat.

He could have killed her, right up until she said that. It wasn't because she'd pointed out that she wasn't the threat to Alex. He *knew* that. She was a roadblock, though, and he could dispose of a roadblock. With most of them, he could do it without any guilt, although if he had to hurt *her*, it would haunt him. But he could have done it.

But she'd cleared the biggest roadblock of all. He wanted two things—to protect his nephew. And kill the boy's father. But his nephew was the one reason he couldn't go after the father.

Problem solved.

Tightening his hand, he lied . . . again. "You think I won't do it. You think I haven't?"

He'd done a lot of things in his life. Killed. Lied. Stolen. Fucked his way to whatever information he had to get out of women and then he'd walked away. But he'd never slept with a woman and killed her in the morning. Never. There was no way he could start with this woman. And now he couldn't kill her, either—

Didn't even know if he could force himself to hurt her. Walking away was becoming something too difficult to fathom.

Her gaze held his and she leaned against the door, unperturbed by the pressure of his hand against her throat. Her fingers were tangled in the wrinkled, worn fabric of his shirt, and he wanted to see her peeling that fabric away. Wanted to peel her clothes away and learn every blessed inch of her.

"I think you can do just about anything you set your mind to," Vaughnne said, her voice husky. "I'm hoping you'll decide that the best option here is to go after the real threat. But you do what you have to."

Then she smiled at him and pulled her hands away from his shirt, lifted them up, and placed them by her head.

The look on her face was like a punch to his gut.

Challenging. Hungry. Insolent. And . . . waiting.

Waiting.

Like she knew exactly what he was going to do. Snarling, he shifted his hand on her neck, hooked it around, and hauled her against him. "You should have used that gun," he muttered against her lips. Desire, so blistering hot, tore through him and he shoved her shirt up until it caught under her arms. He leaned back to stare at her, breathing like he'd just run ten miles.

Simple black cotton cupped her breasts, and it was the most erotic thing he'd ever seen. He'd made love to women who wore silk and satin and diamonds to bed. And the most amazing sight was Vaughnne, still wearing all her clothes, and still wearing that challenging smile on her face. He reached up and trailed his fingers along the edge of the bra, down to the front clasp. With a quick flick, it opened and he pushed first one cup aside, then the other. Her nipples were deep, deep brown, swollen, and already tight.

Bending his head, he caught one in his mouth and listened as a soft gasp shuddered out of her. She reached up to cup his head in her hands and he stopped her, catching her wrists and trapping them together in his hand.

That boiling hunger rose inside him as she tugged against his hold and he lifted his head, glaring at her. "You said I should do what I have to," he rasped, leaning in to sink his teeth into her lower lip. "That's exactly what I'm doing. And it's my way, Vaughnne. All my way."

Her breathing hitched in her throat, her lashes sweeping down over her eyes. "And I'm what you should do? Seriously?"

"In this moment? Yes." Because he couldn't think, not until he'd done this. Skimming his hand down her torso, he freed the button of her jeans.

"Well, if you're that damned determined, you should check my back pocket." Vaughnne's lashes lifted, and once more, that glint was in her eyes. *I dare you* . . . she seemed to say.

Gus had never been able to say no to a challenge. And he was having a very hard time now. Slipping his hand around, he checked her pocket, and when he tugged out a small foil packet, he lifted a brow. "You must have been really certain you could talk me into not hurting you." He dragged the edge of the condom packet across the exposed skin of her belly.

"Nah. Just really, really hopeful that you'd see reason. You seem like a reasonable guy, after all."

"Reasonable." Yes, because all reasonable men fucked women in a hospital room when they ought to either be out eliminating monstrous men or chasing down their nephews. Both.

But for the first time in years, he realized that he could breathe. His gut told him that Alex *was* safe. No, he didn't know the man Alex was with, but he did know Vaughnne. He *did* trust her. And she wouldn't take the boy's safety lightly. He could breathe . . . he could think about the next step. After this.

After this, he'd think. And he'd prepare. Get ready. That would take days, perhaps longer. Nothing he could do from here. In this very moment, the only thing that mattered was her. This moment.

Holding Vaughnne's eyes with his, he let go of her hands and turned her around. "You better have more than one. We'll need them later."

"Later . . . who said I'm going with you?"

He shoved her jeans halfway down her thighs and smoothed a hand over her rump. "You're going. Whether you choose to, or I take you, you're going. Because if I don't succeed, you're going to let your . . . *boss* know that he will have a ghost haunting him."

He touched her between her thighs and nearly went to his knees when he felt how wet she was. How hot. Scalding him. "If you make a sound, everybody outside this room will know what I'm doing to you," he said softly as he tore his jeans open. "And just so you know, I don't really care. You don't want anybody to know, you better be quiet."

A shudder wracked her body and the sight of it made him smile. He dealt with the rubber, slipping the wrapper into his pocket before rolling the thin latex shield down over his length. Tucking the head of his cock against her entrance, he gripped her hips.

Glancing up, he watched as she braced her hands against the wall.

Then, with excruciating slowness, he pushed inside her. She groaned, straining against the confining material of the jeans still tangled around her legs. "Be still," he muttered.

She sucked in a breath and pushed back against him instead.

Swearing under his breath, he gripped her tighter and fought the need to slam into her. So tight. She wrapped around him so tight, so hot. Like a dream. Sweet, tight, hot . . . strong. She moved back against him even as he pulled back and then surged forward, working another inch inside her. A soft, ragged whimper escaped her, her hands fisted against the wall, her spine undulating as she rocked backward.

He smoothed a hand up her back, shoving her shirt higher, wishing he had the time, wishing it was the right place to strip her down to her skin so he could see that strong, lovely body of hers naked. Instead, he surged deeper, deeper inside, swallowing back the groan that rose in his throat as the muscles of her pussy clutched at him, tighter, tighter . . . so slick and sweet.

"*Carojo*. Be still, *corazón*," he muttered as she arched back, vising down around him like a fist. "Damn it, be still."

"Hell, no." She braced her hands against the wall and shoved back against him as he tried to catch his breath, tried to steady himself.

A minute. He needed a minute—

Vaughnne moved a second time, a third time, riding him like she didn't give a damn that he was a moment away from shattering. Like it didn't matter that he wanted nothing more than to drive himself so deep inside her and lose himself. Swearing, he tangled his hand in her hair and crowded her closer to the wall. "My way," he rasped against her neck, sinking his teeth into her skin. She shuddered against him, and once more, those sweet, hot little muscles in her pussy milked him, gripped him, squeezing him, driving him to the very brink.

"Then you better do something," she said on a ragged gasp. "I'm dying . . ."

* * *

His hands, his body, everything about him seemed to surround and dominate and control her. *His* way? She might have laughed if she'd had the breath. If she had *her* way, she would have torn away from him, tumbled him to his back, and ridden him until neither one of them could see straight.

Instead, she was trapped between him and the wall . . . her heart slamming so hard against her ribs, and her legs barely able to hold her up. His fingers dug into her hips, and she sucked in a ragged breath, only to have him drive it out of her as he drove inside her again, this time all the way in, so hard and so deep. He held there, for just one second, linked to her—she whimpered and pushed back against him. Just like that . . . just like—

Then he pulled back out and she wanted to cry, she felt so empty.

Using his hand on her hair, he tugged her head around her and she groaned as his mouth caught hers, a deep, drugging kiss. His tongue traced the line of her lips, so gentle in contrast to his demand on her body. It was painfully erotic, painfully intimate, and then it was done and she hissed out a breath as he tugged her from the wall and they pivoted, all without breaking the connection.

"Bend over, Vaughnne," he ordered.

Her head spun as she saw the seat of the wooden chair in front of her. The one he'd wedged in front of the door. Her entire body went hot as she swayed forward and gripped it to steady herself.

Catching her breath, she braced her body.

But all he did was trail his fingers along her spine. Up to her neck, then down. "The next time I take you, I'm going to strip you naked." He bent down low, pressing his lips to the sensitive, exposed skin of her back. "I'm going to learn your every secret, learn what makes you gasp, what makes you whimper, what makes you moan."

That would be you . . .

If she'd had the breath, she might have said it out loud.

If she'd had the control, she would have whispered it into his mind.

As it was, she could only let it echo through her own mind as he gripped her hips.

He pulled out, slow . . . pushed back in that same fashion. Slow. But there was nothing gentle, nothing seductive or careful about it. It was thorough. A taking. A marking. A claiming.

Deep inside her, she felt him swell, felt the head of his cock stroking her. She angled her hips and twisted—*there,* she thought helplessly. *Right there—*

And although she hadn't said anything, he knew. Gus shifted, changed the angle of her hips, and slammed into her. "Like that?" he rasped, his voice just barely above a whisper.

If she could have answered, she would have.

But then he did it again. A third time. A fourth.

And by the fifth, she was already coming and it was sheer self-preservation that had her swallowing the broken, desperate cry.

* * *

VAUGHNNE had a lot of practice in knowing when she was the object of scrutiny. A lot. She'd been the freak back home, and word had started getting out about her a month or so before her dad had thrown her out on the streets. Nothing like having the kids at school, church, and even your own cousins staring at you during Sunday get-togethers and whispering about what a weirdo you were to give you that little insight into people.

Yeah, she knew when she was being stared at behind her back.

And she knew when she just *thought* she was.

This was totally the latter, and she knew it. Nobody was looking at her as they strode down the corridor.

Now Gus? He was being stared at and not just by the nurse who was scrambling to notify the doctor on call that he was leaving against medical advice. The nurse had tried to enlist Vaughnne to help her out, but Gus didn't need to be here. The nurse was just doing her job; Vaughnne got that and she understood it, but Gus wasn't going to hang around to make anybody's life easier.

The security guards were the big problem, and she just hoped Gus would keep his cool until they got off hospital property. Especially since she'd had Jones go to the trouble of collecting Gus's weapons and bringing them to the room before he'd vacated the premises.

If they caught too much attention, it was just going to attract trouble they didn't want or need.

Of course, if they had the trouble on *their* tail . . .

An idea settled in the back of her head, but it was one that she'd have to think through before she did anything. She needed to know where they were going first, needed to check in with Taylor and make sure Alex was safe, needed to know if Gus was going to be stupid—

Casually, he reached over and stroked a hand up her back, rested it on her opposite shoulder as they came to the elevator. When she would have slowed, he kept walking.

"We've got two people trailing us," he said quietly as he leaned in and pressed a kiss to her neck. "Are they yours?"

Vaughnne blinked.

That . . . no.

That didn't seem possible. She'd know.

She'd feel it.

Then she remembered just what they were dealing with. Reevaluating, she shook her head. Focusing her thoughts down into a narrow stream, she whispered them into his mind, *No. I would have been told. And don't say anything else. Avoid thinking about them if you can. Avoid any direct thoughts, period.*

She didn't know if he'd follow what she was saying or not. Hard to explain psychic shielding to a nonpsychic, although it was entirely possible. Taylor used it all the time. All it took to have a *closed* mind was to project that mental door. Strong telepaths could and did get around it, but it took more focus, and the typical homegrown psychic wasn't trained well enough to do it and still trail them. It took more advanced training, and in Vaughnne's experience, *training* just wasn't all that easy to come by outside of units like Jones ran.

Of course, he didn't have the monopoly on trained psychics, but she doubted that was what they were dealing with.

Even if they rattled one of them, that would be good.

She didn't like the fact that she hadn't picked up on their presence. She was *good* at that. It was why she was here—

"They are in uniform. A man and a woman," Gus murmured as they continued to walk. "One is dressed like a doctor. The woman looks to be a nurse."

As they rounded the corner at the end of the hall, she fought the urge to look back. Casting Gus a quick look, she lifted a brow.

He mouthed. *Run.*

They ran.

Bypassing the stairs, dodging through the ebb and flow of people, they left the medical-surgical floor where Alex and Gus had been kept for the past few hours. As they rounded another bend in the hall, Vaughnne felt an odd prickle and she hissed. Instinct had her slamming a hand against a wall just before a shove would have sent her to her knees.

Now *that* she felt.

And when she looked behind her this time, she saw them.

The fake doctor was the one who'd shoved her. She figured that out from the odd glint in his eyes just before she felt another shove. The woman next to him looked cool, composed. And she watched Vaughnne with absolutely no expression.

It was when she reached out and touched the doctor that Vaughnne figured out what the bitch was.

And just *why* she hadn't picked up on anything.

The bitch was one of the subclasses. Jones had spent the past few years working on categorizing and understanding the psychic abilities, and he had taken it to an art. Vaughnne was one of the ones he'd spent a lot of time pairing with others, just to see what would happen when the psychics worked together or tried to merge their abilities.

There was really only *one* ability that worked well with Vaughnne's and it was one of the subability classes. One of the filtering gifts, like this woman had. It was the *only* reason Vaughnne recognized it, too. Even from this distance, she recognized that odd, muffling sensation of the woman's mind.

She'd block shit. She could either silence the gift in Vaughnne's mind, or she could amp it up.

The bad thing about the subclasses, while they weren't necessarily all that much of a danger in the psychic arena on their own, if you paired them with the right partner, they got dangerous.

Quick.

And this guy was a telekinetic.

Paired with that bitch, he might be able to level the whole damned hospital.

We need to get out of here, she told Gus, shoving off the wall.

SEVENTEEN

Jones had told her he'd leave a car in the garage.

He'd also told her that if she didn't remove herself from the premises in a very short amount of time, he'd be unleashing holy hell.

She suspected that meant he'd be putting his people on Gus's very fine ass in an attempt to bring him in.

All things that wouldn't go well. If he'd decided Gus was a person of *interest*, he'd put his best people on it and it wouldn't end until there was bloodshed. Probably lots of it. And she didn't know what it would take to stop Gus.

It would take a hell of a lot, she thought.

Or maybe just a bullet. That was one fact she was almost painfully aware of as they moved through the parking garage. She noticed the placement of the cameras, watched as they moved back and forth. They wouldn't catch everything, she didn't think. A few blind spots, just at the end of the aisle, and right . . .

Shit. That spot right ahead of them. Her skin prickled and she tugged on Gus's arm, bringing him down to a snail's pace.

There was a funny way of talking in a garage. You can say something and the words would go nowhere. And then you could *whisper* something, and it almost echoed.

She waited until she heard *nothing*.

She didn't hear the doors close.

She didn't hear footsteps.

But she knew they weren't alone. It wasn't even a prickle of awareness on her skin. It was just instinct. And as they walked, she said in a low voice, "We need to hurry. He's keeping the boy at the safe house, but we've only got so much time to get there or he's just going to take him in. If he goes into custody, it will be hell trying to get him out."

"They can't just take my kid away," Gus said. He looked over at her and she saw the knowledge glint in his eyes. And she was also painfully aware of something else. As he moved, he shifted his body, placing it behind hers.

Not cool, that.

How could he go after his brother-in-law if he was taking a bullet?

She didn't know the answer to that. She didn't care. What she did know was that they needed to be in the car Jones had left. Just around the corner—that next blind spot.

Both she and Gus hit the ground at the same time and she groaned as her sore muscles screamed out at her. She rolled and jerked her Glock up, aiming it in the face of the man.

He just smiled and held out a hand to the woman with him.

The weight that slammed into Vaughnne's arms was so heavy, she thought an elephant had dropped down on them.

Gus swung out with his legs and the two psychics went crashing down, but that wasn't going to last for long.

Vaughnne rolled to her feet, an order forming in her mouth. But the words died before she could really even give voice to them. Somehow Gus had arrowed in on the one who was the biggest danger. Silver flashed through the air, flying toward the woman. The subclasses were often misjudged by a lot of the psychics Vaughnne had worked with. But anybody who could suppress or boost her gift was a problem in her mind.

The subclass was no longer a problem. For a moment, she stared at the blade buried in her chest and then looked up, an expression of blank astonishment on her face. Clumsily, she reached for it, but her aim was off and she toppled over to the side before she even made contact. A trickle of blood seeped from the corner of her mouth.

"Anton," the woman whispered, and the word was faint, almost like a ghost had whispered it.

That soft, broken sound shattered the other psychic's stillness and he turned, lunging himself at Gus.

Gus shot him between the eyes and the odd, muffled pop of the silencer seemed even more disturbing than the woman's dying whisper.

Swallowing the bitter, nasty taste of bile rising up in her throat, Vaughnne looked at the woman. There was a chance she might not die if she got help now. A faint chance.

Crossing to her, she eyed the woman narrowly. "Do you know it's an innocent boy you're trying to kidnap?"

Lashes flickered over the woman's eyes. Dull confusion shone back at Vaughnne. "It's a job. Money . . ." She shuddered.

Turning her back, she looked at Gus. "Get your knife."

As he did that, she checked the cameras again. They should still be in the blind zone, but damn it. This was getting dicey already and they were still in the damned garage. Grabbing the man's ankles, she hauled him between two of the cars. She hadn't even straightened from his body when Gus dumped the woman on top of him.

"You would have tried to help her if she had answered the right way, wouldn't you?" he asked softly, his pale eyes unreadable.

She stared at him. "I don't entirely know what the right way is." Then she turned her back to him and made her way around the front of the car. He could stand there and glare at her or he could follow.

Security could show up at any second. So could any number of visitors, and for all she knew, these two had partners somewhere. They needed to get out of the hospital before bystanders got hurt. She had no problem compromising herself or crossing her own lines to go after a monster, but letting innocent people get hurt was a line she couldn't and wouldn't cross.

She didn't bother to look backward. Gus was behind her before she'd even gone five feet.

But if she thought the discussion was over, she was so very, very wrong.

* * *

BORROWED time. Esteban was now operating on borrowed time and he knew it. The men he'd sent after Alejandro had failed. The first pair . . . well, he'd allow himself the one mistake.

But then there had been nothing but more mistakes.

Every which way he turned, he was outsmarted or outmaneuvered and now he had it confirmed that the boy's uncle was no longer operating alone. A woman had been seen with him.

He didn't know who she was, but this changed things.

Matters were even worse than he liked to think. Too many knew how badly things were going.

He'd updated the profile on the site with a vague reference that hopefully people would realize was an increase in the reward.

One of them had outright said, *And what good is that if I end up drooling down my hospital gown?*

They knew what had happened in Orlando. Somehow they knew.

He no longer wondered just how many of them were legit.

Too many of them were very skilled. Too many knew exactly how badly things were going and it seemed the wiser ones were pulling back.

Options were becoming too limited for him now.

The boss had already called him home. He was driving in that direction. Driving. Not flying. Señor Reyes would expect him to fly, but the señor could fuck himself. Of course, he didn't want to appear like he wasn't following orders. But he wanted to think his options through. One last time.

He could run, of course.

There had always been that option, but if he ran, and if he was caught . . .

His gut twisted and his bowels felt watery even thinking about it, but he still had to consider running. It wasn't an option that left him filled with happy, pleasant thoughts.

The other option . . . just thinking about it made him feel better. Peaceful. That decided him. Mind made up, he turned off the interstate. It only took a few hours to reach the spot he had in mind. He ignored a call from the señor and had a moment of terror when he thought he'd spotted a car that appeared to be following him. But it hadn't been. Thankfully.

Up ahead, the road branched and he hit the turn signal, pressing down on the brake as a bunch of guys on motorcycles roared around him. The thick, dark green of the cypress trees seemed to surround him. It was pretty here. So very green. He'd always enjoyed this area. Hot and humid, but that was Louisiana.

Taking the keys out of the car, he grabbed the computer bag from the seat next to him. Before he climbed out, he wiped it down, careful not to leave any fingerprints. He did the same at the trunk when he pulled his small carry-on from the back.

Options. He'd spent so much time thinking about his options and so much time living in fear lately. His best bet had been finding the kid, getting back to the boss, but with each passing day . . . no. The odds had gotten slimmer and slimmer, and now, they were just about nonexistent. He'd never thought that Gustavo Morales would cost him this much. He'd always expected it would be the boy he had to worry about.

After all, Gustavo had been a well-known philanderer. The señor had had him investigated and Esteban had done the same. Nothing in the man's past led Esteban to think he would have proven to be such a problem. He played at life. He went to parties, even did some modeling. *Modeling*, of all things. He hadn't been very successful at it, but the man floated around and didn't appear to succeed at anything, except sleeping with women.

Rumor had it that he wasn't above playing man-whore to some of the more financially well-off women in Mexico.

He never should have been an issue.

Yet, Gustavo had been the problem from the beginning.

Reyes had said that Gustavo wouldn't be a problem. But the man had been wrong. The bastard. Esteban let himself think that way . . . now. As he made his way into the swamp, he decided it was okay to finally think about the señor in whatever way he chose. He'd never *thought* that Reyes was the one who passed on the . . . weird . . . abilities to his son, but he hadn't wanted to take the chance and he'd always been careful to monitor even his personal thoughts when it came to one Ignacio Reyes. But no more. There wasn't any point, not after tonight.

He reached the rickety old dock and eyed the surrounding area.

This would do well, he thought. Very well. A mosquito landed on him as he knelt to catch the rope tied to the dock. He caught the rope and untied it, absently humming to himself as he worked. It felt nice, he thought. Having a plan in mind. Taking the stress, the burden off his shoulders. He didn't have to worry anymore. Not now.

Once he'd finished untying the boat, he took his personal documents, both the real ones and the fake ones, and put them in his carry-on. Then, with a quick look around, he tossed his computer case into the deep, brackish water. Maybe it would be found. Maybe it wouldn't. But it wasn't his concern anymore. Neither was Reyes. Neither was the boy. Neither was that bastard Gustavo Morales.

If he had been feeling benevolent toward the señor, he could have left his information where the man could put it toward some sort of use, but he wasn't feeling benevolent. At all. If anything, some part of him almost wished the boy luck. The boy, not that *cabrón* Morales. Morales could rot in hell, right along with the señor. Right along with Esteban.

Of course, if he *really* wanted to wish the boy luck, he could call off the psychic wolves, but there wasn't time for that. He had to take action before the señor decided to send somebody after him. In all likelihood, there were already people looking for him.

No. If the boy was going to survive, he'd do it on his own, without any help from Esteban.

Eyeing the narrow little boat, he climbed in.

There was just one thing he really needed.

He pulled it out, stroking the cool metal idly. It would be full night soon. He could hear the odd, eerie music of the night creatures. He rather enjoyed it. He'd go deeper into the swamps before he did anything.

It was almost over.

He'd enjoy the quiet of the swamp. And then he'd die there . . . his way.

* * *

REYES lowered the phone to the desk.

Esteban wasn't answering.

It was an irritation more than anything else, but if he didn't return his calls soon, Reyes would be very upset.

Esteban didn't want to see Reyes angry. Things were already not looking well for him.

Absently, he glanced up, eyeing the door. Usually, when he was feeling frustrated, one thing made it better.

Nala.

But she hadn't been her normal self lately.

Ever since she'd slipped away from him for a few days. He closed a hand into a fist, remembering. Perhaps he shouldn't have been so hard on her when she came back. And she *had* come back. She'd come back—he hadn't tracked her down, although he'd certainly tried. It was like she'd disappeared into the wind.

That was part of why he'd been so angry. If she left again . . .

No.

She wouldn't. She knew now what would happen.

Brushing that thought aside, he focused on the matter at hand. Esteban. His missing son.

Reaching for the phone, he made a call. It was time to bring Esteban home. Time for a changing of the guard, so to speak.

"Jorge. Please come to my office."

* * *

SLUMPED in the chair, Nalini kept her back against the wall, the laptop on her legs and her expression bored.

Even when Ignacio came her way, she didn't look away from the screen, although she did shut down the screen to the website she was hacking into. That damned site, *The Psychic Portal.*

He settled on the lounge next to her and stretched out his legs. "Are you still ignoring me?"

She reached for her glass and took a long, deep drink of the sweet rum concoction. It was about the only thing she trusted to numb the pain just then. When she'd made it back to Ignacio's

villa, he'd smiled at her, kissed her . . . and then slammed a brutal fist into her face. *You are never to leave here without my
permission, Nala. This is the only warning you'll receive.*

Her face felt like it had been hammered and that wasn't far
off. Ignacio was a buff guy. She could have avoided the hit, but
she'd rather he not *know* she could. She'd already revealed more
than she'd wanted to, just by disappearing. He knew she *could*
get away from him, and she also knew he'd sent men after her.
Knew that they'd been rather useless at finding her.

That wasn't good.

So she'd taken the hit, much as it sucked. Sometimes a woman
just had to do lousy things. He'd pay for that hit sooner or later.

Right now, she was having fun ignoring him. It was pissing
him off, too. She really liked that.

A cruel hand reached out and closed around her wrist.

Thank you for making this so easy. She turned her head and
listened for about five seconds as he said gently, "I will not toler-
ate being ignored, Nala. I let you pout for a short time, but it's
done." He gestured to the laptop. "I wish to make love to you.
Put that away."

She touched her tongue to her lip, watched as his gaze lowered to her mouth. She was kind of tired of behaving. She'd been
doing it for too long already. "You know what . . . I've got a better idea."

* * *

"WHY did you bother asking her anything?"

Vaughnne just stared at the window in the coming night. Her
gaze was blank and her face was serene. She didn't look all that
bothered by the fact that she'd just seen him kill two people, but
he knew better.

Something was bothering her and he'd get to the bottom of it.
He had to know just how far he could trust her, just how far

she'd go. She said she wanted Alex safe, but while he'd do *any-thing* to see it happen . . . he doubted she'd do the same, doubted she could say the same.

"Because I needed to know," she said when he continued to stare at her.

"Why?"

Her lashes swept down low for a minute. "The agent in me gets it. I know why they were there and I had very little, if any, doubt, that they *knew* what they were doing, that they knew they were after a kid. Did they stop to question *why* somebody was after a kid? Question his motives? His reasoning? Any of that? I don't know. And the agent in me knows this . . . they didn't care. They had a job to do and that's all that mattered. I know that. I get that. I've seen some damn shitty stuff, doing the kind of work I do—that's *why* I do it. To help put a stop to it. But there's another part of me that just . . . doesn't. And I had to know. I had to ask."

"You still want to trust people," he said softly. He turned his head and stared out at the scenery as it raced by. The highway lights blurred around him and he kept watching the mirrors, waiting to see sirens. Vaughnne had a police scanner in the car and they'd heard the alert go out once the bodies were found.

That had been more than an hour ago. He'd heard them talk about a "disturbance at the hospital," but so far, he and Vaughnne hadn't been connected to it. He hoped it wouldn't happen because having his description splashed on the news wasn't going to do his situation any good.

But if it happened . . .

He pushed the thought aside and focused on Vaughnne. "You must see the lowest forms of life out there, *corazón*. The work you do. How you lost your sister. Yet you still think you can trust people."

"Oh, I know I can trust some," she said softly. "But this isn't about *trusting* people. It's about not being willing to believe everybody out there is a monster."

Gus closed his eyes. Life was easier when he trusted nobody. Nothing. When he kept his focus solely on the boy. When his life revolved around Alex, it was simple. It was complicated now and he didn't like that.

Memory flashed through his mind and his blood heated as those memories rose up to whisper, *Oh, you didn't like it? Didn't like fucking her? Don't want to do it again?*

His heart thudded against his ribs, hard and heavy, and he resisted the urge to open his eyes and look at her. He'd have her again. He already knew that. But it was more to ease that hunger than anything else. It had to be; there was no way he'd let himself need anybody. No way he'd let himself want anybody in his life. It was hard enough just letting himself love Alex, knowing how easily that could be shattered and lost.

"How far do we drive tonight?" Vaughnne's voice cut through the dark, edgy hunger and he bit back a curse.

"Drive until you can't see straight," he said sourly. "Then pull off to the side of the road and I'll take over."

A smirk twisted her lips. "Okay, then. And I assume I head toward Mexico, right?"

* * *

Drive until you can't see straight.

She was tempted to jab him with something sharp. Or thump him over the head with something heavy.

Granted, she'd be biting off more than she could chew, but the jackass brought out the worst in her and she couldn't help it.

Still, he'd be surprised at just how far she could go without sleep.

If she hadn't had the shit walloped out of her in the past few days, between *him* slipping her the damned drugs and the car wreck, she could manage another day or so without it.

Day was bleeding away into night when she had to pull over. The brilliant lights of the gas station were what drew her, and anxiety pounded in her as she filled up the gas tank. She had the keys in her pocket, but that wasn't going to keep Gus from taking off. Nothing was going to keep him here if he didn't want to be here—she knew that.

Still. She had to use that damn bathroom and she was hungry.

As she finished topping off the tank, she ran through the list of options in her mind and it didn't take a very long time to ponder each, and toss them aside. The *ideal* option would be knocking him out for a while so she *could* go deal with her bladder. Then she'd know he'd be here when she got out.

The only problem with that scenario . . . she blew out a sigh as she screwed the gas cap on. There was no way in hell she'd be able to knock that guy out. Wasn't going to happen. Not unless she figured out a way to do it from a good ten feet away. Maybe she could shriek him into unconsciousness.

As she started to circle around the car, her bladder screaming, the door opened.

Gus climbed out and stared at her over the hood of the car. He had his bag slung over his arm. She'd noticed that he kept that bag very, very close. "We need to stop for a bit. I have to make a few phone calls and we need to hit the restrooms, grab a bite to eat. You're also going to get in contact with your . . . boss. Jones. I want to know about Alex."

She eyed him narrowly. Okay. No point in letting him know how completely on board she was with the restroom idea, she figured. Restoom, food, all good things. Calling Jones? Not such a great idea, but hell. She wasn't surprised. Actually, she was . . . she was *very* surprised he hadn't pushed for her to do this earlier.

Running her tongue along her teeth, she said softly, "I'll call Jones. Last. And I'm staying on your ass the entire way."

A slow smile tugged up his lips. "Think I'm going to try and ditch you now, Vaughnne?"

"Wouldn't surprise me."

"Stop worrying about that. It's not an issue. You're in this until the end, because if I fail, *you* are the one who is taking responsibility for my nephew. You stepped into this and you gave your word you'd see him safe. I'm holding you to that."

Briefly she wondered just how she was going to do that if she ended up dead along with him. Because that was what he meant by *fail*. A polite, pretty way of saying, *If I end up with my throat slit or worse, you're picking up the ball.*

That had already been taken care of, though. Even if Gus didn't realize it. Nobody would or *could* watch after a kid like Alex the way the people in her unit could. Not that he was going to be communal property exactly, but somebody in her unit would make sure he was cared for. Loved. *And* trained.

Once that kid was trained, there wasn't going to be a person alive who posed much of a threat to him, she suspected. Once he was trained, he'd see to his own safety.

As Gus turned toward the travel plaza, she debated on whether or not to leave the car where it was or trust him enough and let him out of her sight so she could move it.

In the end, she decided she'd make a show of faith. Somehow she didn't think he was bullshitting her about her being in this to the end. Maybe he hadn't meant for that to be reassuring to her, but it was.

Yeah.

It was.

If she didn't have to worry about him ditching her at every opportunity, she could focus on the bigger problem.

Alex's father.

As she started the car, Gus glanced back over his shoulder, one brow lifted. She gestured to the front of the store and started to nose the car around. At the last minute, though, she pulled around to the store, over near the back. There wasn't exactly any place that was hidden in the shadows here—bright lights lit up the area, and out beyond that pool of light, darkness and the stretch of road awaited. But she didn't want to leave the car right out front.

As she climbed out, Gus appeared at the end of the sidewalk where it curved around to the front. His pale eyes glittered in his face as he watched her and her heart jumped and danced around in her throat, just looking at him. Really, that man was just too beautiful to exist. It wasn't fair to the female population. Not at all.

Spit pooled in her mouth and she had to swallow just to keep from drooling as she moved to meet him on the sidewalk.

"We going inside?" she asked, trying to act like she wasn't desperate to touch him. Desperate to see him, be near him. How had he hit her like this? A few weeks ago, she'd been stuck behind a desk, dealing with bitching headaches and wondering when she could get back out in the field.

And now, here she was, still dealing with bitching headaches, back out in the field . . . and standing in front of a man who had come to mean way too much to her, especially considering how very little she really knew about him.

He lifted a hand and brushed a stray curl back from her face, tucking it behind her ear. "If you were smart, you'd try to lose me once you were inside the store. Take off, steal a car, and get away from here. Before it's too late. Once they connect you to me, do you understand you may never be able to go back to your life?"

"I've never been much on doing the smart thing. Just the thing that felt right." She shrugged and tried not to react as he shifted his attention from her hair to her mouth. He cupped her chin in his hand, stroked his thumb along her lower lip. The light touch sent all sorts of sparks and heat dancing down her spine and she wanted to shudder. Shiver. Quiver. She *was* quivering. And hungry, so damn hungry for him, but this wasn't the time, wasn't the place. Not that they were likely to have *that* anytime soon. "Besides, how likely am I to get away if I tried?"

Lashes swept low. "If you ran now, I might let you go. You never should have gotten caught up in this. I've got enough blood on my hands. I . . ."

His voice trailed off and then he shook his head. "Come on. We're wasting time."

"Yeah, and there's none of that," she said, sighing. Edging around him, trying to ignore the ache spreading through her, she started to the store. "I'll call Jones once we're done with the pit stop and grabbing up some food for the road. I've got cash if you don't."

There was no answer. She couldn't hear him behind her as she headed into the store.

But he was following her. She was excruciatingly aware of that fact.

* * *

THEY bought some throwaway cell phones.

Gus had several of them stashed in his bag, but he didn't want to use them until he had to, so before they left, he peeled off a few twenties and bought two more, added a few cards to their purchases so they would have airtime. Vaughnne stood next to him, her right hand hanging loose, her left thumb hitched in her pocket as she stood there, a bored expression on her face.

She might look bored to anybody else, but he recognized that look.

She was watching. Noticing everything.

The door opened and a gust of hot air blew in, and even

though her expression never changed, he imagined she could tell him everything about the person who'd just walked in.

Of course, he'd also noticed.

A trucker. Big guy, nearly six foot five, black, his beard going gray and his head smooth and bald, shiny in the bright light. He wore a faded T-shirt with Mr. T on it, and although it hung loosely on him, it couldn't disguise the muscular build. Automatically, Gus cataloged how the man moved, decided the guy knew *how* to move and probably knew how to fight, as well.

But he was older and he looked tired, like he'd spent the entire day on the road.

He also had a direct look about him, and if Gus had to kill him, he'd do it quick and easy.

It was normal, for him, to note everything about everybody and decide how he'd kill somebody. Some people would die slow, because if he made it slow, he could get information out of them. Others, he'd kill fast because they'd never talk, or if they did talk, it would take too much time, and time was one thing Gus never wasted.

The man looked like one who knew how to take pain.

Stop it, a soft voice murmured into his mind. Shifting his eyes to the side, he eyed Vaughnne narrowly.

She lifted a brow at him, and once more, her voice rolled through him. *Stop. He's just a trucker. If he was more, I'd know. He's not.*

He wondered how she was so certain, when *she* had been the one to point out to him that there were psychics who could hide themselves very, very well—she hadn't sensed the two earlier. And Alex hadn't ever sensed a thing from her.

But then again, Vaughnne and Alex were two very different creatures. Even he could see that.

Alex might be a wildfire, deadly and strong, but Vaughnne was forged steel. Equally deadly, equally strong. And she had control.

Control . . . questions, demands, burned inside him, and abruptly, he was tired of not having those answers. Especially when there was somebody who could answer them.

As they paid for their purchases, he decided, then and there, he'd get the questions.

"You want us to get these activated for you?" the kid behind the counter asked.

"No." Gus looked away before the kid could offer anything else, and in another few minutes, they were out of the store. He took a slow look around the parking lot even as they headed for the car, his mind already focused on those questions.

"How am I calling Jones?" Vaughnne asked softly.

He pulled his phone from his back pocket and pushed it into her hand. "We'll toss it once the call is done. I assume you know the number."

"You assume correctly."

As she went to open the driver's door, he stopped her, gesturing to the other side of the car. As Vaughnne went to climb into the car, she paused, her body tensing. The expression on her face had the hair on the back of his neck standing on end.

"I don't think I'm making that call yet," she said softly, tension threaded through her voice.

He just nodded as they slid into the car. Those answers he wanted would have to wait. From the corner of his eye, he could see her muscles tighten, then relax, like she was readying herself.

"A couple of people," she murmured. "I feel something."

"A white Explorer just pulled into the far side of the parking lot. Do I stay here or pull out?" he asked, jamming the key into the ignition. Asking for advice on which move to make felt foreign, but this was her territory. He should have listened to her before this. It was high time he did so.

Vaughnne looked around and then gestured as a large group of people came pouring out of the travel plaza, heading for a couple of cars parking a few spaces down. "Pull out when they do. Enough commotion will distract them for a minute."

"Once we're on the road, we have to move," he said grimly. He kept his gaze on the white SUV, watched as it disappeared out of his line of sight.

She gave him a lazy smile. "Yeah. That would be wise." That lazy smile remained firmly in place even as he placed his bag in her lap and it didn't even wobble as she lifted a brow and unzipped it. "Damn, Gus. You believe in coming prepared, don't you?"

He didn't respond as he backed the car up, moving with the others she'd pointed out.

She slid him a look. "Do us both a favor and keep pace with them for a few minutes. Trust me, even if they notice us, they aren't going to want the attention of the cops, so they are not going to be speeding or any crazy shit."

He didn't give a damn if the cops noticed him or not, but even as he went to tell her that, she cut him off. "If we end up in a high-speed chase heading through southern Mississippi, it's not going to help either of us. And while I can *probably* help with things as long as you don't piss off the locals, if they see these?" She gestured to the bag in her lap and shook her head. "All bets are off. I may be FBI, but I still have to follow the law. And none of these look terribly legal to me."

He shot a look in the rearview mirror while the skin on the back of his neck continued to crawl. "I'm not worried about the legalities, Vaughnne." The white Explorer wasn't behind them. Yet.

"I get that. I suspect you think you've crossed the point of no return, and I understand. But don't you think it would serve your purpose to at least *get* to him before we both go down in fiery crash?"

He curled his lip. "None of the cops around here would be able to stop me."

She rolled her eyes. "Your arrogance is so appealing, really.

But how about this . . . *none* of the cops around here have done a damn thing to you, and if this ends up in a high-speed chase because you won't pull over for them, people will get hurt. Think about that . . . for five seconds. I'm probably throwing my career away as it is, but I'd rather not let anybody innocent get hurt while I'm at it."

He clenched his jaw as he stared out the window, too aware of the long, mostly empty expanse of highway wrapping around them. The cars they'd followed out of the travel plaza had just headed east.

But so far, the white Explorer was still back at the plaza. "I'll try to behave," he said.

Try.

"Why aren't they following us?"

"They might not have known we were there." She shrugged and glanced back at the plaza as the road curved around. A few seconds later, it was gone from their sight. "Sometimes a psychic just gets a blip, a flash of some place or thing. It could have been that. They could have somebody who gets visions and they were looking for us because of that. Who knows? It doesn't matter as long as we avoid them."

"That's going to make this fun," he muttered, pushing his baseball cap off. He tossed it into the backseat and shoved his fingers through his hair while various plans of attack ran through his mind.

"Is that website still up?" he asked.

"I don't know." She pulled her phone out. A few seconds later, she angled the display toward him. "Yes. And the fucking ad."

"*Mierda.*" The damn website. Alex . . . was he safe?

He didn't know that one crucial thing.

But he did know somebody was chasing after them.

"If they've found us, could they have found him?" he asked softly.

Long, painfully quiet seconds stretched out before she finally answered, "It's a vague possibility, but unless they've got an army, they'll have a hard time getting him away from Jones. It's not just one man he's got watching him now, Gus. It's an entire unit who'll take care of him. And they are all very, very good at what they do."

EIGHTEEN

WHEN they split up at the hospital, Tucker had to make a choice. It wasn't an easy one and it wasn't a fun one, but it was necessary.

Jones and the kid went one way, with a woman Tucker didn't know trailing along behind them in a sleek little convertible Jaguar. He wasn't much for modern cars, but he had to admit, that was one nice-looking car and he had no idea how she afforded it on an FBI agent's salary. And she had to be with Jones. Even though she had it all wrapped up nice and neat, Tucker felt the power of her mind even from a block away.

While those three headed north, Vaughnne remained at the hospital.

Since he'd promised Nalini he'd watch over the kid, he headed north, too.

And all through the night, he followed them. Bit by bit, in a rhythm so subtle he barely noticed, he realized the "glow" of the boy's mind was ebbing away.

Not in a dangerous way, exactly. He could still *feel* the kid, the same way he could sense the pretty psychic in the Jag. But he wasn't radiating so bright. Some weird shit. Made it harder to track him, really, because that wild power was the one thing guiding him, and eventually, he had to move in closer to keep them all where he could sense them.

When they pulled over for dinner at a fast-food place, he pulled in for gas at the station across the street, filling up and adding a few gallons to the gas cans he kept in the back for emergencies. All the while, he watched the cars across the way, ready to take off, and grateful Lucia had convinced him to keep emergency supplies in his car. Emergency supplies including water . . . and food. The energy bars tasted like shit, but since he couldn't exactly hop over to McDonald's—

"Hey!"

He jerked his head up and looked across the street.

Hell.

It was the woman.

She held a bag in one hand, the other was propped on her hip, and she stared at him with a grin.

* * *

"WELL, well, well . . ."

Taylor had met more than a few men and women who had made it clear they'd rather die than join his merry little band of misfits. He was looking at another, he suspected.

It was a damn shame, because he'd managed to get a little bit of information out of Joss Crawford about this guy.

Tucker was the only name he'd been given, but he'd unearthed more on his own.

He went by Tucker Collins . . . now.

Up until he'd disappeared at the age of fifteen, he'd been known as James Tucker Friend, son of Meredith Friend, adopted by the late Senator Bartholomew Friend.

Old Bart had been a man that Taylor didn't think he'd like, judging by some of the information he'd come across. Taylor made his living on information, after all. And he suspected his information was more than . . . accurate. Bart had been found dead the night of his fiftieth birthday and his stepson missing. Foul play was suspected, of course, but everybody believed the stepson was kidnapped. Meredith still routinely made very passionate pleas on the anniversary of her husband's death, pretty little pleas for information on the whereabouts of her only child.

She had red hair, like Tucker did.

Dark eyes. *Cold* eyes.

He didn't have to wonder what she'd do to find her kid. He had heard all about the body trail that had followed Tucker over the years, but that wasn't a problem for him. Not when he had an idea just what old Bart had been doing only moments before he was found dead in Tucker's room by a maid. One who was new in the household and had panicked, calling the police instead of running to the missus, who had been outside with her guests.

Police and private investigators had searched far and wide for the boy. None of them had found him. Taylor didn't have to wonder just how a boy of fifteen had evaded law enforcement officials. The man in front of him looked to be the type who could do almost anything he needed to. Hide, flee, steal, kill.

As Tucker came striding toward him, the air around them went hot and tight, and although there wasn't a cloud in the sky, it seemed like there was a storm dancing on the horizon.

Alex leaned in closer to him, and absently, Taylor reached up, rested a hand on the boy's shoulder.

"He thinks you're taking me away," Alex said softly.

"Don't worry about it," Taylor promised even as he shifted his body to guard the boy a little better.

Taige was just two feet away. If he had to have this confrontation here and now, he figured Taige was a decent person to have with him. She was one of his bloodhounds, but she also had a decent telekinetic gift and one she'd honed into a weapon. Hopefully they wouldn't have to do anything out in the open, but Tucker Collins was a wild card. Taylor could read people pretty damn well, and he suspected Tucker was willing to do anything and everything to accomplish his goals.

"I'm not going with him," Alex said softly. "He wants to take me back to Florida . . . or somewhere. There's a woman. It has something to do with a woman. I don't know her. She can't help me."

Abruptly, Tucker stopped in his tracks, and even though he was ten feet away, Taylor suspected he'd heard the kid. Alex gulped and Taylor squeezed his shoulder. He wanted to tell the kid not to worry, but it was a waste of breath. At this point, *he* was a little worried. He had some level of control over his agents—*usually*—but Tucker wasn't one of his and control was out the window and screaming on its way down to earth.

"Kid . . . stay out of my head," Tucker said, his voice quiet, despite the fact that it managed to carry over the distance that separated them.

Alex flinched.

Taige snorted. "Oh, take a flying leap, pal. He's not *in* your head. He's still trying to learn some control and all those random thoughts are out there like bits and pieces of a song. You don't want him hearing anything? Then you better just stop thinking until he knows how to close all those doors."

Tucker cut a glance her way and his eyes narrowed.

She just smiled serenely at him.

As he went to take a step in her direction, she angled her head to the side. "Nah. I think I like you better there, pal."

Taylor *felt* that. That odd twist when she was using her abilities. He wasn't psychic, but as much time as he spent around them, he knew how to recognize when they were using their gifts, and he suspected the reason Tucker had stopped was because he had no choice.

"I don't like it when people pull shit like that," Tucker said. His voice was neutral. But that odd, heavy feeling, like a storm surging closer and closer, increased.

"Promise me you'll be a good boy and I won't." Taige shrugged, looking unconcerned. "I heard about what went down in Orlando, you know. Word travels. We heard reports of somebody fitting your description on the scene there and I have an idea of what happened with the slave ring, too. I have my own theories on what you can do, so unless you plan on behaving? You can keep your distance."

The lights in the parking lot all flashed on, burning hot and bright—so hot, they exploded. People screamed in surprise. Alex flinched. Taylor clenched his jaw as he watched the display play out between Taige and Tucker. Taige just smirked. "You think *that* is going to freak me out, buddy?"

"Nah. I think you're too stupid to be freaked out. But you can take it as a warning . . . I don't need to be *close*—"

He didn't get another word out, and Taylor sighed. If anybody else had been standing close, they'd see what he saw. The way Tucker's throat went in, like an invisible hand was squeezing it. In a way, that's exactly what it was. Taige's gift . . . the way she'd honed her telekinesis into an offensive skill. He'd actually been at the receiving end of it a time or two and it wasn't pleasant.

"I don't need to be close, either. Thanks to the demonstration, I can feel what it's like when you're . . . amping up." Taige smiled.

Tucker's face was turning red now. But unlike a lot of people, he wasn't clawing at his throat. Wasn't struggling to get away from something he couldn't see. Control. The man's control was something else, Taylor mused.

"Now, I'm going to let go and hope you'll see the sense in all of us playing nice," Taige said softly. "And please . . . don't swear around the kid, and keep in mind, he's been through more hell than most of us can imagine."

She released her grip on him, although the only obvious signs were the slow return of normal color to Tucker's face and his one, single gulp of air. He continued to glare at her, his eyes like black death on her face. "Woman, you've got no idea the hells I can imagine," he said quietly.

"Point taken," she said, inclining her head. "But whatever hell you can imagine, whatever you've been through, does it justify scaring him? Making it any worse on him than you have to?"

*   *   *

THANKS to Tucker's little temper tantrum, they ended up leaving the McDonald's and buying some KFC. It worked out better anyway, Jones figured, even if the food was a heart attack waiting to happen. He'd gotten used to having more junk food in his diet, thanks to Dez, and he managed to eat it without grimacing. Much.

Alex, though, he seemed to inhale the food in front of him. As long as Tucker wasn't looking at him.

Finally, they finished eating and Taylor had the boy gather things up to throw away in one of the nearby trash cans. It was safe enough to let him walk around. Taige would know if it wasn't.

As Alex left the table, they all mutually stayed quiet until he was out of hearing range, although he never once left their sight. "Any chance I can talk you into coming back in for a while to help with him?" Taylor asked softly.

Taige made a face at him. "I'm not the only one who has a handle on the kind of shit he has in his head, you know. You've got others. Use them. Sync me up to Joss and have him do it."

Taylor shook his head. "Joss is all wrong for the kid right now. He needs . . ."

Taige grimaced and looked away. "I know what he needs. Let's get things settled first." Without saying anything else on the matter, she looked at Tucker. "You're not taking that kid. I don't care who you're working for, who she is, what her claim on him is—"

"Do you all ever talk to each other?" he asked, cutting her off. "I'm working with Nalini. She asked me to keep an eye on him, but that agreement *never* involved me letting the FBI get their hands on him. He's just a kid."

"Nalini?"

Taylor smoothed his tie down. "Another freelancer, Morgan. But she got with Tucker here on her own. I have no idea what her agenda is."

She shrugged. "Fine, whatever." She looked back at Tucker. "Yeah, he's just a kid. But he's a kid who has the ability to kill somebody with his mind. He needs to be trained before he does just that."

From the corner of his eye, Taylor saw Tucker's reaction. Or lack of. It was a very careful lack of. "It's likely if he did do just that, it would be somebody who deserved it," Tucker finally said after a long, tense silence.

"Not the way he's been forced to use his gift," Taylor said. "He's got a knack for picking up on danger and his . . . guardian, uncle, whatever . . . knows it. He's been using the kid as a walking, talking lie detector."

Tucker tensed.

Taylor turned his head and looked at the other man. "One of the people he had the boy read was Vaughnne. Alex told me about it. He wasn't careful enough and she collapsed."

Alex glanced over their way, and Taylor gave him an easy

smile, keeping his surface thoughts neutral. The kid gave him a weak smile. "What do we do, Tucker? Let him go around, barely controlling a gift that could kill people?" He rose from the table, still watching Alex. "Some of you learn control easier than others. Out of necessity, maybe, or because it's in your makeup. He's not learning it and he's going to get stronger over the next few years."

"So you . . . what? Imprison him?" Tucker's mouth twisted and the air went hot, tight once more.

"No." Taylor tucked his hands into his pockets. "There's a far cry between imprisoning a person and *training* him. Once he's trained, he'll be a weapon in his own right and he can watch out for himself. But for now, he's not just a hazard to others around him. He's a hazard to himself. And you saw that for yourself. Those men who tracked him down were trailing him. You know that."

"He's just a damned kid," Tucker said, his voice rough.

"So was I," Taige said softly. "I was a kid when it came on me. I bet you were, too. My daughter? She's just a couple years older than Alex is, and she may well be as strong as he is. And I can tell you this . . . she's better adjusted, better controlled, and far less likely to attract the *wrong* attention from people, because she *has* been trained. So . . . what would you do? Let him out loose in the world where he's hunted . . . *again*? Or have him trained, and *protected* while that takes place?"

"His parents should get to decide that," Tucker said, and then he swore, turning away. "Shit. He doesn't have any, I'm betting, does he?"

"We don't know. He isn't telling us and I'm not prying," Taige said softly. "He's got the guy we left back in Atlanta, and I think he's family, but that's not the same as parents, I know. I know he cares about him, and I know he's doing his best. But his best isn't getting that kid trained, and at some point, Alex needs to decide . . . does he *want* to be a walking, talking lie detector or would he like to learn to use what he has before the gift gets out of hand and he damages somebody? What will that do to him, huh? You got any idea, electro-boy?"

Tucker sneered at her. "If he's damaging somebody that's trying to damage him, more power to him."

"And if he's damaging somebody who *isn't* trying to hurt him?" she demanded. "What then? Can *you* imagine being a kid and knowing that you hurt somebody who had never once done a damn thing to you?"

Something flickered across Tucker's face, darkened his eyes. That dark, dark brown deepened to near black and his expression went tight. Finally, he turned away.

"What does *he* want?" Tucker asked softly.

"Why don't you try asking him?"

Tucker glanced at him, and then as one, they all turned to look over at the river where Alex was. Or *had* been. Taylor kept from jumping, barely, as he realized that Alex had closed the distance between them, in complete silence. With a dark, sad look in his eyes, the kid focused on Tucker. "I'm doing what I want." Then he looked over at Taylor. "I want to call my uncle. He's worried."

* * *

HER skin prickled. The buzz was unmistakable, and although she saw nothing when she craned around in the seat, Vaughnne knew they'd picked up a tail.

Hopefully it was the white Explorer.

Hopefully.

She didn't want to think that they had more than one group following them just then.

Sighing, she reached down into the floorboard and pulled up Gus's bag. She looked over just as he glanced at her. "We've got company coming," she said sourly. "I don't know how far off they are, but I can feel them."

A black brow winged up as he shifted his attention back to the road. "How come you can feel it now but not back when we stopped for gas?"

"Could be a variety of reasons," she said, shrugging. "There were a bunch of people—that makes it harder for me to single anything out. It could be they are searching for me, so they aren't shielding as hard. My only real psychic ability is telepathy. It's . . . well, I guess you can call it my *active* gift. But a lot of us have some limited passive skills that allow us to sense this sort of thing. We just feel different. If whoever it is isn't shielding, or isn't shielding as much? He'll stand out more and I'm more likely to pick up on his vibes."

"He?"

She made a face. "Could be a she. Gut says he, but who knows?"

"Any idea how many?"

"Nope." She shrugged and studied the contents of the bag. It was a bad boy's treasure trove, she decided. Weapons of beauty, for sure. And just about every damn one of them was illegal for civilian use. "I'm going to guess two, because working in teams would appear to be the MO for these goons, but for all I know, it's four. That's not likely, though. I doubt they'd want to split the money that many ways."

He shrugged. "If the risk goes up, the money goes up. Mercenaries are going to be smart and bring in as many men as they need. It's already been made clear this isn't going to be an easy job."

"Gee. Thanks for making me feel better."

"If you wanted to feel better, you should have left back at the gas station. You should have left with Alex. You should have never gotten involved." The words were grim. His face, though, was unaffected. He had that sleepy, sexy look in his eyes, and his mouth was relaxed, almost smiling.

Scary bastard.

Before she could let herself get unnerved, she looked back down into the bag and studied the weapons. "How do you want to handle this? We already know what they are doing and why. So no reason to talk to them."

"Now, Vaughnne, it almost sounds like you're talking about just outright killing them," he murmured.

Her gut clenched. "That's not what I'm talking about." Not entirely. But if she could get them off their ass without worrying about them coming after her again . . . yeah. She could go for that.

"Do we have a few minutes before they catch up to us?"

Vaughnne sighed. "Probably." Her gut wasn't exactly screaming at her yet. Once it was screaming at her, they'd most likely be in sight. When they were in sight, then they'd have to make a decision—

Or not, she realized as Gus shot off the expressway. She hissed out a breath at the sudden movement, the seat belt cutting into her skin. The bruises on her made a rather loud complaint, but she bit back any sound she might have been tempted to make. After all, as Gus had said, if she'd wanted to feel better, she shouldn't have come.

"If you can feel them, can they feel you?"

She looked around at the rather isolated bit of highway he'd decided to follow. The expressway was already fading behind them. Blowing out a breath, she said, "Yeah. They'd do better if I'm not shielding. I guess you want to use me as bait, huh?"

"I just want them to follow us." He had an odd note in his voice.

She made a face. "Sounds like *bait* to me." Didn't matter much, she supposed. She'd done it before. She could do it again. Wasn't anything she liked, but she could handle it. Letting her shields down wasn't much different for her than peeling off her clothing. One layer at a time. It left her feeling exposed, just as if she'd decided to strip herself naked in the middle of a public parking lot or something, too.

And as she let the last layer of shielding drop, she was painfully, almost brutally aware of that other presence, a too-hot buzz along her senses. "Yeah," she whispered. "They can feel me, all right."

Gus didn't answer.

She thought about reaching into the bag and pulling out one of the weapons, but in the end, she settled on the Glock that the Bureau had assigned to her. It was hers, and she knew the feel of it, the weight of it, how it settled in her hand. She appreciated that particular weapon rather well. "You want to give me an idea just what the plan is here?" she asked as he took a sharp left off the highway.

They were barreling down a narrow little country lane now with absolutely no regard for speed limits or anything else.

"The plan? Eliminate the threat." A ghost of a smile danced around his lips for a second. "That's the plan." His eyes seemed to take in everything, although she didn't know how. They were driving so fast, she could barely take in anything beyond the scenery blurring around them.

"You got any idea where we are?"

"Somewhere in Louisiana, close to the Texas border. I've been here." He was quiet for about five seconds and then said, "Hold on."

That was about all the warning she had before he slammed on the brakes. It wasn't enough of a warning and the seat belt cut into her skin once more. "Man, I really want to wallop you, and hard."

"Wallop?"

She sneered at him as he turned down an even narrower road, winding, all but obscured by the undergrowth. Green surrounded them. "Yeah. Wallop. Hit you across that thick head of yours," she snapped.

"A day or so ago, you called it beautiful."

"You are beautiful." She tugged against her seat belt and shifted around, staring out the window. "You know you're beautiful and you use it. I think you should have been a damn female."

He surprised her by laughing. "So I'm . . . what . . . using my masculine wiles too much?"

"You use them like a weapon. And again, you know it." There wasn't anybody back there, but unless they knew the road, she doubted they'd take it at the breakneck speed he'd just used. He took another road. "Just where in the *hell* are you going?"

"Hiding the car. Somebody used to live back here. He's dead now, but we can use the place for cover."

She thought about those words, wondered if she should try to get more information about whoever he was talking about. Then ultimately, figured it wasn't worth it. "Why are we using the place for cover? Why hide the car?"

"Because if we're going to deal with our tail, it's better that they aren't discovered right away," he said simply. Abruptly, the trees opened up around them.

Vaughnne looked around, eyeing the ramshackle little building in front of her warily. That thing couldn't even be called a cabin. "What in the hell is that?"

"It's called a house. People live in them."

"That's not a house. It's not much bigger than a damn closet," she said, shaking her head.

"Well, he lived in it. He could have bought something much bigger, too, but he liked it here. Was easy for him to hide." Gus shrugged and pulled the car around behind the house. It was big enough, barely, to conceal the car. But it wouldn't conceal *them* unless they stayed inside the damn car or went inside the house. She wasn't convinced she wanted to do that, though. It was too little. Too confined.

"Come on. We'll go inside."

Of course they were. She stared at the ramshackle pile of boards morosely as she jerked open the door and climbed out. The hot, muggy punch of a Louisiana summer smacked her in the face the second she did so. Ignoring it, she shut the door, still gripping her Glock with her free hand. Joining Gus on the step, she waited as he picked the lock. It didn't take but a few seconds, although it was a pretty complex lock. Hell, the lock looked like it cost more than the damn house.

In under a minute, they were inside and she found herself staring at a place that was actually remarkably . . . charming, considering the outside. Other than a thick layer of dust, it was well kept, a neat little bed up against a wall, a minuscule kitchen, and a bathroom tucked up in the corner. No TV, though. Just the bed, the kitchen, the bathroom. "Wow. He was into luxury, wasn't he?"

"He wanted to escape from life . . . wanted peace. This was what he considered peace." Gus shrugged.

Vaughnne took another, longer look around, her gaze lingering on the bookshelves. Empty now, but they looked like they were handmade, built into every empty space available, including the areas over the door, along the windows, above the bed. A little place, easy to clean, secluded. Just her and a few books . . . well, she wouldn't want to live like that for always, but it might not be a bad vacation, she supposed.

"Did you know him from . . ." She trailed off, uncertain how to finish that sentence.

With an odd little smile on his face, Gus glanced at her. "He was a contact. We knew each other. I wouldn't say we were friends, but we weren't enemies." He shrugged as he moved over to the window, situated so he could see outside without fully exposing himself to whoever might come driving up. "I respected him, I can say that much."

"I take it you don't say that often."

Silence stretched out for a long moment and then he said, "No. I don't often say that."

She didn't say anything else as she crossed the narrow floor space. The skin along the back of her neck was crawling and blood roared in her ears, getting louder, louder. "They are getting closer." She moved to stand beside him, gripping the butt of her Glock while a voice in the back of her mind started to ramble on in a panic.

What are you doing?

You can't be doing this.

You shouldn't be doing this.

What are you doing?

Her mouth felt dry.

It had been one thing to take action in the hospital, although she realized Gus had done most of that. There had been an active threat.

It was another thing to stand here in the shadows of what looked to be an abandoned little shack while they waited for a couple of people to drive up so Gus could . . . could what?

Her mind filled in that blank happily.

It was like shooting fish in a barrel.

And yet these fish were vicious and predatory, ready to kill to get what they wanted.

Information on Alex.

She *knew* what they were going to do if they didn't *get* what they wanted. Or rather, what they'd try to do. But still, it was a cold, heavy weight in her gut, the knowledge that she was getting ready to cross that line.

Watch the lines you cross, Vaughnne. I understand the desire, but I can't help if you go too far . . .

A year ago, she couldn't have stood here. Even as nervous as she was, with all these doubts raging inside her, she knew she couldn't have done this. But losing Daylin had done something to her. Seeing Alex . . . being near him, knowing the kind of fear he lived with.

Yeah.

A hand touched her arm.

She looked up.

Gus stared at her, his eyes cool, unreadable. "Go into the bathroom. Lock the door. I'll handle this."

She knew what he was doing. Giving her a way out. Shouldering the responsibility.

Part of her wanted to let him do just that. Her heart slammed hard against her ribs as she shifted her gaze back to the window. She could hear an engine now, faint, off in the distance. It wasn't coming at them in a roar, so they must be taking their time on that narrow, uneven road.

If they were smart, they'd just park the car . . .

Abruptly, the engine went silent and she cursed and slammed up the shields in her mind. Hopefully they'd just come to the logical conclusion but just in case . . . no point in taking chances. She focused on Gus and focused her thoughts down to the narrowest stream possible, speaking only into his mind. She had trained with some of the best, and if they couldn't pick up on her thoughts when she didn't want them to, she should be okay. But Gus was a different matter. *Don't think anything about what you're doing. Act and react, but don't broadcast your thoughts. They might have a telepath with them.*

She went to break the contact and then paused. Reaching out, she fisted her hand in his shirt, staring up into his eyes. *I told you . . . I'm with you, got it? I'm not hiding in the bathroom like a little girl.*

Gus slid a hand up her back, curving it around her neck and tugging her closer. "You keep throwing your chances away. Sooner or later, they will all be gone," he said softly, leaning in to press his lips to hers.

She sighed as he pulled away. Just that light touch had heat spreading through her, a hot, delighted shimmer that she wanted to wrap herself in. Wrap herself in, lose herself in. Except now was so *not* the time, not when the alarm in her head was slowly getting louder and louder.

He glanced around and then grabbed his bag. "Come on. Let's go outside."

"Outside?" She eyed his back as he headed for the little door at the back.

He didn't answer and she purposely avoided thinking about anything, staring at nothing more than his back, his hips, the long length of his legs. He moved through the door, and Vaughnne had to admit, leaving the hot, confining air of that closed-up little cabin was almost a relief.

She felt terribly exposed as she followed him out of there, although it was just her imagination. Nobody was watching them . . . yet. But they were close. So very close. Her heart raced, her breathing sped up, her muscles had that odd tense feel to them. Deliberately, she made herself relax. Rotating her neck, she eased through the tangle of trees and brush, following along behind Gus. He seemed to know exactly where he was going, she decided. And once again, she had to admire how he moved.

He moved, and he moved well.

He found an area for her, gestured to it, and she tucked herself behind it, not the least bit surprised that she had a fairly clean field of vision ahead of her, although she was mostly out of sight because of the way he'd positioned her.

She shot him a look, saw that sleepy smile on his face as he settled in his own position. It wasn't long, though, before his face went smooth and blank. His eyes were cool, and butter wouldn't have melted in his mouth. He waited behind a tree maybe ten feet away. He eyed the gun in her hand and shook his head as he unzipped his bag.

She closed her eyes as he took out the Heckler & Koch MP5. He checked it with quick, competent hands and loaded it in the same fashion. As he slipped the strap over one shoulder, she swallowed the knot in her throat and looked back at the house. *I'm an FBI agent. Is this what I need to be doing . . .*

The thought was still circling through her brain when she felt something nasty settle in her mind.

I can't do this. I can't. I can't do this—

Her legs were wooden. Mechanically, she felt herself starting to rise as those thoughts tripped through her mind. *I can't do this. I can't—*

Something crunched under her foot and the sound of it penetrated her mind. Dazed, she looked around. Something edged against her thoughts. *Can't do this. Can't . . .*

"Not right," she mumbled, reaching up to smack her hand against her temple. The butt of her weapon smacked against her head, hard, and the flash of pain cleared the fog from her head. It was enough to snap the alien hold on her mind.

Fuck—

Jerking her head up, she saw Gus, realized he was coming toward her.

Stop. I'm fine, she told him, shaking her head.

Like a scummy rope, the unseen psychic had wrapped his gift around her brain and tried to drag her places she didn't want to go.

Bastard was a controller.

A few, a *very* few, had the ability to coerce others to do

things. Nalini Cole was one of them, but she actually had to be touching the person and her skills were . . . odd. This one apparently *didn't* have to be touching his target.

We got problems, she said into Gus's mind, not bothering to shield her voice. It took everything she had just to fight that pull. Sweat broke out on her skin and she dropped down on the ground, digging her hands into the damp earth, anything to ground herself as she fought that pull on her mind.

It *hurt*, and the harder she fought, the more it hurt.

A hand touched her arm and she looked up, saw that Gus had come to her side.

"What's wrong?" Gus murmured, his voice calm, unaffected.

Somebody there can force people to do shit. Look for him. He'll be focusing—She wasn't even able to finish the thought as the strain on her brain increased. Biting down on her lip, she slammed her hands against her skull, but it didn't even touch on the pain there. *Damn it, damn it,* damn *it*—

She slammed up her shields, the ones she'd lowered when she tried to draw them in, but it was hard, so hard to concentrate, and it felt like she was trapping him inside those shields with her. Him. That nasty, slippery presence. It was like having a giant, mutant slug trapped inside her head, in the innermost part of her.

But as she formed one set of shields, then another, and another, some of the pressure on her brain eased off. Panting, she slid Gus a look. "They ought to be close now, really close."

He lifted a hand to his lips.

She sucked in a breath, a second one. Okay. Better now. That pressure was still there and the intensity of it increased, but instead of a rope that was trying to drag her away, it was more like a raging thunderstorm. She wasn't inside a house—she felt like she had an umbrella over her head, though. It was enough to protect her from the impact. It worked.

She focused on Gus. *Do you see them?*

He gave a small, almost imperceptible nod.

Watch for a reaction . . . whoever reacts, take him out.

Maybe she should thank the son of a bitch who'd just tried to mind-rape her. It made this easier. Controllers were dangerous. If they used that ability without any sort of care . . . yeah. He'd made this a lot easier.

She gathered up her control and narrowed her thoughts down. It was like weapons practice, really. Just a different sort of weapon. She had a line of sight, thanks to what that son of a bitch had tried to pull. With her mind's eye, she could see that line, that connection that led her to *his* mind . . . and once she was there, she unloaded.

A shriek rose up—yeah, she'd been right. They were close.

An odd little *pop* echoed through the air.

Somebody swore.

She didn't have time to process that, because a hand appeared in her line of vision. She reached up blindly and found herself on her feet a second later, staring up into Gus's face. Her head was screaming at her but that pressure on her brain was gone, too. "He's dead," she said softly.

He didn't respond.

She didn't guess there was any point.

Out behind them, in that little field behind the house, somebody called out, "Y'all can't avoid all of us, not for forever. Just tell us where to find the kid and this all stops."

She snorted. Yeah. Sure it would stop.

Gus stroked a hand down her arm and then crowded her back against the tree. She didn't know what he was doing, or why, and just then, she decided she was maybe okay with that. She was out of her element here. She worked on task forces. She'd been shot at before, had been hunted before, and done her share of hunting before, but it had all been within the confines of the law. On her part, at least. There were rules in her world.

She'd left her world behind and she was still struggling to adjust to that.

Gus dipped his head and whispered in her ear, "Any idea what he can do?"

She turned her head and looked at him. Then, silent, she shook her head. Whatever the guy was, he either wasn't very strong, or he was very, very smart, and very, very good because she couldn't feel much more than the faintest buzz from him.

"Y'all really want to come out of there now. Come on now," the unknown psychic said. "Don't make me force it."

Don't make me force it. Those words sent a shiver of trepidation down her spine. Force it. Force *them?* His partner had already tried that, ended up dead for his trouble. Just what was he going to . . .

An odd crackle reached her ears. Familiar, that sound. She hissed out a breath and jerked her head around to stare at the orange glow. It shimmered off in the brush about a dozen yards away. "There's the first one," he called. "Do I have to—"

The words ended in a scream and Gus was already striding out of the trees, his Sig Sauer in his hand, the Heckler & Koch hanging from his shoulder. "Bring my bag," he said over his shoulder.

Vaughnne stared at the flickering orange flames for a minute longer, watching as they raged higher. "Don't kill him yet, Gus. We need him."

* * *

DON'T *kill him yet*, she says.

Gus crouched down by the man and shot out a hand, fisting it in the bastard's hair. "You want to try and burn me out of there, hmm?"

The man clutched at the bleeding hole in his belly. "Fuck you," he rasped.

Gus took his weapon and pressed the muzzle to the sensitive

underside of the man's chin. "That hole in your gut isn't going to kill you," he said softly. "Not for a long, long while. So I have time to make you suffer."

"Gus."

He looked up as Vaughnne came closer. "Wait for me by the car," he said shortly. She was already upset by this. He'd known it would happen, that she would see the monster inside him. He could handle that. But he'd rather her not see it.

"Stop," she said, grabbing his wrist and tugging until he eased up.

"Stop?" He stared at her. The *cabrón* had been ready to burn her and she wanted him to *stop*?

"If you don't stop, that fire can burn out of control. You want that?"

He wanted to say he didn't care, but realized he couldn't *entirely* say that, not without lying. Perhaps he wasn't as far gone as he'd always thought. He didn't want to think of this quiet little place gone, lost to a fire.

Sighing, he looked back at the bastard on the ground and instead of pressing the muzzle to the man's chin, he dragged the tip of it down his torso, along his hip, and then jammed it hard against his scrotum. "Here is the deal, *cabrón*. You're going to put that fire out now. If you don't, I'm going to kill you, *ojete*, in the slowest, most painful way you can possibly imagine. And if you can't imagine a slow and painful way, let me know. I'll give you some ideas."

The man sneered at him.

Gus shifted the Sig Sauer to his other hand and reached down, grabbed the man's penis and twisted. Once the man's shrieking had faded away into whimpers, Gus started to speak. "The first thing I'll do? I'm gonna pull your balls out through your nose. If that doesn't get your attention, I'm gonna slice your dick off. In pieces."

He let go and smiled down at the man. "Have I made the matter clear now?"

The man sucked in a breath and nodded.

"You'll put out the fire?"

"Are you going to kill me when I do?"

Gus smiled. "No."

And he wasn't lying. He had questions. After he was done with those questions, though . . .

Vaughnne stood just to the side. From the corner of his eye, he could see her face, grim and unsmiling. Some of her tension eased and she blew out a sigh. "The fire is dying. I'm going to go check, make sure it's out. Don't kill him before I get back here, Gus," she warned.

He didn't answer.

Once she was gone, he pressed the muzzle of his weapon against the man's groin. "Here is where we can start to play, *ojete*. I can put a hole in you. Right here. Or you can answer my questions. You ready to play?"

The man wheezed out a breath in response.

"I'll take that as a yes."

* * *

VAUGHNNE made it back to the area as quick as she could and the warning was still a scream in her head. The fire was out. Awesome. Gus was still crouched over the pyrokinetic. *Not* awesome.

He had his gun pressed against the man's groin and Vaughnne grimaced a little. The man looked ghost-white and he was babbling out answers so fast, she could barely process them.

Gus didn't look to have that problem. The man finally stumbled to a stop and Gus twisted the weapon against his scrotum. "You're sure that's all you know, *cabrón*? There's nothing else?"

"No. Nothing." His eyes were wide, locked on Gus's face like he'd never seen anything so terrifying in his life.

It was a scary thing to look at a man and know he could, and would, kill you without any remorse, without blinking an eye.

"And what was the latest update on the website?"

"Not much." The pyro licked his lips and wheeled his head around to look at Vaughnne. "Word is out about her." Something that might have been hope bled into his eyes. "Hey, I hear tell you're a cop . . . you . . . you can't let him kill me."

She lifted a brow. "Word is out about me?"

He nodded, a quick, awkward bob of his head. "One of the mods can see things. She gets all technical with it, calls it remote viewing and shit, but she knew there was law enforcement working this—described you, this place . . ." His words ended in a whine as Gus reached up and laid a hand on his throat, squeezing lightly.

"You need to be useful," Gus warned. "Or you die. Tell me something I can use. Don't look at her and expect her to help you."

Vaughnne took a few steps closer and knelt down by the man, careful to stay out of reach. "I want to know more about the others. How many are still chasing after the boy, do you know?"

"No." He whined and clutched at his bleeding gut. "We don't work like that. But—" He broke off.

"But what?"

He hunched in on himself, refusing to speak.

Gus sighed. "This man, he likes having me hurt him, I think." He let go of the bastard's throat, but before he could do anything else, the man's breath gusted out of him.

And he started to talk once more. "It's Gemma. One of the mods on the board. The one who saw this place, who knew about you. She's telling people they need to pull off the job 'cuz it's death all over. People listen to her. The smart ones, at least. I wasn't going to take the job. But it's so much money . . ."

Taut, heavy moments of silence stretched out, and when Gus abruptly stood, Vaughnne almost came out of her skin. And when he lifted the gun, leveled it at the man on the ground, she had hers in her hand. It was pointed at Gus's head. "Don't," she said softly.

He didn't even look at her.

"Gus, if you shoot him, I'm shooting you. He's bleeding out, you've now scared him shitless, and he's getting too weak to do anything," she said. The man was pale, and getting paler by the second. He'd die if he didn't get medical help. And she wasn't ready to cross that line. She didn't *want* to cross that line.

Gus's finger tensed. She could see it. "Gus, please. Don't do this."

The man sobbed.

"He was ready to kill you," Gus said gently. "He can, even now. With that ability to use fire? And you would try to save him?"

"It's not about saving him. He hunts kids. He's scum, and I know that. This is about saving me . . . and you."

He looked at her now, and in the depths of those beautiful eyes, she saw a flicker of something. Surprise, maybe.

"Saving me." He shifted the gun away from the man, but she didn't think for a minute that this was done. "Saving me, how?"

"He's not strong enough now to go throwing fire around. Pyros have to work harder, and if he's weak, he can't handle it. He's not the threat he was a few minutes ago. He's wounded, and he's unarmed. If we go around killing the helpless, we become just like the monsters."

Thick black lashes fell down, shielding Gus's eyes. "Vaughnne, I already am just like the monsters. It's one of the reasons I was able to keep the boy alive."

She shook her head. "No."

Another long, tense silence and then finally he knelt back down. She held her breath as he changed his hold on the weapon and swung out, using it to club the man across the head. Her breath gusted out of her and she almost went to the ground in shock. "You cannot save me, Vaughnne," he said softly. "I'm already lost. But you can pretend to save yourself . . . for a little while longer."

NINETEEN

T HE hotel had seen better days, that was for certain. It was mostly vacant, on an isolated little strip along the Texas interstate. The terrain had gone from lush and green to flat and brown, with scraggly little bushes that looked like they struggled to stay alive.

Kind of like the hotel.

Punch drunk with fatigue, she looked toward the highway, half expecting to see another SUV, a sedan with black windows . . . something ominous. It had been quiet for more than a day, ever since she and Gus had left the pyro tied up on the porch of that tiny little shack back in Louisiana.

She'd called Taylor. He'd said he'd handle it.

No telling how he was handling it, but she'd kept an eye on the news in that area. No reports of fires springing up out of the blue, so she didn't have to have *that* on her head.

And nobody else had caught up to them yet. The best she

could do was hope they could get some rest before anyone new showed up on her radar. A couple of hours, she thought.

That was all she wanted.

"Are you thinking about running?"

She looked behind her as Gus came out of the bathroom.

She'd already showered and changed into some clothes he'd picked up for her earlier in the day. The tank top and yoga pants were comfortable enough to sleep in, but if she had to move—or fight—she could.

The only direction she really wanted to move just then, though, was toward the bed. She was so damn tired. Turning away from the window, she decided she'd do just that. This might be her last chance to get any decent rest for a while, right?

"No," she said, shooting him a dark look. "I'm not thinking about running. For the hundredth time. If I decide I'm going to run, Gus, you're not going to see me doing something so obvious as staring yearnfully out the window."

A moment passed and then he echoed, "Yearnfully? Is this really a word?"

"Oh, bite me," she muttered. She stretched out on the bed closest to the door. She had her Glock on the table right next to her, and out of habit, she reached for it, checked it. Loaded. Ready. It didn't do much to ease any of the weight on her mind.

She put it down and closed her eyes.

Five seconds later, she jerked up in the bed as Gus lay down next to her, shirtless, wearing nothing but a pair of loose-fitting gray pants. Low-slung, they revealed far too much for her peace of mind. But then again, everything about Gus was too much for her peace of mind. "What are you doing?"

"Lying down." He rolled on his side to face her. "You should do the same."

She glared at him. "There are two beds."

"There are." He reached up and touched her lips, and her skin all but buzzed from the light contact. "But I'm going to be closest to the door. And even if you move to that other bed, Vaughnne, once we've both had some rest, I plan on being inside you again. Before we leave this room, if nothing else goes wrong."

She gaped at him.

Part of her wanted to sneer at him.

The other part wanted to forget how dog-tired she was and just crawl on top of him, take him *now.*

"You know, that's a terribly romantic proposal," she said, shooting for sarcasm. Hopefully it would keep him from realizing just what she was thinking. Feeling. *Wanting* . . . "But I'm thinking I might pass. You have it in your head that it's a foregone conclusion, pal, the two of us getting it on again. Whoever said it was going to be a repeat?"

He just stared at her, and after a minute, a faint smile tugged up the corners of his lips. "Why don't you get some sleep, Vaughnne?"

"Are you going to move to the other bed?"

"I'm staying closest to the door." He stroked his thumb across her lower lip and then lifted his hand, settled it between them on the bed. That was when she saw the gun—that Sig Sauer he carried around like it was a pacifier. "If you don't want to share the bed, then you can move to the other one."

She should do just that. Really.

But instead, she lay down.

From the corner of her eye, she could see that smile of his. Infuriating. She rolled away from him and gave him her back. The guy was hot as hell, too beautiful to be real. And arrogant as all get-out.

Knowing that last part didn't make it any easier to convince herself she wasn't going to have sex with him once she woke up.

She already knew what was going to happen.

Assuming they had the chance.

* * *

THE phone rang.

Nalini rolled up off the bed, grabbing the phone as she moved. She checked the caller ID and looked up to see Reyes glaring at her. Her hold only lasted for a short time when she wasn't in physical contact, and she had no desire to stay in physical contact with this guy indefinitely.

Tying him up, though, that always worked.

"Hello?" She smiled at him as she brushed her fingers over his brow, establishing the connection, looking for what she needed. He made it too easy. He was greedy and grabby and wanted everything. She twisted those needs and used them against him. Sinking the compulsion deep inside him, she promised him, *You can have what you want . . . me. Hurt me as bad as you want. After you help me. Again . . .*

It was all lies, but he didn't know that. Didn't have to, either. He'd figure it out once the compulsion wore off, but it wouldn't help him then. *You're going to tell them everything is fine.* She set the guidelines mentally as she spoke with his second in command.

They'd all looked at Reyes as though he'd lost his mind when he told them that everybody was going to leave. He wanted a few days alone with his lady. That was the lie Nalini had offered him last time. She wouldn't be mad at him for hitting her, she'd never leave again, she'd do him *however* he wanted her to . . . and damn, the guy was a freak. *However* he wanted sometimes included the kind of violence that women sometimes died from.

As a voice jabbered on in her ear, she held Reyes's gaze, watched as his eyes went unfocused, and she felt it when her hold on him snapped into place. "Yes, he's here . . . we've been . . . well, I can't tell you that, but he was still in bed."

She smiled a little as she put the call on speaker. She kept one hand on his cheek as they lapsed into Spanish. Some part of him tugged against her hold, and she wrapped her will more tightly around him, felt him acquiesce.

"No, no . . ."

Reyes smiled, a dazed, blissed-out look on his face as spoke to his second, *Yes, yes, everything is fine. No, you are not to return yet. Yes, we are well . . .*

"*Mañana . . .*"

Nalini swore silently and pressed harder on his mind. *Not tomorrow. Tell him to call.*

Reyes went white around the eyes under the strain of her hold, but his voice was steady as he relayed just that to his second in command. She was pushing her luck, she knew it. But she was going to finish what she started here, and she had to finish dealing with the website, too. All of that took time, and she kept having to stop and reinforce her damn hold on Reyes every time he had a phone call.

They spoke for another few minutes and then the call disconnected. She broke contact with him, but he continued to sit there, a dazed, happy look on his face, almost like he was high.

"If somebody gets to sit around looking all strung out and happy, why can't it be me?" she muttered as she headed back to the desk.

"Come here, Nala," Reyes said, his voice low and heated. "I can make you happy."

She made a face. The only way he'd make her happy was when she left him far, far behind her. She didn't know if she'd be able to do that without killing him or not. The option was looking less and less likely, too. This fixation he had on the boy wasn't going to end unless he died, but that would bring about a whole other mess of problems. When men like Reyes died, people noticed, and she hadn't come in equipped for that. This should have been a simple information-gathering operation. It was proving to be the most screwed-up disaster ever.

But she couldn't walk away . . . not from that boy.

As she checked the progress on the psychic site, she glanced up at him. "Why the boy, Reyes?"

Something else she'd like while he was feeling cooperative—answers.

"The boy?" he echoed.

Something flickered in his mind. Her hold was slipping. Already. Son of a bitch.

It should have lasted longer than that. Instead of looking at the computer, she remained where she was, staring at Reyes. "Yeah. What's the deal with the boy?"

"He's my son," Reyes said, his voice thick, the words coming reluctantly. "He's mine."

"Yours?" she echoed. "So you miss him, then? You love him? Want to bring him home and . . ."

His lip curled. "Love him. No. Until I knew what he could do, he was just useful to keep his cunt-mother happy. A man in my position needs a beautiful woman at his side. She served her purpose. But then I realized what he could do. And he's my son. He will come home."

Useful . . .

Nalini gathered up her hair, securing it at her nape as she settled back behind the computer. Well, that solved that riddle. The images of the night the woman died still weren't clear. This wasn't the man who killed her, but he was behind the attacks on the boy, was hunting him down like a wild animal. Not out of love, but because the boy was *useful*.

She tapped at a few keys and *finally*—she had the information she needed. What she *really* wanted to do was take the entire website down, see it crash and burn, but Jones might need the information on it to track people down. Too much vigilante shit taking place on it, and that was just bad, bad news. Somebody needed to blow that thing wide open.

But she'd hacked in a mod's ID with enough clearance to delete that profile. She already knew where it had originated from . . . *here*. Esteban. The *missing* Esteban. She'd heard Ignacio ordering his men to find the *cabrón* and bring him in, but she had a funny feeling they wouldn't be finding the man. He'd had a desperate look about him when he'd left here . . . how long ago had it been? Almost two weeks ago? She couldn't even remember. Maybe three? Closer to three, she thought. All the days were running together. But Esteban's eyes, yeah. That she remembered. He'd had the look of a desperate man, and since he hadn't found the boy, she had a feeling he'd be doing almost anything to avoid coming back here.

Still, while she was on the inside, she collected as much information as she could. There were others here that had caught her interest. Nobody wanted to catch Nalini's interest. Ignacio had, and look where it had landed him.

First, screen shots of everything and she saved them, e-mailed them to a personal account. She'd access it later and start researching. Once she was away from here. Then she deleted the *job* listing, wiping it off the server, as well as any and all responses to it. She couldn't do anything if it had been cached anywhere on the Net, but if it wasn't an active job posting, maybe some of the people on his ass would stop. The pragmatic sorts, at least.

After she'd done that, she took care of the protective measures to make sure nobody could get on the computer and find out what she'd been doing. Reyes was no computer genius but he had plenty of them around.

By the time she was done removing all traces from the computer, so much time had passed that Reyes had thrown off all signs of the compulsion, and when she looked up, he was watching her with the soulless, dead eyes of a killer. "Why are you asking about Alejandro?" he asked gently.

"Who?" She smiled at him, the coy, promising smile that had

suckered him into bringing her here. Of course, it hadn't *just* been a smile. She'd thrown in a few casual touches, a few whispered innuendos, basically getting him all hot and bothered.

Now he was icy and cold, like he was already planning the ways he wanted to kill her.

"My son."

She blinked at him. "You have a kid?"

"Don't play the stupid *puta* with me, Nala. I know what you are, what you can do. Is that why you hunt him? You want him for yourself?"

She studied him for a minute. "You would think something like that, wouldn't you?"

She shut down her computer and stood up. She needed to find anything and everything she could that had belonged to the boy, or to his mother. Once she had those things, she had to destroy them. He had already figured out what she was, so he'd figure out there were more. Ignacio hadn't been the brains behind *The Psychic Portal* move, but since he knew there were others out there, she didn't want him to have any decent tools within his grasp if he decided to reach out to others to help look for his son.

"How do you know about my son?"

She smiled at him. "Madame Nala sees all, knows all."

The look in his eyes told her he didn't know if he believed her or not. She managed not to laugh in his face. If he thought she was some all-seeing, all-knowing thing, it might work to her benefit.

He wasn't just going to buy it, though. "You don't think I will just believe that, do you?"

"I don't care what you believe, Reyes." Nalini shrugged. "Doesn't matter jack to me. Why don't you sit there and mentally jack off as you think about the way his mama cried when you hit her because she said she'd leave?"

Direct hit.

She saw his lashes flicker, the only sign that she'd been right on target. But she knew she had. She'd been living in this hell for too long and she'd picked up enough impressions. From the house. From the jewelry he'd given her. From *him*.

"You don't know what you're talking about," he said after just a few seconds too long.

"No?" She shrugged and started to gather up her things. After she went over the house, she had to get out of here. She had to do this fast, too.

As she strode past him, he jerked against the chair. "Let me loose, Nala. Now. If you don't . . ."

She paused and looked over at him, smiling a little. "You'll what? Put your hands on me? Haven't you seen what happens when you do that?"

His mouth spasmed. "I don't need to touch you to make you pay. A bullet in the back of your head will suffice."

"You have to catch up with me first." She shrugged and left the room. The clock was running. She had to gather up anything that could be used to find Alex. She had to gather up anything and everything of hers, but she'd already taken care of most of that. A few other pieces of information.

So much to do . . . so little time.

* * *

Gus expected to sleep lightly, or not at all.

He was in bed with somebody else, and that shouldn't be conducive to restfulness.

It was something of a surprise when he found himself drifting to slow awareness. Slow . . . pleasant . . . awareness.

He took stock of his surroundings, mentally taking note. Had anything changed? Dirty, smoke-stained ceiling overhead—all of that had been the same as last night. Ugly art on the walls—it had been just as ugly the night before. Thick, blackout curtains on the windows—the only change there was the thin stream of light filtering in through the narrow gap. Hotel room—a piss-poor excuse of a room.

Damn, what he wouldn't give to take Vaughnne to a place of luxury, where crystal and gold glinted, where the bed was as soft as a cloud and the cotton sheets felt as smooth and soft as silk against her skin as he lay her down to make love to her.

Instead, they were in this old, run-down pile of bricks that had seen better days.

His brain processed everything else, even as he dwelled a little longer on the fantasy. He still had his weapon, gripped in his right hand. And his left hand . . . he closed his eyes and let himself linger in the moment. A few more seconds, he decided, couldn't really hurt anything, could it? If this was all they'd ever have, why not enjoy what he could?

Vaughnne muttered in her sleep and snuggled in closer, her face tucked against his neck, her arm slung over his waist. She was as close to him as she could be without crawling on top of him, and if she decided to do that, he wouldn't mind.

He'd actually enjoy it. He'd love to see her riding him, freeing his hands to touch that strong, limber body.

Heat spread through him as he thought of it, and he had to fight the urge to bring that hot fantasy to life, right then, right there. His dick insisted that he'd warned her. He'd told her he planned on having her again, and if she wanted that not to happen, she should have gone to the other bed.

But the other part of him remembered how she had looked at him with sad, somber eyes the previous day when she'd pulled a gun on him.

Saving me. It was a lovely, naïve thing that she thought he could actually *be* saved at this point in his life. He'd killed. He'd stolen. He'd long since grown immune to the wet sound a bone made as he broke it. He'd done so many awful things, and up until Alex had come into his life, he'd been about ready to go down in a blaze of glory, too. Tired of it all.

Now he was still tired, but mostly, he was tired of running. Tired of being afraid of what would happen. He didn't fear for himself, but for Alex. Now for her.

She thought she was saving him.

So he could let himself be a little less of a monster and not be the greedy bastard he truly was.

If she wanted him—

She woke up.

* * *

SHE'D expected to get maybe an hour of sleep. Two, if she was lucky.

That was how life had been going ever since she'd hit Orlando, after all. Nothing went the way she'd hoped.

But when she woke up, her head wasn't muzzy with exhaustion, and her body wasn't raging in fury at the thought of getting out of bed. It was just growling a little.

And Gus lay in the bed next to her.

His long, lean form, so strong, so warm. His hand curved over the swell of her hip, and as she lay there, his fingers spread wide, for just a minute, as though he was learning the feel of her. She wanted to do the very same thing to him, spread her hands open and learn every damn inch of his body.

She caught her breath, remembering what he'd told her.

But instead of him rolling her onto her back, when he moved, it was to pull away.

"We need to get on the road," he said, his voice level. Emotionless.

She sat up, staring at his naked back. "The road?" she echoed. What had happened to all his talk about getting her naked? Getting inside her again?

"Yes. I have to make a few calls about getting us across the border." He glanced over his shoulder at her. "I take it you didn't bring your passport?"

"Actually, I do have it." Although illegally entering a country was probably going to be the least of her crimes by the time this was all said and done. And just *what* had happened to getting her naked? She stared at him a minute longer, but all he did was shift off the bed, crouching by the bag he'd left on the floor.

And that was it. Watching his bowed head, she realized his mind was already on other things. *Fine. I'm not going to let him see I'm put out over this. I'm not. And I'm not put out by it. I'm . . .*

Climbing out of bed, she headed to the minuscule bathroom and locked herself inside.

Oh, the hell I'm not.

Emotion tangled inside her, too complicated to really put her finger on. Hurt? Yeah. There was some of that, for certain. Bruised pride? Maybe a little. Okay, more than a little. It was arousing, knowing somebody *wanted* you. *Really* wanted you . . . and then to have him *not* want you? It was a punch in the gut. The hurt and bruised pride twisted in her, but it went deeper than that. She couldn't even figure out everything she felt, either.

Disappointment seemed like such a minor word for the empty ache she felt inside. It went too deep for just mere *disappointment*.

"I don't have time for this," she muttered. Squaring her shoulders, she made herself stare at her reflection. She looked sad and miserable and lost, like a girl who'd been stood up by the cute guy in high school.

That wasn't going to cut it. She had a job to do, and it was going to get ugly before it got better. Hell, it might not *get* better for her. She'd already acknowledged that fact. But if she walked into this looking like a whipped puppy, then it was just going to snowball into one hell of a bad mess, and that, she did not need.

Taking a deep breath, she shoved everything aside. So Gus

didn't seem to want her the way he'd made her think. In the end, that didn't matter. Not to the job, at least, and the job was why she was here. The job and only the job. Having the hot and sexy Gus along the wayside had been both a bonus and a complication, but in the end, he wasn't the focus.

Alex was.

She'd been sent to Orlando to watch over a kid.

Somebody else was taking point on that job now, but that didn't mean she was done. Her current objective was to keep that kid safe, and the threat to him had grown exponentially. She had to get her game on and stay focused.

With that in mind, she turned away from the mirror and stripped out of her clothes. She needed to shower and clear her head. She needed coffee, but they'd grab that on the road.

Game on, she told herself as she climbed under the miserable, stingy spray. *Game on*.

* * *

THE woman who ducked into the bathroom had been quiet, somber, and he couldn't help but think he'd hurt her. He wouldn't let that get to him. He was used to hurting women. Not physically, but when the job included assignments like seduction and espionage, people did end up with their feelings bruised, their pride.

It wasn't so easy to shrug it off when the woman was Vaughnne, and he told himself that maybe he'd misunderstood her. After all, she'd told him he was arrogant, had mouthed off to him before they fell asleep. He was just respecting her wishes, really.

The door to the bathroom opened and the woman came striding out, wearing nothing but a bath towel, her hair pulled back and away from her face. Her eyes cut to his, and any sign of sadness or pain was completely gone.

She looked arrogant now. Arrogant, aloof, and the light in her eyes was one of warning.

He stood by the door, waiting, watching.

And damn near swallowed his tongue as she stood in front of the neat little stack of clothes and dropped her towel.

Beads of water still clung to her shoulders, rolled down the slope of her breast as she grabbed a pair of panties. Black. It seemed black and white were her preferred colors in wardrobe choices, so that was all he'd grabbed for her, but he would love to see her in red silk. Blue satin. Emerald green. Anything. Everything. Nothing.

His heart slammed against his ribs as she pulled the panties up over the taut, round curve of her ass. Then she shot him a dark look. "If we need to get on the road, don't you think you should get ready?"

Ready? If he were any readier, he might die of a heart attack.

She stared at him for a moment and then looked away, that disdainful expression still on her face. She reached for her bra and he locked his gaze on her breasts, memorized those curves for the few brief moments he had left to him. Perfect, he decided. Just about perfect. Full enough for his hands, nothing more and nothing less, her skin that soft, warm brown, and her nipples were a deeper, darker shade. Puckered, and tight, too.

¿Qué carajo? What was he doing? She wanted him. He wanted her. Saving her . . . from what? Himself? She'd said a hundred times if she'd wanted to leave, she'd do just that. And if she tried, he'd let her. He'd already decided that. Because he didn't need the assurance that she'd look after Alejandro. She would already do it. That was just who she was.

So what or who was he trying to save her from?

He dropped the bag he was holding.

Vaughnne shot him another dark look as she reached for a shirt. "You know, if you'd wanted to stare at my tits, you should have done something about it earlier. We need to get going, right?"

Closing the distance between them, he caught the lapels of the black shirt before she could start to button it up. "It can wait," he said gruffly. Dipping his head, he pressed his mouth to the curve between her neck and shoulder.

Vaughnne stiffened.

He breathed in the scent of her skin, warm and soft, smelling of the lousy soap the hotel had provided, and something else . . . female, unique to her. The lotion she slicked on her skin, maybe. He didn't know, but the scent was enough to drive him mad. Raking his teeth along her skin, he caught the collar of her shirt and dragged it down.

She shoved her hands between them. "Hold on there, pal," she said, her lip curling.

He lifted a hand and cupped her face, dragging his thumb across her mouth, watching as hunger danced in her gaze even as she edged backward.

"I'm not a plaything." She glared at him. "Hot little pillow talk last night, and then this morning, it's all serious shit, but five seconds later, you want to put your hands on me again? I don't do this hot and cold stuff, Gus."

"Gustavo." He leaned in, flicking his tongue across her lower lip. She tensed. "What?"

"My name. It's Gustavo. And I *always* want to put my hands on you, Vaughnne," he whispered, teasing the entrance to her mouth, but she still wouldn't open for him. "But last night, you talked as though that wasn't what you wanted. I thought perhaps I'd respect your wishes . . . for once."

If he wasn't mistaken, some of the tension eased from her body. "You were trying to play the nice guy?"

"It's not a role I'm used to." He caught her lip between his teeth and tugged. "Perhaps it is arrogance. I know women. I

know when they want me, and if they don't, I know how to *make*
them want me. You want me . . . and if you didn't, I could make
you. But then you do silly, naïve things like try and save me. And
I lay in bed this morning thinking I didn't want to *make* you
want me. If you wanted me . . ."

Earlier, she'd fisted her hands against his chest, the tension in
her arms keeping him from pulling her close. Now, she sighed
and stroked her hands upward, sliding them around his neck.
"Gus . . . Gustavo . . . you know, you really strike me as the typical Casanova—you should know everything there is to know
about women. So how can you be so damn stupid?"

"I'm not . . . not usually. But you undo me. You make me forget everything . . . make me *want* to forget everything, even
when I cannot." He skimmed a hand up her back and tangled it
in the long, dense tail of her hair. "Let me take you to bed,
Vaughnne."

"I've got a better idea." She leaned back and the slumberous
heat in her gaze was like fire in his veins. "Let *me* take *you*."

* * *

HIS eyes went hot. So hot, they blazed like silver fire. She pushed
against his shoulders, watching him, waiting . . . and he acqui-
esced, moving backward and letting her push him back onto the
bed. She rolled her shoulders, shrugging out of the shirt she'd
never gotten around to buttoning up. He sat on the edge of the
bed and she stood in front of him, catching his shirt in her hands
and dragging it up over his head.

He didn't do a damn thing to help her, just sat there, watching
her with those burning, hungry eyes.

It was almost as erotic as his touch. She went to her knees in
front of him and toyed with the button of his jeans until he went
back on his elbows. She trailed the tips of her fingers across his
belly and watched as the muscles quivered under his skin.

Before she could get too distracted, she reached for the bag she'd left on the floor and hauled it closer, dipping a hand into the interior pocket where she'd stashed the rest of the condoms she'd bought. She pulled out one, wished they had the time to indulge in a hell of a lot more.

But this was all they had.

Something tightened in her throat.

For all she knew, this might *really* be all . . .

Stop it. This wasn't the time, wasn't the place. She had to enjoy it, right?

She tossed the foil packet down on the bed next to him, looking back at him, holding his gaze for a minute. "You ever wish we had an entire night for just this?"

His hand came up and cradled her cheek. "Only from the minute I saw you."

Her heart clenched in her chest.

"Yeah?" She forced herself to give him a cheeky grin. "Maybe if we don't both end up dead, we can take that night."

Before he could say anything else, she reached for the button of his jeans and slid it free. He was already hard and she had to work the zipper down, aching inside at the feel of him under the sturdy denim. Hard, solid, thick. He pressed against the boxers he wore, a heather gray that was soft under her fingers as she caught both the jeans and the underwear in her hands.

He lifted his hips for her to drag the material down, and she caught her breath at the sight of him.

"You . . ." She licked her lips. "You're not circumcised."

"No." His gray gaze locked on her face. "Does that bother you?"

Closing her hand around the base of his cock, she leaned in and pressed her lips to his length, and hunger twisted through her as he shuddered. It gripped his entire body, and when she lifted her head and flicked her tongue over the tip of his cock, he swore, a harsh, guttural phrase in Spanish that she had no hope of understanding. Whatever it was, it was sexy as hell, and the look on his face was almost enough to make her come.

She caught his head in her mouth and sucked on him.

He grabbed her, his hands clenched on either side of her skull as he surged upward.

She sucked him deeper, deeper, until he nudged the back of her throat, and then she eased back upward. Pulling away, she fisted him in her hand and dragged it up, then down, slowly, watching him. As the foreskin moved down, she leaned forward and licked the head of his cock. He swore and jolted, jerking up against her. His hands tangled in her hair. "Again," he muttered. "Do it again, *corazón*."

Heat gathered inside her, spreading through her on a slow burn as she did just that, using her tongue to tease his head. Vaguely, she remembered reading that uncut guys were more sensitive, so she was careful not to pull on him, although damn, it was hard to think because everything she *did* do seemed to send him higher, and higher.

She sucked him back in, taking him deep, feeling him bump against the back of her throat. Gus groaned and then, as she lifted up to do it again, he moved.

She moved . . . but not because she planned to. In a blur of speed and motion, she was on her back with him crouching between her thighs. He hooked his hands into the waistband of her panties and stripped them down her thighs. "You drive me crazy," he muttered. "Absolutely out of my mind."

He grabbed the condom from the bed and tore open the packet. She heard it rip and pushed up onto her elbows to watch as he unrolled it. He pinched it up near to the top and she cocked a brow, trying to memorize just how he did that, because if she had the chance, at some point, she'd actually be the one doing the taking here.

His gaze, heated and hungry, swept over her, and her heart slammed up into her throat as he came down on top of her. He caught one hand in his, and it struck her as absurdly gentle, possessive as he nudged against her entrance. She wanted to say something . . . anything . . . but words didn't want to come.

"Look at me," he ordered, his voice harsh and hungry.

She lifted her gaze and the look on his face, stripped of everything but that raw, naked need, hit the very heart of her. They watched each other as he slowly sank inside and Vaughnne had never felt more exposed, had never felt more vulnerable. Her breath hitched in her throat as he pulled back, the swollen head of his shaft stroking over sensitized nerves, and instinctively, she tightened around him, lifting her hips to draw him back in.

His hand tightened on hers as he surged deeper, harder. She moaned, closing her eyes. He let go of her hand and cupped her face, his thumb pressing against her chin. "Don't close your eyes, *corazón . . . mi vida.* Watch me. Let me watch you."

Forcing her lids up, she stared at him.

His gaze was hooded, intent on her face as he withdrew. This time, as he sank inside, he moved up, riding higher on her body, and she cried out as the movement had him rocking against her clit. She reached down, gripping the taut curve of his ass and arching up.

He did it again, and again, but right before the climax would have broken over her, he stopped.

"Gus, please!"

"My name." He nipped at her lip. "Say *my* name."

"Gustavo . . ." She shuddered against him as he shifted once more, this time moving back and settling on his knees, catching her legs and hooking them over his forearms, opening her. "Damn it, you're killing me."

A faint smile curved his mouth as he swiveled his hips against her, the slant of his body driving him against her in just the right way. Vaughnne tensed as the pleasure gripped her, wrapping around her and pulling her tighter, tighter . . . "Gus, please." It ripped out of her in a whimper. "Gustavo . . ."

He rolled forward, her legs still hooked over his forearms, and the action drove him deep, so deep—he swelled, pulsed inside her, so hard, she felt bruised, and it was amazing, but he *still* wouldn't let her come. Twisting against him, she worked her arms free and speared her fingers into his hair, lifting her head up to cover his mouth with hers. This time, *she* was the one to sink her teeth into his lower lip, and when he shuddered against her, she tightened her inner muscles around him. "Stop it," he muttered.

* * *

"*CARAJO.*" He lifted his head, panting as he stared down at Vaughnne. She tightened around him yet again, the slick muscles of her pussy milking him in another tantalizing, teasing caress. That strong, sleek body of hers would drive him out of his mind, just as he'd expected. So many things he wanted to do to her . . . do *with* her. And there was just time for this.

"I won't stop," she whispered, looking at him with rich, dark brown eyes, a wicked smile on her face. "You're trying to drive me crazy. I'm going to do the same to you. I—*Gus!*"

He drove deep, slamming home and shuddering as her cry bounced off the walls. Her head arched back, the slim line of her neck exposed. Her pulse beat a wild tattoo in her neck and he wanted to press his lips to that delicate spot. Wanted to lick away the bead of sweat he could see forming just there on her temple. But he couldn't think, couldn't breathe. All he could do was surge inside her again, again, shuttling in and out as she tightened around his cock, until it was like he was working back and forth inside a silken fist.

Ragged breaths escaped them both and he could feel that rising tension inside her. This time, instead of trying to hold it off, he let it grab her, let it grab them both. It wasn't enough. Wouldn't ever be enough, he knew. Shifting, he let go of her legs and banded his arms around her, shaking as she did the same to him.

Locked in each other, he thought.

They were trapped, each possessed by the other.

Her ragged whimper echoed in his ear as she started to climax. He wanted to hear it again, and again. Blood thrummed in his head as he tried to hold back, but the need was a roaring dragon and it consumed him.

The inner muscles of her sheath gripped him, milking him convulsively, and he couldn't fight it. "Vaughnne," he rasped into her hair, clutching her tightly against him as he surrendered to that wild, almost painful need . . . to her.

TWENTY

I**T** had been a very long while since he had been forced to take action on his own.

Ignacio now had men who took care of things *for* him. But those men weren't here now and there was simply no way he was going to let that little *puta* get away from him.

She wasn't in the room now and he could finally think.

Finally. Every time she touched him, his ability to think just shut *down*, but she'd been gone for a little while and his mind was his own once more. His mind, his body . . . his *rage*. How long, he wondered? How long had she been controlling him?

His wrists were slick with blood, but the cable tie wasn't coming loose. It wasn't going to come loose, either.

He had to figure out a way to get free.

Of course, she had decided to do all of this in *her* room. Naturally, she had no weapons in here. A bunch of silly baubles and useless female sundries on the dresser but nothing he could use, even if he could get manage to get the chair he was tied to over there.

Think.

He had to think.

There was a way out of this; there had to be. He just needed to think it through.

His men, of course, would return in a few days and he would express his displeasure at them for so easily trusting what they'd been told. It didn't *matter* that he was the one who had told them to leave. They should know he'd never order all of them away. It left him, the entire operation, vulnerable. Fear was a nasty, cold streak inside him as he thought about it. His rivals were many. Most of them wouldn't dare come to his home, he knew, but if they had any idea how helpless he was right now . . .

Nala was going to pay for this.

She was going to suffer. Focusing on that forced the fear back where it belonged. Under control, where nobody else could see it. Wise men accepted fears, he believed. Accepted them, dealt with them. He'd accepted. He'd dealt with it. And now he'd make her suffer, because while a wise man might accept fear and deal with it, there was no reason to like it, and no reason to roll over like a whipped dog when somebody screwed him over.

Twisting his wrists against the cable tie, he shot another look around the room, ignoring the hopelessness that crashed through him yet again. The best chance, he thought, would be to try and get the chair over to her dressing table. There were a bunch of little trinkets there. Mirrors, heavy glass bottles. Not ideal, but the best option.

Watching the door carefully, he eased the chair over. One slow inch at a time.

He moved about a foot and stopped, waited. No sound of Nala. No sign of her.

He moved another. And another.

He was less than eighteen inches from the table when he heard a dull thud from downstairs. Swearing, he shoved closer to the dresser and tried to twist around, rising awkwardly, trying to claw for something.

Anything.

His fingers scrabbled against something that felt like cool, hard glass—

A footstep sounded outside the door.

"Señor?"

* * *

URGENCY rode her hard as they drove across the dark, busted road.

Vaughnne had used her passport at the border, sweating under her shirt the entire time, because she was absolutely certain they'd realize, somehow, that Gus had cleverly concealed the weapons he wasn't supposed to be transporting. She was equally certain they'd suspect something about his passport. It wasn't his name on it. Well, maybe it was. If it was, then he'd lied about his real name to her.

The name on the passport was Miguel Hernandez. About as typical as John Smith, she suspected.

But they'd crossed the border without a problem and she was that much closer to crossing a line. She'd already crossed some, but none of them were anything that would be the end for her.

Not yet.

But it was coming.

She swung back and forth between not thinking about it and trying to overthink it. Did she want to do this? Did she try to call Jones in and see if there were *legal* lines they could take? But what *legal* lines would actually work?

None. She tried to think it through. She knew for a damned fact that both the US government and the Mexican government had gone after Ignacio Reyes more than once, and each time, they'd failed to shut him down. There were no *legal* reasons to keep his child away from him. Alex could claim he'd abused him, but Vaughnne knew how that worked. It was a toss of the dice as to whether or not he'd end up back with his father, and this couldn't be left to chance.

Nor could they try and have him arrested based on what he'd done to Alex.

She laughed bitterly just thinking about that one. *You see, Judge, he used the boy's psychic ability to track down and murder some people who were going to raid the drug compound he runs. No, no . . . we don't have proof of it, but the kid's mom and his uncle believe it happened that way . . . yes, we're certain the boy is in danger . . .*

What *legal* recourse did they have?

She couldn't see one.

Reyes had a long, long reach, and if the boy didn't want to spend the rest of his life running, Reyes had to be out of the picture. Some of her fellow agents would frown on her for this, but Vaughnne didn't see things in black and white. Some people didn't need to be on this earth. She wouldn't cast judgment on the man simply for being a drug dealer and she wouldn't have gone after a man on her opinions of him alone. But the man had abused his son. He'd used his son to kill. If he got his hands on the boy, he'd do it again.

No child should be put through that. No *person* should be put through that.

If Vaughnne had to compromise herself, risk herself, land herself in jail . . . worse . . . whatever, to save a kid from that kind of hell, then so be it. She knew what she was doing, and even if it was a hard-ass choice to make, she knew what the right choice was.

Sometimes, the right choice was just the lesser of two evils, but she knew what she had to do.

One thing lifted some of the weight from her shoulders,

though. She'd checked that awful website. It still existed, sadly. But the ad for the infamous *item* was no longer up.

Hopefully nobody else would come hunting them. They didn't have time—

"Why are you so tense?"

Gus's voice was a soft, velvet murmur in the night, but it did nothing to ease her ragged nerves. She felt like she'd chugged about two gallons of Monster and her adrenaline levels were cranked up on high. It wasn't even just *what* she was doing. Her brain had been sending out little warnings all day long, and the later it got, the louder those warnings got.

Looking over at him, she shook her head and then focused on the windshield again, staring out at the moon-drenched night. "Something's wrong. Or going wrong. I don't know. How far away are we?"

"Twenty minutes by car. I'd planned to ditch it and walk in."

"No." The word tore out of her, and even though she suspected he knew this sort of thing a hell of a lot better than she did, there was no *time* for walking.

"If we drive in, he's going to know," Gus said quietly.

"We don't have time. Something is wrong. I feel it, Gus. Really, really wrong."

His hands tightened on the steering wheel. "Alex?"

Vaughnne shook her head. "It's not him." She'd already checked with Taige. The kid was safe, safe as he could be, tucked up at headquarters, and the other woman had already made headway getting him to shield himself, and that right there would make him less of a target.

"It's not him," she said again. Her gut was tight, cold, and hard. Her muscles, though, despite the fear, felt oddly loose and that, in and of itself, was enough to make her trepidation soar even higher. Everything in her was braced and ready for trouble. "We can't take our time right now, Gus. Please. You . . ." She blew out a breath and then looked over at him. "You have to trust me on this."

*   *   *

IF she was wrong and they blasted in there the way she seemed to want, they were both going to be in so much trouble.

Gus was used to trouble. He could handle it.

But risking her wasn't an option he wanted to take.

He wanted to get her out of this *alive*.

If she was right . . . what had her so worried? *Who* had her so worried?

In the end, though, he supposed it didn't matter.

They were here.

They had a goal.

And Vaughnne was a woman he'd decided he needed to trust. Perhaps if he'd trusted her, as she'd asked him to do from that day on the street when Alex was so ill, some of this, perhaps *all* of it, could have been avoided.

Please . . . you must promise me . . .

Consuelo had whispered those words to him, a few short years ago. An eternity ago. A lifetime ago.

Keep him safe. No matter what it takes, mi hermano, *you must keep him safe from his father . . . starting now.*

So he had. He'd started then, doing the very thing that would keep Reyes from finding them. Doing everything he had to keep the monster from tracking them down.

"He must die," Gus said quietly as he continued to speed through the night instead of pulling the car over. He passed by the area where he'd planned to ditch the car. They continued to drive through the night, chasing the moon. "No matter who is there, what is there, no matter what happens, he must die. It is the only way Alex will be safe."

"I know."

* * *

BRUISES were expected.

The cable ties around her wrists and ankles were expected.

Even the brutal backhand was expected.

Nalini blinked the cobwebs from her mind and focused on the man in front of her just as he was drawing back his fist again. Pain exploded through her face as he struck her again, but she swallowed back any sound she might have made. Head averted, she sucked in a breath and ran her tongue over her teeth, checked her jaw. Nothing felt broken.

She wiggled her wrists, but there was absolutely no give in the restraints. No give in the restraints, and she didn't have a lot of options around her, either. They'd moved her at some point. She didn't like the looks of the small, dark room she was in, either.

For some reason, it made her think of a coffin. Or a grave.

A place where she was going to die, she realized. Die, restrained to a stupid chair with a couple of cable ties, all because she hadn't gotten the hell out of there fast enough.

Damn, what she wouldn't give to be a bad-ass bitch like Black Widow just then. Just bust up the chair and bust up the bastard in front of her while she was at it. Wasn't going to happen that way, though. She was going to die here, and she wasn't going to see her mission through. The son of a bitch she'd been chasing for so long was going to get by unscathed for what he'd done. Ignacio was going to survive this. They all were. Everybody but—

"Look at me, *puta*."

Slowly, she swung her head around and stared at Ignacio's right-hand man. His name was Jorge. He was mean as a snake, and although he pretended otherwise, he was too smart. He was also wearing a pair of gloves. That was a problem. If there was skin contact for even a second . . .

Through her lashes, she stared at him for a minute, holding her breath, hoping he'd edge close enough.

But he was careful, keeping just enough distance between them that she couldn't wiggle around to touch him, not even a bit.

"The señor says I can do whatever I want with you now," Jorge said, smiling at her.

"Whatever?" She doubted that. She suspected Ignacio had figured out how she worked and he wasn't going to risk having her pull Jorge in. She licked her split lip, the taste of blood a metallic wash on her tongue. "He said you can do *whatever* to me and you decided you were going to just hit me?" She laughed and tugged at her bonds. "He told you to beat the shit out of me, didn't he?"

He shot out a hand, fisting it in her shirt.

"You stupid little bitch. I'm going to have a lot of fun with you, you know that?"

"This?" Despite how much it hurt, Nalini made herself laugh. "*This* is how you have fun? Whoever taught you about women seriously neglected their lessons, *hijo de la chingada.*"

His face went red.

Nalini just smiled, keeping her mask in place.

His hand shot up to her face and squeezed, squeezed . . .

Through the pain, she tried to focus. So hard to do it. His gloves. Damn the gloves. No skin-to-skin contact.

"That's enough for now, Jorge. I want to ask her some questions."

With blood pounding in her ears, fear cloying in her throat, Nalini sucked in a breath as Jorge's hand fell away from her face. Turning her head, she stared at Ignacio as he appeared in the doorway of the dim room. The star-studded sky was at his back, the moon shining down on his black hair, casting his face in shadow.

Then he came inside, shutting the door at his back.

He had showered and changed, dressed in a suit that cost

more than she would have made in a month working for Jones in the Bureau.

Jones. She'd needed that out and she hadn't had time to so much as call.

Life really was a bitch, she decided. A mean, sucker-punching bitch.

As he came to a stop in front of her, she spat out a mouthful of blood at his feet. Nalini watched his eyes narrow in distaste as he moved his shiny, slick shoes back from the small bit of saliva and blood.

So careful with his clothes, with his shoes, with his home. So arrogant.

People around him scraped by for every damn thing they had. People died acting as his mules . . . died or were jailed, and they took the risk because they felt it was their only option.

A monster, that was what stood in front of her. One who sent mercenaries after his son, so he could . . . what? Use that kid?

The frustration she'd been feeling abruptly died.

Okay, so she hadn't gone after the bastard she'd promised herself she'd find. But she hadn't wasted the past few weeks, either. This son of a bitch wasn't going to touch the kid, and she'd had a bit of a hand in that. She'd help save a kid from dealing with some of the hell she'd had to deal with. It was enough.

Ignacio's face smoothed and he came closer, sat on the bed across from her. "You have proven to be such a problem, Nala . . . or is that your real name?"

"A name," she said, heaving out a sigh. "What's in a name, really?"

Jorge moved to stand behind her, tangling his hand in her dreads and twisting so hard her scalp screamed at her. She smiled through the pain. "Is that the best your trained monkey can do, Iggy? Come on. I had schoolyard punks pound on me harder than this."

There was a table just outside the narrow pool of light, and she watched as he turned and reached for something. Her gut clenched as she saw what it was. A knife. A big-ass machete. "We're going to talk, Nala. About my son. How you know about him. Where he is. How I can find him. And for every time you fail to answer me, I'm going to cut off a finger. If we go through all your fingers, then I'll move to your eyes. I'll save your ears and tongue for the last. Am I understood?"

Horror twisted inside her, but she didn't let herself babble in fear.

In the end, there wasn't a damn thing she *could* tell him, really.

The boy was probably safe, but she'd deliberately avoided learning anything about him. Defeat settled over her and she slumped in the chair. "You might as well start cutting, then. Have fun getting bloody. I don't know where he is, who has him . . ." Then she lifted her lashes and stared at him. "Even if I did? I'd lose my eyes, my ears, my heart, my kidneys, every damn thing I have before I'd turn some poor kid over to the likes of *you*."

Ignacio simply smiled.

TWENTY-ONE

"WE walk from here."

From where he'd stopped the car, he could see Reyes's villa.

His gut was tight and every sense was on red alert.

It was too quiet.

Too quiet and the skin on the back of his neck was crawling, like something or somebody was breathing down on him.

But there was nobody there.

He wanted to ask Vaughnne if she felt something, but she was focused on the big house, sprawling out under the silvery sheen of the moon. It was as though something had enchanted her, and she just couldn't pull herself away. Even as he went about ready-ing himself, checking his Kevlar vest, knives, the Sig Sauer, slip-ping the strap of the Heckler & Koch MP5 over his shoulder, Vaughnne was moving toward the house.

"Vaughnne."

She didn't even slow down.

"*Esta chingadera,*" he muttered, grabbing the vest he'd found among her belongings and heading off after her. He caught her arm right before she started down the hill. The scraggly, low-lying bushes would offer them some concealment, but she was *not* barreling toward that house without some sort of protection. What had he been thinking, bringing her here . . .

Abruptly, Vaughnne stopped and looked at him. "Whatever happens, you didn't make me come, got it?" She caught the vest from his fist and pulled it on.

"I thought you didn't read minds."

She shrugged. "I don't. But what you're thinking, for once, is actually written all over your face. I'm here because I gave my word I'd watch over that boy. And I know too much about Ignacio Reyes. People have been chasing after him, trying to shut him down for years, and they are no closer to doing it now than they were a decade ago. If we're going to make Alex safe, then we have to do it the hard way."

He lifted a hand and touched her face. "It's my problem, Vaughnne. My responsibility, and I'll accept the risks. If you cross this line, there may be no turning back for you. You don't need to do this."

A sharp scream, female and full of pain, rang out from the house.

Vaughnne swore and turned. "Yeah. I do."

* * *

Fear was a strange thing.

Sometimes it was like an icy tickle down the spine.

Other times, it was a dragon screaming inside her brain.

And it could hit on so many things in between.

Right now, her fear was a nasty little twist in her gut, and in the back of her mind, there was a voice, almost like she was talking to herself. *Hurry, Vaughnne. Have to hurry. Have to hurry!*

There was another scream and everything in her wanted to run, barrel into that house.

But she couldn't. Had to be smart. Had to creep across the ground, following Gus's oddly reluctant lead. All along, he'd been warning her, making her very aware of just how far he'd go, what lines he'd be willing to cross—just about *all* of them. And now they were here, and he wanted her to . . . what? Leave? Let it go?

While he went on ahead and probably got himself killed, she knew.

He was ready for it. She wasn't stupid. She knew the look on a man's face when he was ready to face down death. She'd seen it more than once. There had been a time or two when *she* had worn that look.

But she hadn't come down here to walk away now.

Another scream rang out, and they were close enough now that she could hear a voice as the scream faded—it had come from the building ahead, set apart from the big house. So close. It was so close.

Where is everybody? she asked, searching the perimeter.

He'd already done a check for the guards and hadn't seen a damn soul. That bothered her. A lot.

He looked at her and shook his head minutely, but she didn't know how to take that. Did that mean he didn't know? There wasn't anybody? What?

They inched forward another few feet, following the sound of that voice.

Low and smooth, it sounded like the voice of an educated male, the accent all but gone. "Come now, Nala . . . there's no reason for this. If you answer my questions, I will not hurt you . . ."

Nala—

That name sounded an alarm in Vaughnne's mind.

But then she heard the voice. A woman's. Ragged and hoarse, but familiar, all the same. "Why . . . don't . . . you go fuck . . . yourself?" she panted.

Nalini—

Shit . . .

She looked at Gus. *He's got one of the agents in there, Gus. I know her.*

Gus didn't respond.

At all.

The sound of Nalini's next scream was almost enough to freeze the blood in Vaughnne's veins.

Desperate and so full of pain.

Her muscles bunched, tensed. Gus must have sensed what she wanted to do, because his hand came up and gripped her arm, his fingers squeezing with deliberate strength.

She let him guide her over to the building, all but hugging it as she listened to Nalini inside. Begging now . . . She was begging, whimpering, and crying.

Where the hell is everybody? You acted like he'd have a small army here, Vaughnne said, searching the night-dark terrain, but she saw *nothing.* The buildings were there, but there were no people. Save for those they could hear behind them.

The screaming had stopped, dying away into low, soft sobs.

"Do I start cutting off fingers now, señor? Cutting up her pretty face didn't do much," somebody said.

Reyes? Vaughnne wondered. She had to see him. If she *saw* him, she could get a link in on his mind. That was all it would take.

"Nala, you are so foolishly stubborn. Talk to me, and this can end. Here, we can do something easy; it will not hurt the boy. Just tell me this. How did you manage to send my men away?"

Next to her, Vaughnne felt Gus tense. She was terrified now. Nalini had monsters in there *with* her, but if Gus thought she'd endanger that boy . . . *She won't say anything, Gus. She won't.*

His long, lean body vibrated next to hers and she could feel him readying himself.

I have to see inside, damn it. I can't work if I can't see in there. Her ability was limited that way; the first time she used it, she had to *see* somebody. And once she saw whoever was torturing Nalini, the bastard was going to hurt.

Slowly, Gus's fingers uncurled from her arm and she crept forward. Mentally, she reached out to the other woman. *Man, Nalini, you landed yourself in a shitload of trouble. How did you manage that?*

She didn't know if Nalini recognized her, and she wouldn't get much of a response, either. Nalini's gifts didn't work like that.

But she couldn't let the woman think she was in there, alone and left to die, either.

A harsh, low groan left the woman, still hidden by the walls that separated them. The window was a few feet ahead and Vaughnne had to inch forward every damn millimeter, watching where she placed her feet, watching everything around her. Her skin crawled.

Nalini, where is everybody?

"You . . . moron," Nalini said. There was so much pain crowding her voice it hurt to even hear it. "Haven't you . . . figured out what I do? *I* made *you* send them away. They wouldn't . . . listen to me." She broke off for a minute, panting.

There was a whisper of sound and then the man's voice. "Hold off, Jorge. I want to hear this. This . . . this could be useful."

Nalini laughed. "Oh, I'm not going to be useful . . . to you. At all. Trust me. Anybody who touches me does it . . . at his own risk. You had your hands . . . all over . . . me. I made you . . . send . . . them all away. They are too scared *not* to listen. Except Jorge, apparently. He came running . . . back, the jackass. Like a little . . . puppy. I bet . . . if you asked him to suck you off, he'd . . . do it."

"*Puta.*"

Ah. That must be Jorge . . . Vaughnne eyed the distance to the window. A foot. She was going to be in range soon. Very soon.

Did you hear?

She glanced back over her shoulder, saw the slow dip of Gus's head. But something told her that he didn't buy anything out of Nalini's mouth; he didn't trust her. He didn't trust *anybody* but he'd never trust something coming from Nalini now. She was being tortured and Reyes thought she knew something about Alex. To Gus, that made her suspect.

* * *

NALINI was almost numb as Ignacio waved Jorge away. "Now, now . . . I'd promised we wouldn't hurt her if she answered the question. Although, Nala, I do not care for your foul mouth."

"Yeah?" She sneered at him. "Too fucking bad."

"This really is your last chance. The injury to your face can be . . . well, it may or may not heal well. If I start cutting off fingers, Nala, you'll never be able to use that beauty of yours to blind a man again."

She smiled, the cut on her lower lip splitting wide. He planned on killing her—did he really think she was that naïve? "Did I blind you, Iggy?"

Damn it, Nalini. Shut up. The voice . . . Nalini frowned as it came to her mind again and she almost believed it wasn't wishful thinking. Maybe . . .

Something danced just out of the corner of her eye. A flit of movement, a dark shadow lost to darker ones outside the window.

"Iggy . . ." She sucked in a breath. "Maybe I can help. A little."

A pleased smile curved his face.

I've got a line in now, Nalini. Get ready.

She closed her eyes and wondered just how in hell she was supposed to get ready? "Yeah. Whatever . . ."

In the next second, Ignacio jerked upright like a marionette yanked on his strings.

His eyes rolled back in his head and he clamped his hands over his ears. A rapid-fire spate of Spanish exploded from him, and her pain-flooded mind took a few seconds to translate.

What is that terrible noise? Shut it up, Jorge!

She thought that was what he said.

Jorge answered back, shaking his head. *"No, no oigo nada."*

"You . . ." Ignacio whispered, his eyes wide and glazed while he continued to cover his ears. "You are . . ."

He went white.

Jorge fisted his hand in her dreads. "Whatever you are doing, *puta*, stop it, now." He pressed the edge of his knife against her neck.

And then, a muffled pop sounded.

It was followed by a thud.

Nalini was only vaguely aware of the fact that Jorge's hand had fallen from her neck. All she could see was the man—long, lean, and lethal—coming through the window with death in his eyes.

Death . . . in his eyes, in his hands. On his soul.

You . . . she thought, dazed.

*   *   *

THE woman was drenched with her own blood. Restrained for now, cable ties holding her in place. He didn't spare her more than a glance because she didn't matter.

All that mattered was Ignacio Reyes, and the man was all but clawing at his ears. An attempt to silence Vaughnne's voice, Gus supposed.

"Vaughnne."

"I'm done," she said, edging around him.

He stared at Reyes, waiting until the man lowered his hands, until he looked around. His gaze sought out Jorge. When he saw the corpse on the floor behind the other agent, there was only a flicker of his lashes to betray his emotions. No sign of fear showed on his face, in his eyes.

Nothing.

"So." Reyes kept his body averted.

The man was a fool, thinking that would hide what he was doing.

"You finally return, Gustavo," Reyes said as he drew the gun out.

"For you." Gus smiled. "I always did want to come back for you."

"And where is my son?"

"Where you'll never get him."

Reyes laughed, the malicious chuckle echoing through the room for a long, lingering moment. He spun around, already lifting the Derringer he'd been using his body to conceal. It didn't bring Gus as much pleasure as he'd like to aim, squeeze.

The man went down with a scream, the weapon falling from his hand, his arm rendered useless.

"A useful piece of advice, *cabrón*," Gus said, striding over to him and kicking the Derringer away. "Hide the weapon better. Don't let me see it until you're ready to pull the trigger."

He pressed the muzzle of his Sig Sauer to Reyes's temple. "You have no idea how many times I've thought of this moment."

"Go ahead, *hijo de la chingada*. Kill me. Just like you killed my wife."

* * *

THOSE words froze the very heart of her. Vaughnne lifted her head and looked at Gus's profile.

She never should have looked.

He must have felt her stare because he turned his head, glanced at her for just a second. Less.

And the bastard bleeding on the floor moved, shoving back and swiping out with his uninjured arm.

When he moved again, he had a knife in his hand.

Time slowed down to a crawl and she saw Gus jerk back, saw him lifting his weapon even as Ignacio Reyes shoved the blade into Gus's side.

"Die, you stupid *cabrón*."

Two shots rang out.

Vaughnne had no idea which one killed him.

The one she put through his head, or the one Gus put through his heart.

But Ignacio Reyes was down, his eyes sightless and fixed on the ceiling. Blood oozed from the wound to his right forearm. All of it spilled on the floor, turning it a deep, deep red.

Looking up, she stared at Gus.

But he'd already turned his back.

"He killed the boy's mother," Nalini said, her voice tight and low. "I saw it, Vaughnne."

Picking up the pocket knife she'd been using to cut Nalini free, she focused on just that task. Just that.

"Did you hear me?"

"I heard you," she said quietly.

She'd heard her. She even believed it was true. Not so much because Nalini insisted.

But because of the very plain and simple fact that Gus wouldn't look at her.

TWENTY-TWO

"*You must promise me, Gustavo.*"

"*Consuelo, stop this foolishness. Come now. Put your arms around my neck.*" *Urgency was a constant alarm in his head. The boy was safe—he'd called in so many favors to get here, and Jimmy Doucet was at the door, clutching a terrified Alejandro in his arms. There weren't many he'd trust with his family, but the old Cajun was one, and he had come without asking a single question.*

Gustavo went to pick up his sister, fury twisting in him as he felt the odd, almost pulpy feel along her right side. So many ribs, broken. "No," she said, flinching away and then gasping as even the pain from that tore through her. "I cannot go with you, 'mano. Listen to me, you have to get him away. I will slow you down and he'll get Alejandro. He can never do that. Never. You must promise me he'll never touch him again. Never find him."

"*He won't,*" *he said, trying to calm her.* "*Now let's go before they realize we are here.*"

"I can't walk," she said, shaking her head. "I can't run."

She started to cough and there was blood trickling from her mouth when the fit finally passed.

"Gus, if we're going, son, we gotta go now," Doucet said, his voice low and urgent.

"Have him and Alejandro wait outside," she said, her voice softer, weaker.

Once the door closed behind him, Consuelo closed her eyes. "I'll never make it to the border. And if you take me, all of you die."

He froze at the look in her eyes. Despite the pain she was in, despite the blood and the bruises, she watched him with an eerie sort of calm. "Listen to me, 'mano," she said, her voice getting weaker. "I know you do not understand, but please try. I know what will happen if you take me. He'll catch us. I . . . I've seen it, Gustavo. He'll catch us. He'll kill you . . . I'm dead already. And he'll do as he wishes with Alejandro. You have to protect him now."

"No," Gustavo said, shaking his head even as denial roared inside him. He brushed her hair back. "Come now. Hold on to me."

"I've seen it," she whispered. And then she told him just what she'd seen.

He froze. And then, defeated, he dropped his head onto the bed next to her, closer to sobbing than he'd ever been in his adult life. There was no room for tears, he knew, but they wanted to come nonetheless.

Back when she'd been a child, Consuelo had been a child whom many had mocked. She did see things. Mamá had believed her, had insisted their grandmother had been the same. Neither Mamá nor Gus had the ability, but Consuelo . . .

"You can save my son, Gustavo. But you cannot save me. I cannot even move. It hurts to breathe, hurts to even lie here.

Please . . . you must promise me. Take him, keep him safe. And don't . . . please don't let Ignacio hurt me anymore. If he tries to make me talk, I . . ." She shook her head and reached for his hand. "I can't keep fighting him."

Unwittingly, he lifted his weapon hand, the one still clutching the Sig Sauer to stroke her brow. She caught his wrist and lifted it, guiding the weapon to her temple.

He jerked away. "Consuelo!"

"If he finds me alive, he will try to make me talk. I am not as strong as you. Please, Gustavo. You must protect my son . . . you must do this for me."

*   *   *

HIS gut roiled, even now.

The guilt he'd kept buried raged to the surface as he moved out of the dark, dank little building.

It had been there that he'd found his sister. She, too, had been tied up. But she'd been tied to a cot, left naked and uncovered, so every violation had been there. For all the world to see.

And because he had made her a promise, to save Alejandro, he'd left her. Just like that, after he'd put a bullet through her heart.

There was a soft whisper of sound and he turned, saw Vaughnne standing in the doorway, her friend's arm slung over her shoulder.

Vaughnne stared at him.

He returned that gaze without blinking, letting her see every ugly truth on his face.

"If you are going to ask if it is true," he said, schooling his voice into a bored, flat tone. "Don't bother, Vaughnne."

"I won't. I can already tell it is. I just want to know why."

The other woman was pale, so deathly pale, and she stared at Gus with eyes that were an odd mix of horror and fury. And in her hand, she clutched the Derringer that Reyes had tried to use on him. It was, yet again, leveled at him. "Vaughnne, we need to go. It doesn't matter *why*. We have to get out of here before the rest of Reyes's men show up. I don't want to die here, not just because you need to know *why* he killed his own sister."

The look in her eyes was scathing and cold, but it didn't affect him. He didn't care what that woman said.

Vaughnne, though . . . the look on her face . . . it cut something deep inside him. It left a wound he wouldn't have imagined possible. Still, he didn't let it show as he looked from one woman to the other. "You should go. Get out while you can."

"Are you going to answer me?"

He resumed his study of the night sky. And when she walked away, he closed his eyes. Blood dripped from the wound in his side, but he ignored it.

It was done, then.

Alejandro was safe.

He'd kept his promise.

He'd always thought it would kill him in the end.

This, he thought, was actually worse.

* * *

"You have no idea how much trouble you could have caused."

There were only four of them in the room at the moment. Vaughnne and Nalini, along with Joss Crawford and Dr. Melissande Grady. Grady was settling Nalini into a chair that had been dug up from somewhere—an armchair, not one of those hard-ass chairs the rest of them would be in. Nalini looked like hell. She'd lost a decent amount of blood by the time Vaughnne was able to get her to a hospital, and the long, narrow line of sutures on her face stood out in stark relief against her pale skin. Grady murmured to her softly and Nalini nodded, and even that careful movement hurt like hell. Grady touched her shoulder and then moved away.

While Grady was playing doctor, Joss was busy ripping Vaughnne a new asshole.

"Were you trying to get yourself thrown in jail?" he demanded. "Trying to cost yourself your job? Cause an international incident or what?"

She gave him a sweet smile. "Well, if those were my intentions, I obviously *failed*, right? After all, I'm not in jail, there was no international incident."

He waited a beat. "But do you still have a job?"

"Well, that's not really up to you." She settled back in her seat and stared outside. They'd just gotten out of Mexico early that morning, and although it was damn late and she was damn tired, she hadn't been given the option to go home and rest.

No, she was at headquarters, getting debriefed. Well, *waiting* to get debriefed.

It had taken every last bit of Grady's considerable diplomatic skills to get them out of Mexico so quickly. She'd lied through her teeth, too, while Joss stood in the background, looking brooding and menacing, which he did rather well.

Now they were waiting for the boss. It struck her as kind of odd that he wasn't already there, but it was one of those random little thoughts that passed through her mind and then faded.

Just like every other thought of the past few days.

She couldn't think.

Couldn't focus.

Couldn't sleep.

Couldn't eat.

Nothing seemed to matter anymore, not since the moment she'd turned her back and walked away from Gus.

If you are going to ask if it is true . . . Don't bother, Vaughnne.

Don't bother. Like it didn't matter at all if he'd killed his sister.

Don't ask? Screw that. She *knew* it was true, she'd seen it on his face. Just as she'd seen the misery hidden in the back of his eyes. The misery, the pain. The grief. *There had to be a reason*, she told herself. She could feel it, in the very bottom of her soul. The man she'd come to know might be a killer, but he wasn't a cold-blooded monster.

She damn well should have asked. Should have pushed. Yeah, there were reasons, all right. And fuck him to hell and back if he thought she just *shouldn't bother to ask*.

Her gut churned as she continued to stare outside at the streets. It was late, but the streets were still crowded with cars and buses, people moving along the sidewalks.

What had happened?

Her mind spun, twisted with the possibilities. Had his sister been hurt? Sick? Maybe—

Before she could finish that thought, the door opened and she turned her head, watching as Jones came striding through the doors. He had a man with him, a man that Vaughnne was pretty damn certain she didn't know.

She was *equally* certain that he could cause all kinds of problems. He stood solid, straight as a soldier, shoulders back, and even though he wasn't obvious with it, she had a feeling he'd already looked and judged everybody in the room. Looked, marked the weaknesses, the strengths.

She didn't much care for that.

"I'd like everybody to meet Antonio Moran. He's in from Mexico . . . he has a few questions about a fire that took place at a private home, an hour west of Monterrey."

A fire—

West of Monterrey.

Just like that, and her heart almost stopped. She kept her face blank, though, even as her pulse started to race, as her skin went cold and clammy and all the air squeezed out of her lungs.

A fire—

The world stopped spinning. She'd almost swear to it.

She'd taken Nalini to a hospital in Monterrey. They'd driven east. The home hadn't been burning when she left. Jones wouldn't have the guy in here if it was just some random house.

Gus—

Her heart went tight and cold, and there was a scream lodged in her throat.

"I'm attempting to locate a person of interest. I think he might have answers about the fire." Moran studied her face. "You might have met him while you were in Mexico."

"I was just there to help a fellow agent, Señor Moran," she said, moving forward to take a seat. Despite her best attempts, her voice came out a little rougher than she liked. "She needed backup, so I was down there for that, and only that."

That was the story they'd decided to go with. Nalini had been on an assignment; things had gone to hell. It wasn't too terribly far from the truth. Except for the fact that Vaughnne hadn't been sent to help Nalini, and she hadn't been in Mexico on any sort of job . . . but . . . well. If Jones decided to come clean and let her fend for herself, she'd deal with it then. She'd made her choice.

"The house belonged to a man who has been under intense scrutiny by both my government and yours . . . Ignacio Reyes."

"Reyes." A knot swelled in her throat, so large and hard, she could barely talk. Her hands were sweaty and she swiped them down her jeans before reaching for the bottle of water waiting on the table. "Ignacio Reyes. Yeah, I'm familiar with the name. Were there any fatalities?"

"We are still investigating at this point."

When he didn't elaborate, she shot Jones a glance, struggling to keep her face blank even though all she wanted to do was jump over the table and demand that he tell her what in the hell was going on. Anything. Everything.

The calm look on his face shattered every last nerve she had and she knew he knew something. Hell, he might know *everything*. This was Taylor Jones, damn it.

Instead of attacking him, she looked back at Moran. "Exactly what can I do for you, then, señor?"

"I just had a few questions."

Vaughnne leaned back in her chair and laced her hands over her belly. Maybe that would keep them from shaking so much. "Well, I'm not sure how much help I can be, señor. Reyes was a bastard, but we focus more on missing persons and crimes against children in this unit." She paused then added, "It wouldn't hurt my feelings, though, if I heard he'd died in the fire."

A faint smile came and went on Moran's face. "I imagine a great many feel the same way, Agent . . ."

"MacMeans. Vaughnne MacMeans." All the bureaucratic games she had to play. What the hell was going on? "So were there fatalities? Reyes or anybody else?"

Moran studied her face for a long, long moment, and she had a feeling the question hadn't been quite as subtle as she'd hoped. Hard to be subtle, though, when her heart felt like it was bleeding inside her chest. *Gus . . . damn it, Gus. What did you do?*

"We're still in the process of investigating, Agent MacMeans," he said, inclining his head. "I'm actually not here for information on Reyes, though. I'm looking for information on somebody else. A man, about your age, perhaps a few years older."

"This would be your . . . person of interest?" She made herself smile.

Gus.

As he placed his briefcase on the conference table, Vaughnne tried to breathe around the ache in her chest. Tried, but it was so damn hard. Her heart felt like it was broken and she wanted to demand answers but she had already messed things up so bad and she knew it.

Then Moran pulled out a slim file from the briefcase and

opened it. A second later, she saw a picture. Her heart jumped into her throat and she was so very glad she'd had years to learn how to hide her reaction. When she saw Gus's averted profile, everything inside her felt frozen. Ready to shatter at just one blow.

Unblinking, she stared at the grainy image. Oh, it was him. There was no denying it, even though it was a lousy picture. All she could see was his profile, the carved line of his jaw, the ball cap turned backward.

"Does he look at all familiar to you?"

She made herself sigh and lean forward, studying the picture under a pretense of trying to see it better. *Gus* . . . "Hell, that could be *anybody*, Señor Moran. Well. Not *anybody*." She jerked her chin toward Jones. "It's probably not him. It's not Crawford." She flicked a glance at the quiet, brooding agent by the wall. "Not too many people have a mug like his. I don't think it's you or me. But it could be a million men."

No. Just one. One who'd proven to be rather good at blending in.

She wanted to reach out and snag the picture from Moran, clutch it close, and ask if he had more. Ask if he had news about Gus.

But she didn't.

Something big was going on, and although fear curdled inside her heart, she wasn't going to say a damn thing until she knew more. Not a damn thing. Too many things could make a bad situation even worse. For her . . . and worse, for Gus.

Moran held her gaze for a long moment. "Does that mean you do not know him?"

"It means I don't *know* if I know him." She hoped the ache in her heart wouldn't show on her face. *Why* . . . those had been her last words to him.

Had he set the fire?

That was a stupid question, she realized. Of course he had. The real question was, had he gotten out?

Her heart lurched, just thinking about it. Gus had always acted like he wouldn't be surprised if the trip to Mexico turned out to be a one-way thing. But Alex, what about Alex?

What about me . . .

If Gus was dead . . . *no!* She shoved the thought aside before it could even settle. *No.*

She'd get answers. Somehow. Once she had them, then she'd deal . . . somehow.

She peered at the image, head cocked. Tears burned inside her throat, in her chest. *Gus . . .*

"It could be almost anybody, sir," she said softly.

"Yes." He stared at her, his gaze unreadable. "I suppose it could."

* * *

JONES returned nearly thirty minutes after he'd escorted Moran out.

He spoke to Nalini, and although Vaughnne was right there, she couldn't recall much of anything he said. It was like he was speaking another language.

But then Nalini left, Grady following along behind her. Joss lingered a few more minutes and then he left as well.

The door shut and the tension in the room almost shattered her, and she was hovering on the brink as it was, about to come out of her skin. She'd spent every second of the past half hour on her iPhone, trying to unearth details about the fire, but she hadn't learned anything. The boys down in Mexico were keeping that little mess locked down tight. There wasn't even any information about Reyes's death, and *that* should be front-page news.

Feeling the weight of Jones's stare, she made herself look away from the phone and focus on her boss.

His steely blue eyes should have made her nervous.

But she was already sick with fear, pain. What the hell did it matter if her job was in jeopardy just then?

"The man you lied to is one of the higher-ranking diplomats," Jones said, his voice a cold slice in the room.

She lifted a brow, refusing to let herself react. "Hey, did you see that picture? Shit, I can find you five men in this damn building *now* who could probably pass for that guy in the picture."

"You could," he agreed. "Give me twenty minutes and some hair dye, and *I* could pass for the guy in the picture. But you knew who it was. I saw it in your eyes, Vaughnne, and if that man knew you at all, he would have seen it, too."

Spinning away, she paced over to the window and stared outside. "What do you want me to say, Jones?" she asked softly. "I can't help him. I don't know where Gus is. Where he was going. What he is planning."

"Did you know he was going to blow the house up?"

She closed her eyes. "No."

But maybe she should have thought that through. Gus wouldn't have risked leaving any sign that might lead to Alex. If Reyes had left anything behind that could point the way to the kid, then Gus would have razed an entire country to the ground to protect his nephew.

Blowing up a house? He wouldn't even think twice.

"Was there any word about him?" she asked.

A heavy, taut silence weighed between them, and finally, a soft sigh drifted from Taylor. "That's why he was here, Vaughnne—looking for information. He didn't say it in as many words, but that was my take on it."

"He could have been in the house," she said, and a lance of pain went through her, so deep, so crippling, it almost drove her to her knees. Not Gus. No. It hurt even to think about it. But the thought was there, settling in her mind and growing roots. She couldn't knock it.

"If . . ." She had to stop and clear her throat before she could continue. "If he was, then that means Alex has nobody, Taylor. Nobody. He's a gifted kid who has had a life of hell. If he's lost his uncle . . ."

"Maybe his uncle should have thought of that," Taylor bit off. Then he swore.

She turned around to look at him, watched as he reached up to tug at his tie. She had to focus, see this through, even if her heart was bleeding inside. "But that's not Alex's fault."

He gave her a dark look. "I know that."

"So what happens to him?" She'd promised. And no matter what, no matter how much she hurt, she'd see that promise through. "You can't just send him back to Mexico. He has nobody. Has nothing. And—"

He lifted a hand, staring at the wall. "You know I'm not going to do that, Vaughnne, so just stop." He tugged his askew tie off, glanced at it, and then sighed, draping it around his neck so that the ends hung free. "Even if it wasn't for his . . . circumstances, he's a victim of the situation. But he's got months ahead of him before he'll have his gift under control. We have to make sure he's trained before he ends up another target. And we have to keep him safe. Assuming, of course, his uncle doesn't show up." His lip curled. "It just might be *easier* if his uncle never showed his face again."

"Shut the hell up, Jones," she said, the words flying out of her mouth before she could silence them.

When Taylor shifted his gaze to her, she stared right back at him. She'd already jacked this job up. What did it matter if she said what she thought *now*?

His steely eyes bored into hers and she lifted her chin. "What?" she demanded.

"You might want to check the attitude, Vaughnne," he said softly. "You have caused so much trouble, I don't even know if I can begin to fix all of this, so cut the bullshit."

"Cut the *bullshit*?" She gaped at him. "That man was willing to do *whatever* it took to protect his nephew. *Whatever* it took. All they *had* was each other and Gus might be—"

Her voice cracked and she spun away, lifting her hands to hide her face. She couldn't do this. Not here. Not now.

Behind her, she heard a sigh. A moment later, Taylor tugged on her shoulder. She jerked away, but he just pulled again, and a moment later, she found herself caught in Taylor's arms, her face pressed against his chest. The terrified tears were still trapped inside, though. She couldn't let them out. Not here. Not now.

Taylor was more than just her boss. He might be a straitlaced bastard and the world saw a cold piece of work, but he was the closest thing to family she had. But she wasn't ready to break around him. She closed her eyes, clenched her hands into fists, and made herself breathe. She had to breathe, had to function and focus so she could ask him what she needed to know.

One minute after another slowly passed, but finally, she thought she could manage. "Do you know anything?"

His chest rose and fell on a sigh. He squeezed her gently and then eased back, studying her face. He still looked pissed, she decided. But his eyes were a little less icy. "Some, yes." He moved away and took up a position at the window, staring outside. "Moran is mostly on a fishing expedition, Vaughnne. If he knew where Gus was, he wouldn't be fishing."

A few seconds of silence passed and the ache that might have hope swelled inside her. Taylor flicked her a glance. "Dead bodies are usually pretty easy to locate in a fire, you know. If you weren't so . . . close to this, you'd have already come to that conclusion, I guess. If Gus was one of his, he would have already done what was necessary to ID him."

"One of his . . ."

A faint smile came and went on Taylor's face. "Give me some credit, Vaughnne. I've pieced some things together about him, you know. And I know what kind of operation Moran runs. Although if I'd had any clue who Gus was *before* this . . ." His voice trailed off and he shook his head.

"You would have done exactly what you did," she finished. "A kid was involved. You and I both know . . . kids are worth it." She closed her eyes. "One of his. Why didn't he go to Moran back then?"

"Too many corrupt people," he murmured. "Reyes had a very, very long reach. I imagine he didn't want to risk the boy."

"No. He wouldn't have taken the chance." She rubbed her eyes. She pushed all thought of Gus out of her head. She'd think about him later. When she could actually do it and not worry about others seeing her fall apart. "What's going to happen with Alex now?"

"For now, he stays where he is," Taylor said, his voice flat. "Until we know more, there's nothing else that can be done."

Until we know more—

She started to tremble. The need to break weighed heavily on her.

"Vaughnne." Taylor looked over at her. "Go home. Come back tomorrow. We'll start cleaning things up then."

She nodded and tried a weak smile. "Should I bring a box to clean out my desk?"

"No." He folded his arms across his chest and resumed his study of the parking lot. "*I* might need one by the time this is over, but we'll cross that bridge when we come to it."

* * *

Gus had planned to do . . . something.

He didn't know what.

But he'd planned to do . . . something when she came inside.

She came inside, a dazed, almost drugged look on her face, like she didn't know where she was. Who she was. Part of him wanted to grab her and shake her, scold her for her carelessness, because she didn't even look around.

He wasn't hiding. The room was dim, but he stood in the corner, leaning against the wall, and all she had to do was look around and she'd see him.

But all she did was shut the door and flip the locks.

Then . . . she stood there.

Her back to him. Her shoulders rose and fell rapidly, and distantly, he was aware of the harsh sounds of her breathing filling the room. She leaned forward and pressed her forehead to the door. A sob ripped out of her. She slammed a fist against the door and the sound of it caught him off guard.

Anger and grief rolled from her, and he felt frozen there. Guilt flooded him and part of him wanted to slip out of the room, disappear, and leave her alone with whatever hurt her.

The other part of him wanted to go to her and haul her against him, make her tell him *what* had hurt her . . . so he could kill it. Fix it. Whatever. He didn't know which one he was supposed to do. He was good at *killing* things, but fixing them? Not so much.

This wasn't supposed to happen.

He wasn't supposed to care . . . not for anything or anybody.

She wasn't supposed to matter, yet she did. More than anybody or anything, save for Alex.

He didn't want this inside him, but there it was.

She slammed her fist against the door and screamed, and he just couldn't take it anymore. Shoving off the wall, he crossed the floor. He didn't know what he was going to do, what he was going to say—

"Damn you, Gus." The words came out in a ragged sob.

His heart jumped into his throat.

She was crying . . . over him.

He almost tripped over his feet, his shoes scuffing on the hardwood floors.

She gasped and whirled around.

He saw her hand go to the weapon strapped to her waist, and he moved, catching her wrist and pinning it to the wall.

Her eyes went wide, damp and glinting with tears, as she stared at him.

"Gus . . ."

"Damning me finally?" he whispered.

She sucked in a breath and reached up, fisting her hand in his shirt. "You . . . you're okay."

Reaching over, he caught the weapon and tugged until she let go of her Glock. He laid it down on the small table to his left. "I wouldn't go that far." He cupped her face in his hands. "Why are you crying, Vaughnne?"

She sniffed and reached up, swiping the tears from her face. "I'm not." She lifted her chin and glared at him.

"Of course you're not." Unable to resist another moment, he lowered his head and pressed his mouth to hers. She tasted of tears and her and he was starved for her. He lifted his head a fraction. "If you don't want this, then you better stop me . . . now."

Her response was to reach for his shirt and strip it off.

If he were any sort of decent, he'd slow this down. Talk to her. He'd be lying if he tried to tell himself he hadn't come for this. He hadn't come *only* for this. He'd wanted to touch her, feel her underneath one more time . . . to take her in a bed and take his time with her.

One night. One night when he didn't have to worry about all the burdens he'd carried for so long. One night when all that mattered was the two of them.

But Gus had stopped worrying about being decent a long,

long time ago. So as his shirt fell to the floor, he reached for the neat little line of buttons marching up the center of her prim white shirt. "You look so neat and put together, Vaughnne," he murmured, freeing first one button, then another, watching as he bared one inch of skin at a time. "I'm going to enjoy watching you come apart for me."

She leaned back against the door, her hands falling to hang loose at her sides. "I've been doing that almost since the first second I laid eyes on you, sugar." A smile curved her wide, sexy mouth, but it didn't quite reach her eyes, and if he'd let himself look, he knew what he would have seen.

She knew, he realized. Had some idea of just why he was there.

And it just made him that much more of a bastard. But he didn't care.

When he reached the final button, instead of pushing the shirt off her shoulders, he let it hang open, revealing the narrow line of her sleek torso, the lace edging of her bra. He traced one finger down the midline of her body, stopping when he reached the waist of her trousers, the sturdy leather of her holster. Still holding her gaze, he unbuckled it, unbuttoned her trousers.

Vaughnne stood there, silent and watching him with solemn eyes. He leaned in and nipped her lower lip, pressed a kiss to her neck, moving in a line straight downward until he was kneeling in front of her.

She wore a pair of low-heel ankle boots and he tugged them off, setting them neatly by the door. Vaughnne kept a tidy little nest, something he'd noticed when he let himself inside. He wouldn't leave any sign of himself when he left . . . other than what he was doing to her now. Glancing up at her, he saw her lashes were closed, her head was tipped back, and her hands were braced against the door, curled into tight fists that left her knuckles bloodless.

He wanted her clutching at *him* that tightly.

Wanted to hear that smart mouth, the cocky attitude that had driven him insane the past few weeks.

But when he tried to reach for the words to say something, anything to tease it out of her, he couldn't find them. So instead of saying anything, he leaned in and pressed his mouth to her belly as he caught the waist of her trousers and dragged them down over the swell of her hips, her thighs, down until she could step out of the puddle of material.

Rising, he stood in front of her, arms braced on the door by either side of her head, waiting for her to look at him.

Seconds ticked away, and finally, she lifted her lids, staring at him with dark, unreadable eyes.

He opened his mouth, determined to find *something* to say. Something. Anything. It shouldn't be this hard to find a handful of words. He'd lived most of his life by them. Glib lies, charming little half-truths . . . all of them said to people who meant less than nothing. And here he stood with a woman who meant everything and he couldn't find anything to ease the pain he sensed was inside her.

Before he managed to find even *one* damn thing to say, Vaughnne reached up and laid her hand on his cheek. "Take me to bed, Gus," she said quietly. "We can have that one night now, right?"

TWENTY-THREE

His face was stark, his eyes so hungry and hot, they burned as he stared down at her.

For the first time, she felt almost nervous. Almost anxious. It seemed like there was something brewing inside him. She could feel the storm of it, but whatever it was, Vaughnne knew it wasn't going to change anything.

She'd realized why he was here within seconds of laying eyes on him.

He was here to say good-bye.

Maybe he was going to say thanks. Maybe he was going to tell her to stay out of his way. Maybe he was going to tell her to stay silent. Maybe he'd say a lot of other things. But one thing he'd definitely say . . . *good-bye.*

Fine.

She could live with that, because she knew what mattered the most . . . he was alive. Whatever had happened in Mexico after she'd gotten Nalini out of there, he hadn't died. Gus was alive and she would be okay with whatever else might come. Because she knew he was alive. Maybe she'd never get all the answers she needed, maybe she'd never have anything more than this . . . but she knew he was alive. And he'd done what he'd set out to do. He'd made sure Alex was safe.

Slowly, he reached for her, and as he wrapped his arms around her, she curled hers around his neck, shuddering at the feel of his body pressed against hers again. Over the past few days, she'd missed this . . . wondered if she'd ever feel it again, and it had *sucked*. But then Moran had shown up and she'd had to wonder if Gus was just *gone*. That vivid, burning blaze of him gone . . . and that had hurt so much she had thought she was dying inside.

He boosted her up, and she wrapped her legs around his waist, her breath catching as it brought him in contact with the sensitive flesh between her thighs. She pressed her brow to his. "My bedroom is down the hall."

He found it unerringly and she realized he'd probably spent some time poking around her house while waiting for her. She should be pissed about that. She might be later. Matter of fact, she'd almost make a mental note to do that, just to distract herself from the misery that waited for her. But for that moment, she didn't care. He was here. One more night. They were together. One more night. That was all the mattered. She'd worry about everything else after it was over.

Once they were inside her room, she unhooked her legs and let him guide her to the floor. Settling down in front of him, she rested her hands on his chest, vaguely aware that she'd started to shiver.

Gus noticed. He stroked his hands down her arms. "You're cold."

"No." She wasn't cold, at all. Emotion crashed and swelled inside her and she ached, so full of want and hunger and need and confusion. She didn't know exactly *what* she was. But it wasn't cold.

Swallowing, Vaughnne smoothed her hands down his chest and hooked them in the front of his jeans, tugging him closer.

He came and they tumbled back onto her bed. The feel of his weight on her was almost a painful pleasure, and she curled her fingers into his arms, arching up against him, clutching him closer. "Naked." His hand tangled in the front of her shirt, dragging it out of the way, down her arm until the material caught around her elbow. "I should have gotten you naked before I let you get us on the bed."

She ran the insole of her foot down his calf. "Look who's talking. You're still wearing your jeans." She might have said something else, but he'd tugged the cup of her bra down and dipped his head, catching her nipple between his teeth. As he tugged on it, pleasure blistered through her and the ability to speak died. The ability to *think* seemed to die.

Gasping, she shoved a hand into his hair, held him close.

He rolled on the bed, bringing her on top of him. Then he stripped her shirt and bra away and forced her to sit up. Vaughnne groaned, bracing her hands on his shoulders and glaring at him, but he wasn't looking at her. He cupped her breasts in his hands, plumping them together and circling her nipples with his thumbs. His touch, the way he watched her . . . she looked down and stared at his hands. Those beautiful hands, stroking over her flesh, bringing her more pleasure than she'd thought it was possible to feel.

* * *

HUNGRY for everything he could get, Gus watched as Vaughnne's head fell back, the ends of her long, dense curls falling almost to her ass. Grabbing the skimpy strings that rode high on her hips, he jerked, tearing her panties away and tossing the scrap to the floor. He surged upward and tangled a hand in her hair, twisting it around his fist and tugging her mouth to his. "Unzip me."

She watched him, her eyes heavy-lidded. Then she eased back, wiggling around until she could work the button, the zipper of his jeans. The light brush of her fingers against his flesh was a painful, sweet little tease and he wanted more. Needed more, a lot more than the one night he was going to give himself.

Once she'd eased the zipper down, he nudged her away and pulled a rubber from his pocket. Yeah, he'd come here for this, no denying that. Tossing it onto the bed, he shoved his jeans down, kicking them and his shoes off before rolling onto his knees and kneeling above Vaughnne. Her hair spread out around her, one thick lock curving around her breast. The dark circle of her aureole peaked through. She had a smile on her face. A sexy, female little smile . . . one that said she knew what he wanted, one that said she wanted the same thing, and it only made the hunger inside him burn that much brighter.

It was a picture he'd keep with him, he thought. Much better than that last one that had haunted him ever since she'd walked away in Mexico.

He tore the condom open and his hands actually shook as he unrolled it down over his length, fumbling more with the damn thing than he'd done since he was a teenager. And all the while, she watched, the smile slowly fading from her face until there was nothing on her face but need. He came down over her. "Hold on to me, *mi vida*. Hold on."

As she wrapped her arms around his neck, he settled between her thighs, shuddering at the heat waiting for him. Warm and welcoming . . . so soft.

He reached between them to guide himself home, groaning at the feel of her, shuddering as she yielded to him, the tight, clutching fist of her pussy closing around him as he slowly sank inside.

He sought out her mouth and the pleasure was like glory as she sank her teeth into his lower lip, as she rocked up against him, her hands, her body, urging him on. He sought out her wrists, guiding them over her head and pinning her in place.

"Slow down." If all they had was tonight, then he'd make it last.

At least, he'd try.

Vaughnne twisted beneath him, clenching down around him so that all those tiny little muscles inside gripped him, stroked him. He shuddered and withdrew. "*Carajo* . . . stop it, Vaughnne," he rasped against her mouth.

Her response was to catch his lower lip between her teeth again. When she bit him, he swore and surged deep inside her.

She cried out, the sound of it echoing through him. Her hands strained against his hold and she twisted, arching closer, harder. A flush spread out under the soft, warm brown of her skin and he dipped his head, pressing a kiss to the elegant line of her collarbone.

"Let go of my hands," she demanded.

* * *

HE stared down at her, the misty gray of his eyes boring into hers, hot as molten steel. Slowly, his fingers uncurled from her wrists, the pads of his fingertips tracing down over one arm, across her shoulder, and up her jawline until he could cup her face. He arched her jaw upward and took her mouth, his tongue echoing the rhythm of his body as he started to pump deep, deep inside her.

She wrapped her arms around him, sinking her nails into the ridge of muscle along his back, a scream rising inside her, only to lodge, breathless, in her throat. Too much . . . too much . . .

He drove into her, so hard, so fast, stealing the breath out of her.

And climax shimmered right *there* . . . just out of reach. Then, just when she was certain she would die from the painful pleasure of it, he shifted, moving higher on her body and changing his angle. At the same time, he tore his mouth from hers and set his teeth on the curve where her neck met her shoulder. As he bit down, the climax exploded through her and she thought she was just going to die from the pleasure of it.

* * *

THE faint, gray light of dawn was streaming in through the slit in her curtains when Vaughnne awoke. There wasn't a sound, but she came awake the moment Gus rolled away from her. She already ached for him; he hadn't even left yet and she was lonely.

She was going to miss him.

Every day for the rest of her life. It shouldn't happen like this. Damn it to hell, it shouldn't happen like this. If she was going to fall for a guy, why couldn't she have fallen for one she could *keep*?

She rolled onto her side and watched him climb out of the bed and her heart skipped a beat. Wistful, she bit back a sigh. Then again, she was being stupid. She had absolutely no desire to undo a minute with him. Maybe she couldn't keep him, but the days she'd spent with him burned brighter on her memory than any other she could recall.

If she had to settle for something vivid like this that would end in heartache, or something just . . . mediocre that she barely recalled a few months, a few years later? This was better, she thought. She hoped she could remember that later on down the road when she was cussing him out for leaving her.

He didn't speak as he dressed. She didn't bother saying anything. There was no point in trying to get him to change his mind. He'd already decided what he needed to do. He wasn't there looking to see if she *wanted* him even. If he'd shown any sign of that, then she'd be all over him, giving him all the reasons he needed to stay.

But he'd come with a purpose in mind.

So fine.

Let him go.

Swallowing around the knot in her throat, she told herself she could get through this. The first few days would be the worst, right? After her father had thrown her out, once she'd gotten through the first few weeks, the first month or so, she'd figured out how to get along and she'd been okay. This couldn't really be any worse than that.

In the dim light, he turned to face her after he'd pulled his shirt on, and she rolled onto her back as he came to sit on the side of the bed.

He reached up and touched her cheek. "Thank—"

"If you say *thank you* to me, I'm going to break your nose," she warned softly.

A faint smile danced across his face, there, then gone. "Do you really think I can leave without saying thank you for helping me with Alex?"

She sat up and leaned in until they were nose to nose. "Anything else and I'm punching you, Gus. I did my job. Period."

"Your job . . ." He sighed and pushed her hair back from her face. "What you did, were willing to do, was so much more. We both know it. But if that is how you want it . . ." He shrugged. Then he reached over for something on the nightstand.

She hadn't noticed it before. The sight of it made her heart slam against her ribs for some reason and her chest ached.

It was stupid, maybe. No reason for a piece of paper to make her hurt, she thought. Especially when she hadn't seen what was on it. But she already hurt, just seeing him hold it, his head bent as he stared down at it. Although it was too dark for him to read it, it was as though he was committing whatever words were on that paper to heart.

"Alex is with your boss."

And the pain in her heart ripped deeper through her, if that was possible.

Swallowing, she nodded slowly. Unable to sit there, naked save for the sheet and blanket pooled around her waist, she climbed out of bed and padded over to her dresser. She tugged open a drawer and pulled out a shirt at random. It fell to mid-thigh, covering her decently, but she still felt exposed so she pulled open another drawer and fished out a pair of yoga pants. "Yeah, he's still with Dez and Taylor. He's made some progress from what I've heard."

"Progress."

The sound of his voice, hollow and empty, set off warnings in her head.

Slowly, she turned to look at him.

"I did what I could, you know," he said quietly. "I did everything I could think of . . . letting him practice on me until I was almost immune to the headaches. I read so many bullshit websites, searching for any *useful* information I could find that might help him. And I still failed him."

"You didn't fail him." She stared at his bent head, feeling like she was bleeding inside. "You just don't have the tools needed to teach him this. He can get that from somebody else. It doesn't mean you failed him."

He lifted his head and stared at her. "He was almost taken because I didn't protect him well enough, didn't give him the tools he needed to protect *himself*."

He surged up off the bed and started to pace, a sign of restless, reckless energy she'd never seen from him. "He's making progress . . . I saw him." He stopped and spun around until he was staring at her from across the room. "I went to the house yesterday, where Jones is keeping him, and I saw him. He looked almost *happy*, Vaughnne. It was like the burden he has carried all these years was just gone. In just a few days, these people have given him what I was never able to."

"You can love him. You're his family . . . that's a bond nobody else can replace," she said.

"His family . . . *esta chingadera*." He turned away. "His *family*? Like that is the answer to everything? You know what I did, yes? To his mama? To my *sister*? I killed her, Vaughnne. Tell me now, what kind of *family* am I?"

"Why?"

He turned, the look in his glittering eyes full of rage and pain and grief. "Because she asked me to. Because I had to. Because if I didn't, Reyes would catch us and kill us all. And if I *left her alive*? Reyes would just torture her more before she died."

Then he went to his knees, slowly, his hands coming up to cover his face as a sob ripped out of him. Just one . . . that slow, ugly sound coming from the very core of his soul.

She'd known. In her heart, she'd known there were reasons . . . and she'd known it had left a scar on him. Blinking back the tears, she went to him.

Because she asked me to . . . because I had to . . . She didn't know if he'd welcome her touch now, but when her fingers brushed across his skin, he reached out, quick as a wish, and hauled her against him, so hard and sudden, it knocked the breath from her.

With his face buried against her neck, he started to speak. "She called me . . . from the village. I already told you that. But Reyes was already after her and caught up with her just minutes after she hung up. She acted like she was trying to run. He didn't know she'd made the call, and just took her back home. He started to beat her. By the time I got there, he'd beaten her . . . so badly . . . too badly. He'd shattered the bones in her legs, let her know that it was because she had run. He'd broken her ribs. And he did it all while Alejandro watched. The boy had to *watch* as his father tortured his mother, almost to death." He paused, his chest rising, falling in hard, heavy pants.

She lifted a hand to his cheek and just waited.

"I couldn't save her." Stark, haunted eyes lifted to hers and he said it again, "I couldn't save her. I told myself I could and I even tried to take her out of there, but she wouldn't let me. She . . ." He looked away, a nerve pulsing in his cheek as he lapsed into a long, heavy silence. "Alex got it from her . . . this . . . whatever he has. I know he did."

"It runs in families," she said quietly. "I got it from my dad. It's in the genes, just like a lot of other shit. The color of your hair, your eyes. This isn't any different."

He nodded stiffly. "He got it from her. She . . . she saw things. Sometimes things that had already passed, but it was from long ago. But other times, she saw what *would* happen—the future, I guess. She told me that if I tried to take her, Reyes would catch up with all of us and we would all die, except Alex. There would be nobody there to take care of him. He'd be a prisoner, trapped in that monster's home, just a tool, forced to do what Reyes wanted and be beaten if he refused. That would have broken him."

It likely would have. Or maybe Alex would have become a monster like his father. Vaughnne didn't know which was worst.

"She made me promise," Gus said quietly. "Before she would say anything, she made me make her a promise . . . there she is, my little sister, in so much pain, begging me to promise her something. And I would have done anything to make it better for her. So she tells me that I have to take care of the boy. I tell her I will. And then she tells me . . ."

His voice hitched. Vaughnne leaned in and pressed her lips to his cheek. "You don't have to do this."

But he didn't even seem to hear her. Tears dampened his cheeks as he continued to speak. "She tells me, in vivid detail, what she has seen if I try to take her out of there. She tells me that she will not live through the night, because she is bleeding inside. I don't know if she knew that or if she just guessed . . . she'd been going to school to be a nurse before she met Reyes. But she believes she is dying, and looking at her, I think she was right, even if I didn't want to believe it. I couldn't let myself believe it. I had to save her. That was all I wanted to do. Save her. Instead, she sends Alex out of the room—I had a man with me. Jimmy Doucet. It was his place we went to in Louisiana. He died a year later . . . cancer took him. He . . . *mierda*. He was the closest thing to a friend I had. But it was just the two of us. A quick job, in and out. He takes Alex out and I have my gun. She takes my hand and points to her head, tells me to kill her."

* * *

You must promise me . . .

Even now, those words danced through his mind. Horror, pain.

No . . . Consuelo, stop this. You're coming with us. Now come. It will hurt, but we will be fast.

No . . . you must do this . . .

Then she guided his weapon hand to her head and told him again what she had seen.

He will find us. He kills you first, from outside the hotel. Then, your friend. It's a nice hotel. You didn't want me to suffer and you brought a doctor. There are casts on my legs and I cannot even move from the bed when he comes through the door. Alejandro tries to run to me, but before he can, Ignacio grabs him. Then, while my son watches, that monster kills me.

He could still feel the way her hand had brushed his hair back from his face. The way their mother had used to do.

You can save my son, Gustavo. But you cannot save me. I cannot even move. Please . . . you must promise me. Take him,

keep him safe. And don't . . . please don't let Ignacio hurt me
anymore. If he tries to make me talk, I . . .

He'd tried to pull his hand away, horrified at the sight of his
gun so close to his sister. She hadn't let him.

If he finds me alive, he will try to make me talk. And I am not
as strong as you. Please, Gustavo. You must protect my son . . .
you must do this for me.

"She begged me," he said softly. "Begged me to kill her.
Begged me to keep him from being able to hurt her again. Begged
me to protect her son."

Vaughnne's hand stroked his neck and he realized absently
that he was rocking. She was curled up on his lap. He didn't even
know how that had happened, but it had, and the two of them
were rocking, while she held him with soft, strong arms.

"If he'd beaten her that badly, you know she would have slowed
you down. If she was bleeding inside, if he had hurt her that bad,
it might have been impossible to save her," she said softly.

He stiffened. "It doesn't matter. If I'd been faster . . . if I'd
killed that bastard sooner. That *cabrón hijo de su puta madre*—
if I'd killed him the minute I realized who my sister had married,
then none of this would have happened."

"And Alex wouldn't exist."

He closed his eyes as the bitterness of guilt chased through
him. Yes . . . that was something else he knew. "I never cared
that he was a drug lord," Gus said softly. "Mexico is overrun
with drugs. Many people there worship men like him. They are
like folk heroes. There wasn't much talk about Reyes, because he
was careful. Always so careful. I should have paid closer attention, but I was never in the same part of the country, and if you
look at a man like him too carefully, people notice. I looked, but
I was careful about how I looked and I didn't look too deeply.

"I was arrogant," he said, his voice bitter. "I thought I would
have known if he was a man that should concern me. I knew all

the dirty secrets, and he was greedy and vain, but there were never stories about him being abusive or cruel. But I didn't look at him hard enough. Consuelo paid for my arrogance."

Vaughnne stroked a hand down his arm. "She was a grown woman. If she knew what he did, and married him anyway . . . you can't take responsibility for her choices."

"Can't I?" He shifted his eyes to her. "I could have looked deeper, but time and again I pulled back because I feared it would be discovered. That my connection to her would be discovered. That my cover would be blown. My *fucking* cover. I was this rich, foolish playboy. I'd fucked and gambled my way into money, forgotten my family . . . Only the lowest of men do that in Mexico. Family is everything. It was the only way to protect them, though." He sighed and shrugged, staring off into nothing.

He laughed bitterly. "Looking back now, I don't know what is worse. If people had noticed there was a connection between us, and if she suffered for that? Or if I had just done exactly what I did. Either way, she would have suffered for it. This way, she died. And no matter what, Alejandro has paid the price. He has lost his mother. Has lost most of his childhood."

Most . . . what a lie. Alex had never *had* a childhood. The boy had been a pawn to his father, and although Consuelo had loved him, tried to protect him, she just hadn't been strong enough. Not with Reyes in the picture.

But Reyes wasn't in the picture any longer.

And in a matter of days, perhaps weeks or months even, Gus was going to make sure that anybody who knew about Alex died. It was the last thing he had to do, eliminate those men who had been with Reyes for years. Once he'd hunted those men down, Alex would be safe.

But he couldn't do that with a child at his side.

It was like cutting off his arm—or cutting out his heart—as he eased Vaughnne off his lap. "The boy has nothing," he said, keeping his voice flat. "I am his family, but I have never provided him with the security he needs. The stable home. He doesn't even have the chance to go to school or be a regular boy. *That* is what I want for him."

Rising to his feet, he bent over and scooped up the document from the floor. From the corner of his eye, he saw Vaughnne rise.

When he lifted his head, he saw the knowledge burning in her eyes. "Don't," she said, shaking her head. "Don't you do this to that boy."

"It's the best thing I can do for him," he said simply. "You love him. I see it in your eyes. Family isn't just who you are born to. It's those you find in your life . . . those who love you. You made him your family when you took him in your heart, Vaughnne. And you can make him happier than I can. He doesn't have the threat of his father hanging over his head so he doesn't need a hired killer hovering over his shoulder as he sleeps. He needs somebody to love him, to give him a home. Somebody who understands what he *is*, and how to make certain he gets that training he needs."

"He needs the people he loves." Fury made her voice shake.

But he knew he was doing the right thing.

"I'm leaving the documentation you'll need." He nodded to an envelope on the nightstand. "You have his birth certificate. Proof of my relationship to his mother, a letter she wrote naming me his guardian. Now I'm naming you."

"You can't just *give* him away!" she shouted. "He's a child. A person, you son of a bitch. He's got feelings, too, you bastard, and this is going to destroy him."

"I've done nothing but destroy him, destroy his life, bring him pain for the past few years," Gus said. "I did what I had to because it was necessary to protect him. And that's what I'm doing now. Protecting him. He needs a real life, Vaughnne. I can't give him one." He headed for the door.

"What makes you think *I* should?"

He paused in the doorway, smiling a little. "It won't be because you *should*. If you did what you *should*, you never would have gone to Mexico. You never would have gone after the men who hurt your sister."

She narrowed her eyes at him.

"Yes. I know about that." He'd learned as much about her as he could in the past few days, calling in favors, bribing, threatening. He had to make sure he was doing the right thing, he'd told himself. In truth, he'd just been hungry for what he could learn of her. For anything about her. "You took leave, just to hunt them down. You don't always do what you *should*, Agent . . . do you?"

"Obviously, we make a great pair," she said, her lip curling in disgust. "Except I don't abandon the kid who loves me."

He arched a brow. "Exactly. That is why he should be with you . . . he loves you already. Don't disappoint him as I've done so many times."

TWENTY-FOUR

*D*ON'T *disappoint him.*

As Taylor guided her down the steps to the TV room in the basement, Vaughnne tried to steady her breathing. Tried to quell the fury still burning in her heart. Yeah. She'd expected anger would carry her through, but she hadn't expected it to be like *this*.

As she rounded the corner and saw Alex sprawled on his belly, next to a dark-haired girl with a headful of wild curls, she sucked in a deep breath. *Breathe, Vaughnne. You can do this.*

Then, out of spite, she focused her thoughts and reached out.

She knew when she touched a mind. Could always feel it—it wasn't much different, to her, than touching somebody's hand, or seeing the way a person reacted when she said their name. She could just . . . *feel* it.

And she felt Gus's reaction as she said, *I'm getting ready to break this kid's heart, you son of a bitch. Wherever you are, I hope you're having fun.*

Then, because she was feeling pithy, she added, *Don't suppose it ever occurred to you to try this with me together? This kid could use two people in his life who love him. We could have both given him a home . . . I would have been happy to have you in my life, Gus. But you're too much a coward to try it.*

She didn't even have to worry about a response.

That was the beauty, sometimes, of her gift. A curse at other times, but just then, it was welcome. She didn't want to *see* him, didn't want to hear from him. Not when she was going to have to break this poor kid.

"Jillian."

The girl looked up.

The name was familiar, and Vaughnne stilled as the girl sat up and turned around. The teen focused a vivid pair of blue eyes on them.

Jillian. Jillian Morgan.

Shit, the girl was already a borderline legend back at headquarters and she was still in high school.

This was the girl Taige had rescued all those years ago, and if the rumors were true, the kid was already feeding Taylor bits and pieces of information that sometimes led to their cases being solved.

Narrowing her eyes, she focused on Alex and then looked over at Taylor. She never did hear just *how* he'd learned about Alex's presence in Orlando. She'd assumed it had something to do with Nalini, but standing there, looking at Jillian, she realized she'd been off base. *Way* off base. No wonder he'd been so fucking vague about things.

She told you about him, didn't she?

Taylor's only response was a flicker of his lashes.

If she'd been wrong, he would have said so. But he didn't. Not then. And never once, after that.

Looking back over at the girl, Vaughnne watched as Jillian

came to her feet, a diminutive thing, maybe five feet two, at the max. All curls and dimples and big blue eyes. But under the shields Jillian had wrapped around herself, Vaughnne sensed a power that almost made her teeth ache.

"Hi," Jillian said, smiling at her.

Vaughnne smiled back, although she had to force it. Smiling was the last thing she had inside her just then.

"Jillian, your mom is about ready to go."

Jillian sighed and looked over at Alex as he sat up. "I've gotta go, Alex. I'm going to try and talk them into staying a few more days if I can. But if I can't, I'll call you."

Alex tucked his chin against his chest, his cheeks flushing a dull red. "I don't know how much longer I'll be here. My uncle . . ."

Jillian looked over at Vaughnne.

Too young, she thought absently. That girl was way too young to have that kind of wisdom in her eyes. Wisdom . . . and sadness.

"It's okay. I'll find a way to keep in touch," Jillian said, bending down to hug the boy's skinny shoulders.

She was halfway across the floor before he looked up. "Bye, Jillian." The look in his eyes was one that hit Vaughnne straight in the gut.

Loneliness. Such loneliness. She knew what that was like. She remembered how it had felt, the first time she'd ever really made a friend.

He needs a real life . . . That was what Gus had told her.

Yeah. The kid needed a real life. Needed friends. Needed a home and stability and structure, and for all that was good and decent, he needed to know how to control the wild gift inside him. But why in the hell couldn't he do that with Gus in his life?

It was a question she had no answer for, she knew.

But she couldn't let that get in the way.

She had to focus on Alex now.

Crossing the floor, she sank down in the spot where Jillian had been, watching as Alex continued to play the video game. "You seem to be pretty good at that," she said softly as Taylor and Jillian left.

"I'm lousy at it," he said. But there was a bit of a smile on his face. "Jillian is good at it. I could get better. But . . ." Then he shrugged. "Gus will be coming for me soon and we won't have the money for things like this. It's fun, though."

"Actually . . ." She blew out a breath and opened the folder. Gus hadn't just left the legal documents. Taylor was already doing what he could; he'd started that ball rolling once Vaughnne had talked to him. Still, all in all, this was just a nightmare in the making.

The good news, Alex was underage and hadn't had any say in what the adults in his life had done. His mother was dead, his father was dead. Taylor would go to the wall to keep the boy from going back to a place where he'd be in danger and the man had a lot of pull, knew a lot of people who owed him favors.

The bad news . . . it was going to be a rough road before this all settled down, and she had to break Alex's heart.

Withdrawing the letter Gus had written for the boy, she held it out. "He isn't coming back," she said gently. "I'm sorry."

* * *

Gus didn't set the house on fire, although part of him wanted to see another piece of that hell go up in flames. These men had known about Alex. He was careful, leaving no sign of himself, and unless the authorities there were very, very good, they'd assume exactly what Gus had wanted them to assume. A card game between two friends, gone very, very wrong.

The last pair had an unfortunate accident while driving.

There were three more who had been in Reyes's inner circle.

They would be the hardest to track down, though. After this, they would all be more cautious. And the others were smarter, had taken more care.

It was going to be harder, from here on out.

Still, once he had eliminated the final few, he'd . . .

He'd what?

Gus really didn't know the answer to that.

He stopped on the beach, staring out at the almost painful blue of the Pacific while that question echoed inside him. He'd what?

"Killing your way through Mexico, Gustavo?"

He tensed at the sound of that voice. He had his weapon, tucked under his shirt at his back. But it was a question, really. Could he draw it before the man behind him shot him?

Antonio Moran had made him who he was. What he was. The older man was in his late fifties, but he was still one deadly son of a bitch. Slowly, he turned and eyed the man who'd held his leash for almost fifteen years. Up until Gus had slipped that leash to go rescue his sister.

He'd failed there.

But he wasn't going back on that leash, either. If he hadn't been so afraid of the hell he could bring to Consuelo's door, perhaps he could have saved her *and* Alejandro.

"Nothing to say?"

He just stood there as Moran crossed the sand to stop just a few feet away.

"I've got a number of dead bodies that I can track back to you, and you're just going to stand there and stare at me like you'd rather see me dead than speak," Moran said, sighing a little.

"There's not much reason to speak, is there?"

Moran inclined his head. Then he shifted his gaze and looked out over the water. "I am sorry for your sister. For the problems you've had these past few years. If you had come to me . . ." He stopped and shrugged. "But there is no reason why you would have."

"Reyes would have done anything to bring his son home. The man was an abusive monster and he had contacts everywhere. He even had men on your payroll, and we both know it. Now . . . why would I have come to you?"

"I would have protected anybody you brought to me," Moran said softly. "Surely you know that."

"I believe you would have *tried*." Gus did believe that much. "But you cannot control all of those under you, not when you knowingly allow rats to exist under your thumb, just to see what crumbs they'll leave."

"I'd never put an innocent child in harm's way," Moran said.

Gus laughed humorlessly. "I wasn't much more than a child when you dragged *me* into this."

"But you were never innocent." Moran shrugged as if that made all the difference.

"I'm not coming back," Gus said. "If that is why you are here, you waste your time. You might as well kill me now."

Moran made a *tsk*ing sound under his breath. "And here we were, having such a nice conversation. Have I threatened you at all? Insisted that you come back?"

"There is no other reason for you to be here."

Moran tipped his face back to the sun. "Perhaps I just wanted to see for my own eyes that you were still alive. You stayed hidden for a long time, Gustavo. And you went after a very dangerous man."

"You made me for just that purpose."

Silence fell and then Moran nodded. "Yes. Indeed I did."

He reached into his pocket and held something out.

Gus ignored it.

Moran just let it fall to the sand. "You feared staying close to your family because of the life men like us lead, Gustavo. I can respect that. I understand it. I even pushed you to do just that. But you don't have to continue this life . . . you got lost in the world once. Do it again, *mi amigo*. Get lost and take care of that boy. Give him a real life."

Gus bit back his response and stayed where he was, ignoring whatever it was on the sand as he stared out over the water. He could never fully escape the past he had here. It would always find him, he thought. He couldn't create a new life out of nothing.

Moments passed. He didn't know how much time passed. He was alone on the beach. Moran had left, leaving behind nothing but a sealed envelope. Scowling, Gus knelt down and tore it open. The letter inside, the documents, all they did was make him scowl. A new birth certificate, a new passport . . . the promise of a new life. What . . . what was this?

A new life. Meaningless, now. Alex was gone. Vaughnne . . . *Mierda*.

Even as he thought of the futile, fanciful impossibility of it, something brushed against his mind. It was faint at first. Then harder, and louder, like something was slamming against his skull—from the inside.

Vaughnne . . . her voice an echo, like it was coming to him through a tunnel. Or maybe over thousands of miles.

I'm getting ready to break this kid's heart, you son of a bitch. Wherever you are, I hope you're having fun.

Don't suppose it ever occurred to you to try this with me together? This kid could use two people in his life who love him. We could have both given him a home . . . I would have been happy to have you in my life, Gus. But you're too much a coward to try it.

He tensed, holding his breath as he waited for more.

"Vaughnne." He closed his eyes and whispered her name again.

But she couldn't hear him. That wasn't her gift.

And he didn't have any.

* * *

ALEX was a quiet shadow at her side as she led him into her apartment.

It wasn't much.

The second bedroom was mostly used as an office, but she'd already figured that problem out. She could move her desk into her room. It would be cramped, but that wasn't a problem. The bookshelves would go into the living room. Problem solved.

She flicked on the light and automatically checked the room, wishing she'd sense some dark, quiet shadow hiding in wait.

He'd changed his mind.

He'd realized he was wrong.

Something.

Anything.

But they were alone.

She knew it.

So did Alex.

"He's not coming back." It was the first time Alex had spoken in over three hours.

She locked the door and then looked over at him. His eyes, so like his uncle's, met hers, and the pain there all but broke her heart all over again. She'd known this would happen, she thought absently. The very first time she'd seen that kid, she'd had a feeling he'd break her heart, and she'd been right.

"No, Alex," she said softly. "I don't think he is."

He nodded, his eyes taking on a dull, lost look.

Unable to stop herself, she crossed to him and caught him in her arms.

Slowly, he wrapped his arms around her waist and rested his head on her shoulder as he started to cry. "I'm sorry, kid," she whispered. "I'm so sorry."

"Why did he leave?"

Closing her eyes, she wished she could figure out the right way to answer that. But there was no right answer when a boy's world had just been shattered . . . again. "I think he believes he's doing the right thing. He's a smart guy, your uncle. But he's not very bright sometimes, huh?"

A hard sob shook him. "He left me. He really left me."

It was a pain that she understood. No, her parents hadn't left her. They'd thrown her away like she was nothing more than trash. *Worse* . . . they'd thrown her out, in fear and hatred. Hugging him tighter, she said softly, "I know, Alex. I know. You'll get through this, I swear. And I can promise you this, as long as God lets me, *I* will be here. I won't leave you, I won't throw you out. I'll be here for you . . . I'll love you and take care of you and I'll fight for you and with you. I'm not your mom and I'm not Gus, but I'll do my best for you, I swear."

Whether it was the right thing to say or not, she didn't know. But it was all she had.

TWENTY-FIVE

IT was a rare thing for her to wake up and smell food cooking. *Very* rare. As in it never happened. Not even in the past two months since she'd starting sharing her home with somebody else. Sharing . . . as in making somebody else part of her life.

It was a weird adjustment to make; making somebody else part of her life.

But as weird as that was, she still couldn't quite accept what her senses were telling her.

Breakfast. Made by somebody else. Did Alex know how to cook?

Turning her head, she eyed the clock with a scowl. It was seven. On a Saturday. Alex up early . . . and *cooking*?

Scowling, she sat up and tried to figure out how she felt about a kid cooking breakfast in her kitchen. Granted, this was a kid who had more responsibility thrown at him than was really fair, and yeah, he kind of knew his way around a kitchen. Kind of, as in he knew how to make hot dogs and macaroni and cheese. But she'd thought that was it.

Still, they could discuss that after she had some bacon.

Her mouth was watering as she paused long enough to put on a bra and something other than the spaghetti tank she usually slept in. She'd gotten used to not being able to sleep in nothing, but all the little adjustments were strange.

She wasn't even down the hallway when the door to the room she'd given Alex opened. He stood there and gave her a sleepy smile. "You're making breakfast?" he said.

Her heart jumped into her throat even as adrenaline jumped up to high. She stared down the hall toward the stairwell. *Go back into your room for a minute, Alex.*

He blinked at her, frowning.

Then he cocked his head and peered down the steps.

Something flitted through his eyes, and before she could grab him, he was running downstairs.

She caught him halfway down. *Did you not hear me?* she demanded, putting enough volume into her mental voice that she saw him flinch. *Wait in your room.*

"But it's Gus," he told her. "I can feel it."

The strength wanted to drain out of her legs.

Shaking her head, she pointed up the stairs and hoped he'd listen. Part of her wanted to believe him. Who else would be in her house cooking bacon?

But she'd taken a kid into her home and that meant she'd protect him. Even against bacon-making intruders who might or might not be his uncle.

Slowly, Alex pulled back and nodded, trudging back up the stairs. She eased her way down them, although considering how much noise they'd made just now, was there really any point in being quiet?

Her heart slammed hard against her ribs as she pressed her back against the wall, peering around the corner. There, just there, on the long skinny table behind the sofa, she spied a ball cap. It wasn't hers. It wasn't Alex's. Seeing it made her heart ache even more.

She took a deep, slow breath and eased forward one more step.

"One thing I can manage well enough is breakfast."

At the sound of his voice, she sagged back against the wall. Not certain she trusted her ears or her eyes, she stood there. Was she awake? Yeah. She was pretty certain she was.

"It won't be warm, though, if you two don't come in here soon."

Lifting her head, she focused on the man standing in the doorway.

He wore a pale blue polo, the closest thing to dress wear that she'd ever seen him in. His eyes rested on her face, and the look in his gaze was cautious.

Vaughnne didn't know whether she wanted to throw *herself* at him, or the nearest heavy object.

"If you're going to break that kid's heart again," she said, focusing on the most important thing, "I'm going to hurt you in so many ways."

He shook his head.

What that meant, she didn't know, but she had to hope it meant something. Because just then, she heard a creak on the steps, and when she leaned over to look, she saw Alex there, a look on his face that melted her, even as it infuriated her. "Come on down, Alex."

She barely had time to move before he was blasting past her.

Seconds later, the boy was wrapped in his uncle's arms. And she had to admit, even if she'd cried herself to sleep a few times over the past couple of months, it was a sight that did her heart good.

Then Alex jerked back and punched Gus in the arm. "Tell me you're not leaving again," the boy demanded. "You . . . you . . . you stupid *cabrón*. You tell me you won't leave me again."

Gus's brows arched over his eyes. "I ought to tell you to watch your mouth, but I suspect I deserve that." Then he sighed and leaned in, pressing his brow to Alex's. "No. I'm not leaving. We're family, Alex. We should be together."

Alex hugged him, sniffling.

Over the boy's head, Gus stared at her.

She inclined her head. "Took you a while to figure that out. I told him a while ago . . . you're a smart man, Gus, but you're not very bright."

"No." His voice was hoarse. "Not very bright at all."

Vaughnne padded down the last few stairs and eased around them. "I'll make sure the food doesn't burn. You two should probably talk and all, right?"

She could feel the weight of his gaze burning into her, but she didn't look back. He'd come back for Alex, and the boy needed him.

So do I, her heart screamed. But she wasn't a lonely, scared child. Gus didn't owe her anything. Maybe she wanted him. Maybe she needed him. Maybe she loved him—

As she flipped the bacon out of the skillet, she blinked back tears. Okay, no maybe about it. She did love him. Craved him. He was like a drug in her system, and the past couple of months hadn't gotten him out of her blood at all. But he'd come back for Alex—

"I think it's the three of us who need to talk," Gus said.

Her hand shook as she turned the burner off. He'd already made eggs, scrambled with salsa and cheese. They smelled good. They would taste like sawdust, but she'd make herself eat. Turning around, she eyed him. "I don't much see what we have to talk about, Gus."

"If *we* are going to give him a family," Gus said, moving deeper into the kitchen, "I think there are a number of things to talk about."

We . . .

Her breath caught as he reached up to cup her face in his hands. "That's part of why I came back . . . I want *us*, Vaughnne. All of us. I want Alex. I want you. I want a family. Starting now."

Her knees gave out on her, and if she hadn't been standing next to the counter, if Gus hadn't been right there, she might have wilted to the floor.

"Is it too late for me to have a chance with you, Vaughnne?" he whispered, pressing his brow to hers. "Did I mess it all up?"

She reached up and grabbed his wrists. "The only way you could have messed it up was if you didn't come back at all."

He stared at her, with misty gray eyes that could burn like molten silver. And then, something she'd never experienced happened. A smile, one that knocked the breath right out of her, lit up his face, and changed everything about him. "I'm sorry it took me so long, *mi vida*," he murmured, leaning in and pressing his lips to hers.

She hummed against his lips as he kissed her, soft and light, both of them too aware of Alex standing a few feet away.

When he pulled back, she reached up, touched his lips. "What does that mean . . . *mi vida*?"

"It means 'my life.'" He pulled her against him with one hand and then turned to Alex and held out his other hand. The boy rushed over to them. "It took me long enough, but I finally found it."

Glossary

carajo fuck

corazón heart (endearment)

(ése/éste) cabrón hijo de su puta madre (that/this) fucker son of his bitch/whore of a mother

esta chingadera this shit

hijo de la chingada son of a bitch/whore

'mano brother

mi hijo my son (familial term of endearment for a male child)

mi vida my life (endearment)

mierda shit

no, no oigo nada no, I don't hear anything

pendejo/cabrón asshole, idiot, moron, fucker

¿qué carajo? what the fuck/hell?

¿qué carajo clase de mierda jodida es ésta? what manner of fucked-up shit is this?

tío uncle